STARBURNER

Claire Luana

Leigh Anne—
Happy reading!

Claire Luana

To all of you who've read and loved the Moonburner Cycle.
Thanks for helping make a dream come true.

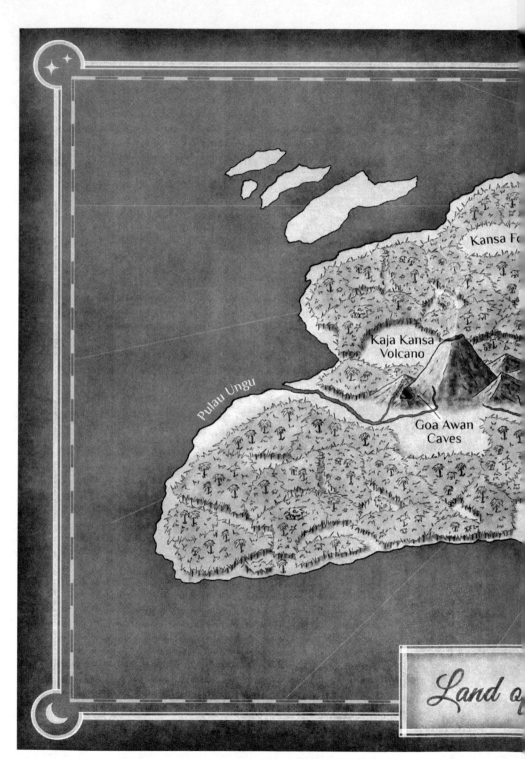

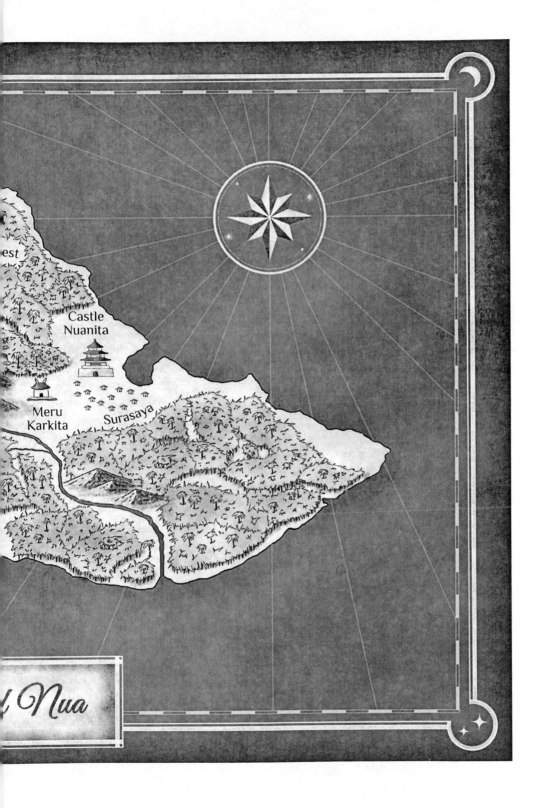

PROLOGUE

The forest was ablaze, a raging inferno of heat and smoke that reached towards the castle with grasping fingers. Vikal watched helplessly as birds and insects took to the air, as animals large and small rushed careening out of the flaming forest towards the aquamarine sea.

The creatures hadn't needed to set the blaze—these monsters—these soul-eaters. They had done it for spite. Or perhaps for sport. When the first plumes of smoke danced skyward, he and most of his men had been already pinned hopelessly behind the walls of his castle, trapped with only the knowledge that the thick stone was a flimsy barrier to keep these enemies at bay. At least a few had escaped—Bahti and Kemala, whom he had sent to warn as many people as possible to flee. He prayed they were safe, that they had flown from the city of Surasaya and not looked back.

It had been six days. Six days since a flash of green light across the sea had heralded the arrival of a fleet of strange ships borne by jet-black sails. Six days to transform his kingdom, his very life, from one of joy and prosperity, to this hellish inferno. To a last stand that was sure to fail. It had been remarkably efficient.

Vikal watched mutely as a wall of ten soul-eaters emerged from the forest, seemingly impervious to flame in their black armor. They looked like insects beneath their shiny black plate; they stood straight like men, but each creature's four long arms and sharp claws screamed the truth. They weren't human. He didn't know what they were. He had seen nothing but shadow and green-glowing eyes in the dark of their helmets when he and Sarya had gone to greet them, armed with little more than foolish pride. He held one of his twin blades loosely in his hands as the soul-eaters reached the castle gates and began banging on them with blows as powerful as a battering ram. He held his staff, his totem, in the other. Sarya. She had wanted to see them, to welcome these newcomers to their land. He could refuse her nothing, not when she jutted out her plump pink lip in mock affront, wearing down his resolve with honeyed kisses. She was the queen, after all, and he wasn't the type of king who would forbid his wife anything. So Sarya, a wreath of jasmine crowning her ebony hair, had been the first to welcome their new visitors, to offer them peace and prosperity and friendship. She had been the first to be sucked dry—to turn to ash within the silk of her magenta sarong.

Vikal had played the memory over in his mind so many times that he now saw it when he closed his eyes. Burned in his vision—his wife's face twisted in agony as the bulk of black armor bent over her, wrapped her in its four arms as if a lover. The sound of bursting wood broke him from the vision, and he opened eyes wet with refracted tears. He coughed as the smoke billowed across the castle wall, bearing ash and death on its wings.

"Your Majesty."

He turned to find Cayono standing at the top of the stairs. His friend had a gash over his left eye from one of the many skirmishes they'd had with the soul-eaters, but the blood had long since congealed and crusted. Their attacks against the soul-eaters after the initial disastrous attempt at peace had all been utter failures. They had found no weapon that could touch the creatures, and each skirmish had only lost Vikal more men. Their short-lived guerrilla warfare had turned into a full-on-retreat to Castle Nuanita, the seat of his rule. He saw no path to victory this day.

"They have broken through the gates," Cayono said.

Vikal sheathed his sword in one of the scabbards strapped to his back and squeezed his friend's shoulder. Cayono had given Vikal his first bloody nose when they'd been playfighting at the age of six. It seemed fitting that they would go out together. "It has been an honor, *bak*. My brother."

"For me as well." Cayono's deep voice was thick with emotion. "Let us show them that we Nuans are not without honor. We fight to the end."

Vikal gave a curt nod. Ready or not, it seemed the end was here. But in truth, he found himself ready—bone-weary to his soul. Sarya had been his light, his reason for living. He didn't want to go on without her.

The two men hurried down the stairs from the castle wall, jogging towards the sound of men fighting and dying. Three of his soldiers, clad in the green and gold livery of Nua, stumbled into them, fleeing from the horrors that strode towards them, filling the space under the castle wall.

"Steady," Vikal said, and it seemed to hearten his men. They formed a rank behind him and Cayono, weapons ready.

The first soul-eater through the gate stepped from the darkness into the sunlight of the courtyard, its green eyes glowing. "Soul-eater," Cayono said, spitting at its feet. One of the creature's arms shot out and buried its claws in the leather armor Cayono wore, raising the man off the ground as if a child. Cayono, to his credit, showed no fear, and swung his sword at the creature, striking its armored torso with a resounding clang. Vikal lunged for the soul-eater, bringing his sword down on the creature's outstretched arm hard enough to send a ringing vibration through Vikal's entire body. The blow should have severed the creature's arm, but it hardly dented its armor.

Two of the soul-eater's other arms shot out, taking Cayono's head in its hands, almost tenderly. Vikal's thick brows furrowed. *What was it doing?* When the soul-eater had embraced...*taken* Sarya, it had bent over her, sucking her essence into itself. Now, it seemed as if the creature was sending something into Cayono. Green energy pulsed between the monster and his friend, like an unnatural tether from the dark chasm of the creature's helmet snaking into Cayono's horrified face.

Vikal bellowed and hacked again at the creature, trying to pierce the seams of its armor, to get through somehow. Another soul-eater appeared before him, seizing Vikal by his jacket, lifting him up as he kicked wildly at the creature, screaming in anger and futility. The creature holding Cayono was setting him down now, releasing him. Vikal stilled for a moment in shock. *Was it letting him go?* But then his friend turned to face him, and hope turned bitter in his mouth. Cayono's eyes were vacant, glowing green. He stood, swaying gently on his feet, his tanned face slack. The creature had infected him somehow. Was it...controlling him?

"No! Cayono!" Vikal bellowed, scrambling against the creature who held him, wedging his booted feet against the creature's chest and pushing, straining against it. It was no use. The creature seized his ankles in one of its claws, while holding his jacket with the other. Its last two arms came up to his temples, cradling his head in its claws. He thrashed against it, fear rising like the evening tide. Take his soul. Fine. He didn't want to live without Sarya. But to be a slave to these creatures…to be used by them…it was an unholy thing, too terrible to comprehend.

He screamed in anguish as the green light entered him, filling him with its sickly poison. He screamed until the energy clamped down on his vocal chords, silencing him with a mute command. His mouth shut, his body relaxed. The creature put him down and he swayed next to Cayono, his body compliant, waiting for its instructions. But in his mind, he was still himself. In his mind, he screamed, and screamed, and screamed.

BOOK ONE

CHAPTER 1

A streak of silver slashed through the sky, leaving a tail as straight and true as a shooting star. A clap of thunder and an explosion of colors followed, filling the night with sparkling arches that fell towards the city skyline like shimmering raindrops.

The crowd erupted into applause, the cheerful light from their lanterns bobbing like ships on the sea.

"That's the biggest one yet," Quitsu said, appearing in Rika's lap with a nimble leap.

Rika started in surprise at the sight of the silver fox seishen, causing her horse to dance sideways beneath her. She steadied him with her knees, giving his chestnut flank a pat. "Quitsu, you gave me a fright."

"You'll live," he said, curling against her, pressing his warm fluffy back into her stomach while he turned to watch the expanse of cheering and waving citizens.

"It's a miracle Colum hasn't blown his eyebrows off, experimenting with that powder," Rika said as another two fireworks shot up into the sky—one spawning tiny pops of red, the other flashes of purple and gold.

"Those and a few other parts he'd miss more dearly," Quitsu remarked.

Rika chuckled.

"Is that a smile I see?" Quitsu turned, peering at her with black button eyes. "My mission here is accomplished, then."

"Your mission?"

"Your mother bid me remind you that this is a celebration. There's no need to look so stone-faced. You'd think someone had died, not that we're commemorating the fact that twenty years ago we vanquished the greatest foe our world has ever seen."

Rika sighed, pasting a fake smile on her face and waving at the crowd. It was hard to make out faces in the dark, but the lights held aloft by the crowd stretched as far as she could see, back through the streets and alleys of Yoshai. She supposed they could see her, what with the line of attendants walking alongside the royal family bearing bright paper lanterns. "Tell Mother there's no way I could forget the brave deeds that were done that day, when she and Father destroyed the tengu, saved the gods, and returned our land to safety and prosperity. I would not dream of dampening the festivities."

"Rika." Quitsu tsked. "You used to love hearing stories of the Battle of Yoshai. You and Koji would beg me for it every night before bed. This was your favorite festival, year after year. I can't believe you've outgrown it so completely. What's wrong?"

Ahead, the parade stretched up the hill towards the palace, where the nobles would join them for feasting and dancing. Her mother and father rode before her on two golden lionhorses, Queen Kailani and King Hiro of the consolidated lands of Kita and Miina, waving to the crowd with broad smiles. Her mother's silver hair, the trademark of her magical moonburner abilities, was woven into an elaborate crown, while her father's golden locks—marking him a sunburner—fell loose around his shoulders, bound only by a golden circlet. They both wore lavish clothes richly woven in the colors of their country, silver and gold, navy and red. Her father's seishen companion, Ryu, a golden lion who stood almost as tall as Rika did, padded next to Hiro. Her parents together looked happy. Regal. Practically divine. She fingered a lock of her own plain black hair before tossing it back over her shoulder. "I'm not feeling very festive this year," she finally replied.

Quitsu turned to examine her with that inscrutable fox face, and traitorous tears sprang to her eyes. She ripped her gaze from his, watching another firework as it exploded over the crowd in a riot of color. She pulled in a deep breath.

"Your powers will come, Rika." Quitsu's voice was gentle. "You'll see. One day you'll look back at this time and laugh at how worried you were."

"I'm almost seventeen," Rika said, her misery flaring to anger at Quitsu's words. "Of course I'm worried. No moonburner in history has had her powers develop this late. Usually they come at twelve or thirteen."

"No moonburner in history? Performed a thorough study of all of history, have we? Even the parts that weren't recorded?"

"I've done a lot of research," Rika retorted. "Plus, I overheard Nanase saying as much." Female magic wielders—or moonburners—drew power from the light of the moon and were able to turn it into light, or heat, or flame. Males wielded the power of the sun to the same effect. Rika, apparently, was as magical as a ball of wax.

"Your mother couldn't burn until she was eighteen," Quitsu said.

"But someone purposefully put a block on her powers. And her hair turned silver anyway. That didn't happen to me. My hair is still black as coal." She stilled her hand, resisting the urge to tug at her locks again. Yanking them out at the roots wouldn't get them to grow back silver.

"The Oracle prophesied that your powers alone would save this land from the greatest threat we have ever faced."

"Maybe the Oracle's gone senile," Rika grumbled. "Because unless we're talking about my ability on the dance floor, I don't think I'm going to be saving anyone."

"The Oracle is most certainly not senile," Quitsu scolded. "Unpleasant, enigmatic, grumpy as a koumori getting a bath, but not senile."

Rika cracked a smile at that.

"I know sixteen-year-old princesses aren't very good at it, but be patient," Quitsu said. "All will work out how it is supposed to."

Rika nodded, taking in a deep breath and letting it out. Quitsu was right. True, she didn't have her moonburner powers yet. And true, they were later in arriving than she had ever read about in the history books. But that didn't mean they would never come. Perhaps they were just waiting to arrive with...a bang, she thought, as another firework exploded amongst the stars above her.

"Rika, mind if I ride ahead?" Her little brother, Koji, had trotted up beside her, an arrogant smirk pasted between the few sparse hairs he liked to call a beard. "Getting bored back there; plus, I figured all the burners should ride together." He clicked his tongue and his steed reared magnificently, causing the crowd to murmur in awe. A wave of applause followed as he cantered ahead and fell into line behind her parents.

Rika's spirits plunged back into blackness as she struggled to keep a twisted scowl off her face.

Quitsu sighed. "I see my valiant efforts to urge patience and faith are wasted with your brother around."

"Does he have to be so...ARGH," she exclaimed, curling her hands into fists around the reins, unable to find a word that encompassed the entirety of Koji's state of loathsomeness. She wished she was an only child. She wished he had never been born. She wished she could wipe the smug little smirk off his smug little face...

"He's not fooling anyone with that attempt at a beard," Quitsu remarked. "Those whiskers look like gingko trees in the desert. Confused about how they got there and doomed to a life of loneliness."

Rika laughed despite herself, trying to hold back more tears. The truth was she didn't hate her brother. Sure, he was an annoying little brat who got on her last nerve. But the truth was she was desperately, hopelessly, jealous. Because Koji, even though he was only fourteen, was a sunburner. His hair was fully golden. His powers had come in over a year ago, and he lorded them over her on a daily basis. But more than that—Koji had Enzo, his seishen. He was a golden unicorn, with a mane and fetlocks that flowed like blowing autumn grain. His coat glistened over strong muscles and his horn twisted like a sugared candy, tapering to a delicate point. Like all seishen, Enzo was a creature of legend, a supernatural companion who had journeyed from the Misty Forest to find her brother. Destined to spend his life bonded to him.

Rika stroked Quitsu's downy fur as their parade neared the palace gates, trying to keep her gaze from sliding to her brother and Enzo. She looked at the crowd, at the lights strung across the palace walls, at the torches angled up to illuminate the sandstone walls of their home. She was grateful for Quitsu's presence leaning back against her. Quitsu was her mother's seishen and had been with Queen Kai since she'd been seventeen. He had helped her find her way out of the desert, had been with her when Kai had first become queen, defeating the evil Queen Airi. He had been there when they had saved the goddess Tsuki and defeated the tengu demons. Quitsu was a comfort, but he was temporary. On loan in those moments when Kai saw Rika struggling.

What she wanted was a seishen of her own. She deserved one. More than Koji did, anyway. She had been a good princess her whole life, had done her duty preparing to be queen. Learning diplomacy, history, military strategy, language, science, mathematics. She had given up sunny days and adventures with friends, time for astrology and art and the things she really wanted to do. She knew what it took to be a good ruler—to be as fair and honorable as her parents were. Her brother, on the other hand, had run around like a feral child, refusing to listen to anyone or do anything but play in the armory.

And now, what did they have to show for their respective upbringings? She enjoyed a crushing loneliness and fear that her powers would never come. That all her sacrifices would be for nothing. Because by law, the queen had to be a moonburner. No powers, no crown. No purpose, no point. And Koji, for all his antics, had everything she had ever wanted and would probably step in to rule in the face of her failure. It was a bitter pill to swallow.

They rode through the palace gates to shouts of applause and the sound of music and revelry. The party had already begun while the royal family made the annual parade through the city. Rika reined her horse to a stop and Quitsu turned to her. "It's a night for celebration. You must find something to be glad for."

She nodded woodenly, and he turned, smacking her in the face with his fluffy fox tail before jumping to the ground. She watched him go as he trotted up to join her mother where she was already greeting her guests with smiles and embraces.

Rika straightened, steadying herself. *Find something to be glad for. Something. Anything.* She nodded. Otherwise, it would be a long, unhappy night. It would be a long, unhappy life.

CHAPTER 2

Rika was the first human to the breakfast table the next morning. She found Ryu, her father's seishen, sitting by the giant fireplace, licking a great golden paw.

"Morning, Ryu," she said, rubbing the sleep out of her eyes. "Everyone else still in bed?"

"They're up," he rumbled, "but there is a lot of cursing the second bottle of sake. I thought it best to remove myself."

Rika smiled and sat down, her stomach rumbling at the sight of the food that had already been laid out on the table. She poured herself a cup of green tea and began piling her plate with an assortment of fruit, fluffy white rice, and slices of smoked fish.

The celebration hadn't been as terrible as she had feared during the parade. Her two best friends, Oma and Sadele, had found her soon after she had dismounted and whisked her into an evening filled with dancing, sneaking sake, and eyeing the cute sons of Yoshai's nobles. Her parents, caught up in their own celebration, hadn't paid any attention to Rika, and Koji had thankfully left her alone. All in all, it had been a pretty good night.

Rika was mid-bite when her parents breezed through the door. Her father had his arm around her mother and was nuzzling at her neck while she playfully swatted at him. Rika swallowed thickly. Ugh. Her parents were always all over each other. You'd think after twenty years of marriage, they'd be sick of each other. Kai finally pushed Hiro away with more force and seemed to register Rika's presence.

"Darling!" Kai said, coming around the table and kissing Rika on the top of her head. She snagged a berry off Rika's plate, popping it in her mouth. "That tea smells heavenly. Pour me a cup?" Kai slid into the seat next to Rika while Hiro took the chair at the head of the table, rubbing his face vigorously to wake up. "Did you have fun last night, panda?" he asked, using the nickname that had followed her since she'd been a baby. Apparently, she had been ridiculously chubby. "We hardly saw you with all our guests."

"It was great," Rika said, forcing a smile while she poured her mother a cup of tea. "A perfect night."

"It *was* a perfect night," Kai said, taking the cup from Rika and passing it to Hiro. "So clear—perfect for the fireworks. And unseasonably warm. You always know how to pick the most auspicious dates. What did you say? Last night was a conjunction of the blue dragon constellation and the kinsei planet?"

Rika poured a third cup of tea and handed it to Kai, who wrapped her hands around it like it was sacred, breathing in the trails of hot vapor.

"Yep. Master Fortin and I calculated the angles ourselves." Master Fortin was her astrology teacher. She tolerated the rest of her lessons as part of her royal duties, but her favorites were astronomy and astrology. She had begged her parents for months for tutors in those particular subjects. They hadn't seen it as a necessary part of her curriculum. But for Rika…being out among the moon and the stars….it was the time she felt the most clarity, the most herself. That, and her fighting classes. Somehow the dance of fighting made sense to her. It was an art form of its own. She didn't care for archery or throwing knives, but whirling with the staffs or swords in hand-to-hand combat… She smiled despite herself at the thought of the last class, when she had landed two blows on Armsmistress Emi. Those were good days too.

Her smile crumbled as her brother slouched in, still in his crumpled pants and shirt from the night before. Quitsu padded behind him. "You didn't need to send Quitsu in to attack me, Mom," he grumbled, collapsing into a chair across from Rika. "I barely got any sleep as it is."

"Staying up late isn't an excuse to shirk your duties the following day," Hiro said. "The kingdom doesn't sleep in late if we do."

"Besides," Kai said brightly. "I thought today we could spend some time together as a family."

"Mother, no," Rika and Koji both protested, their eyes meeting in surprise at their unexpected alliance.

"I had plans to go to the beach with Oma and Sadele today," Rika said, thinking quickly. "We haven't gone in forever, and it's supposed to be sunny today."

"And Armsmistress Emi was going to work with me and Enzo today on some joint fighting moves we could do. We need to learn to work together."

"Joint fighting moves?" Rika snorted. "What, is he going to spear people with his horn?"

"I'll have him start with you," Koji said, throwing a grape at her with narrowed eyes.

Rika picked up a piece of fish to lob back at him when Hiro's voice cut through their feud. "No throwing food at the table. Rika, put the tuna down."

She dropped it on her plate, glaring at her brother. Why couldn't she have been an only child?

Kai sighed, looking between her children. "Are you sure you can't make an exception? I feel like I hardly see my babies anymore."

"We're not your babies anymore," Koji said. "I'm a sunburner with my own seishen."

Rika opened her mouth to make a quip about his "beard" but saw the warning look from Hiro and shut it. "You're fourteen," Hiro said. "You have a lot left to learn. Including a little humility."

"Mother, I'm sorry, but I really want to spend the day with Oma and Sadele," Rika said. "Some other time?"

Kai patted Rika's hand. "Of course. Maybe we can spend the day together," she brightened, looking at Hiro. At that moment, a servant entered, dropping a pile of scrolls onto the table next to Hiro. He winced. "Duty calls, my love."

They spent the rest of the meal in silence, as they usually did, both her parents buried nose deep in scrolls and letters pertaining to the business of the kingdom. Rika pushed the food around on her plate, no longer feeling hungry. She didn't really have plans with her friends today; she just didn't think she could stand to spend the entire day with her magical family and their seishen.

It wasn't that she didn't love her parents—she did—and she knew she was lucky to have them. It was just that she didn't fit. She looked around the table, eyeing her mother, her silver hair pulled into a messy bun, a pair of reading glasses perched on her nose. Her mother didn't look her near-forty years of age—she was willowy and strong, with a smattering of freckles across her small nose. Rika herself took more after her father, with his square face and striking features, but she had gotten her mother's freckles and small, thin build. She wasn't sure where the little gap between her two front teeth had come from. Koji was an immature, gangly version of their father but was already tall and sprouting more muscle than was fair. He would be as handsome as Hiro when he was grown, Rika thought begrudgingly. Some of the girls at the festival last night already had their sights on him. Gold and silver hair aside, she looked like part of this family. But the hair was impossible to ignore. As much as she wished otherwise, it was plain to see she didn't belong.

Rika dressed in a pair of white leggings and a long lavender tunic belted with a braided obi of silver. She had to make herself scarce today, so her parents didn't catch her in her lie about going to the beach. The town of Yoshai in which they lived was about an hour's ride from the southern coast of Kita-Miina, or Kitina, as they had taken to calling it for short. After her parents had wed and defeated the tengu, they had merged the two lands under joint rule. If Rika's powers ever came in, she would rule everything from the Akashi Mountains in the north to the frothing oceans in the south, and all the lands in between. *If* her powers ever came in.

She walked through the palace, enjoying the sunlight streaming through the broad windows. The palace had been built on the highest hill in the city and was tiered, so nearly every garden, walkway, and room had a sweeping view over the checkerboard city down to the sea. The water was as blue as she had ever seen it today, shimmering like a ribbon of jewels in the distance. The palace was filled with gardens, and Rika had explored every one. There were a few that were her favorites, including the one she found her feet had led her to now. It held a sundial set in the ground, as well as other carvings that Master Fortin had explained marked the movements of the moon and planets. Around the dial were climbing jasmine vines and flowering orange trees that attracted butterflies and flitting hummingbirds. She loved to watch the hummingbirds darting about so fast their wings looked invisible.

Rika took a seat in a spill of sunshine, her face turned to bask in the morning glow. The crisp spring was giving way to warmer days of summer, and she, for one, was ready. She loved the heat—it seemed it was never hot enough for her, even when the rest of the palace was complaining about the steamiest days of summer.

"Come to my garden yet again?" A lilting voice rang out. "You always seem to find yourself here."

Rika jumped at the intrusion. "Roweni. This isn't your garden. And I like it. It's my favorite."

A diminutive woman emerged from the flowering bushes, a tiny silver owl seishen on her shoulder. The woman had short, silver hair and violet eyes unlike any Rika had ever seen. She was the moonburner Oracle. According to Kai, she had made many prophecies over the years— prophecies that were uncannily accurate. But there was only one Rika cared about. The one that said that Rika would have magic someday. That prophecy was the only reason Rika hadn't completely lost hope.

"It is my favorite too," Roweni said.

"It's big enough for two," Rika said defensively, though in truth, she would have rather have been alone.

"Perhaps, but your troubles take up far more space than they have a right to."

Rika bristled, standing. The woman was always impossible to talk to. "I'm sorry to inconvenience you with my woes. If your prophecy showed signs of ever coming true, I wouldn't be so concerned."

"My prophecies always come true," she said. "But rarely in the way we expect."

Rika was twirling the end of her black hair between her fingers and angrily dropped her hand. "I can't wait anymore, Roweni. Some days I feel like I'm going to explode. If I'm not magical, then fine. I'll deal with it, move on with my life. Koji will take the crown, and I'll go…tell horoscopes in some backwater town. But the not knowing, the wondering…I can't take it anymore."

"You must."

Rika ground her teeth in frustration. "I've dissected the prophecy a thousand times! *Dark shadow falls, great danger calls; the first-born's power fights at last hour.* Was there nothing more? No explanation, no other verses?"

"I am not a reference book, child," Roweni said. "Don't you think I would ask for more explanation from the universe if I could get it? Some clear direction?"

Rika sighed, pacing across the face of the sundial. "I know. I'm sorry. Perhaps I need to find the answer elsewhere. I've looked everywhere in this palace, the library, nothing. Maybe I need to go journey to find Tsuki, to ask the goddess for insight. Or the seishen elder." She had grown up hearing of her parents' exploits in dealing with these wise and ancient gods. Surely, they would have insight into her circumstances. A thought occurred to her. "Maybe I could go to the Misty Forest and find my seishen. Why should I wait for it to come to me? Perhaps it's waiting for me there!"

"Seishen come when they are ready. And when you are ready. You know that. You can't force it," Roweni said.

Rika closed her eyes, despair coiling deep within her. "I feel like...I'd rather throw myself off the palace walls than wait one more day." A light flashed behind her closed eyelids, like one of the prior night's fireworks had exploded. "What was that?"

Roweni's seishen, Giselli, was fluttering in the air, its little wings whirling with agitation. Roweni was looking out towards the sea, her face an inscrutable mask.

Rika followed her gaze, and her heart skipped a beat. On the horizon, a shadow had fallen across a broad swath of the glistening sea—as if the sun didn't reach. There was a patch of...darkness.

Roweni and Rika both drew to the end of the garden, pressing themselves against the balcony wall. Rika squinted, shading her eyes with her hand. *What was it?* She hissed in a breath when she made it out. It wasn't a patch of shadow or darkness.

It was an armada.

Ships with billowing, black sails, packed so tightly that no blue was visible between them. Thousands of ships.

"Where did those come from?" Rika whispered.

"Great shadow falls. Great danger calls," Roweni said. "It seems your wait is over."

CHAPTER 3

Rika found her mother striding through the hallways towards the royal council room, her seishen Quitsu trotting at her side. "You've seen them?" Rika asked breathlessly.

"Impossible to miss." Kai nodded.

Rika fell into step beside her mother. "Can I sit in on the council meeting?"

Kai looked at her daughter sideways, considering. "You may observe. Not a peep out of you, understood?"

"Understood," Rika said eagerly. "Mother...I was with Roweni when the ships appeared. She said...a great shadow."

Kai frowned, and then her eyes opened wide. "She thinks this concerns your prophecy?"

Rika shrugged. "Maybe."

"You must be pleased as a fox in the henhouse," Kai said.

"At a threatening armada at our shore? I'm not that selfish, Mother," Rika said. But inside, she was jumping with excitement, twirling and spinning. Of course, she didn't want any threat to come to her homeland. But the prophecy seemed to say her power would manifest when the threat arose. Maybe her wait was truly over...

They reached the council room and Kai pointed at a chair at the far end of the table. "Sit. Listen."

Rika sank into it, shoving her hands under her knees to keep them from shaking with excitement. The council room was built like so many at the palace of Yoshai, a long chamber full of windows that let in the remarkable view of the city and sea. A long, black polished wooden table paralleled the row of glass that now held a perfect view of the stain that darkened their crystal sea. Rika couldn't help herself, she stood and went to the windows, pressing her nose to the glass. The ships were reaching the shoreline, and had begun to spread to make the landing. There were *so many* of them. Kitina had no significant naval force, as it had no enemies that would attack by sea. Or so they had thought.

She turned as her father and Ryu entered, and Hiro enveloped Kai in a comforting embrace. "Daarco and Emi are on their way, as is Master Tato. Nanase had some business in town, but I sent a messenger to fetch her."

"I sent for Colum," Kai said. "He's the most extensively traveled of us all. Perhaps he knows something."

"No doubt he stole something from these people and they're here to get it back," Hiro said, and Kai swatted at him. Hiro wrapped his arm around Kai's shoulder, and they walked to the window beside Rika. "You'll sit in?" he asked.

Rika nodded.

"I've never seen anything like it," Kai said, her face grave. "It's hard to imagine they come in peace."

"Not in such numbers…and with black sails." Hiro shook his head. "Who are they?"

"Where did they come from?" Kai asked. "Our sailors have traveled as far south as three months' provisions would take them before turning back. They've never found evidence of any land that direction."

"When they appeared, there was a flash of light. Did you see it?" Rika asked.

Kai and Hiro both shook their heads.

"One minute, they weren't there, and then the next minute they were. Like…"

"Magic," Kai finished. "But what kind of sorcery could manifest a fleet of vessels? And, presumably, men to sail them? There's no way someone could use burning for such a purpose."

"We have to assume it's a new kind of magic," a new voice said from the door.

They all turned, and found a tall, willowy man with golden hair and a stack of books under his arm. Master Tato, the chief librarian, and a member of her parents' council. He had always struck Rika as too young, and frankly too handsome, to be interested in a lifetime buried in dusty books, but they seemed to be his true love. Rika had only hazy memories of the prior historian, Master Vita, as he had passed away of old age when she'd been five. But those memories of his half-moon spectacles and halo of his bright white hair were much more suited to the post of librarian.

Master Tato was followed by Armsmistress Emi and General Daarco, who was head of the country's military forces. They were married and had one daughter, Rika's friend Oma. They were also two of her parents' oldest friends, and they all spent a lot of time drinking sake and laughing together around the dinner table. Oma and Rika would always sneak away from those dinners as soon as they could to find their own fun. More often than not, Koji would follow, whining until they let him tag along on whatever adventures they had. He hadn't been doing that as much since he had gained his powers. Actually, Rika thought with a little frown of dismay, she and Oma hadn't spent as much time together in the few years since Oma's moonburning powers had appeared, either.

Rika, mired in her thoughts, realized with a start that everyone had sat down. Ryu and Quitsu had curled up next to each other in a patch of sunlight spilling onto the floor. She hurried over and took her place, trying to look meek and concerned.

Her parents' friend Colum chose that moment to breeze into the room, his curly, gray hair bobbing as he walked. "'Bout time for a little adventure around here!" he exclaimed, settling into a chair and propping his boots up on the table. They were at Rika's end. She wrinkled her nose and he winked. "Been positively dull. You're all getting fat and lazy."

"Colum, always a pleasure," Hiro said dryly. Perhaps "friend" wasn't the right word to describe Colum. Acquaintance? Strange uncle-type whom they tolerated with half-fondness and half-weariness? That was more appropriate. Colum was an adventurer who had traveled across their land, but his weather-beaten face still managed to look surprisingly youthful. He had settled down in the past years with his wife, a moonburner named Mesilla. They lived a quiet life on an island to the southwest of Yoshai, as Mesilla didn't like to be around people. Rika had gathered that the woman had ghosts in her past. Her parents didn't like her for some reason. And they liked everyone.

"What'd you think of those fireworks last night?" Colum asked. "Impressive, no? I'm glad I came to visit; now I can be in on whatever hijinks we come up with to foil these invaders."

"We can't presume they're invaders, or that we'll be taking any action against them," Kai said. "They're foreign ships landing on our shores. That's all we know right now. We shouldn't jump to conclusions."

Rika had noticed that her mother seemed to lead the council meetings, while her father played a supporting role. She wasn't sure how they had settled into their roles, but she hoped if she was ever queen, she could find a king who was similarly confident enough to not need to take charge all the time.

"Hard to jump to any other conclusion with black sails," Colum said under his breath.

"Maybe black is a color of good luck in their culture," Hiro suggested. "Maybe it's to pay homage to their sea god, who rules the dark depths of the sea."

"Yah, yah. Maybe some apprentice accidentally squirted squid ink over the lot of them so they had to dye them black to salvage 'em." Colum snorted. "We could speculate for days. But maybe, and far more likely, they are designed to intimidate."

"Can we table the issue of the sails?" Kai said wearily. "Master Tato, is there anything you can tell us about these new arrivals? Have you ever read of such a thing? Of another land to our south?"

Master Tato ran a nervous hand through his golden hair in an unconscious gesture. "I've never come across mention of lands other than Kita or Miina in my studies. And, I might add, I went through a bit of a phase in my younger years where I fancied the idea of being an explorer. I did extensive cartography research in both the libraries of Kyuden and Kistana. I will comb through the library here, in Yoshai, for any mention, but I'm afraid I have very little counsel to give you at this time."

Kai nodded. "It was a long shot." She paused, seeming to steel herself for her next question. "Colum, what about you? Have you seen any mention of such things in your travels?"

"Why, thank you for asking, queenie." Colum dropped his boots off the table and leaned forward. Rika didn't know how Colum got away with such impertinence to her mother. She could only imagine that the familiarity went back years.

Colum continued. "I've seen something. In a treasure case in the remote corners of Kita. I was in a cavern that served as an ancient burial ground for a past civilization..."

Hiro pinched the bridge of his nose, shaking his head. "You're a graverobber now, too?"

"You want to hear the story or not, Your Majesty?" Colum asked.

Kai waved him on.

"Inside the cave was a carved tomb that must have housed a real big shot. He was buried with all sorts of goodies—jewels, coins, golden goblets, you get the idea. But what concerns us today was a map I found. A map of the stars."

"Like for navigation at sea?" Hiro asked.

"No, like for navigation *among* the stars," Colum said, his voice hushed. "Between the constellations were what I could only describe as paths. I thought it was fanciful—a stylized depiction of what some artist thought could be out there. But what if there really were a way to travel between worlds?"

"It's a remarkable thought," Kai said.

"Do you have this map? Could we examine it?" Master Tato asked, leaning forward eagerly.

"Nah. Sold it years ago."

"Of course you did," Hiro said.

Kai shook her head with wonder. "To think there could be other unexplored worlds..."

"Clearly," Master Tato interjected, "these newcomers have some magic that enables them to travel at great speeds, whether across stars, or oceans, which seems far more likely. Otherwise, how else would they have appeared so suddenly?"

"So these foreigners have started exploring," Kai said.

"Or invading," Colum said, picking at his molar with his pinkie.

"Our next step is obvious. We must go to these people and welcome them. I refuse to treat them with hostility until they show it's warranted," Kai said. "To do otherwise is to risk starting an unnecessary war."

"I'll go," Hiro said. "I'll take our most elite warriors with me, and Ryu. We will provide a royal welcome."

"I'm coming with you," Kai said.

"One of us should stay here, my love," Hiro said softly, taking Kai's hand. "If they prove hostile, we should not have both monarchs in harm's way. It's not wise."

She frowned. "Then I'll go, and you stay here."

"If this is a patriarchal culture, they might respond better to negotiating with another man."

Kai rolled her eyes. "If they're matriarchal, they'd respond better to me." Rika's parents looked at each other, conducting the kind of silent debate that only married people know how to do. It seemed that Hiro proved victorious, as Kai was the one who broke eye contact. "Fine. Hiro will go. I'll stay here and tend the hearth."

He chuckled. "Running the country is hardly tending the hearth."

Armsmistress Emi cleared her throat. "Is it wise to send a monarch at all? Is it not an unnecessary risk? Send an emissary, a messenger. Take their temperature."

Hiro shook his head. "I don't want to risk offending them by sending someone without the proper authority. Besides, I want to take their temperature myself. Me and my men can take care of ourselves."

"I think it's a necessary risk," Kai said. "Master Tato, I'd like you to accompany Hiro. You're good with languages and perhaps can lend some aid in communicating."

Master Tato inclined his head. "As you command."

Rika had watched the exchange silently, but inside she was jumping up and down. She bit her lip in indecision but ended up blurting out: "I want to go too."

All heads swiveled towards her. "Absolutely not— "Kai began but was cut off as Koji swung down from the rafters in the corner of the room, dropping onto the floor.

"If Rika gets to go, I want to go too!"

CHAPTER 4

"Koji!" Kai scolded. "How long have you been hiding there?"

Rika snorted. That much was obvious.

Hiro threw his hands in the air. "Why have the gods seen fit to punish me with such obstinate children?"

"What did I do?" Rika asked, wounded. "I should go because Roweni thinks that the great shadow from my prophecy is the fleet of ships on the water."

Hiro's head swiveled up at that, and he looked searchingly at Kai. She nodded grimly. "It could be."

"If the prophecy is correct, my power is necessary to defeat these invaders."

"If the prophecy is correct," Hiro said, "these newcomers aren't here for trade and cultural exchange. The prophecy speaks of great danger. I don't think it's a good idea to send you into that before we know what we're dealing with. We might need to make a quick exit."

"I agree," Kai said. "I'm sorry, but it's too dangerous. Until we know more, you stay here. And you definitely stay here, Koji. I'll deal with you later."

"But, Mom," they both began.

"End of discussion." Kai's voice cracked like a whip. "Now unless anyone besides my children has anything else to add, Hiro should ready his team."

Rika crossed her arms over her chest, slumping in her chair. It wasn't fair. The first time in sixteen years where her powers might have a chance of manifesting, and she wasn't allowed anywhere near it.

The adults stood, beginning to file out of the room. Her parents talked by the door in hushed tones, Kai tracing her fingers along Hiro's ear and jaw. Ugh. Rika looked away. Emi was rounding the table and leaned down beside her. The moonburner's face was half-scarred from a fire that had occurred when she'd been young, but it somehow only served to accentuate how beautiful the rest of her was. "It was a valiant attempt. But don't be so hasty to rush into danger, panda. I have a feeling we'll all see plenty of action before this plays out. Your time will come. Be patient."

Rika attempted a half-smile. "I know. Thanks, Emi."

Emi stood, squeezing her shoulder as she walked around the table and slipped her hand into Daarco's outstretched palm.

Koji stood at the door, the last to leave besides her. He paused. "They were never going to let you go. You can't protect yourself without any powers."

Rika narrowed her eyes and exploded out of the chair, running towards him. She grabbed his arm before he knew what to do and twisted it behind his back painfully like Emi had taught her. Then she stuck her finger in her mouth, wet it with her tongue, and waggled it in his ear.

"Ugh, Rika, stop! Gross! You're hurting me!" Koji cried, his voice squeaking in protest.

She grinned. "Tell me again how I can't defend myself without powers?" She felt a heat growing around her wrist, warming before it became a searing pain.

"Let go," he grunted, and she released his hand, stepping back in shock, cradling her wrist to her body. As soon as she released him, the pain stopped. She looked down. A red welt circled her wrist, growing angry and puffy.

"You sunburned against me?" She couldn't believe it. Students were forbidden to burn outside of training. Plus, it was always forbidden to use burning to harm someone.

Koji shrank from her, his face a mix of emotions. "I told you," he said. "You can't fight someone with magic."

"Just get out, Ko," she said, suddenly unable to stand the sight of him. She pointed to the door. "Go!"

He fled, and she sagged against the door frame, hissing at the pain. She'd need to go to the hospital ward and get a poultice to soothe the pain. Tears stung her eyes, but she welcomed them this time. They left hot streams down her cheeks, fueling her anger. *Be patient. Wait. It's coming; you'll see.* That's all anyone ever told her! Well, she was sick to death of waiting. And she wouldn't do it anymore. It was time to take matters into her own hands.

☾

After stopping by the hospital ward for a cooling balm for her wrist, Rika skulked about the palace eavesdropping on her father's preparations. Hiro would lead a team of three sunburners (including Master Tato) and two moonburners. The beach where the foreigners had landed was only about ten leagues from Yoshai, and so they would ride lion-horses, rather than flying on golden eagles, with the hope that they would give the invaders time to prepare for their presence, rather than see a sudden landing as a threat. They would set up camp on the outskirts of Antila, the little fishing village on the seaside. From there, they would send an emissary to invite the leader of the new arrivals to treat with them.

In the meantime, Rika made her own preparations. Her excitement was like a taut bowstring; it took all of her self-control to hold in her excitement. As much as she wanted to, she knew she couldn't tell anyone what she intended, not even Oma or Sadele. She packed her supplies: her cloak and a change of sensible clothes, her hunting knife, flint for starting a fire, thin leather rope to set a snare for game, a small medical kit with herbs, gut and a needle for sewing wounds. Both her mother and late grandmother were excellent healers, and though Rika wasn't as passionate as they were, it *was* a sensible skill, so she had soaked up as much knowledge from them as she could. She threw a bedroll and a waterskin on the pile and went to the kitchens to steal some food.

Though Rika had grown up amongst these sandstone walls all her life, her clandestine mission lent a sense of newness to them. Suddenly, there was someone lurking around every corner, intent on foiling her plan. At one point, she heard her mother's voice, and she darted into an empty room to let the queen pass by. She didn't want any probing questions.

Much to her chagrin, Rika wasn't a very good liar. Or perhaps her parents were just able to sniff out a lie at fifty paces.

Luckily, the cook wasn't so discerning and swallowed Rika's cover story about a hunting trip without blinking. Rika helped herself to dried meat and fish, a few apples, a packet of nuts, and some hard cheese. She didn't think she was going to be gone for more than a day or two. It would be enough. She swiped a hot honey cake on the way out, blowing to cool it as she called a *thank you* to the cook. The sticky pastries were her favorite, and she was feeling tremendously pleased with herself by the time she got back to her room, licking the sweet crumbs from her fingers.

Hiro's team was to leave at sundown. Rika and Koji were summoned to the main courtyard to say goodbye. Enzo trotted next to Koji, too regal for words, his golden mane fluttering in the wind. Rika shot Koji a look of as much venom as she could muster, and for once, he looked away, rather than meeting her glare with one of his own. Clearly, he was still feeling guilty about sunburning against her and scalding her wrist earlier. Good. He *should* feel bad. What he had done was inexcusable. To use magic to harm was forbidden, except in cases of self-defense. And he could hardly argue that her arm-twisting justified true self-defense. It was a move Emi had taught twelve-year-olds how to elude. She huffed, tossing her ebony hair over her shoulder. It didn't matter. She would be gone from here within the hour, on her way to her destiny, to challenge these invaders and finally get her silver hair and magic and her seishen. When she returned, he would have nothing to lord over her. She relished the prospect.

Hiro and Kai were wrapped in a tight embrace, murmuring into each other's ears. When they finally pulled back, they shared a long kiss, and Rika looked away, drumming her fingers in impatience. *Yes, the whole kingdom knows you're desperately in love,* she thought. *Let's get on with it!*

Hiro went to say goodbye to Koji first, placing a big hand on the side of his son's face. Ryu stalked at his side like a shadow. "Take care of your mother while I'm gone. No pranks or provoking your sister or running off. This is a dangerous time, and your mother needs to be focused on running this country, not chasing her errant children."

Rika swallowed her guilt at that. Mother would be fine. She'd leave a note.

Koji nodded as Hiro continued. "I love you, son. Be safe." He pulled him into a hug. They were the same height now, Rika realized. Hiro still dwarfed Koji with his bulk, but they were even, head to head. When had her brother gotten so big?

Then Hiro turned to Rika, his green eyes full of concern. He drew her to the side, where he could speak to her without her brother hearing. He took her hands in his own and kissed one. His hands were calloused, rough. "My little girl, you're all grown up. More beautiful and smart than your mother and I could have ever hoped."

"Dad—" Rika rolled her eyes.

"I'm serious. This world has treated you unfairly. Made you wait and wonder about something that should have been your birthright. And you have handled it with grace and poise. Most of the time." A smile flicked across his face, and she swallowed the lump in her throat.

"You must be patient a bit longer. I know you must be thinking of the prophecy, but we don't know what we're dealing with here. Don't try anything that could put you at risk. Promise me."

She averted her eyes, examining veins of the stones beneath her feet, nodding.

"Say it."

"I promise." The words were a whisper. *I'm sorry, Father,* she thought, *but I can't make that promise.* Guilt needled at her. She hated to lie to him. But she must. And he must believe her. She straightened, meeting his eyes. "I promise. But don't talk like this. It feels like you're saying goodbye."

"I don't know what we'll be facing. A warrior prepares for all outcomes."

"No," she said. "Prepare to come home. That's the only outcome we'll accept."

He chuckled. "As stubborn as your mother. I'm a fool, but it only makes me love you more." He pulled her into a hug, and she closed her eyes, breathing in his scent of oiled leather and fresh mint. He released her and turned. She knelt and opened her arms to Ryu to give him a hug too, squeezing his fluffy lion mane tightly in her arms. "Keep him safe, Ryu," she whispered in his ear as his wiry whiskers tickled her neck.

"I always do," he rumbled back.

"Take care of Master Tato," she called to Hiro. "He's hopeless with a sword." The librarian was far enough from her that he didn't turn as his name.

Hiro winked at her and strode from the courtyard—Ryu at his side—in an instant shedding the skin of father and husband and king, and donning the aspect of warrior. He didn't look back.

Rika managed an encouraging smile for her mother, who stood, her hand to her heart, worry lining her brow. Then Rika was off, turning and slipping through the corridors back to her room to grab her bag and bedroll. She quickly changed into plain clothes—thick, chocolate brown leggings, a deep purple tunic belted with a plain leather obi, and sturdy lace-up leather boots, worn in from years of training, hunting, and riding outside the city. She twisted her long, black hair into a bun, securing it with two wooden hair sticks. She wanted to jump with giddiness. She was ready.

She took the servants' hallways through the palace, making her way down to the stable. The lion horses, the huge hybrid creatures favored by armored sunburners, were kept in a separate stable from the horses, so this one was relatively deserted. She pulled her horse's tack off the wall and slipped inside his stall, dropping her bag. "Hello, Michi," she said, giving the bay a scratch behind the ears. He shook his head, seeming surprised to see her. "We're going on an adventure," she whispered, sliding the bit into his mouth and the halter over his flicking ears.

She finished saddling Michi and stole across the stable to scoop out a small bag of grain to add to her food stores. There should be plenty of grass for Michi, but he liked oats, and he would be in a better mood if she had a little treat for him at the end of their ride. Michi huffed at the bag in curiosity as she stuffed it down beside her cloak and other food. "For later," she whispered.

Rika opened the stall door and led him out into the starry night, her heart thundering in her chest. They walked towards the side entrance of the palace, Rika cringing as the iron shoes on Michi's hooves clanged against the stones of the courtyard. The sound seemed deafening—she was sure her mother would come running any second. But no one did. At the gate, the guard nodded to her but didn't inquire where she was going. She could hardly believe her good fortune. It took all her restraint to keep the smile of glee off her face as they walked under the arch of the high palace walls. On the other side, the smile broke out in earnest as she swung up onto Michi, nudging him forward with her heels. She had done it. She was on her way!

CHAPTER 5

Though Rika wanted to urge Michi into a gallop, she reined him in when they were a few streets away from the palace, settling into his rocking gait. It wouldn't do her any good to attract attention by trampling some innocent Yoshian citizen in her haste to get out of the city. Rika almost never traveled anywhere without at least one or two guards, and so it felt strange to be alone. Strangely freeing.

It took her about half an hour to make her way through the winding streets of the city, past street vendors offering fragrant vats of spicy noodles, people drinking sake at sidewalk cafes, shopkeepers blowing out lanterns and locking their doors for the night. Yoshai was by no means a perfect city—it had its share of crime, poverty, and unrest—but Rika loved it. Everything felt so deliberate, as if some divine hand had planted the buildings where they sat. From the colorful tile roofs to the fragrant blooming vines clinging to sandstone walls, right down to the ornamental grates covering the storm drains. There was a loveliness and care about it that she hadn't seen when she visited Kyuden or Kistana, the other seats of her parents' rule. According to Kai, Yoshai had been buried under the desert for most of her childhood, and it had only been the act of Taiyo, the sun god, that had raised it again. So perhaps there had been a divine hand in the city's original creation.

Rika was headed for the Dragon Gate, a small pedestrian entrance in the southwest corner of the city. It was named for the elaborate carving of a serpentine dragon that slithered around the arched opening—so lifelike, its scales seemed to ripple as you walked beneath. Hiro and his soldiers were leaving through the main southern gate—the Sea Gate—and she planned to follow them south on a parallel track. Close, but far enough to stay out of sight. Once Hiro had made camp and it was too late to send her back, she would present herself. She'd have to take whatever punishment her father saw fit to give her, but whatever happened, it would be worth it. She would be right in the thick of things, the perfect spot for her powers to come to life.

The land south of the city walls was made up of rolling farmland that gave way to tall, sweet-smelling grass. Here, the cloudless sky stretched wide, a velvet blanket dotted with glittering stars. With no walls to keep them at bay, it seemed as if the heavens stretched down low, reaching out to touch her. The constellations winked cheerfully at her—the black tortoise that guarded the northern star, the red phoenix standing in the south, the white tiger in the west. Her favorite constellation, the clever fox, seemed especially close, starlight wagging the cluster of five stars that made up its bushy tail. She stretched a hand up, imagining she could scoop him up and bring him down to Earth, to ride on her saddle like Quitsu. When her neck began to ache, she finally looked back to Earth, giving the fox a little wave goodbye.

She rode for an hour or so in silence, listening to the clicking of the wild koumidi, the little bats whose tame brothers they used to send messages. The air was warm, but a wind blew from the south, bringing the tang of salt and something else. Something that tasted bitter on her tongue. She shivered, her skin prickling, her senses roaring to awareness. It was then that she realized that she was being followed.

She wasn't sure what first clued her in. The nervous swiveling of Michi's ears, perhaps, as if he were searching for something. Or maybe it was the sound of the grass slipping past the muscular legs of a beast. Beast, or man? Rika resisted the powerful urge to turn about in her saddle and confront the interloper, knowing that it was hard to defend herself on horseback. Should she kick Michi to a gallop and put distance between them? But that might alert her father to her presence. The road wasn't far from her current position, and he likely had at least one man scouting around their position as they traveled. No, if this person intended her harm, they would be doing a better job of stalking her. If they were here to fetch her back to the palace, they would have announced themselves. That left just one person it could be.

She reined in Michi, making a show of yawning, stretching her arms wide. She swung down from the saddle, her knees popping. She opened one of her saddlebags, rummaging around for a piece of dried salmon. She actually was hungry. A break couldn't hurt. She stood, munching, watching the dark horizon where she knew the ocean to be. She took a swig from her waterskin. A twig crunched behind her. She whirled and darted for the noise, tackling it into the thick grass.

"Oof!" Her follower went down like a sack of rice, landing flat on his back. Rika's knee pinned his chest, her belt knife held aloft in one hand.

"Ow, Rika, get off me!" Koji said, squirming beneath her. "Are you going to stab me?"

"I should," she said. "I'd finally be rid of you."

Koji's seishen, Enzo, emerged from the darkness, leveling his long horn at her. It wasn't close enough to be threatening, but she took his point well enough.

She pushed off Koji before standing up, causing him to wheeze out another breath. She sheathed her knife and offered him her outstretched hand. "Happy?" she asked Enzo.

The seishen straightened. "Very," he said.

Her eyes opened in surprise as Koji took her hand and hauled himself to his feet. Enzo didn't often talk to her, not like Quitsu or Ryu. He and Koji kept to themselves, a secret friendship of whispered confidences and jokes. A friendship she wasn't welcome in.

She shook off her surprise and resumed glaring at Koji, her hands on her hips. "Ko, what in Tsuki's name do you think you're doing here?"

"Same thing you are," he protested.

"You're confronting a threatening darkness that your powers were prophesied to defeat?" she asked.

"Okay, not exactly the same thing. I don't want to miss the action," he said. "I'm fourteen. I've been training my whole life with Armsmistress Emi and the other sunburners. This is the first exciting thing that's happened in...our entire lifetimes. I'm not going to miss it!"

He had a point there. There had been war and strife when her parents had been young, but her own childhood had seen nothing more exciting than tavern brawls and villagers grumbling about taxes. Things had been remarkably peaceful. Still. "I'm not here to be part of the action. I'm here so my moonburning powers manifest. Because according to

Roweni, if they don't, we're all screwed. You'll just get in the way."

"I won't," he said. "Enzo and I will…observe. I want to see these foreigners. Do you think they have three eyes and blue skin? That's what my friend Jino said."

"Jino's an idiot," Rika said. "I bet they look exactly like us." She sighed. "Is there anything I can say to convince you to go back to Yoshai?"

"No," he said, sticking his chin in the air. Rika grimaced. She recognized that stubborn look. She was the one making it most of the time. There would be no convincing him to return. "Fine," she said. "You and Enzo can ride with me. But when it's time to tell Father I'm here, you'll hide. I have a good excuse for why I've come. You're just nosy."

"But then I won't get to see the foreigners!" he protested.

"You can watch from a hillside. You'll be able to see how many eyes they have and everything. And then you won't get in trouble with Dad for sneaking out." *At least until you get back to Yoshai*, Rika thought, *and Mother flays you alive*. But Koji wasn't thinking that far ahead. *Typical boy*, she thought. He clearly liked the idea of having this adventure without getting in trouble with their father. "Agreed," he finally said.

"You have to do exactly what I say, though," she warned.

"Unless it's stupid," he countered.

"Fair enough," she said. "Let's go. Father should be nearing Antila. He'll set up camp soon. If we get to a good spot nearby, we can get some sleep."

Koji seemed content to let her lead, and they mounted up, riding in silence. Rika tried not to stare at Enzo, but it was still disconcerting to see her brother riding a golden unicorn. She still hadn't gotten used to his seishen.

They slowed to a stop as the lights of Antila came into view. Rika could just make out a tent going up by the light of four orbs the moonburners must have cast. In the distance, along the black line of the sea, hundreds of green lights glowed. No, not hundreds. Thousands. They stretched as far as the eye could see, floating eerily in the air.

"Look at all of them," Koji whispered.

"What's making that green light?" she asked, more to herself than to Koji. The illumination was unlike anything she had ever seen before. Her mother was right. Whatever had borne these ships here, whatever made that light, it was magic unknown to the burners of Kitina.

"Maybe they're here to trade," Koji said weakly. She glanced at him. His face was drawn, pale. It seemed the reality of this adventure was coming home to roost for him. Who was she kidding? For her too.

"Father will be able to reason with them. He faced demons from another realm, remember?"

Koji gave her a grateful smile and she felt a twinge of fondness for her brother. "You're right. If he and Mother could free the gods, destroy the tengu...he can handle these guys."

"Now, I just have to figure out how to let Father know I'm here with minimal yelling."

"Good luck with that," Koji said. "Remember when that litter of chinchillas got loose in their chambers, and he didn't realize his pants had a hole in them until halfway through that royal dinner?"

Rika cackled at the memory. "There couldn't have been a worse place for a hole." She laughed. "Remember how red his face got?"

"And that vein in his neck started to bulge? I thought it was going to explode, and a spurt of blood would come out of the side of him!" Koji pantomimed the explosion, and Rika held her stomach as she laughed. She had never seen her father so furious. But he couldn't say a word, not until the dinner was over and his guests had left.

"I can assure you"—a deep baritone voice sounded before them—"that his fury over the trouser incident will pale in comparison to the rage you two will face tonight."

Koji and Rika froze as Ryu, their father's seishen, stalked out of the tall grass as silently as a wraith.

"Both of you. Come with me."

CHAPTER 6

Rika couldn't help the feeling that she was walking to the gallows as she and her brother followed Ryu towards their father's tent. Koji, for once, was silent beside her. Even Enzo's head was down, his horn skimming the ground. This was going to be much, much worse than the trouser incident.

She had wanted to present herself to her father on her own terms, to prepare her case for why she should be allowed to stay. This wasn't at all what she'd imagined. How had Ryu even found them? As if he had heard her thought, Ryu rumbled, "Seishen can sense each other's presence. Even communicate telepathically across short distances. Something you might want to keep in mind for future rebellious acts."

Rika glared at Koji and Enzo. They had given them away! If she had come alone, she would have been fine. Koji seemed to shrink under her gaze, and Enzo looked away. She'd deal with them later. For now, she had to brace herself for the gale force winds of her father's anger.

The burners who had accompanied Hiro were still finishing erecting the tent, tying the sturdy bamboo poles to the crimson fabric. Hiro stood in the middle, stock still amongst the flurry of activity. Even from behind, Rika could see that his muscles were tensed, his fists balled in fury. Her heart hammered in her chest. On a whim, she seized her brother's hand and squeezed it. He squeezed back—his palm sweaty.

"So," Hiro finally said, after the silence stretched so long she thought she would scream. He turned, his eyes pinning them like arrows. His face was red—thunderous. "Instead of performing valuable reconnaissance, Ryu has had to waste his time bringing my errant children to me. Do you think this is a game we're playing here?"

"No," they both murmured, their eyes glued to the ground.

"Do you think it is sport?"

"No."

"Do you think I forbade you to come because I am a spiteful father, intent on depriving you of fun? Do I forbid you to do things without good cause?"

"No," they both said, though at this point Hiro was getting going, and Rika thought his questioning was more rhetorical.

"I forbid you to come here because what we do is dangerous. And I do not want to put my beloved children and the heirs to this nation's future at risk. Does this seem so unreasonable? So intolerable for you that you must disobey me?"

"No—"

"And now you put me in the impossible position of deciding whether to send you home with an escort, depriving me of valuable burners whom I need here, or allowing you to stay in this dangerous situation."

Rika looked up at that. "You must let us stay," she blurted out. "We'll stay out of the way. Watch from afar. But you might need my power…"

"I am a sunburner and a king!" he thundered. "I do not need my teenage daughter's assistance with affairs of state!"

"But the prophecy…" she said weakly, his words stinging as surely as if he had slapped her. She felt her chance to see her powers manifest slipping through her grasp like sand.

"Prophecy be damned. I will not be ruled by a few words uttered a decade ago by an unhinged Oracle! Now, I have made my decision. You will return to Yoshai at once. One of my sunburners will escort you, and if you give him a peep of trouble, you will both be locked in your rooms for a year. Do I make myself clear?"

Rika's face flushed with anger and shame as she nodded, looking at the swirls on the carpet that had been laid over the grass. This was all Koji's fault! If he and Enzo hadn't given them away, she'd still be tucked away out of sight, ready to present herself at the perfect moment. She could kick herself. Why had she agreed to let them travel with her?

Hiro heaved a massive sigh, deflating a bit. "I do this because I love you and I fear for you here. If anything happened to either of you, your mother and I—"

"Your Majesty!" Master Tato ducked inside the tent, his eyes wide as full moons. "There's movement from the beach. Something...*someone* is coming."

"Now?"

Master Tato nodded, wringing his thin hands.

Hiro turned to Rika and Koji. "You two will sit in the corner and say *nothing*. Ryu and Enzo will guard you. Am I understood?"

They both nodded eagerly, Rika's heart fluttering in her chest. This was it. The shadow would be revealed, and if the invaders tried anything, her powers would manifest to save them. She wanted to dance with glee, but she kept a serious expression on her face, forcing her shaking hands behind her back, so her father wouldn't see them. She would be quiet. Until he needed her.

As Rika, Koji, and the seishen retreated into the corner of the tent, Hiro quickly donned his jacket and buckled on his sword belt. He flipped open one of the saddlebags they had brought and pulled out his golden crown, resting it atop his head. Rika knew that the crown was more than an accessory—it was a well for sunlight, catching and holding it so the wearer had something to burn at night. The other sunburners, who had no similar relics, were as helpless as ordinary men at night, though they all had extensive weapons training. Except poor Master Tato. Rika didn't think the librarian was particularly handy with a sword. At least the group had the two moonburners to defend them—their power was most deadly at night, when they could pull light from the moon and burn it into heat or fire or lightning. Plus, the seishen could be deadly if cornered. Though Rika had grown up treating Ryu like a pet, she knew she wouldn't want to cross him in a fight. There was plenty of firepower in this tent. They would be able to face whatever came through that door.

Four of the burners fell into position in a row behind Hiro while the last sunburner went outside to great their "guests." The wait stretched long and wide, but finally, when Rika thought the anticipation would kill her, she heard murmured voices outside.

A man was the first to duck under the tent flap. He looked unlike any of her people. Dark hair swept over his brow, and he had olive skin, as well as thick, arching eyebrows framing eyes that glowed an eerie green. Like the lights over the sea. He was handsome—strikingly so—as tall and broad as her father. Black leather armor stretched over lithe muscle that moved with Ryu's cat-like grace. The man surveyed each individual standing in the tent, and when his eyes swept over her, a chill crawled up her spine. Despite the pleasant packaging, this man frightened her.

Then he stepped aside to allow the next member of his party to enter the tent. At this sight, Rika forgot all about the man. This…this was the threat. This was the great shadow, the sweeping darkness. This was, in a word—evil.

It stood two heads taller than her father and was clad in black chitinous armor, almost like scales. Its claw-like fingers curled into fists on the end of unnaturally long arms, and the arms, she realized in horror, numbered four. Whatever this creature was, it wasn't human. It wore a black helmet that covered its head, but where its face should be…was only darkness. Darkness and two orbs glowing sickly green. In one of its hands it held a wooden staff covered in an intricate pattern of vines and leaves.

Hiro backed up a step and tightened his hand on his sword hilt. The creature stepped aside, and another entered the tent, looking identical to its fellow. Except this one, she noticed, was missing two claws on one of its hands. She wasn't sure why she noticed it, but the sight returned some of her failing courage. If it could lose fingers, it could be killed.

Hiro squared his shoulders and faced the horrors before him. "Welcome to the land of Kita-Miina," he said formally. "I am King Hiro, one of the rulers of this land. I am pleased to welcome you to our shores. I look forward to talking with you about how our two great races can coexist in peace. We believe we have much to learn about each other, and much to learn from each other."

Rika was amazed that her father's voice was clear and strong, without a hint of fear. Suddenly, the bedtime stories of her parents fighting demons and winning came into vivid color. Pride swelled within her.

The creature with three fingers turned to the man who had entered with them. Rika had forgotten about him, but he stepped forward. He began to speak, his eyes flashing with that same eerie green. He had a pleasant voice, deep and melodic, but the words he spoke were strange and garbled. Nonsense. Hiro looked at Master Tato, who shrugged helplessly. Whatever this language was, it wasn't one the librarian had encountered. Clearly, the creatures couldn't understand the dialect Hiro spoke.

Hiro paused for a moment, but then stepped forward slowly, taking his hand off his sword. He extended his hand to the creature in a gesture of friendship. The creature extended one of its own arms, wrapping its claws delicately around Hiro's hand. Hiro gently pumped his hand up and down, and Rika blew out a breath she hadn't realized she was holding. A handshake. It was a good start.

The creature tightened his grip, causing Hiro to grunt in surprise. Ryu, who had been sitting at her side, was on his feet in a flash, a low growl rumbling in his chest. He didn't approach, no doubt not wanting to make a threatening movement. The creature pulled Hiro towards him, bending its face down towards Hiro's own. Her father stepped forward—once, twice. What was the creature doing?

Rika looked to the black-clad man, who stood stiff as a board, his hands clenched into fists at his sides. His eyes were fixed on the ground, away from the creature and Hiro. The muscles in his strong jaw were working, as if he were grinding his teeth. As if he were bracing himself for what was about to come.

Horror swelled in Rika's heart and she cried out, though she had promised she wouldn't. "Father! Get back!"

But it was too late. The creature's arms shot out and wrapped around Hiro like four lassos. The creature hovered over Hiro—a monstrous shadow bending him backwards like a bow. A scream ripped from Hiro's throat, a sound of such agony that it was almost inhuman.

Those in the tent exploded into action. Ryu leapt for the other creature while one of the moonburners cast out at the man with a fireball. The other moonburner targeted the creature holding Hiro, sending blinding bolts of lightning into its black-clad body.

Rika stood frozen to the spot, her hands clamped uselessly before her open mouth. She couldn't look away from her father, from the sight of the creature wrapped around him in an embrace so close it was almost…intimate. Hot tears splashed down her face as Hiro's face began to blur, as if the creature was…pulling Hiro into the dark chasm where its face should be. No. Where its mouth should be. Hiro continued to scream as the other creature batted Ryu away like a kitten, sending him tumbling into the side of the tent. The man had dispatched one of the moonburners, his swords piercing her through. Rika saw these things in the periphery while she watched in numb horror as the creature sucked the life from her father. Where were her powers? What could she do?

Ryu let out a grating snarl as he tried to rise to his feet but stumbled, landing on the carpet with a shuddering crash. What was happening to him? Why couldn't he stand?

"Father," Koji whispered. His voice was small and high, like it had been when he'd been a boy. Rika wrenched her gaze back to the creature, but what it held in its arms was no longer her father. It was a gray husk in sunburner red. Empty.

The creature straightened, letting the clothing fall from its outstretched claws. The form clunked to the floor, borne by the weight of Hiro's sword and crown. But there was nothing between the velvet and linen. Nothing but dust. Rika looked at Ryu through a blur of tears, just in time to catch his eyes as he withered away, his once-proud golden body dissolving into ash.

Rika's knees collapsed beneath her, and she fell to the ground, numb and disbelieving. They were gone. Her father was gone.

CHAPTER 7

Silence blanketed the tent, broken only by the sound of ragged breathing. In and out. In and out.

As if watching from afar, Rika realized the sound was coming from her. The last moonburner had ceased her assault on the creature, watching in mute horror as her king was turned to ash. But she came back to herself—launching herself at the creature with a wave of fire before her. The monster stood unflinchingly as the flames enveloped it. When they died away, it advanced—totally unharmed—upon the moonburner. The fire hadn't slowed it a step. It reached out black-armored arms and grabbed the moonburner's navy uniform, pulling her into the same strange embrace it had leveled at her father. The moonburner screamed, flailing in its iron grip, her silver hair whipping about her face. "What are you?" she managed, but the creature ignored the question, intent upon its prize. A sob escaped Rika's lips as the moonburner's face began to blur.

The sunburner soldiers attacked the other creature with sword and spear, but it grabbed the spear-wielding man, pulling him close. It lowered its shadowy helm to the burner's golden head while the other man hacked uselessly at it with his sword, howling in anger.

Rika's wide eyes flew back to the other creature, the one that had taken her father. The moonburner, already fading to ash, turned a face cracked with graying skin and mouthed a single word at Rika. "Run!"

The creature hissed in frustration, a high-pitched clicking scream that grated against her eardrums. Rika met Koji's terrified eyes and began to crawl towards the corner of the tent. If they could wriggle under, they could take Enzo and ride for Yoshai...warn her mother...

Rika screamed as a hand wrapped around her ankle, yanking her back towards the center of the room. She turned to find the man in black leather, his green eyes glowing like emerald coals. She fought against him, landing a vicious blow with her boot to his jaw. It hardly fazed him. With one swift motion, he tossed her by her ankle into the center of the tent. She tumbled to a stop in the pile of her father's clothes, gagging as her hands scrambled in the powdery ash that was all that was left of her father. Her flailing fingers brushed against her father's sword hilt, and she grabbed it, clinging to it like a lifeline.

A navy-blue uniform collapsed onto the carpet next to Rika with a shower of ash. The creature—the soul-eater—had finished off the moonburner. Rika shied away, crawling back, dragging the sword with her. She bumped against a pair of boots and looked up to see the dark-haired man holding a knife to her brother's throat, his other hand twisted painfully in Koji's golden hair. Enzo was backed into the corner of the room, rearing and tossing his head, his horn swinging in dangerous arcs. But the man seemed to understand that Enzo wouldn't do anything to risk Koji, and so he had subdued the seishen more effectively than the bars of a cage.

The last sunburner was being sucked dry by the other soul-eater now, and Master Tato, the last member of her father's party, was huddled in a ball against the far wall, his knees drawn up to his chest.

When the sunburner's empty armor clanked to the carpet, the soul-eaters turned as one. First they looked at her, then at Koji, then at Master Tato. She felt like a pig at the slaughterhouse, having her fate decided for her.

The soul-eater who had taken her father turned to Master Tato, and he cowered from it, scuttling as far as he could against the wall of the tent. "Take them," he said, pointing a shaking finger at her.

Rika narrowed her eyes, a surge of anger cutting through her terror. He was a sunburner, sworn to protect the royal family.

"I'm a historian," he said. "Scholar. Librarian. I have much knowledge about this world. About its people. Their defenses, their resources. I could help you."

Rika's jaw dropped. Not only was he willing to sell her and Koji out, but to save his own skin, he would sell out their whole civilization?

"Master Tato," she hissed, the fire of her fury burning away the fog of fear and disbelief. "Don't do this."

He ignored her, keeping his focus on the soul-eater's black form.

The soul-eater turned to its brethren and spoke in that hissing, clicking language it had used before. She wanted to clap her hands over her ears, but she held them at her sides, one hand tight around the sword hilt. It seemed the creatures reached a decision, because the one with all its fingers advanced on Master Tato and buried its claws in his tunic, hauling him to his feet. Master Tato whimpered, squeezing his eyes shut. But the soul-eater didn't take him in its embrace as it had the other burners. Instead, it took his head between two hands and breathed out a green mist that glowed like swamp gas. Master Tato squirmed but couldn't help but breathe it in. As soon as he took a breath, his movements stilled and he went stiff. Then his eyes flared the same green as the other man's, and the creature dropped him to the ground, where he stumbled but caught himself, swaying on his feet. Master Tato's face was strangely blank. And those eyes.

As soon as Tato's feet hit the ground, the soul-eaters turned on her and Koji, the last two alive and free in the tent. Enzo reared with a fearsome whinny, his golden hooves flashing through the air, his teeth clacking viciously. The man in black leather twisted his knife more tightly against Koji's throat and Koji cried out in pain. A trickle of blood ran down towards his collarbone.

The soul-eaters must have seen the threat that Enzo posed, because the one missing fingers moved towards her brother, its claws outstretched.

"No!" Rika cried, rushing to stand before her brother. She didn't know what had come over her—what had finally moved her feet. Whether it was bravery, a desire to protect her brother, or cowardice, not wanting to watch him die too. But either way, she couldn't do nothing anymore. "Take me," she said. "He is heir to the throne. If he dies, my mother and our armies will hunt you down until every last one of you is dust on the Earth."

"She lies," Master Tato said, his voice monotone. "She is the heir."

The soul-eater took a step forward, its armor clanking. It took all of

Rika's restraint to stand her ground. The thing was immense—she hardly came up to its chest. "I care not for heirs or bargains or peace. This land is ours. We will take what we want from it. Your armies are flies to be brushed aside." Its breath smelled sour, like sulfur from a hot spring. Bile rose in her mouth and she swallowed thickly.

"You're wrong," she said. Her voice was small. It was all she had, this small bit of defiance. She wanted to scream, to beg, to collapse over her father's clothes, weeping. But she wouldn't. She wouldn't let this beast have the satisfaction. And then she realized it wasn't all she had. She still held her father's sword limp in her hand, its heavy tip trailing behind her on the carpet. That's how she would go out. So she summoned her training—the years on the sparring ground with Armsmistress Emi— and swung the sword with all her might, right at the crease in the creature's armor where helmet shadowed its shoulder.

The sword made contact with the creature's outstretched hand with a clang. It had caught it in the air, its movement impossibly fast. It wrenched the sword from her grip and flung it across the room. Master Tato had to scramble out of the way to avoid being clubbed by it.

The creature's claws shot out and wrapped around her throat, jerking her into the air and against its hard armor, its other arms wrapping around her, its claws digging into soft flesh. Breath left her as her body smashed into its breastplate. She tried to scream, but nothing came out.

It let out a strange hissing noise that Rika realized was laughter, but she was too wrapped in fear and pain to feel the outrage she should. It leaned over her, bowing its body over hers how it had her father's, and its piercing green eyes plunged into her soul. She felt it swimming through her thoughts, her memories, gathering them to it, ripping them from their rightful home towards the unnatural vortex of its magic. She railed against it, struggling to hold on, to fight it, to deny it the sustenance it so desperately craved. And as she grabbed for a handhold, a grip, anything to keep her mind and her soul in her body, her mental scrambling brushed against something. Something warm and bright and good and *strong*. Something strange, but familiar at the same time. She gripped it desperately, not knowing what it was—a piece of herself, or this world perhaps. But it held fast, held firm, and she pulled more of herself back into herself. She heaved herself away from the soul-eater, its power sucking at her like quicksand. But blessedly, she broke free of its hold and found herself fully back in herself—her mind, her body, her soul where it should be. Firmly, securely inside her body. And there was something new. When she had broken free of the soul-eater's grip, her handhold had loosened as well. It was tumbling towards her as if a rope had come untied.

The soul-eater was keening its strange sound, its claws still firmly affixed in her body, but its eyes were glowing like fiery green embers. She could feel anger radiating off it, through the strange unearthly connection between them, and she could feel power growing, surging towards her, energy enough to make her hair stand on end.

The soul-eater seemed to feel it too, because it looked up from her with confusion, its grip loosening. Rika pulled her feet up and kicked against its armor, twisting herself out of its grip, its claws tearing from her skin in furrows of pain. The walls of the tent flapped in an unnatural breeze and for a moment, all grew still.

A jet of pure white light tore through the ceiling of the tent and exploded into the soul-eater, enveloping it in a brightness so sharp it burned through Rika's closed eyelids. Stunned by the ringing in her ears and the blinding of the flash, it took Rika a moment to realize that the soul-eater who had seized her was on the ground, shimmering ivory flames licking across its broken body. It was dead. She had killed it. Something was rising above the smoking corpse, a shimmering mist that undulated and rose towards the freedom of the hole in the tent and the starry sky beyond. The mist looked like...people. With a start, Rika realized what they were. Hundreds of souls, floating, spinning, faces with strange features cast in relief and abandon.

The black-haired man had dropped his knife from Koji's throat, overcome with shock at the sight of his dead master. Enzo wasted no time and barreled at the man, his horn lowered like a spear. The man leaped to the side just in time, rolling towards Master Tato. The lone remaining soul-eater came for Rika, hissing and clicking, its talons outstretched. She scrambled away, stealing precious seconds while her mind tried to work out what had just happened. And how to recreate it. What had she done? How had she done it?

Koji pulled himself onto Enzo's back. "Come on, Rika!" he cried, holding out a hand to her. As Rika rose to make a run for him, a sharp blow landed on the back of her head. She crumpled forward, falling to the ground with a crash. She rolled over, gasping, to find a blurry Master Tato standing above her, a war-hammer held high. He had clubbed her. Rika couldn't believe it. The librarian had hit her. She tried to scramble away, but her body was sluggish to respond, her thoughts no better. The remaining soul-eater clamped his claws around her, hoisting her into its arms.

Enzo pawed the ground near the door of the tent, rearing in fury. "Rika!" Koji yelled again. Rika tried to pull at the thread of power she had felt a moment before, but whatever it was now slipped from her grasp.

"Go," she croaked to Koji, motioning with her hand. "Run! Tell Mother…what happened…one of us…warn them…"

Koji's face was streaked with tears, and he bit his lip as Enzo danced beneath him, clearly torn over abandoning his sister.

"Enzo, save him!" she croaked, hoping the seishen had more sense than her brother.

The last image she saw before darkness overtook her was a seishen's golden tail disappearing into the night.

CHAPTER 8

Rika awoke to pain. Her head throbbed and her body felt wrung out and exhausted, as if she had just run up a mountain pass. She turned her head gingerly to take in her surroundings. She was lying on her back on a hard table, a tent of black fabric above her. The flap of the door was propped open, and she squinted into the sunlight beyond. It was daytime. She must have been unconscious for hours. She tried to sit up and found that she couldn't. A stab of panic lanced through her. Was she paralyzed? She looked down at her body and saw that she was held down by thick leather straps—her wrists, ankles and chest affixed to the table. Fear clawed at her insides as she jerked her arms against the straps.

A shadow passed in front of the sunlight and she froze, craning her neck to make out who entered the tent. It was the black-haired man— the one who had helped the soul-eaters murder her father. "Don't struggle," he said in the deep honeyed tone she had heard yesterday. But something was different. His voice—it had inflection. Personality. His handsome face—rather than the blank featureless mask she had seen as he grabbed her by the ankle and dragged her across the tent—was now twisted with something that looked akin to regret. And... "Your eyes," she said with surprise, her voice nothing more than a hoarse whisper. They no longer glowed with the soul-eater's unnatural magic. They were still green, she realized, but a light, lovely hue like fresh-cut lemongrass.

He stepped in close and bent over her. She jerked away reflexively but was anchored in place by the leather bonds. "We have little time. They are coming. When your magic killed Twelve, it freed me from their compulsion." His breath tickled her ear.

"Twelve?" she asked, curiosity overcoming her revulsion at the murderer's closeness.

"They are called by numbers, not names. It is not important. No one has ever killed a soul-eater before. At least not that I have heard of. They are frightened of you—and intent on learning the secrets of your magic so they can rip it from the world. I am to torture you until you reveal it to us." The words he spoke were clipped, his accent peppering her language with staccato rhythm.

"Torture?" She yelped.

Deep voices sounded outside the tent. Cold fear twisted her stomach in an iron grip.

"They are coming," he said. "I need you to pretend I am hurting you." He looked back at the tent flap, where tall black shadows hovered outside. "Do you understand?" he whispered.

She didn't, but she nodded sharply as two of the soul-eaters entered, together with Master Tato, strange green eyes blazing. She narrowed her eyes at him. *Traitorous coward.*

"This puny creature killed Twelve?" one of the soul-eaters asked. She cringed at its grating voice.

The other one nodded, stepping closer to examine her. Still out of reach, she noticed with some small bit of satisfaction. It was the soul-eater with three fingers, the one that had killed her father. It now held the strange staff that had been in the hands of the other one last night. Perhaps it had taken it after the death of the other?

The soul-eater spoke again, without looking at Master Tato. "What can you tell us of her magic, historian?"

"Her magic is unknown in our world," Tato said, his voice flat. "The primary form of magic is drawn from the sun and the moon. In women, the ability to burn the light of the moon manifests physically in the form of the hair turning silver. As you can see, her hair remains black. It appears that she did something new. Something unknown to me."

"Something new," the creature seemed to sneer. "You promised that you would be of use to us. Yet you know nothing."

"There was a prophecy. It was foretold that she would confront a great shadow. It is believed that your armies are that shadow."

The black-haired man shifted slightly at this, watching Master Tato with veiled interest. The mention of the prophecy had peaked his interest for some reason. Could she truly trust that this man was on her side? Someone who had offered himself to be a slave to these horrible monsters? Who had stood by as his own kind were turned to ash before his eyes? While her father…Rika's mind stuttered over the thought as tears pricked at the corner of her eyes. With a silent apology, she shoved the thought away. She couldn't fall apart now. She needed to be smart. Like her mother. What would Kai do? *The most unlikely alliance is often the most effective.* Her mother's words, spoken in the midst of a torturously long lesson on foreign policy. She looked back at the black-haired man, his eyes fixed on the floor, his stubble-covered jaw working. No, she couldn't trust him. But that didn't mean she couldn't use him.

"Does this prophecy speak of others like her?"

"No," Master Tato said. "I believe she is the only one."

"So we kill her and our problem is solved," the soul-eater said. Rika glared at it, struggling against her bonds.

"I believe so," Master Tato.

"Unless this fool is wrong," the three-fingered soul-eater said, its green eyes glittering with malice.

The black-haired man inclined his head in a respectful bow. "Seven, the girl might know of her own power. Know if there are others. Let me question her. If I learn nothing, I will end her."

The two soul-eaters looked at each other and conversed in their hissing, clicking language. The one the man had called "Seven" made the decision. "Do it. If you learn nothing by nightfall, she dies."

Some of Rika's tension melted at the sudden reprieve. Her life was now in this strange man's hands.

"You." The other soul-eater pointed to Master Tato, who straightened at the word. "Stay with them and observe."

No! Rika thought. With Master Tato watching, reporting back to the soul-eaters…the black-haired man would actually have to torture her. Her stomach flipped.

Master Tato inclined his head in agreement and the two soul-eaters swept from the tent.

"You—Tato is your name?" the black-haired man said. "Fetch me a bucket of cold water and a brazier to heat the coals."

"I'm supposed to observe."

"You can at least be of use!" the man snapped, and Master Tato jumped, shuffling out of the tent.

The man must have seen the fear in Rika's eyes because he leaned over her. "I have an idea. It's going to be all right. But when I signal, you'll need to scream like you're in the worst pain of your life. Do you understand?"

She nodded, swallowing the lump in her throat.

"We make it through this day, and tonight we escape. Understood?"

"Escape?" she asked, hope blooming like a cherry blossom in her chest.

He nodded, his green eyes blazing with intensity. "You can kill soul-eaters. That makes you the most precious treasure in the world. I will not let them kill you."

"Okay."

"Be still," he said, squeezing her hand. His hand was warm, his palm calloused. "I will return."

"Not like I could go anywhere," she grumbled, fluttering her arms uselessly in the leather straps.

☾⁺

When he returned, the black-haired man—she needed a better name for him—filled the tent with horrors. He heated a brazier until the coals were red-hot and placed two pokers in the fire to heat. He rolled out a little leather case with wicked-looking metal implements, whose purpose Rika could hardly even guess. Rika's heart thundered in her chest as she tried to stay calm. Even knowing that he said he was going to go easy on her, she broke out in a cold sweat at the sight of the torture implements. There were so many ways to hurt a person. She hadn't known. Her mind spun in panicked circles, cursing her idiotic decision to come here. What a fool she'd been. To think that she could defeat something so evil, an armada of ships bearing monsters that she couldn't have imagined in her deepest nightmares. To think that she could fight something that not even her father, a seasoned warrior, could stand against. She squeezed her eyes closed, her heart wrenching at the thought of Hiro. The raw ache inside at his absence felt real—physical. She wished he were here now. She would run into his arms, wrapping herself in his embrace of mint and leather. She would bury her face in Ryu's thick mane, crying until her tears were spent. But those were comforts that were gone from this world. Even if she survived this, she'd never feel them again. What kind of world was it without her father? A dark one indeed.

The black-haired man pulled a poker from the fire, drawing Rika's attention. The glowing end of the iron filled her vision as he stepped beside her and a sob escaped her lips. She squirmed, fighting the leather straps. Whatever the man did here, it would hurt...there was no going easy, there was no pretending. He stepped right next to her, so his bulk blocked Master Tato's sight, and from a pouch on his belt, he pulled a piece of raw meat. He looked at her intently before plunging the poker into the meat. She was so surprised she almost forgot her part in the theatrics, but a wide-eyed look from the man was enough to remind her. She let out a blood-curdling scream, arching her back, thrashing against her restraints. The smell of burning flesh filled the air, making her gag, and she screamed even louder, almost able to believe that the burning flesh was her own.

He pulled the poker from the beef and slipped the meat back in his pouch before turning to place the poker back in the fire.

Thus, they commenced what could perhaps be described as the most elaborate ruse ever concocted. Master Tato, who had been squeamish and soft as a historian, had not had his disposition improved by enslavement to an evil soul-sucking race. He sat in the corner, his skin pale and sweaty, trying to avoid looking at what the black-haired man did.

Rika, for her part, almost started to enjoy herself, screaming out her anger and fear and sorrow while the man pretended to stick needles under her fingernails or pour water over a cloth covering her face. Never did he truly hurt her, and as the hours ticked by, she began to feel a true appreciation for the black-haired man. Whatever he had been when his eyes had glowed green, now, he was her savior.

As the sun began to set, the man wiped his brow, sitting down heavily in a chair beside Master Tato. Rika watched him, though she pretended to moan and twist with the pain. He took a swig from a flask that he pulled from his belt and offered it to Master Tato, who took it gratefully, taking a large gulp.

The man clapped Master Tato on the back. "It's not for everyone," he said. "No shame in it."

Master Tato nodded, and the man stood, stretching. His back popped. Master Tato swayed in his chair, his eyes fluttering. Rika watched with interest as his chin drooped onto his chest. He was out.

"What…" She cleared her throat. Her voice was croaky from screaming. "What did you give him?"

"Sedative," the man said. "He should sleep for a few hours, but be none the wiser. Enough time for us to get out of here."

He crossed the room and began to unbuckle the straps holding her to the table. "What's your name?" she asked.

"Vikal," he said.

"I'm Rika."

"Nice to meet you, Rika," he said, unbuckling the last strap around her chest. He offered her his hand, and she took it, using his strength to pull herself up. Her body groaned in protest from the hours it had been held down on the hard surface. "Are you ready to get the hell out of here?"

She nodded, adrenaline singing through her veins. Her father's sword leaned against the chair Tato slumped in, its hilt decorated with a golden dragon with red ruby eyes. Tato must have removed it from the other tent. She grabbed it, buckling the scabbard securely around her narrow waist. "Now I'm ready. Lead the way."

CHAPTER 9

The southern sky was painted with the navy and gold of a dying sunset—the low light turning the sea of black tents and ebony-lacquered ships burnished bronze. Rika stood outside the corner of the tent, flighty as a wild thing. She was too exposed. Vikal bent down and retrieved a black bundle from beneath the corner of the tent before shaking it out and wrapping it around her. A cloak. He fastened the garment beneath her chin and pulled up the hood, as if she were a child unable to dress herself. Though if she were being honest with herself, she wasn't sure her hands wouldn't shake too much to fasten the clasp on her own.

He looked down at her and her breath caught at the nearness of him. Who was this man? "Stay close behind me. Let me do the talking if we encounter anyone. Any…thing."

She nodded. "Did my brother escape?"

"Yes," he said. "His steed was fast as the wind. My… The soul-eater's scouts could not catch him."

Some small bit of tension uncoiled from her spine. Thank the gods. Koji had escaped. Which meant that he would warn their mother about the creatures. Give her time to prepare for war.

"Can you swim?" he asked.

Another nod.

"Good. We are stealing a boat."

She opened her mouth to question him further, but he was already striding across the grass-covered dunes towards the ocean. She hurried after him, falling into step behind him like a shadow. The camp was strangely silent. There were men who wore the same black leather as Vikal, who walked about the camp on business for the soul-eaters, but the creatures themselves were nowhere to be seen. The number of ships was staggering, however. Even if there were only a few men and soul-eaters per ship, the invading force had to be in the thousands. Her parents…no, she thought with a choking correction, her mother had perhaps one hundred sun and moonburners, if you included those in training. Only a dozen of those had seishen. The gift of burning was rare, after all. Perhaps five thousand soldiers, if the reserves were called up. After twenty years of peace, much of their military apparatus had been dismantled. There was simply no way Kitina could withstand this force if it was brought to bear.

A man in leather was approaching them, walking up from the undulating line of surf. Rika tensed. "*Bak!*" Vikal called, raising a hand. He repeated the word, and then began conversing with the man in a foreign tongue. It was not the clicking, scratching language of the soul-eaters; it was melodious and lilting, almost like song. In the low twilight, the other man's green eyes glowed like twin campfires. Did he see that Vikal's eyes no longer glowed? Would he notice? The moment stretched on for what felt like an eternity, and Rika was forced to take a shuddering breath, able to hold it no longer. Finally, Vikal grunted an affirmation and the man nodded in deference, trudging on through the soft sand.

"What language is that?" she whispered.

"Later," he hissed.

She bristled at the reprimand but fell silent, following along behind him, quiet as a ghost.

They reached the water's edge and he removed his boots, tucking them securely in his belt. He began wading into the water. "What are you doing?"

"You said you could swim."

"I can, but that doesn't mean I want to."

"We are taking that boat," he said, pointing to one bobbing a few hundred yards out to sea, a glowing green light at its prow. "Taking one of the rowboats off the beach would be too obvious though. So we swim. Or you can stay here."

Rika glanced over her shoulder at the city of black that polluted Kitina's sugary sand. No way in hell she was staying. She sighed and waded in after him, her skin goose pebbling at the cold of the water. It wasn't frigid, but it certainly wasn't bathwater. She tried to judge the distance to the boat, shoving down her trepidation. She didn't think she had ever swum so far. She looked back at the beach and caught sight of an armor-plated soul-eater moving in the distance. Determination flared in her. She would swim halfway around the world to get away from those things.

She slipped into the water and began stroking her way towards the boat in smooth, easy motions. She paused for a moment to unbuckle the cloak at her throat, letting the water bear its heavy weight away. The clothes she wore were heavy, but the sword scabbard was the real weight, pulling at her middle, arresting her progress. She didn't care. It was all she had of her father now. She would drown before she abandoned it to the depths of the sea. At that moment, a bit of brackish seawater slopped into her mouth, making her cough and splutter. Perhaps it would come to that.

Vikal's lungs burned like fire and his muscles felt like lead weights when he finally reached the boat. He had been too long in the soul-eaters' captivity, standing about like a mute automaton. Who was he kidding? One moment enslaved to those leeches was too long. But now he was free. Thanks to that tiny girl.

He ruffled his hand through his thick hair, shaking out the water. She was approaching the stern of the vessel, paddling slowly, struggling to keep her head above water. There was a ladder on the back, and she hung on the bottom rung for a moment, heaving in a breath. He watched all this from the corner of his eye as he began to unfurl the sails. He had looked back at her a hundred times during their swim, making sure she wasn't struggling too much. Though he didn't want to coddle her, he couldn't risk losing her. He had meant what he said. She was precious.

He unwrapped the mainsail as with a little sob of effort, the girl rallied her strength and heaved herself over the rail. She collapsed in a puddle of seawater on the deck.

"You brought that sword?" Vikal asked, pausing. "Foolish girl. It is a miracle you did not drown." What had she been thinking? There was no room for sentiment here.

"I'm not"—Rika gasped—"a foolish girl. I saved your sorry self from being enslaved to those monsters. And this is my father's sword. It's all that's left of him, besides ash and memories. I wasn't going to leave it behind."

Rika's eyes gleamed in the moonlight as they stared each other down.

"Very well," he said. She had made it. It wasn't worth fighting about now. He caught sight of a wisp of a form floating against the starboard rail. When he turned his head to look at it, it was gone. Ever since he had been freed yesterday, he could swear he was seeing things. Seeing Sarya. A side effect of the compulsion perhaps. Creeping madness.

Rika did unbuckle the scabbard, though, and tucked it under one of the benches in the stern of the boat. She rose, stumbling against the rail. "Can I help?"

"We must haul up the anchor," he said. "I pull, you coil the rope?"

She nodded and fell into position behind him. He grunted as he hauled the dripping anchor up from the sea-floor, hand over hand. The closer the anchor got, the more his spirits rose. This was going to work. They were actually going to escape.

"Have you sailed before?" he asked.

"A little," she replied. "As a kid." A memory seemed to flash across her gray eyes wreathed by thick, black lashes. She was as thin and willowy as a palm frond, with an ethereal beauty to her oval face, petite nose, and smooth, tan skin. Her coloring was lighter than his own or that of any Nuan, set off by her thick, ebony hair. She was short as well, shorter than most Nuan women, only coming up to his chest. If not for the freckles across her nose and the playful gap between her teeth, he would think her a sky spirit. And perhaps she was, given the incredible power she'd displayed last night.

"What?" she asked. Vikal fought his embarrassment. He had been staring. "Take the wheel," he said. "I will hoist the sails."

She followed his instructions, making her way to the stern to where the wheel stood. Vikal hoisted the main sail, and it unfurled dark as night against the first pinpricks of stars. He was struck by a moment of surprising gratitude for these black sails. White would be conspicuous, even from the shore.

The sails luffed and snapped in a gust of wind and he winced, looking back at shore. Had anyone heard the sound? But Rika sensed what to do, turning the ship to the southeast—the best angle for the wind to catch the sail. She pulled in the mainsheet, tightening the sail.

Vikal finished unfurling the jib, the second sail on the bow of the boat, and the girl tightened it, tying off the rope on a nearby cleat.

Vikal made his way back to the stern and took the wheel from her. "Not bad," he said. She hadn't been lying—she did know something about sailing.

"Where are we going?" she asked. "There are some islands that way. We could hide out in them for a day or two before regrouping and heading to Yoshai. That's our capital. My mother and brother will be there. Readying our people for war."

"Do you have weapons more advanced than what I saw yesterday?"

She crossed her arms. "You mean when you helped them murder my father?"

He winced, keeping his eyes on the dark sea before them. "Though I know it is little consolation, I *was* under their compulsion. I had no control over my actions." He had known it would come to this. He had just hoped they would be gone from here before it did.

"Convenient excuse," she muttered.

"Call it an excuse, but it is the truth. Believe me. Whatever disdain you feel for me, I have for myself a thousand-fold. The things I have done… They will haunt my dreams as long as I live."

"You…knew?" She softened. "You were in there…aware…when your body was doing what they commanded?"

He nodded, the muscles in his jaw working. He wished he could forget—though he knew that the sentiment was cowardice. There was no redemption for the things he had done. He didn't deserve the blessed relief of amnesia. A king who murdered his own people—

"I'm sorry," she said softly.

Their eyes met, and the pity in hers was too much to bear. He didn't deserve it. He had helped the leeches kill her father. Her king. He turned to watch the shore of this foreign land slip away, its hive of green lights burning in the darkness. One light seemed closer, farther out to sea than the rest of the anchored ships. He squinted, crouching down a bit to examine the angle. The light was most definitely closer. Gods, no.

"We are being followed." His voice was flat.

She ran to the rail to look, sending off a stream of curses. "What do we do?" she asked.

"We cannot outrun them," he said. "This ship is sturdy, but not fast. They will catch us."

"So we fight? If they board us, you take any humans, and I'll...I'll try to figure out how I managed to kill that other soul-eater."

He weighed this option. "Even if you could figure out how to use it in time, your power is too bright in the darkness. It will be a beacon announcing us to all the other soul-eaters. We will be overrun before we have gone a league."

She grimaced. "Then what? Take the rowboat, hope they can't find us in the darkness?"

"That will only help us until morning. When they will easily find us and pick us up."

"How about you stop shooting down my ideas and come up with one of your own?" she snapped.

There was one play they could make. She wouldn't like it...but they didn't have a choice. It was the only way. "I have an idea. Hold the wheel."

He hurried to the middle of the cockpit and pulled the wooden top off the pillar that was affixed there. Rika's eyes widened as he set the wooden piece on the ground. It revealed what looked like a compass at first glance—eerie green dials and needles swinging beneath the surface of the shiny glass orb. In truth, it was so much more than that.

"What is that?"

"It is the leeches' astrolabe. Each vessel has one. How do you think they got here so fast?"

"It's used to..."

"Travel across vast distances. In an instant."

"And you know how to use it?"

"I have...observed it in use. I understand the concept." He had watched the spinning of the dials as the soul-eater had jumped them from his home, Nua, to this strange land. He could reverse the process. Hopefully.

"Great. You're going to astrolabe us into the center of a mountain," she said.

"Would you rather have your soul sucked out?" he snapped back, pointing behind her. The ship following them was only a few hundred yards away.

He twisted the dials on the base of the astrolabe, setting the coordinates for Nua.

"We can't leave here," she protested. "We need to help my mother. Help Yoshai. Where would we even go?"

"Home," he said, the green light from the astrolabe beginning to pulse. The light flared so brightly that he was forced to close his eyes, to shield his face from the brilliance. Then the world went wrong, and Vikal lost all orientation. Up was down, sideways was inside. And then...nothing.

INTERLUDE

K ai paced across the armory floor, sweat pouring off of her. Though she and Emi had just finished an intense sparring round, the physical activity had done little to calm her ragged nerves. Her steps carried a limp, her hip smarting from a particularly deft move of Emi's that had landed her hard on the ground. She rubbed it, wincing. "You didn't need to go all 'Armsmistress Emi' on me. I could have broken my hip!"

"You're not *that* old." Emi snorted. Her friend was sitting on a bench, polishing a set of daggers. Her friend's moonburner uniform, with its navy-blue fabric and silver embroidery, was unbuttoned at the neck to let some air in. Emi's full, silver hair was plaited in a thick fishtail braid down her back. She didn't look the least bit concerned that the two heirs of Kitina were missing. They could be dead for all she knew!

"The point of sparring was to quiet your mind. You didn't even make the smallest effort. So, you suffer the consequences for your lack of focus."

"I suffer the consequences of having two obstinate children!" Kai threw up her hands, spinning to begin another line of pacing. "You're sure Oma knew nothing about Rika's plans? She didn't even have a whiff of a hint of where she was going?"

Emi shook her head. "Daarco questioned her about it. I think he was channeling some of his old dark sunburner ways—getting all intense and in her face. Poor Oma was quaking in her slippers. I had to bribe her with rice pudding to even come to the dinner table after. If she knew anything, she would have talked."

Kai smiled. She hardly remembered the old Daarco anymore, angry and sullen and hateful. For so many years now, he had been her faithful general and friend, a true partner to Emi, and a good father. "I wish I knew where they were! It doesn't make sense—Rika and Koji planning anything together. They can't stand each other right now."

"We know where they went. Rika went to meet this shadow, to try to force her powers to manifest. Koji probably followed along like the little brother he is because he can't stand to be excluded."

"I thought Enzo would have had the sense to talk Koji out of something so foolish," Kai grumbled.

"We seishen are only as foolish and headstrong as our burners," Quitsu drawled from the corner, where he was draped over a pile of shields, his chin on his paws.

"I'll choose to ignore that," Kai shot back. "You don't think that Rika would confront these invaders by herself, would she? I didn't raise that foolish of a child?"

Emi shook her head. "Rika may be desperate to gain her powers, but she's been soaking in all those lessons on diplomacy and foreign relations you've been feeding her all these years. She'll know how important it is for Hiro to take the lead in this negotiation. I don't think she's confident enough to think she could manage it herself."

"Let's hope not," Kai said. She closed her eyes, rubbing them wearily. "Hiro, take care of our babies," she said under her breath.

"Did you get any sleep last night?" Emi asked, concern written in her dark eyes.

Kai shook her head.

"Had any breakfast?"

Another head shake.

"Let's at least get some food in you. You can't help them by sheer force of worry."

"It's a mother's most powerful weapon—" Kai began, but her stomach interrupted her with a loud rumble. Kai pursed her lips. "You win this round," she relented.

"I won all the rounds today." Emi grinned, the old burn-marks on her face paling against her brilliant smile.

"Yeah, yeah."

Emi wrapped her arm around Kai's shoulder and squeezed. They rounded the door into the hallway and a servant scrambled to a stop, nearly bowling into them. "Your Majesty!" He panted. "Prince Koji has been sighted riding through the Sea Gate! He's coming in at a gallop. He should be nearing the palace gate by now."

Kai's stomach dropped. What would bring him back at such a pace? Not slinking back with apologies, but at a full-fledged run? "Let's go."

Kai and Emi sprinted through the hallways of the palace, dropping all sense of royal decorum. Quitsu streaked after them like a silver arrow. They dodged servants bearing trays of food and nobles who plastered themselves against the walls in surprise at the queen's passage. It wasn't fast enough. Kai needed to be there now, to see him now.

They burst out the doors of the castle into the main courtyard, shaded with soaring camphor trees. "Koji!" she cried. Her son was across the courtyard, standing next to Enzo, whose flanks heaved with effort. Koji turned towards her with a face red and blotchy with tears. When he saw her, he ran towards her and they slammed together in a fierce embrace. Kai held him in her arms, taking in his solid presence with palpable relief, rocking him as shuddering sobs began to wrack his body.

"Shhh," she said, stroking his golden hair. "It's okay. You're home now. You're safe."

He held her, bowing his head to let his tears fall on her shoulder, wetting her blouse. Kai held tight to her son and her fears, a thick knot deep within her, wanting to know what these tears meant, but also holding on to this moment of not knowing—sensing that soon, everything would be change.

He finally pulled back, wiping his nose on his sleeve. She had never seen him look so miserable.

"What happened?"

"Father's dead," he said, not meeting her eyes. "They killed him. And Ryu. And all the other burners."

Kai felt her knees grow weak beneath her and it was only Emi, at her side in a blink to grasp her arm, that kept Kai on her feet. Hiro...dead. Her mind stumbled over the word, unable—unwilling to wrap around it. It couldn't be.

"Your sister?" Kai asked, grasping for something to distract her from a cascading sorrow that was too great to bear. Even if...Hiro...Rika had to be safe, right?

He shrugged, wiping his nose on his sleeve again. "She killed one of them. Her power, it came and when the thing tried to kill her, she killed it instead. That didn't make the others too happy. She told me to run…she was holding them off…" He looked at her then, misery etched across his face. "I left. Enzo started running, and I didn't stop him." Tears flowed fresh. "I left her. I'm so sorry. I left her."

Kai pulled him into another embrace, her own tears mingling with his as she pulled his cheek against her own. "You did the right thing. If your father couldn't defeat these enemies…you did the right thing. You came back to me. You warned us."

"I'm a coward," he sobbed. "They were hurting her and I abandoned her."

She pulled back, taking his face in her hands. "Sometimes it takes more courage to live than to die. We needed you to live. I needed you to live. When faced with overwhelming odds, retreat is not cowardice."

He nodded, but she saw he didn't believe her. She didn't know if she believed herself. She wanted to scream at him, pound his chest for leaving his sister behind, for going in the first place and putting himself at risk. But she knew, the small part of her that was still in control, that if she did such things, she would lose him forever. And she needed him. He was likely all the family she had left.

"Koji," Emi said gently, putting a hand on his arm. "These invaders. You've called them…things. What did you see?"

"They're not human," he said. "They're eight feet tall, covered in impervious armor. They have four arms with claws on the end. Burning can't touch them."

Kai and Emi exchanged a look of shock. "What do they want?"

Koji shrugged hopelessly. "They called themselves soul-eaters. They…they suck the life from people. I saw… Father and Ryu…they turned to ash."

Emi took Kai's hand, grasping it tightly. Kai nodded with much more calm than she felt. "Why are they here?"

"I think…" Koji shuddered, closing his eyes at the memory. "I think they're here…because they're hungry."

CHAPTER 10

A soft breeze ruffled Rika's hair. Her eyes fluttered open, taking in an impossibly large sky filled with unfamiliar stars. She was lying on the deck of their boat. Gone were the giant tortoise, the red phoenix rising, the white tiger, the blue serpentine dragon. The constellations she had grown up with, her familiar friends…they were gone. Replaced by unfamiliar stars in unfamiliar patterns. She closed her eyes again, shutting out the strangeness, the horror of her present circumstances. It was a dream. It had all been a dream. Her father. Ryu. An armada of monsters intent on destroying everything she held dear. Hot tears leaked from the corners of her eyes and she curled her arms around her stomach, trying to hold in the wracking sobs that threatened to consume her, to deny the reality that her mind insisted upon. This *was* a dream. She'd walk down to breakfast and her mother would be perched in her father's lap kissing him and she'd tell them about the wildest dream she had had over cups of steaming tea.

"Rika?"

She opened her eyes. The strange stars remained, refusing to be banished, to admit they were anything but firm and fixed and real. An ache rippled through her, a quake that shook apart the already-shattered pieces of her heart. Her father and Ryu were gone, and she was here. In this strange place. With this strange man.

"Are you all right?"

She took in a shuddering breath. She would have to face it. To fix it. To make the most of this mess that had so quickly consumed her reality. She couldn't stay lying on this salty deck forever. Rika rallied her strength and tried to sit up, her vision reeling. She groaned, bringing a hand to her head, as if she could hold the pounding inside.

"Easy," Vikal said.

She squinted in the darkness, looking for him. He sat across the cockpit from her, elbows on his knees. The sails fluttered uselessly, flapping back and forth.

"It hits hard, especially the first time. It takes a few minutes before everything works right."

"What'd you do? How'd you work that thing?" Her voice sounded like an echo in her own head.

"The leeches call it 'hopping.' Far more advanced magic than anything we have on our island. I learned when…they controlled me. With this power, you can cross great distances instantly. Travel between worlds."

Between worlds? Rika couldn't wrap her mind around that one, so she set it aside for the time being. "The leeches?"

"It is what we have named them. Leeches. Soul-eaters."

"What do they call themselves?"

"It is not a word that can be translated." he said. "It means something like—deliverers."

"Deliverers?" Rika was incredulous. She adjusted her position gingerly, leaning back against the opposite rail. "They have a high opinion of themselves."

"I saw some of their history when I was under their thrall. They come from the stars. From another world. Many other worlds. They started out by trading—exchanging knowledge of their magic and the worlds for resources. For souls. They would free those who were sick, suffering. They were deliverers, in a way. Then a new queen was born. She was different. Ambitious. Cruel. She killed the old queen and everything changed. They have become these monsters you see today."

"And no other soul-eaters objected to this new queen's plan to start murdering everyone in their path?"

Vikal shook his head. "They have a strange social structure. Like—a beehive. The queen controls the soul-eaters. The soul-eaters control the thralls. No independent thought or action allowed. It is contrary to their nature."

"An army of mindless killers," Rika said. "Great." Her head had mostly stopped spinning. A warm breeze blew from the island, invigorating her with the heady scent of lush vegetation. She hauled herself to shaky feet—and felt her knees go weak. She caught herself on the rail. Okay, too soon. "Where are we?" she asked, looking across the dark sea to a body of land she could just make out in the distance. "It's so warm here. The air feels…thick." Her despair was fading into the background as her curiosity grew. She had never been anywhere beside Yoshai and Kitina. What was this place? A different land mass? A different world?

"Nua," he said, standing as well. His voice was wistful. "My home."

She turned and examined him, leaning on the rail for support. Even in the low light of the starry sky, he was…changed. His spine straighter. His head held high. His skin—there was practically a glow coming off of him. A health and vitality that radiated from his very pores. As if the man needed help being more handsome. And his eyes…was it a trick of the light? His eyes were so vibrantly green, she could hardly believe they weren't lantern light. And—she squinted, looking more closely. Yes! There was a faint glow coming from his forehead under the thick shock of black hair.

"Are you going to dissect me?" he asked with an uncomfortable laugh.

Rika hardly noticed. *What was that?* She stepped forward in a lithe motion, sweeping her hand across his forehead to push back his thick hair. Then with a yelp, she backed away. "What is that?" she squeaked, her hand to her hammering heart.

"It's a long story," he said, a wry smile flickering across his face.

"A long story? Who—what—Vikal, you have *three eyes!*"

He pushed the hair off his forehead with a quizzical look. "I do not know what you speak of. All I have is this tattoo."

Rika's mouth hung open as she looked at the smooth expanse of skin he revealed. She crept forward and peered at it, standing on her tiptoes. It *was* a tattoo. Dark green lines depicting a closed eye, decorated by triangles and dots and sweeping geometry. But she had sworn she had seen…she would bet her life… She shook her head in wonder. Had hopping from Kitina addled her mind?

The tattoo popped open with a blink, revealing a glowing green eye fringed by long, dark lashes.

Rika jumped back with a screech, practically careening over the side of the boat.

Vikal started laughing, a deep guffaw that warmed her core.

Rika's jaw hung open with shock. "Are you—*messing with me?*" she asked incredulously. Without thinking, she stepped forward and punched him in his sizable bicep with all her might.

"Ow." He shied back, still laughing. "Is that how they do things in Kitina?"

Rika whirled, his words smothering her rising mirth. She was horrified by her impertinence. Punching him—it was something she'd do to Koji. Not some strange man—if he even *was* a human man—who had helped murder her father. What was she doing? Standing here joking with him while the soul-eaters were marching on Yoshai? She needed to get back. Now.

Rika stilled her face into a mask of calm before turning back to him. His laughter had died, and he was looking not at her, but at a spot towards the center of the ship. What was he looking at? There was nothing there. She cleared her throat. When she spoke, her words were cold, imperious. As queenly as she could make them. "I admit I'm curious, but we can talk about your third eye later. You made a good call hopping us away from that soul-eater ship. But now, please hop us back. Preferably, a few leagues down from where the soul-eaters made landfall. I need to go help my mother defeat them."

He leaned against the rail, looking at her. His mask had fallen back as well, and his features were hard, his jaw set. The laughing man of a moment before seemed like a figment of her imagination. The ship's rigging creaked and clanked in a gust of wind. A feeling of trepidation washed over her. "Vikal. Take me back."

"I cannot," he said finally. "I need you here."

"What do you mean?"

"You are the only person I have ever heard of who can kill a leech. Even in the memories of the hive, I never saw such a thing. The leeches have taken over most of Nua, but some of my people escaped into the mountains. I need your help to rescue them. And I have friends who were trapped under the leeches' compulsion, like I was. If you kill the leeches that enslaved them…"

"They'll be free," Rika finished, her voice cold. "And what about me. Am I no longer free?"

"Of course you are free."

"Then take me back," she said. She stormed across the deck, retrieving her father's sword and buckling it onto her narrow hips.

"If you go back, you die. The might of the soul-eaters armies are marching on your land. You have no hope of defeating them. You cannot help there. But you can help here. Only two dozen or so remained behind."

"So you would have me abandon my family, my people, my duty? Let them be sucked dry by these leeches while I gallivant around here freeing your friends?"

"No." He shook his head, sighing. "The only good thing about the soul-eater's power is that they do not seem to hurry. They are methodical, moving forward inch by inch. It is unlike fighting a human enemy, where there are tactics and feints and double-crossing. The leeches are straightforward destruction. If your people can hold them off long enough…they might have a chance. You should take that time to master your powers."

Rika opened her mouth to object, but he continued. "I could help you learn. While you help me. Then when you return, you will be ready to fight them."

"My homeland will be a smoking wasteland by then. No. The answer is no. I'm sorry, but I don't have time to help you." Rika stepped up to the astrolabe. "Take me back now. After I save my family, I'll come back to help you here. I promise. I owe you something for helping me escape that place. I repay my debts."

"Go back now and you will not live long enough to help your family or my land. You were captured by only two leeches and a cowardly historian. You think you could defeat a swarm of these creatures? Hundreds? With thousands of men at their disposal? Are you so eager to die?"

Rika narrowed her eyes, glaring at him. True, her first experience using her power had been a little…unpredictable. But she would learn as she went. There wasn't time to waste trying to learn how to use her power. She had let down her father… She pushed the thought aside. It was too painful to confront right now. She wouldn't fail her mother and brother too.

"Just show me how to use the astrolabe. You don't need to come with me. You can stay here and free your people."

"I cannot free my people without you," he said, running his fingers through his dark hair. "You... Your power..." He hesitated, spinning on his heel and turning from her.

"What?" she asked suspiciously. "What about my power?"

He shook his head, shoulders slumping. "You will never believe me. I do not even know if I believe it. All right. We will make a deal. Summon your power and show me you can control it. Then, I will take you back."

She crossed her arms, weighing his suggestion. "What do you mean, control it?"

"Make it do what you want it to do."

"I don't know what it can do, besides kill soul-eaters."

"If you want to go home, find out quickly. Until I am convinced you can care for yourself, I will not take you back. You are too valuable to this world to let you walk into a suicide mission."

"What do you think you are, my father?" Her voice broke and hot tears welled in her eyes. She spun away, not wanting him to see her cry. No, he wasn't her father. She didn't have a father anymore. And soon she might not have a mother.

The deck creaked beneath Vikal's feet and she knew he stood behind her. She didn't turn, didn't accept whatever false comfort he might try to offer. He had helped those creatures kill her father, under a compulsion or not. And now he wanted to hold her captive here while Yoshai was invaded. Rika balled her fists. Not if she could help it.

She closed her eyes, taking a deep breath. She tried to remember how she had summoned her power, going deep within herself to find the firm handhold, the connection between her spirit and whatever had given her aid. She was there in a blink and let out a little gasp of surprise. The strange force had felt subdued before, a single rope tied like a lifeline. Now, the power pulsed before her, hundreds of threads of power ripe for the picking. It was overwhelming. She reached and took the smallest handhold of light, trying to coax it towards her. As soon as her intention fixed around it, the rope, the tether in her mental grip, began thrashing and bucking like a wild thing. And at the end of that thread of power was a presence. Another life force that flipped around her mind, her awareness. Straining against her. It was like lassoing a dragon with a spool of yarn. *Who are you?* she thought, her mental voice tiny and small.

There was no answer, and she pushed down her fear and frustration, ignoring her hammering heart. She had to show Vikal that she could use her power. Just a display of light should do…she gingerly tugged the thread towards her. *Please come here,* she thought. No reason not to be polite. The presence, whatever it was, seemed to take note of her contact. It turned and barreled towards her like a lion-horse stung by a bee.

Rika opened her eyes with a gasp. Vikal had taken a step back. His hands were up warily. "What have you done?"

Rika spun around, looking at the deck, then the sky. "Something." She shivered. "It's like something's coming. I thought…" She let out a breath. "I must have imagined it."

Vikal opened his mouth, no doubt to lecture her on her lack of control over her abilities, when his jaw dropped. His chiseled features flared into view, illuminated by a bright light. Rika whirled, backing into him as she saw in the sky what had lit up the night. A brilliant white comet streaked across the sky, leaving a trail of fiery debris in its wake. It was headed…straight for them.

"Rika…" Vikal said, grabbing her hand. "Jump!"

CHAPTER 11

The boat exploded behind them as the bright object careened into the middle of the deck, sending up a shower of debris and seawater. Rika plunged into the dark water, the ocean churning around her. Water poured into her mouth, her nose—burning her nostrils and making her lungs ache for air as she fumbled for the surface. In the dark tumult, she couldn't tell up from down, and panic pulled at her like an anchor. A bright light whooshed by her in the water, illuminating the turbulence around her. She kicked towards it, following the light, gasping in sweet air as her head breached the surface.

The wreckage was lit like a beacon, and Rika blinked away saltwater, trying to make out the source of the illumination.

"Rika!" Vikal cried, and she spun towards his voice, treading water as he swam towards her. "Are you hurt?"

She shook her head, coughing out the last of the water. "What was that?" she asked, watching in dismay as the ship's mast and sails collapsed into the sea, disappearing below the surface.

Vikal's eyes were wide, watching something behind her. She turned, spluttering as a wave slapped across her face.

"I was hoping you would know," Vikal said.

A crystalline light hovered over the remains of the ship, bobbing in the air. Rika frowned. It didn't make sense. A comet or a shooting star would have sunk to the bottom. But this—it came back up. As it drew closer, Rika found herself swimming away from it, bumping into a piece of the ship's railing. She heaved her elbows over it. At least the ocean was as warm as bathwater. They wouldn't die of cold.

Vikal had found a piece of flotsam to keep him afloat as well. "I've never seen anything like it."

"It almost looks like...a star." It was blindingly bright. And drawing closer. Had she done this? Was this the presence she had felt when trying to draw on her power? A possessed star?

The light came to rest on the end of the wooden railing Rika clung to, dimming from painful to merely bright. It was close enough to reach out and touch, but she stilled herself. It looked...like a bird. "A sparrow?" she asked, awe filling her. "You're a sparrow."

"Is this some quirk of your power?" Vikal asked. "Why did you summon this thing?"

"I am not a thing," the thing said. "I am the night sparrow." Its words came out as clipped chirps, each syllable evenly spaced.

Rika let out a delighted laugh. "You talk?"

"Of course."

An idea struck Rika and her heart leaped in excitement. "Are you my seishen?"

"Your what?" Vikal and the night sparrow asked at the same time.

"My seishen. On our land, some burners have animal companions who are part-spirit, part-flesh. They're connected to the burner's soul."

"Is that what that great lion was?" Vikal asked.

Rika's elation dimmed at the mention of Ryu. "Yes. And my brother's unicorn."

"I do not believe I am a seishen," the bird said. "I am a constellation."

"A constellation?"

"A cluster of stars."

"I know what a constellation is," Rika said crossly. "But what I don't understand is why you fell from the sky and destroyed our boat."

"You summoned me."

"I..." Rika's mouth opened and closed as the creature's words sank in. She looked at Vikal for assistance, but he was no longer looking at her. He stared towards the island, an odd look on his face—something like shock.

Rika didn't know what to make of this strange bird and its pronouncement, but she knew she wouldn't solve this riddle floating in the middle of the ocean. "Can you help us get to land?" she asked. "Do you have any useful skills?"

"No skills," the bird said, alighting in the air. She watched it flap upward, squinting again as the constellation brightened with the movement of its wings. "I do see a rowboat," the constellation called. "Perhaps useful?"

"A rowboat?" That shook Vikal from his daze. "There was a rowboat on the bow of each of the leeches' ships. Did this one break free?"

The night sparrow banked towards the distant island. "This way!"

Vikal and Rika made their way slowly through the debris floating on the slick surface of the sea. And like the bird had promised, a rowboat bobbed in the waves. "Thank the gods." Rika breathed a sigh of relief. Her father's sword was pulling her down once again.

Vikal looked into the boat while the star-bird alighted on the bow like a little lantern. "Oars would have been too much to hope for."

Rika looked back and saw a few splintered boards that were about the right size. "We'll have to make do."

In no time, Rika had corralled the boards and shoved them into the rowboat. Her arms burned from swimming and treading water, but she summoned enough strength to flop into the little vessel while Vikal held the other side to keep it from capsizing. She leaned the other way while Vikal hauled himself over as well.

She handed him one of the boards and without a word, they began to paddle. Rika looked over her shoulder at the wreckage of the ship, and a single thought burned through the fog of her numb and tired mind. "The astrolabe," she breathed, the reality of her situation sinking in. There was no way she would return home now. No way to help her mother or brother, Yoshai or Kitina. She was stuck here, in this strange place overrun with soul-eaters, with only a brooding soldier and a constellation for company. What had she done?

They reached the shore as the sun's first rays broke over the eastern horizon. The little bird launched into the air, soaring over Rika's head. "I return to the stars," it said. "Until another night."

"Wait!" Rika called after it. "Do you have a name?"

"Cygna," it said before banking to the west, away from the rising sun.

"Try not to crash-land next time," Vikal called after it grumpily, hopping out of the boat into the surf. He heaved the boat up onto the beach, aided by the rhythmic pounding of the waves. The rays of the sun gilded his tousled dark hair, illuminating him like a halo. When at last the boat was out of the surf, he grunted, wiping his hands on his pants.

Rika jumped out of the boat into the soft sand. She wrangled her tangled salty locks into a knot and looked up to take in her first real glimpse of Nua.

The island was in a word—breathtaking. Lovelier than a dream. There was much she found beautiful about her own homeland, but this—she admitted begrudgingly to herself—it was a sparkling jewel. The island rose from the sea in soft folds of green jungle before jutting into the sky to meet in a craggy peak. Even this early in the morning, the air was warm and humid, lush with smells of green palm fronds and fragrant flowers. Rika could only imagine what amazing plants and creatures sheltered below the shadow of the rich canopy. "This is your home?" she asked.

Vikal nodded. He had fallen to his knees in the sand and was looking at it with tears shining in his eyes. He buried his hands in the sand, pulling out a handful and letting it sift through his fingers.

"It's pink," Rika said with surprise, bending down and picking up a handful of sand herself. It was soft as flour and squeaked between her fingers.

"I thought I would never see it again." His gaze was fixed on the jungle, and Rika was surprised to notice that the vibrant green of his eyes was reflected in the colors of the thick foliage. "I have you to thank for this. For bringing me home. And we are not too late. They have not burned everything."

Rika swallowed a lump in her throat, his words sparking within her. She looked back at the sky, at the blanket of stars that were yielding their dominion to dawn's light. Somewhere out there was *her* home. And she would likely never see it again. Never see her mother or brother. Never ride Michi through the grass, never play hide-and-seek with Quitsu, never spar with Emi. And no matter what happened, she would never see her father again. She squeezed her eyes closed, trying to block out the memory of his scream of agony, of him turning to ash before her, of her hands scrambling through the remains of his body. Of Ryu, trying to protect them, vanishing into the night. There was no closing out those memories, no erasing them. A vision of Yoshai burning swam to the surface, unbidden—of soul-eaters breaking down the sea gate, burning the palace, sucking the life from her mother. No. It wasn't possible. This couldn't be real.

A sob escaped her lips, and she clapped a hand over her mouth, turning from Vikal. She wouldn't cry. Not again.

"Rika." Vikal placed a gentle hand on her shoulder.

"I'm fine," she lied. "I just need a minute."

"I will help you return home," he said. "I swear it. Once you master your powers and we defeat the leeches here, we will have our pick of their ships. We will return to your land and defeat them for good."

She whirled on him. "How? How will I learn about my powers? I tried to summon some light and I blew up our ship with a sparrow!"

Vikal pressed his lips shut, but the corner of his mouth crept up in a smile.

Rika let out an incredulous laugh and closed her eyes, a tear leaking down her cheek. She shook her head, her sorrow mingling with the ridiculousness of their situation in a strange cocktail that somehow made her feel just a tiny bit better. She welcomed it, clung to it. She wasn't ready to let her sorrow over her father bear her away in its powerful tide. Not now. Right now, she needed to hold herself together.

Vikal chuckled—that velvet laugh again. "That was one powerful bird."

Rika heaved a sigh, opening her eyes. "How am I supposed to defeat these leeches if I don't know a thing about these abilities?"

Vikal stood, brushing the pink sand from his trousers. "I might. First, we find water and food. Then, I will tell you what I know."

CHAPTER 12

They trudged across the soft sand into the shadow of the jungle. Vikal flowed through the forest like he'd been born to it, and at times Rika could swear she saw the plants and vines bow out of his way to make a path. "Do you know where we are?" she asked as they walked.

He nodded. "I know the pink sand beach—Pulau Ungu. We keep towards the volcano Kaja Kansa until we cross a ridgeline, and then we will have a view of the whole of Nua."

"What's a volcano? And what's Kaja Kansa?" Rika asked. The words were unfamiliar.

"It is a mountain that spits fire. Kaja Kansa is its name."

"Fire?" she asked incredulously.

"Not all the time. But yes. When it is angry."

Rika shook her head at the strangeness of it all. But in her world, women burned the energy of the moon. So who was to say that here a mountain couldn't breathe fire?

"Ah!" Vikal said, approaching a tall, leafy tree ladened with rich, purple fruit. He reached up to grab a fruit just out of reach, and the tree bent towards him, relinquishing its treasure.

"I saw that!" Rika said, pointing at the tree accusingly. "It moved! I thought I was imagining it…but the whole forest…it's moving around you!"

"Eat," he said, holding out a fruit to her. "Then I will explain."

Rika examined the fruit in her hand with skepticism, but her rumbling stomach quieted any doubts. She bit into the fruit—or rather, tried. Her teeth wouldn't puncture the thick skin. It was like leather. She gnawed at the fruit with her molars but couldn't get anywhere. "How do you eat this thing?" she asked, glaring at it.

Vikal looked at her and shook his head. In his own hand, he had somehow cracked open the purple skin to reveal sections of smooth, white fruit within. "Do not eat the skin. Here. I will show you." He took her hands, lacing her fingers together. The sensation of his touch traveled up her arms into her torso like an unfurling ribbon, but she ignored it, just as she ignored the lock of hair falling over his eyes. Fruit. He placed the purple thing between the heel of her hands. "Now press," he said, gently pushing her hands together between his own. As more pressure was exerted, the skin of the fruit split in half.

"I did it!" she said, delighted.

He smiled, but as their eyes met, he dropped her hands and stepped back. "I hope you like the flavor. It is very sweet."

Rika discarded the skin and bit into the fruit, letting its juices run over her chin. The flesh was firm but yielded in a satisfying crunch. "It's delicious," she said, taking another bite.

Vikal stripped two huge leaves from a nearby palm and fashioned them into a little satchel, which he filled with fruit. "Ready?" he asked. "I would like to reach the ridge by nightfall. See what we can see."

Rika nodded, chewing the last of her fruit and wiping her sticky hands on her leggings. "Lead the way. And it's time to get talking."

He sighed, stepping back onto the trail the forest somehow made for him. "Yes."

Vikal handed Rika another fruit and she popped it open as they walked.

"Do you have gods in your land?" Vikal asked.

"Yes. We have a god of the sun and goddess of the moon."

"Any others?"

"Just those two. There's a...creator of our world, but he is above the gods. He created them. At least that's what my mother said."

"Are these gods born? Do they die?"

Rika frowned, considering as she chewed. "I don't believe so. They were created, and they always have been. They can die, though. A few years before I was born, they were almost destroyed."

He nodded. "In Nua, in this land, the gods are born like men. They live and then they die. And then they are reborn. It is a cycle we have seen many times over. Sometimes, for whatever reason, it takes many years for a god to be reincarnated. Other times, the god is reborn as soon as the old body is put to sea."

"So the gods are like people? What do they look like?"

Vikal stepped off the path and picked up what looked like an oversized green nut. "They do look like people. They are people. But they are more. They are gods. Other cultures might think of them like…demi-gods? A god's rebirth is heralded by a storm of falling stars. In this way, we know to keep a close eye on the babies who are born that night, to watch if they develop special abilities."

"What kind of abilities?" Rika was fascinated now, the rest of her snack forgotten. Gods as people, walking among them? Suddenly, she stopped in her tracks, looking around at the forest. A vine undulating in the corner of her eye suddenly froze, as if guilty at being spotted.

"You're one of them, aren't you?" she asked. "God of the forest, or something."

He turned. The green in his eyes seemed brilliant here, shining with power and force. His three eyes. The third eye on his brow glowed as well. "Yes. I am the god of green things. The forest speaks to me, and I to it."

She looked around her, craning her head to look up at the soaring canopy, so thick and lush that the hot sunshine barely filtered through. This was all Vikal. He controlled it all. She looked back at him, letting out a steadying breath. "Okay. Nice to meet you, god of green things."

The corner of his mouth tugged up, and he ran a hand through his hair. "It is not as impressive as it sounds." He bent over to pick up a sharp stick, and with one powerful move, drove the end into the ground.

"It sounds pretty impressive," she said, watching as he began to expertly drive the green nut thing onto the stick, shearing off sections to reveal something within. It was mesmerizing to watch him work.

"I could not even stop the soul-eaters from massacring our people," he said, grunting as he pulled off the outer shell to reveal a furry brown ball within. "They burned the forest, barreled over any defenses we put up. We did not stand a chance."

"My father was the most powerful sunburner I had ever known. And they killed him…" She swallowed. "Like he was a helpless child. They're so strong."

"Rika," Vikal said softly. "I am sorry about your father. There is no forgiveness for the part I played in his death."

She looked away, examining the ombré petals on a creamy-white flower—fighting the vise grip around her heart, the burning in her eyes. "It wasn't you."

"But I was in there…I remember—"

"It wasn't you," she snapped at him. She couldn't hear his confession, see the twisted sorrow on his face. Because when she thought about the part he'd played, even knowing he'd been under compulsion…she wanted to rip him apart with her bare hands, dreamy green eyes or no. And she couldn't think like that right now. She needed him. Clearly. She didn't even know how to eat fruit here without him.

"Let's just drop it, okay?" she asked, and he nodded. He fell to his knees a few feet beyond the trail and cracked the brown ball across a rock with a satisfying pop.

"What is that?" Rika asked, grateful for something to focus on other than the memory of Vikal's part in her father's death.

He offered one half of the little ball to her. "It's a coconut. You can drink the water within. And eat the white flesh."

"Oh! We have coconuts. I guess I never saw them…out in the wild."

Vikal took a long drink from his half. "They don't spring to life in neat sections on a plate."

"I see that now," Rika said. Was he making fun of her? But no, there was a crinkle of a smile at the corner of his eyes. She drank her fill, closing her eyes as the sweet liquid coated her scratched and salty throat. When she opened them, their eyes met, and he looked away quickly, breaking a section off his coconut with deft hands.

She cleared her throat. "Tell me more about the gods. How many of you are there?"

They resumed their trek. "There are seven that move through the cycle of birth, life, and rebirth. We are not always here at the same time. In fact, it is rare that we are."

"Do you know each other?"

"There is often an innate connection. When I first met Bahti, we were children. We became instant friends—like we each recognized the divine spark in the other."

"What are Bahti's powers?"

"He is god of the burning mountain."

"Where is he now?"

"I hope that he is sheltering what is left of our people. But he may be dead. Or a thrall."

"Thrall?"

"Under the leeches' compulsion. It is we call it."

"So you hope we can find these gods and band together and defeat the leeches?"

"I think I have already found one."

"One what?"

"A god. Or, I should say, a goddess."

He stopped and turned to her. She blinked in confusion, coming up short. Why was he looking at her with such intensity? But then the wheels of her mind clicked into place and she stepped back, putting her hands up. "Oh no. You think...I'm a goddess?" She laughed incredulously. "Remember the incident with the sparrow explosion?"

"I do. You did not have such power when we were on the beach in your land. Do your powers feel stronger here?"

Rika frowned. The power had felt exponentially stronger the second time she'd tried to access it. "Yes. But maybe it's stronger because I'm getting used to it. It wasn't the first time."

"My power was much weakened when we were in your land, almost non-existent. Now that I have returned, it is strong again. I think your power has strengthened for the same reason. Because it comes from Nua."

"But I'm not even from here! How is that possible?"

"I do not know. In the past there have been generations where one or more of the gods or goddesses were not reborn. We always assumed that they were pausing in the cycle of rebirth for some unknown reason. But what if they were born—only born in another land? Another world? We never knew any world but Nua existed. The astrolabes have changed that. Who knows how many worlds are out there? Perhaps our gods, for whatever reason, are sometimes born far away."

Rika shook her head, her mind refusing to wrap itself around what

Vikal was telling her.

"Sixteen years ago, there was a storm of falling stars unlike any alive had seen before. It was in the heat of mid-summer. I remember it, though I was only four years old. We knew it heralded the rebirth of a powerful god or goddess. My parents were very excited because they already suspected what I was. The priests scoured the island, looking for the babe who had been heralded. But they never found one."

Rika's mouth had gone dry.

"How old are you?"

"Sixteen," she said woodenly.

"And when is your birthday?"

"July…"

"In the stories, the goddess had a great bird that she would ride, a companion of light made manifest. This…Cygna, the sparrow you summoned. Perhaps it is not big enough to ride, but it fits the stories."

She laughed weakly. "Of course my powers would show up in miniature."

"They will grow, with practice. When I was first learning to use my ability, I could hardly make a seedling grow."

Rika turned from him, chewing on her lip. Could this be possible? Did she believe him? True, the ability she had was unlike anything she had ever heard of in the history books of Kita or Miina. And she had felt more raw power since they had arrived here. But if she was a Nuan goddess…why had she been born in Kitina?

"Would it be such a terrible thing, to be a goddess?" he asked gently.

She turned back, taking in his handsome face—worried and cautious. Perhaps it wasn't all bad.

"If I believe this rebirth nonsense…If I believe that I am what you say I am…" She paused. "What am I goddess of?"

"Goddess of bright light."

Goddess of bright light. It did have a nice ring to it.

CHAPTER 13

As the day progressed, the heavy heat of Nua's afternoon settled over them like a blanket. Vikal let it melt into his bones and permeate his muscles, hardly minding the sweat that dripped off him and slicked the leather armor to his skin. He was *home.*

The terrain grew rugged as they neared the ridgeline that would stretch Nua before them—all the way from its eastern to western shores. The trees and foliage helped their passage by leaning out of the way, bowing in deference to their god. Vikal opened his third eye and smiled to himself at the explosion of green tethers tying him to every living plant on the island. He surveyed the land with relief. It seemed his absence hadn't been too detrimental. Here, the threads of the jungle were vibrant and lush, thick with birth and life, death and decay—the cycle of a healthy forest. Beyond, past the ridge and the shadow of Kaja Kansa, he didn't know what he would find. Those threads were twisted—or missing altogether. The soul-eaters had burned much of the forest on their march to Surasaya. How much had been destroyed? And more importantly, how many people were left?

As they walked, Vikal pointed out to Rika the plants and animals they passed—a family of bearded monkeys, a colorful green parrot, the downy white frangipani flowers that seemed too perfect to be real. His makeshift satchel filled with more bounty as he pulled up fruits and roots that they passed. The girl had tied her long, black hair in a knot at the back of her head and drank deeply when they finally found a stream. Though sweat poured off her, rolling down her smooth skin and dampening her stained tunic, she didn't complain, and she kept up his vigorous pace. She was tougher than she looked.

He sighed. Of course she was. She had lost her father and been essentially kidnapped by a stranger who might as well have been her father's murderer. It was a miracle she was tolerating his company at all. Out of the corner of his eye, he caught a whisper of white, a curving smile and undulating lock of hair. When he turned, it was gone. He stifled a sigh. It must be wishful thinking that made him think of Sarya, to think he saw her here in this forest where they had fallen in love. He wished she were here. His wife had had a way of making people feel welcome and wanted, becoming their instant friend. And with Sarya, it had been genuine. She would have known how to help this poor girl.

Rika was looking at him sideways under her thick lashes, her chest heaving from the effort of the hike.

"We should be to the top soon," he said.

"Thank the gods," Rika said. She let out a little laugh. "Or…thank you? Right? Because you're a god?" She shook her head. "The idea takes some getting used to."

"It did for me as well."

"Will you tell me about the gods or goddesses?" she asked. "You said there are seven? What other powers do they have?"

"Of course," Vikal said, grateful for a topic that felt safe. "My friend Ajij is god of the deep sea, and like I said, my other friend Bahti is god of the burning mountain. He's a bit rough on the edges, but he has a good heart."

"Any goddesses?"

"Kemala, goddess of dark spaces. She is really quite sweet," he said hurriedly when he saw Rika's eyebrow raise. "A little intimidating at first, though. And then there is Sarnak, who trained most of us. He seemed ancient when I was a boy—he is practically a fossil by now." Vikal paused, his tone turning somber. "If he is still alive. He is the god of endings."

"Endings?"

"Yes. Death…but not so morbid. We believe all life is circular. When we leave this place when we die, our spirits rejoin the great consciousness. It is an ending of sorts, but not the end. When we are born in a new body, the cycle begins again."

"We believe something similar, I suppose. When you die, your spirit goes to the spirit world, where it may spend just minutes, or years, if you have reason to hold on. But eventually, you pass along. We don't believe you come back, though."

"So once you are gone, you are just…gone?" he asked. "It sounds sad."

A cloud of emotion passed over Rika's face and her lower lip quivered. Vikal could have kicked himself. Speaking of the sadness of her beliefs, after her father had just passed on…

"I've never thought about it much. Before now." Rika managed, her voice thick. "I guess it means we have to make the most of the time we have."

"That is a good way to live, whether you come back or not." *But to only have one chance to get things right on this Earth…what pressure.*

"Are you the ruler of Nua?" Rika asked. "The way you talk about the people…it's like you feel a sense of responsibility."

"I do," he admitted. *Though I have failed them.* "I am…I was…a king of a sort. Our ruler is selected by the people—who make a pledge of faith towards that ruler. If the people are displeased with you and withdraw their pledge, you must step down. I do not know…perhaps things have changed since I left."

"The people would abandon you because you couldn't defeat the soul-eaters?"

"Perhaps the people thought I abandoned them."

Rika was silent.

"And what of you? Your father was…the king?"

"My parents shared power," Rika said quietly. "They ruled together."

"And who would rule when they are gone?"

"Me," she said. "If I ever get back."

He stopped, looking at her. "We will get you back. I promise." He had failed so many people so many times—Sarya, Cayono, his subjects. The capital of Surayasa was overrun, Castle Nuanita taken. Burned and destroyed. But perhaps…perhaps he could find some small piece of redemption if he could help Rika prevent a similar tragedy in her own home. As soon as they defeated the soul-eaters here…

"I thought my land was gone, but here it is. Perhaps the leeches will not do so much damage to your home before we can return."

"I hope you're right."

As they resumed their trek, an acrid smell tickled Vikal's nose. Rika sneezed.

Vikal stretched out his hands, brushing them against the green vines and knobby tree trunks they passed. The threads here vibrated with pain and sorrow. "Something's wrong." The top of the ridge was in sight, and Vikal could wait no longer. He had to know. Had to see. He took off up the mountain, spurred on by a dark intuition. As he crested the ridge, he stumbled to a stop, his legs seeming to turn to stone from shock. Words—thoughts—froze in his mind.

Rika reached his side a few seconds later and rested her hands on her knees, panting. "What—?" she began with a gasp before the words died on her lips.

The island was…a wasteland. A smoking, wrecked slope of blackened, twisted tree trunks. The jungle ended a hundred yards below them, and all that went beyond it, as far as the eye could see, was destruction. Dotted lakes, once blue, sat like stagnant pools of ink, and even the shining ocean beyond the far stretch of shore was putrid with waste.

Vikal had thought there was a limit to the amount of sorrow that could pour from one man's heart. He'd thought he had reached it when Sarya had turned to dust, thought that the well of agony and guilt and rage had run dry. He had been wrong.

Vikal opened his arms wide and screamed, a primal cry of anger and sorrow. A flock of birds alit from the canopy behind them. The cry echoed off the hillsides and valley. He screamed again, picking up a rock and hurtling it down the hillside into the ravaged stretch of forest. He threw another rock, and another before sitting down in disbelief and burying his head in his hands. The trees and bushes seemed to curl around him, a comforting embrace, sharing his mourning. *This cannot be. This cannot be Nua.*

Rika dropped down next to him, pulling her knees against her chest and wrapping her arms around them.

Vikal's broad shoulders shook as he sobbed into his hands. He didn't care if the girl saw him cry. He had no pride left, no honor. Like this island, he was a broken thing.

Rika voice was quiet. "Nua can regrow. If we kill them all, it will."

"It is a fool's errand," he said. "I saw you kill that leech and it freed me, and I thought it changed everything. I was kidding myself. You are one untrained girl against hundreds of them. Thousands. They are powerful beyond belief. They are nearly impossible to kill. They eat and consume and eat and consume. All you will do if you try to go against them is die."

"I will with that attitude," she said petulantly.

"Do not be naive!" he shouted from where he was sitting, grasping her shoulders in one lithe motion. "You forget what I have seen. Every moment I was under those creatures' power, I was aware. Awake. I remember…everything." His hands shook, and his grip tightened, digging into the flesh of her arms. "I killed and slaughtered and maimed for those things. My own people…I might as well have set this fire. They are unstoppable."

She stared at him with unflinching gray eyes, her jaw set. She didn't back down from his ferocity, but matched it with her own. "You said you believe in beginnings and endings. A cycle. Well, these creatures began somewhere, and they will end somewhere. Let it be here. Let it be Yoshai. Gods willing, my home isn't gone yet. For whatever reason, I have this ability. So I'm going to kill as many of them as I can before I go."

He deflated, loosening his grip. His head fell forward and he heaved a great sigh. He was supposed to be a ruler of men—brave, bold—god of all green things, and he was getting lectured by this strange, steely-eyed girl. And gods help him, she was right.

"Let's make them pay," she whispered.

He nodded, closing his eyes. "All right," he said, though he did not believe it could be done. Not really. Not anymore.

Silence stretched between them.

Rika stood and extended her hand to him. He looked from it to her and back again. After all he had done, he didn't deserve her companionship, let alone her forgiveness. But she was all he had. The smallest glimmer of hope that she could change things. And perhaps he was all she had too. So he enveloped her hand in his own and pulled himself to his feet, scrubbing away the tears with the heel of his other hand.

"Where are we headed?" she asked.

Goa Awan. The name of the holy place swam to his mind unbidden. Yes. Goa Awan. But how to explain… "There is a legend that the creator spirits formed Nua on the back of a giant sea turtle."

"Right," Rika said with a little eye roll. "Of course."

"The legend says that the great turtle was best friends with a flying snake, the spirit who formed the sky. The snake was exhausted from setting the sky in the heavens and flapping the stars away from the land with gusts of wind from his wings. So he rested on the back of his friend, falling into a deep sleep. When Nua was born, it formed right over the back of the snake. When the snake awoke eons later, he panicked, finding himself encased in darkness. He thrashed about below the ground, raising the earth into the mountain we see today. Finally, he found his way out, breaking a hole through the top of the mountain and flying into the sky."

Rika nodded. "Great story. Not sure how it impacts where we're going…"

"The snake's attempts to free himself left caves and tunnels under the mountain. They are called Goa Awan. The lost caves. We will find my people there."

"Lost caves… Have you ever seen these tunnels?"

Vikal shook his head. "The island will show us the way." He hoped. If it still found him worthy.

A branch cracked down the hillside, and they both froze. "What was that?"

Vikal held up a hand to silence her and peered into the twisted, fire-eaten forest.

"I see movement," he whispered. A flash of black. And glowing green. Vikal's blood turned to ice in his veins.

"A soul-eater," she hissed. She had seen it too. "Should we hide?"

Vikal shook his head. "They already have our scent. We fight." He drew his twin blades from the scabbards on his back with a ring of steel. "You ready to kill that thing?"

Rika let out a shaky breath, drawing her father's sword. It was far too long for her, but her grip appeared steady, and her stance was practiced. "Ready."

The soul-eater appeared through the blackened limbs of the burnt trees, its ebony plate glinting in the low afternoon sun. It wasn't alone. Five. Five thralls in addition to the soul-eater. Could they fight so many?

Would he be able to hold them off while Rika summoned her power? And then...he saw the face of one of the thralls.

"Gods above," he said, his swords drooping.

"What?" she asked.

"The man with the shaved head. He is my..." Vikal corrected himself. "He *was* my second-in-command." Cayono was alive.

Rika groaned. "So we can't kill him?"

"No. Please. Do everything you can to save him."

"Short of dying, right?" Rika asked.

"Right."

And then Cayono let out a bloodcurdling battle cry and surged up the mountain.

CHAPTER 14

It was not an easy thing—to fight a battle without killing your opponent. Vikal's friend crashed against him with a sound like a clap of thunder. The man bulged with muscle; his arms looked like tree trunks underneath his black leather armor. He wielded an odd axe as his weapon, and Vikal countered it with his blades crossed. "Cayono," he grunted at his friend as they grappled against one another. "*Bak.* My brother. I know you're in there. We'll get you out. Fight it."

Vikal's words faded away as one of the other thralls came at Rika, his short sword held aloft like a banner. She brought her father's sword up and the man slammed into her, his sour breath bathing her as they grappled. With a panicked move that held none of the grace of her training, she shoved him back. He stumbled a few steps down the mountain slope before skidding to a stop and renewing his attack. The man was thin and wiry, but tall, with a long reach. Her sword was too large for her, too heavy, too unwieldy compared to the more compact weapons she was used to. She realized all this in the span of a second between the rush of blood that thrummed in her ears. But there was nothing for it. Her father's sword, impractical as it may have been for a fighter of her size, was the only thing keeping her alive.

She struggled to keep her footing as she traded blows with the man, her feet slipping in the rich earth, her clothing snagging on branches and grasping burnt limbs. No, they weren't fighting on the smooth gravel of an even training ground. She ducked a swipe of the man's sword, diving out of the way, and found herself rolling down the hill, sword torn from her grip, empty hands scrambling to grasp something that would stop her progress.

Rika's outstretched palms scraped and sliced against rough bark and rocks as she fell, but as she slipped past the trunk of a sturdy palm, she was able to hook her elbow around it and stop herself. She groaned as pain lanced through her shoulder—it felt like her arm had been torn from its socket. But that wasn't as concerning as her sword, which lay uselessly in the dirt halfway up the hill. She wanted to lay her face in the ashy soil, but she knew she couldn't. She had to get it. She had to get up. She rolled over—just in time to see another soldier swinging his sword down in a blow aimed for her head. She shied away from the thrall's swing and the blade buried itself in the earth, quivering where her neck had been. She acted without thought, exploding up into the man, hammering her shoulder against his torso. He grunted in surprise and toppled over backwards, rolling down the hill just as she had moments before. She picked up his sword and wiped her hair from her eyes. This was madness.

The other two thralls were standing slightly down the hill, guarding the soul-eater, who stood like a black hole, soaking up the remaining light and brightness of the day. It seemed content to let its minions tire its prey, sure there was nowhere they could go, no way to escape its clutches. Rika narrowed her eyes. To end this fight, she needed to end that leech. But could she grasp her power without a moment to center herself and focus?

She risked a glance up the hill, to where Vikal was still locked in furious combat with the bald-headed man. It was good she did, because she was able to get her sword up in time to parry a wicked thrust by her first attacker. Rika's skull rang with the vibration of the swords clanging together, and her feet slid in the earth as the man pushed with his sword, blackened teeth bared. Thoughts of summoning her power fled from her mind as she focused on the immediate threat. She kicked out, knocking one of his knees out from under him. He fell to one knee but caught himself before careening down the hill. It was all the opportunity she needed. Rika plunged her sword into his throat, gagging as the coppery scent of blood perfumed the air. She pulled her sword out, eyes wide as the man clutched desperately at his neck. Rika's stomach heaved as crimson blood pulsed between his fingers, his life draining away. He slumped forward into the dirt, an accusing stare frozen on his face by death's embrace. She drew in a shuddering breath. She had killed a man. That man was dead because of her.

The man whom she had sent tumbling down the hill was nearly back to her position now, and so she shoved her dismay aside, adding it to the growing pile of sorrows too horrible to deal with. She dodged past him, scrambling down the hillside towards the soul-eater. Its two guards came to life, one pulling a sword from its scabbard, the other pulling two knives from sheaths at his belt. He threw them at her in quick succession, and she dodged, twisting her torso to avoid the deadly projectiles.

Pain bloomed in Rika's stomach, and her steps faltered. She looked down, stumbling, almost losing her footing. A knife blade protruded from her stomach. Red blood flowed freely, staining her obi. Numb disbelief washed over her. The thrall had hit her. The man was pulling two more long-bladed fighting knives from sheaths on his thighs, but the other thrall came at her first, his sword singing a deadly song. Blocking his blow sent a wave of pain and nausea through her. She countered two more blows, but the ending to this encounter stood before her, clear as day. She couldn't fight both of them, not wounded and losing blood. She needed to destroy the leech, freeing these men from its compulsion.

"Soul-eater," she cried, "are you such a coward that you let these men do your fighting for you?" The soldier came at her with a fast attack, and she barely parried the blows. She was slowing. The man with the knives threw another at her, and she dove to the side, landing with a thud. The pain took her breath away, and fire bloomed on her arm. He had hit her again—a glancing blow. She clawed through the pain in her mind, grasping at the threads of power she had felt when she had summoned Cygna. When she had killed the first soul-eater. They eluded her dazed efforts, slippery as eels.

The creature seemed to respond to her taunt, advancing up the hillside. The two soldiers were upon her in a moment, the one with the sword leveling its tip at her throat. She lay back, panting, her blood mingling with the ash of the fires that had ravaged the forest. The soul-eater came to a stop just feet from her, surveying her with its glowing green eyes. "You think me so easily baited?" it hissed, its voice grating in her ears. "I have heard of you. We have all heard of you. My brother was foolish enough to die at your hand. I will not make the same mistake.

I will claim your head for a trophy, and my queen will rejoice."

Her vision swam, the creature becoming two, three black shapes before merging back into one. She was losing too much blood.

"So easily killed," the leech said. "You are little more than bleating sheep."

Rika's eyes narrowed, and she threw open the gates of her mind, grabbing desperately at what she found. *Help me!* she screamed desperately. *Cygna! Anything. I summon you! Kill it!*

The energy responded, pulsing with celestial power. Though she couldn't see, she grabbed for it, yanking it towards herself like a lifeline. The power yielded, streaming towards her in a raging river of pure light. She was tired, and her mind was sluggish. Her effort drained the last ounce of strength from her. The soldier's sword was raised above her, ready to give the killing blow—and she knew she didn't have it in her to evade it.

But before the blow could fall, a jet of crystalline light streaked down from above and barreled into the soul-eater with the force of a shooting star. The intensity of the flash burned her retinas, and she squeezed her eyes shut against the force and backlash of the landing. When she opened them again, blinking away the dust, she saw that the power had eviscerated the soul-eater and tossed the other men off their feet.

The thrall who had been poised to kill her rolled on the ground beside her, groaning, holding his head. When he opened groggy eyes to look at her, they were dark brown—free of the soul-eater's compulsion. *Thank the gods.* The muscles in Rika's body loosened, exhaustion and pain washing over her. The handle of the knife still protruded from her stomach. Her shirt was black with blood.

The former thrall pulled himself onto his knees beside her, speaking words of concern. The language was strange to her—the words meaningless.

Tears leaked from the corners of her eyes as Rika realized her predicament. Without a miracle, she was going to die. She had sat by her mother and grandmother in the healing ward often enough to know what could be fixed and what couldn't. Her wound was grave. Perhaps she could have been saved before she'd lost so much blood...but now...she would leave this world without helping her family. Kitina would fall—her home burned and ravaged like this land. She felt hollow inside. This is what Kita and Miina would look like. If it didn't already.

This is what those leeches did. They consumed and destroyed. She felt so foolish. All she had wanted, all she had prayed for fervently every day of the last four years, was for her power to manifest. And now that it had, it had ruined everything. How could she have been so selfish, so self-absorbed? Had she known that the cost of her power would be her father…her people…her home…she would have stayed away as long as she lived.

"Vikal," she managed. Her voice was distant. Perhaps the gods of this land had some other power. Something that would save her.

"Vikal?" The soldier perked up. "Vikal?" As if he wasn't sure he had heard her right. The man stood, and waved his arms up the hill. "Vikal!" Then more foreign words.

A sob escaped from her mouth. She would die in this strange place, in this strange land. Her body wouldn't lay to rest in Yoshai, with her parents and her people. She would be lost forever. They would never know what became of her.

Blackness swam before her vision, but she blinked, clearing it. She wanted to see Vikal, the most familiar thing she had in this place. The face appeared above her, concern and worry written like the chapters of a book. "Rika! Stay with us. Stay with me." She felt his hands on her face, cradling her head, the dichotomy of his rough palms and gentle touch soothing her.

"I'm sorry," she managed.

Vikal was saying things to someone else now, words she didn't understand, directing and pointing. "Don't be sorry." He turned back to her, crouching over her. His thumb stroked along her cheek. "You will not die. You have a destiny, goddess of bright light. We need you."

CHAPTER 15

Rika was as pale as a lotus flower and as still as a shadow. Her shallow, rasping breath was the only sign that she still lived. Vikal sat back on his haunches, running a bloodied hand through his hair while the other held the hem of her tunic pressed against the wound. His mind rebelled against him, unwilling to form a cohesive thought—beyond one. She was dying. Rika was dying.

Cayono had shaken off the fog of compulsion and fell to one knee beside him. "How…?" he rubbed his forehead. "Vikal. How are you here? Free? Last I saw you were boarding a rowboat bound for a leech ship. It was so strange. Yesterday, the soul-eater's control of me just…fell away. But another, this one, it saw it and took me again. What is going on?"

Cayono's questions darted about Vikal like gnats. There was only one that was important. "Her," Vikal managed. "She is why you are free. Why I am free. Why I am here. All of it. It is her."

"She killed it," another man said, the one who had called Vikal down the slope. "I saw it. She summoned something—and it blew the leech sky high."

"She can kill them?" Cayono's dark eyes blazed with excitement. "Vikal! *Bak!* Do you know what this means?"

Vikal shook his head miserably. "She is dying."

"Save her!" Cayono cried.

"How?" Vikal's voice was weak, twisted. "Maybe Sarnak could heal this, but not me. I do not know healing magic." Not again. He was failing again. First Sarya, now Rika… Was he doomed in this incarnation to be nothing but a wretched failure?

Cayono paused. "The forest. Surely, there is some leaf or flower that could sustain her. Stop the bleeding. Until we find help."

Cayono's suggestion lanced through the haze that clouded his thoughts. The forest. Of course. He wasn't thinking. "Cayono, you are a genius. Hold this. Keep the pressure on," Vikal said, and Cayono leaned forward, placing his hand over the slick wad of fabric.

Vikal dashed up the burnt slope towards the green of the ridgeline above, throwing his third eye open. *Healing,* he thought as he ran his mind along the thousands of green threads that tethered him to the forest. The spiderweb of green filaments revealed by his third eye had once overwhelmed him to the point of vertigo, but over time it had grown familiar, welcome. He searched them desperately now for a miracle that could save Rika. *Something to stop the bleeding. Something for strength. Something to ward off infection…* He ran his mind along the threads of power like strings of a lute, commanding them to sing for him. Two trilled in response, and Vikal redoubled his sprint, charging like the soul-eater queen herself was on his heels. At the top of the ridge he skidded to a stop, falling onto his knees to gather fistfuls of moss that had grown up at his insistence. *To stop the bleeding*—it called to him, revealing its essence. A vine snaked down from a nearby tree and presented a curling end laden with tangerine flowers. He pulled them off, saying a silent thank you. *To give her strength.* He closed his hand gently over his treasures and began his wild descent back down the mountain.

Vikal skidded to a stop beside Cayono and the other two men, who were standing over Rika, watching her with trepidation.

"Her breathing slows," Cayono said. "Tell me you found something."

Vikal opened his hands and took the moss, leaning down over Rika's wound. Blood soaked the ground beneath her—pulsing out weakly as Cayono lifted his hand. Vikal took the moss and packed it into the wound as delicately as he could before holding out a hand without looking up. "Give me something to wrap it with." Was the blood already slowing? Or was it just his desperate imagination?

One of the men quickly unwrapped a black sash from about his hips and handed it to Vikal.

Carefully, Vikal tied the sash tightly around Rika's narrow waist and fastened it securely. Then he took the flowers and crushed them between the heels of his hands, staining his palms orange. He took Rika's head and opened her mouth gently, packing the flowers into the corner of her cheek. How he knew what to do, he couldn't say.

Rika lay limp and quiet. The blood had slowed, but she was so pale. Like the veil of death had already fallen over her. Vikal let out a hiss of frustration. What more could he do? He looked at Cayono and the despair on his friend's face mirrored his own. "You held back..." Cayono said. "Fighting me. You should have killed me. Stayed by her side. If I had died, this wouldn't have happened."

"I threw the knife," one of the former thralls said, his hand hovering over his mouth in horror. My *Gusti,* forgive me." Vikal grew cold at that word. He was not this man's king anymore. He was no one's king. Cayono was right, though he didn't blame Vikal. Vikal should have given any life to protect Rika's. But his attachment to Cayono, his determination to spare his friend, had cost her dearly. And had cost his people their one chance of salvation.

"It is my fault," Vikal said woodenly. "Mine and no one else's."

Then Rika let out a ragged gasp and sat straight up. Her eyes fluttered open before rolling back in her head as she fell towards the earth. With a cry, Vikal caught her, cradling her in his arms, laying her down gently. He looked at her in amazement. Her color had returned, and he felt the strong beat of her heart hammering through her ribcage.

"A miracle," Cayono said.

"If we get her to Sarnak, she could live," Vikal realized, hope unfurling in his chest like a spring bloom.

"Do you know where he hides?" Cayono asked.

"Goa Awan." Vikal slid his hands under Rika's limp body, pushing to his feet. "We'll find him at Goa Awan."

The legend of Goa Awan was an old one, a bedtime tale told to children. Vikal and Bahti had searched for it as boys, as the threads of their power started manifesting. Mostly an excuse to sneak out under the light of the full moon, their search had yielded much adventure, but no concrete results. The island had withheld its secrets from the two boys until they'd started growing up, more concerned with girls than full moon quests. As far as Vikal knew, Sarnak, the God of Endings, was the only one whom the island had deemed worthy of its inner sanctum.

Now, he understood why. The horror of the soul-eaters' compulsion was magnified by the fact that their power opened up your mind to them—laid it bare. The soul-eaters had had full access to Vikal's furtive prayers, his deepening despair, his self-loathing. Emotions, thoughts, identity—the monsters claimed sovereignty over it all. Thank the gods he hadn't known the location of Goa Awan. He would have betrayed his people yet again.

The forest's previous coyness regarding the location of the sacred caves had vanished. The vegetation parted for him, revealing the path, propelling them forward. *Faster, faster,* it seemed to say. He ran as best he could without disturbing the precious cargo in his arms. Rika's eyes flickered back and forth behind her long, dark lashes, her breathing uneven. Her head lolled back against his shoulder, her neck as limp as a flower petal. The plant medicine he had given her seemed to be keeping her alive. No more blood flowed from the wound. But for how long?

"I am dying to hear your story, my friend." Cayono puffed behind them as they traversed up a hillside along a tumbling stream. "Where did this girl come from? How did you find her?"

"Another world," Vikal said. "And dumb luck. I will tell you all if we make it to Goa Awan."

"When we make it," Cayono said pointedly.

"Right."

The terrain was growing steeper, the river fuller. "I know this place," one of the former thralls called from where he jogged behind Cayono. "There's a waterfall up ahead." Vikal felt a stab of guilt that he hadn't gotten the men's names. He was normally better about making the time to get to know those around him, to give his subjects their due attention. But right now, there was only one thing that mattered. Rika. The thought of losing her terrified him, and that fact alone left him uneasy and confused. Surely, it was just what Rika meant that made her so precious to him—she was his only hope of freeing his people and defeating the soul-eaters.

Over the crest of an emerald hill a waterfall came into view—a hazy deluge thundering into the jungle below. The path ended abruptly at a wall of dark volcanic rock, slicked by the waterfall's rainbow mist. Vikal knelt and gently laid Rika on the soft springy undergrowth, stretching his aching arms with a groan.

"Where has the forest led us, Vikal?" Cayono asked, placing his palm on the rock and looking up the soaring expanse. "A dead end? Why would it do this?"

Vikal had been thinking the exact same thing but held his tongue. Perhaps he was still not worthy of the secrets of Goa Awan. Perhaps the island had weighed him—his failures, his crimes against its people—and had found him wanting. Or perhaps—a small frightened voice suggested—he would be retaken by the soul-eaters. A cold wave of panic swept over him at the thought, threatening to pull him under. He couldn't go back. He wouldn't. He'd rather die first. Better die a coward than live a thrall.

"Vikal?" Cayono's voice was gentle.

With a shaking breath, Vikal clawed free of the fears. Perhaps the island wouldn't show him Goa Awan. But Rika needed help. And it had brought them here for a reason. With a worried glance at Rika, Vikal stepped up beside Cayono, examining the cliff face. There was nowhere to go. A torrent of water to their right, a crumbling slope a few yards to the left. From here, the whole of the soul-eaters' devastation was visible, a cruel black scar through Nua's picturesque landscape. "I don't know," Vikal admitted. "The path seemed so clear."

"*Gusti*," one of the other two men said—the taller one. "A few vines up there are acting strange."

Vikal looked up with his third eye open. Sure enough, the man was right. The vegetation was pulsing with movement and life. The path led—up.

"How in the world...?" Vikal said, looking back at Rika.

"We go up?" Cayono asked.

Vikal nodded.

"I have an idea."

And so they found themselves climbing, Rika strapped to Cayono's back with an overabundance of vines. Her head lolled against his burly shoulder, her arms and legs hanging down limply, waving with Cayono's every movement. Vikal climbed below Cayono and hardly noticed the precariousness of his own ascent, so fixed was he on watching Rika's form. "How is she doing?" he called.

"How is she doing? How am I doing!" Cayono grunted. "She is sleeping like a baby! I am the one stuck on the side of a mountain! Man is not meant for these heights. The gods would have made us monkeys."

Vikal knew Cayono's words were meant to lift his spirits, to make him laugh. But his ragged nerves left no room for humor. If the harness slipped...there was nothing they could do to stop Rika from plummeting to the ground far below. He tugged at the threads of the vines holding Rika, infusing them with his own will—ordering, pleading with them to be strong. To hold firm to this most precious of cargo.

"A ledge!" Cayono called. "I think...we might be there!"

Vikal prayed it was true, and with a burst of strength, made his way to where Cayono now stood. Vikal pulled himself up onto a ragged outcropping of rock that ran perpendicular to the waterfall, disappearing behind its spray.

"Is this it?" Cayono asked, massaging his hands.

Vikal scooted over to give the other two men room on the ledge. Without thinking, he smoothed Rika's hair back from her face, tucking it behind her ear. She was so still now, her lovely features pale once again. The adrenaline and energy of the plant medicine was waning.

"Let us hope so," Vikal said. "Rika has little time left."

Cayono inched forward on the ledge, hugging the cliff face as the path disappeared into the roaring darkness behind the waterfall. The tiny jutting of rock opened into a wide tunnel, completely hidden from the outside world. Vikal peered into the dim light but saw nothing. Cayono unwrapped the vines from his torso and Vikal was there ready to catch Rika as she slipped off Cayono's back. "Thank you for carrying her, *bak*."

"It is my honor." Cayono clapped him on the shoulder. "Into the dark?"

"No way but forward."

They crept forward until all light from the entrance had dimmed. There was nothing but rock and breathing, the heavy weight of the unknown.

Vikal didn't know how long they had been moving when a light bloomed in the distance. A strange light. A dim lavender glow.

"I see something," he hissed.

"What is it—woah!" Cayono said, coming up short, his hands raised.

Four men had materialized from the darkness. And four spear points were leveled at them.

CHAPTER 16

"E asy," Vikal said. "It is Vikal and Cayono. We are here to help." *And for help.*

"Out of the way," a gruff voice said, shoving aside one of the men who was now lowering his spear. "You are late," Sarnak said, his black eyes gleaming in the darkness. The man looked the same—orange robes, bald head, lines in his face as deep as the furrows on a fresh field.

Vikal grinned in relief, overcome with gratitude at the sight of his old mentor. "Better late than never."

Sarnak waved a gnarled hand for them to follow before turning and disappearing into the depths of the tunnel, the light of his floating orb bobbing before him. The orb was the most mysterious of the totems of the gods, giving Sarnak the ability to gaze into the past or the future. Or just show off by making it defy gravity.

Vikal and Cayono exchanged a glance before hurrying to follow. They came to a junction in the tunnels and took the left, diving deeper into the blackness. Sarnak stooped low while he shuffled along, though the tunnel was tall enough for even Cayono to pass without ducking his head. The tunnel deposited them into a large room. Vikal looked around, letting his eyes adjust to the purple light that glowed from recesses on the wall, illuminating half a dozen beds of leaves and cloth. A sick ward.

"Come, come," Sarnak said, walking to the bed on the end and motioning for them to deposit Rika. Her breathing was faint, her skin sallow. It was like she was already gone.

"Can you save her?" Vikal didn't think he could bear returning to his people only to fail them once again.

"It is not time for her ending. She will live."

Vikal heaved a huge sigh of relief, stepping back. Weariness swept over him as the adrenaline of their frantic flight drained away.

Cayono clapped a hand on Vikal's back. "Well done, *bak*."

"It was your fast thinking that saw us here," Vikal said.

"Yes, yes, a parade for each of you. Now, there must be silence if I am to do my job," Sarnak snapped, pulling Rika's shirt up slowly to reveal her wound. The stiff shirt fought him, the blood crusting the fabric to her skin.

Vikal suppressed the urge to hug Sarnak. Over his years of training, he had learned to love Sarnak's straightforward gruffness. It was refreshing to hear such truth spoken, especially for a king.

Cayono just shook his head. "I would like to find my sister," he whispered, motioning to the tunnel entrance.

Vikal nodded.

Sarnak, without looking up from examining Rika, shook his hand at one of the little recesses filled with light. "Take a lantern. Dark out there."

Cayono squeezed Vikal's shoulder before grabbing a light and vanishing into the darkness.

"This is unusual, unusual indeed." Sarnak was looking past him, staring over Vikal's shoulder. Vikal turned to look at what he was staring at, but there was nothing. "What?"

"You come bearing ghosts," Sarnak said. Sarnak pointed behind Vikal again, and again he saw nothing. Nothing except a Nuan, hurrying over with hot water and clean cloth. "My *Gusti*." She inclined her head, setting the supplies down. "You have returned."

"I have. With a very important ally. We must save this woman," Vikal said. "She can kill soul-eaters."

Sarnak's head shot up at that.

Vikal suppressed a smirk of satisfaction. It wasn't often he surprised Sarnak.

"Goddess of bright light," Sarnak said, surveying Rika with a keen eye. "Yes, I see it is so. But a stranger to our land."

"I did not know such a thing was possible," Vikal said.

"We will speak of this once she is well. For now, stay out of our way." Sarnak and the Nuan woman leaned over Rika and began to go to work.

Vikal was pacing at the end of the bed when a scream ripped from Rika's throat. She tried to sit up, but he was at her side in a flash, pushing aside the nurse, pressing her back down gently.

"Shhhh," he said, taking her face in his hands, trying to find her within the wildness of those gray eyes. "Rika, stay still. They're sewing up your wound."

She seemed to register his presence and relaxed against the bed. He stroked the velvet skin of her temple with his thumb, speaking to her in Nuan. He didn't know what he was saying—words of comfort his mother used to whisper when he was a very young and sick or scared.

"Where...?" she croaked.

"Some water?" Vikal said to the Nuan nurse, who reached for a bowl and cloth. The woman leaned over Vikal to dribble water across Rika's lips. She gulped it up greedily.

"That's enough for now," he said, gesturing to the nurse with a sharp motion of his head.

Rika glared at him before hissing in pain as Sarnak made another stitch with the needle.

Vikal chuckled. "You can have more in a moment. You seem to have gotten your spirit back. That's a good sign."

A half-smile broke across her face. Her eyelids fluttered. She was slipping back into unconsciousness.

"Sleep," Vikal said. "Heal." He stroked the side of her face until her breathing evened, mesmerized by the sight of her. He brushed her hair back from her forehead, marveling at its softness.

"All right, good job," Sarnak snapped. "Now didn't I tell you to stay the hell out of our way? Over there. Sit." He pointed across the room and Vikal stood, his face flushing at the chastisement.

Vikal walked stiffly to a ledge of stone and collapsed onto it, leaning back. The cave wall was dewy with cold, leeching the warmth from his body, pulling the heat from his cheeks. It felt good. He closed his eyes, trying to forget what he had just found himself doing. What had come over him? He was just feeling grateful that Rika would live. Yes. The girl was a fighter. Strong and braver than he had given her credit for. Her face flashed before him—square jaw, smooth olive skin, that little gap that peeked from between her teeth when she smiled. Ebony hair that had felt so soft beneath his hand. Guilt spasmed in him as he thought of another whose silken strands he used to run his fingers through. Sarya. So different. Playful and full of laughter while Rika was fierce and strong, with iron in her bones. Dear gods, he had no right to compare them. To see Rika as anything but an ally. Perhaps a friend. Never mind what the lore might say.

☾

Vikal found himself wrapped in a dream of Sarya—of their past. It was the day of silence, one of the high holy days of the Nuan calendar. The day where the whole island fell silent, tiptoed about with bated breath so the sea demons couldn't find them, couldn't attack and kill and maim. He had been twelve, playing hide and seek with Bahti and Sarya in the jungle outside Meru Karkita, the most magnificent of Nua's many temples. His sight gave him an unfair advantage, so Sarya and Bahti had made him promise that the jungle wouldn't aid him. He hadn't promised he wouldn't use his abilities to get comfortable, though, so he had crafted an expert hiding place out of a hammock of vines up in the shade of the canopy. He was dozing when something pinched his big toe. He surged awake and squirmed to see what it was, nearly falling out of the hammock. It was Sarya, her hair braided over one shoulder, a delighted look on her face. "I found you!" she exclaimed—before clapping her hands over her mouth.

Vikal dropped down from the hammock, looking all around for witnesses. *You talked!* he mouthed, his eyes wide. The importance of the tradition had been drilled into them year after year. If the day wasn't observed with absolute silence, the sea demons would come ashore, and a sacrifice would be required to placate them—to keep them from devouring all they found in their path.

Sarya pulled herself up straight and dropped her hands. "I'm not afraid," she said, though her voice quavered. "I will be the sacrifice."

A rustling in the jungle to their left made them both jump, and Vikal was at Sarya's side in a blink, his hand over her mouth. They stood as still as stones as the foliage moved. Fear squeezed his chest with a vise grip. Was it a demon? Part of him, the conscious part that knew that this was a memory, remembered Bahti emerging from the trees, squat and scowling, waving away a fly. But this dream twisted the past into something new. It was not Bahti that brushed aside the green leaves—not this time. Instead, a twisted nightmare emerged—a three-fingered hand wrapped in an iron gauntlet, followed by Seven—the soul-eater who now held his totem.

Sarya screamed into his hand as the creature looked down upon them with baleful green eyes, reaching one of its four arms out for her. Vikal was frozen to the spot, small and trembling, too terrified to defend himself or Sarya. Just as he had been when the soul-eater had taken her in real life. "I will feast on the soul of this sacrifice," it rasped, its fingers closing around her arm.

Vikal jerked awake with a shout, cold sweat frosting his brow.

"You were leaping about like a monkey in a lightning storm," Sarnak said, pulling a sheet up over Rika's torso.

Vikal rubbed his hands over his face, trying to banish the image of the soul-eater reaching for young Sarya. "Bad dream," he admitted.

"You will have bad dreams for many moons to come," Sarnak said. "As your mind purges itself of what you saw as a thrall."

Vikal ground his teeth. Those images would never leave him. Not now, not ever. "How's Rika?"

"She will be well in a day or two. She lost much blood."

"Thank you." Vikal heaved a sigh.

"Does she know what she is?"

"Yes. I told her."

"Does she know what it means?" Sarnak asked with a pointed look.

Vikal shook his head. He had been avoiding even thinking about sharing the deeper history of the gods of this island—what it meant for her. "I did not want to complicate things."

"Things are already complicated. She will learn, here in Goa Awan, among her people. You tell her or I will."

"She deserves a choice before she is yoked to me for eternity."

"This is ironic, coming from one who carries the ghost of his dead wife with him like a stone around his neck."

"That is exactly why Rika deserves better. Why the fates should let her be this incarnation. Let her go home to her land. I have nothing to give her, even if she wanted such things."

"You have yourself."

"I am nothing. Not anymore."

"When circumstances strip us down, what remains is our soul. Pure and unadorned. To think otherwise is pure ego."

Vikal exploded from his chair, his hands balled into fists. "Ego? You know not what you speak of. Have you lost the woman you loved? Watched her soul be sucked into ash before you, to know that there would be no solace in death for her, no new life waiting for her to be reincarnated into? Have you been enslaved to the creature who killed her, forced to stand at its side, kill for it, hear its twisted thoughts in your head, scraping against the walls of your mind? When you've done any of those things, perhaps you can have grounds to judge me. To judge what remains."

Sarnak hadn't moved, hadn't blinked at Vikal's outburst. His tone was gentle. "Sarya is free from the soul-eater who took her. She will walk this island again in another body—feel the pink sand between her toes. You are the one holding her now. Your unwillingness to let her go. To forgive yourself for your imagined part in her death."

Vikal paced back against the wall, his hand twitching for his staff. He longed to caress the engraved vines that adorned it, to feel the familiar patterns beneath his fingers. "I don't know how."

"You must discover how. For Rika. She is in a foreign land. You must teach her our ways, make her feel at home for the time she is here."

Yes, he owed Rika that much. "How is it possible, Sarnak? That she was born a world away? Have you ever heard of such a thing?"

"All things are possible. One must only have the imagination to dream bigger. And the universe has endless imagination."

"I would not have believed it, but I see the threads that tie her to the stars. To Nua."

Sarnak nodded sagely. "I see them too. We must help her remember the goddess she is."

"I was hoping you would help her with that. Like you helped the rest of us remember our past lives."

"I will have a lesson with her. But you must help her fall in love with Nua. And with you."

"Nua, yes. But me? No. I'm a ruined man. I've already let one wife down. I won't make that mistake again. She deserves better."

"The fates may not think so."

"The fates can go to hell."

INTERLUDE

The invading army was a dark swarm in the distance, a slow-moving plague swallowing the green quilt of farmland that stretched between Yoshai and the sea. All that stood between this malignant force and her people was a wall of stone and gates of wood. They seemed painfully insufficient.

The wind ruffled Kai's hair, bearing scents of iron and sulfur where it had once borne honeysuckle and grass. The day was warm, however, and the sun shone cheerfully. It felt like an insult to the ache in Kai's heart. Her husband was gone—robbed from her—erased from the world without so much as a goodbye. There would be no body to mourn, no grave to visit.

"How long?" Kai asked, her eyes locked on the horizon. She stood in the upper courtyard of the palace at Yoshai. In this courtyard, she had once met the creator. She had sent two demons back through a rip in the fabric of their world—trapping them in their own dark dimension. What she would give to fight those enemies again. For those allies. At least then she had a plan. An idea. Now, she had only heartache and despair.

"A few hours at most." Nanase stood at her side. Though her weather-worn skin was wrinkled from her years, Nanase still stood tall—her body supple and strong. She had been the headmistress of the moonburner Citadel in Kyuden when Kai had first trained. Kai had always been a little awed by fierce Nanase with her hawk's tail of braids and her fierce reputation. That feeling had never truly gone. Kai was grateful to have her by her side.

"We've evacuated everyone from the land they'll be crossing?" Kai asked.

"Everyone we could get to in time. A few thousand at least. They're being housed in the palace, the temples, schools. Wherever we can fit them. The village of Antila was too close to the soul-eater forces for us to reach. But everyone else is within the city walls."

"How are the preparations going?"

"We are ready to face whatever force they throw at us. Though from Koji's description of what these creatures can do…who knows if it will be enough."

"My mind keeps fighting with itself. I think that no creature can have the powers he described. That there's no way our burners could be so ineffective against them. But then…"

"You believe him."

"You heard him at the council meeting. He's absolutely terrified of these creatures. Even if things were not as he says…he believes they are to the depth of his soul."

"I don't doubt Koji saw something terrible. Nothing short of a nightmare could have defeated the king. But some things we have to see for ourselves."

"We will have the chance soon enough."

"Your Majesty." A cleared throat behind her interrupted their conversation.

Kai turned to find General Daarco striding across the courtyard, clad in red leather armor traced with veins of gold.

"General," she nodded. "How are the fortifications coming?"

"We've reinforced the gates and have set up some nasty surprises on the approach. We have soldiers and burners stationed at all stretches of the southern wall with longbows, rocks, and burning oil. We're ready for whatever they throw at us."

"And messengers have been sent to Kistana and Kyuden to warn them to prepare their citizens to evacuate and shelter inside the cities?"

"They're standing by for instructions from you."

"How are the stores?"

"We brought everything we could inside the walls from the surrounding farms and manors. If we had had more time—"

"How long will we be able to withstand a siege?"

"With the number of people we have in the city…two months?"

Kai exchanged a glance with Nanase. "It's not as bad as I feared," Nanase said.

"Agreed. Thank you, General," Kai said. "We estimate they'll be at the gates in less than three hours. Ready the troops."

Daarco nodded, his golden hair glinting in the sun. Then he spun and was gone, disappearing back down the stairs.

Kai crossed the courtyard and picked up Quitsu from the chair where he sat, sinking into it. Quitsu didn't normally like to be held like a housecat, but he seemed to sense her distress and curled into her lap. Nanase sat down beside her.

"I keep thinking…" Her voice was soft. Had the army's great shadow grown closer in the last few minutes? "What are we holding out for? Two months…two months until what? There are no reinforcements coming. If Koji's right, we can't defeat these creatures with burning. We don't even know if they can be killed. Maybe it would be better to ride out to meet them. Go out in a blaze of glory and battle."

"That's your grief talking. Giving up before we've even begun the fight." Nanase said. "Everything can be killed. We just have to figure out how."

"I don't have the faintest idea where to begin. We know nothing about these things. At least with the tengu…we had something to go on. Legends. Myths. History, however tangled it was. This…this feels like a foreign language."

"We have one clue," Nanase said.

Kai raised an eyebrow quizzically.

"The prophecy. Rika. Koji said she did something. Fought one of the creatures. Killed it."

Kai's heart twisted painfully. Rika. Where was her daughter? Was she dead? Was she being held captive by those monsters? Tortured and maimed…her body broken…Kai closed her eyes, shaking away the rush of worries that threatened to overwhelm her. "We don't even know if Rika is alive."

"Do you think your daughter could pass from this world without you knowing it? That your soul wouldn't feel it? Truly?"

"No. A mother knows," she whispered. She met Nanase's sharp gaze.

"What if she's their prisoner?"

"Then it's lucky they're marching right to our door. We'll get her back."

Kai let out a grunt of laughter. She took Nanase's sinewy hand in hers. "I'm not sure what I did to deserve such wise counsel."

"You were a damn good queen. And friend." They looked together over the dark stain of the approaching army, drawing strength from each other.

Nanase nodded to herself. "I feel it in my soul. Rika is the key. We just have to find her."

CHAPTER 17

Rika swam in and out of consciousness. Strange sights and unfamiliar faces passed above her. At times, she wasn't sure if she dreaming. Or dead. But there was movement and pain—and didn't both mean that you were still alive? Vikal's tanned face flashed before her, his brow knotted with worry. "Stay with me," he mouthed, but his words were distant, as if spoken underwater.

There was darkness—an immense weight of earth and stone bearing down on her. A lavender light that surely must have been a dream. Twisting passageways. Shadowed faces peering through the gloom. Still, Vikal was with her, his arms beneath her, his touch against her temple. He was a tether holding her to this world.

Rika woke to throbbing in her side and memories raging in her mind. She had almost been killed fighting that soul-eater. She had felt so small and foolish as she'd lain there, her lifeblood leaking out into foreign soil. Gods, she had been *excited* when the shadow of the soul-eaters' army had appeared on the waters. Had thought it would mean the arrival of her powers. How naive she had been. How childish and selfish to wish for danger just to satisfy her own need to be special. To fit in. What kind of queen would she have been, to put her own needs before the lives of her people?

Hot tears leaked down the side of her face. She wouldn't be queen anymore. She would never see Kita or Miina again. There might not even be a queen, a land to rule. She'd never see her mother again—Kai would go to her grave thinking Rika had disobeyed her and been killed. She had had everything and appreciated none of it. And now it was all gone, vanished in a flash of black and glowing green.

A light flickered to life, blooming behind her eyelids. She opened her eyes, glaring at the interloper, ready to tell them to leave her alone.

It was a girl, perhaps twelve years old. She wore a cropped blouse and loose skirt that might have once been orange or pink but were now faded to a mute tan. She was lovely, with thick, black hair and wide dark eyes, but painfully thin—her collarbones protruding from her chest. The girl spoke—asking something in the strange melodic language the soldiers had used. She approached slowly, the lantern in her hand emitting a dim lavender glow. In the light, Rika could just make out her surroundings, cast in shadow. They were in some sort of cave.

"I don't understand," Rika said.

The girl crossed the chamber and set the lantern on a little cleft in the rock wall. She pointed questioningly to a bowl next to it that was filled with glistening water.

Rika nodded eagerly.

The girl lifted a ladle of water to Rika's lips, and Rika inched her way onto her elbows to drink, groaning at the pain in her side.

The girl spoke again as Rika slurped greedily.

"I wonder how long I've been out?" Rika asked herself, slowly trying to maneuver herself into a seated position. The blanket that had been draped over her fell, and a fierce blush rose in her cheeks. She was naked beneath. She snatched the blanket back up, tucking it under her armpits. Who had undressed her?

"Where's Vikal?"

The girl brightened, recognizing the name. She pointed out the door, motioning for Rika to come with her.

Rika looked down at herself, clothed in only the colorful blanket. She gave the girl a questioning look, and the girl smiled, a dimple appearing on her cheek. She bolted towards the roughhewn opening to the cavern.

"Wait!" Rika called after her. "What's your name?" She frowned. How best to communicate? She pointed at herself. "Rika."

The girl understood immediately. She pointed at her own chest.

"Tamar."

"Nice to meet you, Tamar." Rika said as the girl slipped into the darkness beyond.

Tamar returned quickly with a bundle of clothing and a bowl of some sort of orange mush topped with a red broth. Though the food was unlike any she had seen before, Rika's mouth watered. The girl handed her the clothes and quickly turned her back. Rika sat up with a groan, her head swimming with the effort. She dropped her legs off the side of the bed and paused, fighting a wave of dizziness. She took a deep breath and immediately regretted it as a stab of pain shot through her side. *Okay. Take it slow.* Rika pawed through the pile of clothing and found underclothes, a long-fitted skirt in a pattern of purple and gold, a white buttoned shirt, and a gold sash.

After dressing, Rika sat back on the bed to eat the mush and broth—woozy after only a minute of standing. The orange stuff was sticky and sweet, the broth warming and spicy. The flavors were strange to her palate but surprisingly delicious. She ate slowly at first, not sure how her stomach would react, but quickly gained momentum. At least she wasn't stuck somewhere with terrible food. When she had slurped the last bits of broth and washed it down with some water, Tamar clapped her hands, motioning for Rika to follow.

Outside her door, nestled against the wall, lay a neat row of green leaves covered in trinkets—flower petals, coins, candles, berries. What were they? Rika left them behind as the dim lavender light of Tamar's lantern continued down the tunnel. She tried to hurry to catch up with Tamar but found herself as weak as a kitten, leaning against the cold stone wall for support. Rika squinted into the gloom as she slowly passed openings into other rooms, searching for inhabitants within. Was this truly the place from Vikal's story? The labyrinth of tunnels felt ancient—she could almost imagine the great snake thrashing about beneath the mountain before breaking free, winging towards the sky.

The smooth floor of the tunnel angled up ever-so-slightly until it deposited them into the next cave. If it could even be called that. Rika's jaw dropped as she craned her neck to take it all in. The cavern was big enough to fit half the palace at Yoshai. The ceiling soared above them, gleaming stalactites barely visible in the gloom. The walls' cracks and crevices glowed lavender, illuminating the space in fairylike light. Rika bent down to look into Tamar's lantern more closely, groaning at the pain in her side. The lantern was filled with a glowing lichen, or fungus of some sort. It must have been native to the cave, and the inhabitants were using it to light the space.

And the inhabitants…Rika could hardly comprehend the number of people housed here. From the tunnel where they stood, a spiderweb of wooden walkways snaked down to a veritable city of fabric tents. People chatted and cooked over fires while children chased each other through the narrow alleys between rows. A woody smell like incense mingled with the smoke from the fires and the ancient scent of the caves, forming a strange perfume that set her teeth on edge. Tamar led the way along the edge of the cave and Rika followed, not sure whether to watch her footing or the people. Vikal's whole city must have been here.

The sounds of murmured conversation and children's laughter died down, fading to silence. Rika looked back to the cavern that stretched below her. The people had grown still and were now staring at her and Tamar. Quiet voices like a wave sounded as Vikal's people realized who she was. "*Dewa*," they murmured. Then the murmurs rose to a buzz—calls and cries of "*Dewa*" echoing through the space. Rika stumbled against Tamar, edging past the girl towards the tunnel leading out of the massive cavern.

In her haste to leave the strange scene, Rika crashed into a hard body, recoiling. Vikal, she realized with relief. She fought an urge to hug him, so thankful was she for a familiar sight. "What are they saying?" she asked, turning back towards the cavern, where the people had quieted again.

"*Dewa*," he said. "It means goddess."

Rika shook her head, trying to shove down her rising panic. "I'm not their goddess. I'm nobody's goddess." Two dead soul-eaters did not a goddess make. Just a few short days ago, before black sails had appeared on the horizon, before her father…she might have welcomed this. But now…she felt like a fraud. She hadn't seen Cygna again since they had arrived and she had so unceremoniously sunk their boat, destroying her only way back to Kitina. She had almost gotten herself killed battling a few thralls. If she was truly these people's goddess, she couldn't help but think that they were in for disappointment.

Concern was etched on Vikal's face. He blessedly ignored her comment. "How are you feeling? Are you sure you should be out of bed?"

"I needed to see…to understand where we were. What had

happened. What… What did happen?"

Vikal said a few words to Tamar, who curtsied and handed him the lantern. He reached out to ruffle her hair, but she ducked out of the way, sticking her tongue out at him before scampering off. Rika raised an eyebrow. "Does she know you?"

"She's my niece," Vikal said, ushering her to walk with him through the corridor. *Niece?* she thought, questions swimming in her mind. She and Vikal hadn't had much time to exchange small talk, and that included personal histories. What other family members might she come across in this place?

"What do you remember?" Vikal asked. He walked slowly next to her, keeping pace with her pained shuffle. His hand hovered behind her like he was afraid she would topple over at any moment. Though in fairness, her knees seemed to be considering that very possibility. Vikal had changed into a pair of green trousers and a white collarless shirt. The dark shadow of stubble was gone from his jaw, and he smelled fresh— faintly of eucalyptus. He looked softer than he had in his black leather. She liked this domesticated version more than his black armor-clad self.

"I remember fighting the soldiers and the leech. I was stabbed. But I killed the soul-eater, right?"

"You did." He nodded. "You fought well, but you were injured. You were near death when we brought you here. You are lucky to be alive." Vikal's voice was grave, his face stony. "You were in a fevered sleep for so long. Though Sarnak said you would live… I still worried."

"How long?"

"Three days."

"Three days?" Rika yelped, her heart sinking. What damage had the soul-eaters done to Yoshai in three days?

"Yes. We came so close to losing you."

Rika didn't miss the word choice. We. Not I. She needed to remember. It didn't matter if the hazy memory of his thumb on her cheek sent the butterflies in her stomach into a maelstrom. Vikal cared about her for one reason, and one reason only. She was a tool to free his people. And he was a tool to get her home.

"How did we get here?"

"After you fell, the forest showed us the way here. It was a close thing."

"Thank you for saving me. Again."

"It was you who saved me, Rika. Without you, I would never have seen this land again. My friends and family. So it is I who owe my thanks."

"We're even," she said, uncomfortable with the intensity of his words.

"Do you feel strong enough to meet the other gods?" Vikal asked. "They are gathered. We're discussing what to do about the leeches."

Rika nodded, following Vikal down the dark tunnels dimly lit by violet light.

"How long can your people last in here?"

He looked at her, and when he answered, his voice was a whisper. "Weeks. If they're lucky. Without the tana root, the people would have starved by now. Going outside to hunt or forage is a great risk. If one person were to be captured by the soul-eaters, they would give up all their knowledge, including the location of this place."

"So what have people been eating? What's a tana root? The orange mush?"

"A vegetable that grows in the ground. Sarnak discovered it in these caves. It is not exciting, but it fills the belly. It can grow in the dark, so the people have been cultivating it in the tunnels by the light of the lava lichen."

"Is that the glowy purple stuff?"

"Yes." Vikal smiled. "You have quite a way with words."

Rika raised an eyebrow. "Was that a joke?"

"I am as surprised as you are," he said. "Goa Awan—Nua herself—has provided everything our people needed—caring for them when I could not. But one cannot live on tana root forever. If we are to survive, we need to strike back soon."

"I'm amazed that they've lasted as long as they have," Rika said. "It's very well organized."

"That is all Kemala. And Bahti. They are Tamar's parents."

"Who are you related to? You said Tamar's your niece, right?"

Vikal hesitated. "We have arrived," he said instead, pushing aside a ragged curtain that hung over the opening to yet another cave, holding it for Rika while she entered.

Three people were gathered around a large table. Though they all had the ebony hair and tanned complexion that Nuans favored, that was where their similarities ended. A woman, dark and lithe, her features exquisite, leaned back in a chair, examining perfect fingernails. Around her throat was a dazzling necklace of what looked like white and black diamonds. It was the type of jewelry Rika's mother would have worn to the fanciest of ceremonies and complained about the whole time. But it suited this woman, as if the dank cave should have dressed itself up, rather than the woman dimming her beauty to suit.

At the other end of the table sat a man of about Vikal's age with a thick, black beard and a warm smile revealing straight, white teeth. Beside him leaned what looked like a man-sized golden fork, as tall as Vikal. Some kind of—pitchfork? The last man stood behind the woman, as menacing as she was elegant. He seemed made of squat bulk and menace, his muscled arms crossed before his broad chest, his jaw set in anger. In the darkness, his eyes glimmered red as rubies. Rika swallowed thickly.

Vikal spoke to the three people in the room in their language before motioning to Rika. "Rika," he said. She gave a little wave.

"Rika, this is Kemala, Bahti, and Ajij."

Kemala, the woman, flourished a graceful half-salute. Bahti, the angry man, merely glowered at her, one of his hands drifting to an ornate dagger at his waist. Was it possible sweet Tamar had come from this man? Ajij, the bearded man, stood and came to meet her. He took her hand and bowed low over it, speaking strange words in a tone filled with welcome. She squeezed his hand, and when he stood, he studied her with eyes as blue as the sea, endless and deep. Between his brows was a tattoo in dark blue ink, identical to Vikal's. Bahti scoffed. Ajij threw him what looked like a lewd gesture as he went back to his chair, saying something.

"You've met Cayono," Vikal said, turning to introduce the tall, muscular man who had just entered from the hallway behind them.

Cayono bowed low and deep. "My goddess," he said, in Rika's language. "I am indebted to you for freeing me twice over. You are truly our saving grace."

"You speak my language?" Rika asked, relief welling at this bit of familiarity amongst the strangeness. Then it dawned on her. She turned to Vikal. "Because he was a thrall?"

Vikal nodded. "Some of the knowledge of the leeches is imparted to the thralls, particularly that which they think is useful, like the language of the land we are conquering. As soon as the first person from your land was taken, the soul-eater hive learned your language. All the way down to the thralls."

Rika's half-smile faltered. The first person taken. Her father. These men knew her language because her father had been killed—eaten alive. She couldn't forget that, however friendly they seemed. She didn't belong here. She needed to get home.

Bahti let out a string of words that sounded spitting mad. Vikal responded in a reproachful tone.

"He doesn't like me very much," Rika observed.

"Ignore him. Bahti is hotheaded. It is in his blood."

Vikal asked another question in his language and Kemala answered this time, shrugging her shoulders.

"Here I am," a gravelly voice said behind them. Rika turned to find a short, wiry man, completely bald, swathed in orange robes. He gave off the impression of age, and wisdom, and…darkness. His eyes were inky pools shrouded in shadow. She took a step back inadvertently. Vikal placed his hands on her shoulders to still her. "This is Sarnak. The god of endings."

Sarnak reached out for her and grasped her wrist in his gnarled one, pulling her from Vikal's grasp. "Our newest goddess is to come with me. There is something I have to show her."

"Come with you? Where?" Rika asked. How did he speak her language? Had he been enslaved to the leeches?

"Sarnak is the keeper of our histories and a master of magic," Vikal explained. "He helped all of us learn to use our powers. I asked him to help you."

Sarnak stood as still as a statute, his hand locked around her wrist in an unyielding grip.

"You trust him?" she whispered.

"With my life," Vikal said gently.

"Very well," Rika said, shoving down her trepidation and letting the strange little man lead her from the room.

CHAPTER 18

Sarnak dropped Rika's hand and reached into his belt, drawing out a small glass orb. He tossed it into the air with a flourish, and instead of falling to the ground, it bobbed before them, suspended in midair as if hanging from a string. A pure light blossomed from within, illuminating the tunnel and lighting their path. "You took your time arriving," he said. His words held the strange staccato cadence that she was coming to recognize as the Nuan accent.

"Excuse me?" Rika asked, forgetting her questions about the strange orb in the face of his comment. "I didn't even know this place existed more than a few days ago."

"To forget your own people," he chided with a shake of his bald head. "What did you do wrong? To get so turned around during your reincarnation."

"Maybe you sent me down the wrong door or plane or whatever during my last ending," she shot back, her hackles raising. Was he blaming her for what—being born in the wrong world?

He looked sidelong at her and coughed. Or was it a disguised laugh? "This is not exactly how it works."

"Then teach me. Rather than judging me."

"I can do both." Was he toying with her?

She rolled her eyes. "Were you under the soul-eater's compulsion?

How do you speak my language?"

"This is a worthy question. My role is unique among the gods. To begin and end—to rule the cycles. All things on this Earth turn in cycles. The seasons, birth to death, the ocean to rain—"

"Right. But how do you speak a language fluently when you've never even heard it before? Or have you?" she asked.

"All people are related. All languages are related too. This is part of the cycle."

She looked at him suspiciously. His explanation lacked something. Like an actual explanation. "You have no idea, do you."

He shrugged, a smile playing across his wrinkled face. "I will meditate on this thing. If I come to understand this secret, I will share it. To oversee the reincarnation of the other gods is part of my duties. My guess is that my soul's role in placing you in this cycle imbued me with this knowledge."

"Your soul's role..." Rika shook her head. "So did you know I was in Kitina?"

They had reached the end of yet another tunnel, and Sarnak paused before the dim doorway, motioning for her to proceed. "This is something we will speak of. All in due time."

She entered a chamber with a soaring ceiling. The cave was sparsely furnished, a bedroll on the floor, a shelf with a few books. The room was lit not by the low lavender glow she had seen elsewhere, but a quicksilver light pouring down from above, bathing the mundane furnishings in a magical ambience.

"This is a benefit of everyone thinking you are a little mad. You get the best room," Sarnak said.

Rika let out a surprised laugh. "Where is the light coming from?"

"To let in the light, a path of tunnels lead from this cave to the side of the volcano. The light of the sky is reflected into this room. This is the best place to practice your magic."

"Practice?" Rika swallowed. She hadn't managed much control in the days since her magic had manifested. She didn't want to blow this man up like she had the boat. Or the soul-eater.

"Vikal said you are powerful but untrained. To do magic, we must first understand it. First we learn. Then you wake. Then we practice."

Wake? Rika wondered. She was already awake. Though in truth, this all did feel like a strange dream.

Sarnak retrieved a book from an indent in the wall and settled onto the floor, patting the ground beside him. Rika sat down beside him, awkwardly tucking her feet behind her. Damn this ridiculous skirt. She wished she had her leggings. He opened the book to the first page, which revealed an image of a dark expanse. The writing was a strange script of swirl and dots—nothing like the writing she was used to. "This is one of our vedas, or religious texts. The one tells our history. The world we know was created from the void by four great creator spirits." He turned the page. "The land we walk on was made by a spirit we call the great turtle. He placed it on his back, where it still rests today. The sky was formed by the flying snake, who fans the currents with his wings. The ocean was created by a great leviathan, whose tail swirls the tides. Underneath the volcano is the dragon, who breathes the fire that fuels the Earth. We take care not to anger him, for when he spits fire, Nua suffers for his wrath. Above this all is the floating sky, where the world of human emotions and love are born and live. Beyond that is the endless sky, where the stars and planets sit. Each of these forms have unique energy and attributes."

Rika peered at the image, at the layers and depictions of beasts. "Vikal told me about the snake."

"To rule the land were created seven gods and goddesses, who are reborn into human bodies."

"Seven?" Rika asked, ticking off the numbers in her mind. If she counted herself—which she wasn't sure she did—she had met six. "Who's the last one?"

The next page of the book depicted seven people, proud and regal and clothed in glorious fabrics and gold. Sarnak pointed to the first. "The god of green things—that's Vikal. He governs plant life and is the first among the gods. The king of kings, if you will. The goddess of bright light—that's you. Then the goddess of open sky rules over the air and the winds. She died many years ago and has not been reborn this cycle. The god of the deep sea is Ajij."

"What's with his golden fork?"

"His trident. It is his totem. I will explain that as well."

"And then Bahti and Kemala, god of the mountain and goddess of dark spaces." He pointed to the last two. "And me."

"So one of the gods govern each of the realms of creation. They all make sense except the goddess of dark spaces," Rika said. "What is her power?"

"This goddess governs humanity, human emotions. Love, joy, hope, hate, jealousy, envy, courage…the best and worst of humanity, the thoughts and emotions that fill the dark spaces of our minds."

"She's not what I would have expected for a goddess of love," Rika said under her breath.

Sarnak chuckled. "It is my belief that the gods and goddesses are reborn with different traits based on the cycle in which they are born. This is a cycle of war and destruction. Hence Kemala is fierce and frightening. This is also why you were born in a foreign land."

"What do you mean?"

"If you were native Nuan, you would have met the soul-eaters when they first arrived. To be captured or killed was the only possible outcome of this encounter."

"Or maybe I would have destroyed them and prevented them from coming to my world," Rika shot back.

"My soul tells me this is not how it would have ended. The goddess of bright light could not have been Nuan in this lifetime. With distance came safety."

She supposed that made sense, if she believed that whoever made these rebirth decisions somehow knew the future. And that was a lot to swallow. She changed tactics. "Tell me about these totems. What are they?"

"Each god and goddess has an item that has been given to them by the creators of old that links them to the energy of the great spirits that separated the world into its forms. To possess your totem strengthens your power immensely. It tethers you to the power of this land and your form. Of the creator spirits. You have perhaps seen some of these totems—Ajij's trident, Bahti's hammer, Kemala's necklace."

Ah. That explained the fancy necklace.

"What is the goddess of bright light's totem?" Rika asked. Part of her refused to believe she actually was this goddess. But the rest of her—the rest of her was curious.

Sarnak turned the page. On one page was an image of a god surrounded by vines and leaves, holding a staff of twisted vines. On the other page was an image of a goddess shrouded in light, constellations bright behind her, her hair flowing in the wind. She held a strange type of sword in her hand, with two curving silver blades arcing from each end of the hilt. "Ooh," Rika said, her eyes widening. Her body thrummed with excitement as she looked at the page, coming alive with the suggestion of power.

"Where is it?" she asked. "The sword? Knife-thingy?"

"It is in the treasure room at Nuanita castle. At least it was when we evacuated. I regret that we did not have time to save it before fleeing."

"The palace overrun with soul-eaters?" Rika asked, dismayed.

"The same one."

"And you say it will make me stronger?"

"Oh, yes. To lose my orb would weaken my powers greatly." Sarnak flicked the glowing orb that floated above them and it twirled, casting twinkling light on the cave walls.

"Where's Vikal's staff?" she asked, peering at the picture.

"This is unknown. He possessed it when he was captured. The leeches likely hold it now, though they may not know of its importance."

An image flared to life in her mind of the soul-eater—the first who had entered the tent the night her father had died. Its dark claws curving around a wooden staff. Was it possible...that creature held the totem? What had become of it after she had killed it? Her stomach churned as she tried to banish the image.

"You said these totems connect us to this land, the source of our power. Vikal said that when he was in my land, his powers were weakened. Do you think that his powers would have remained strong if he'd had his totem?"

"This is likely so."

The page crackled beneath her fingers as she traced the outline of the totem. If they were going to get back to Kitina and defeat the soul-eaters, she would need all the help she could get. That meant Vikal at his full abilities. And her...whatever her powers were...at their strongest. They needed to get these totems back.

"I need not be Kemala to see your mind working in the dark spaces. You wish to recapture these artifacts."

"Is it such a crazy idea?" Though to steal a wooden stick from an evil soul-eater army a world away did sound...kind of crazy.

"This is necessary. But not yet. Vikal has said that your control is inconsistent—your power weak. The energy of your totem would be too much for you until you gain control."

Rika's anger flared. Her power may have been inconsistent, but by her count, she had still killed two more soul-eaters than any other god on this stupid island.

"My people are probably being sucked dry as we speak," Rika retorted. "There's no time."

"There will be only one chance to defeat the leeches. To advance before you are ready will spell disaster."

"Then teach me," Rika snapped. "Then we go for the totems. If I can convince the other gods," she muttered.

"This should not be difficult. They already make plans to attack. Besides, the fates have named you their queen. They will bow to you eventually."

Rika furrowed her brow. *Queen?* "What do you mean?"

Sarnak turned the page of the book back to the image of the seven gods. "The gods and goddesses are bonded. Three pairs, and a seventh, to govern the cycles."

"I don't understand."

"He has not told you yet?"

"He? Who, Vikal? Told me what?"

Sarnak furrowed his brow, the lines on his face falling into shadow. "The god of green things and the goddess of bright light are mates. This is true each cycle. Same with Bahti and Kemala. Ajij has no mate this cycle, unfortunately, unless a new goddess is soon born."

Rika shook her head, trying to process what he was saying. She held her hands up. "Wait, wait. So you're saying that me and…Vikal, we're destined to be together? We're … *mates?*"

Sarnak cocked his head, seemingly unable to understand her reasons to be upset. "As sure as the sun rises in the east. To marry Vikal…to rule Nua. This is your destiny."

CHAPTER 19

Rika leaped to her feet, shock coursing through her like a bolt of lightning. The sudden movement jostled her wound, and she was forced to shoot a hand out against the wall to steady herself. "Why didn't Vikal tell me?"

Sarnak remained perched serenely on the floor. "Perhaps he feared you would overreact."

Emotions swirled through her like a tempest. Surprise, doubt, frustration...but was that...something more? Excitement? Vikal was handsome. Her senses heightened whenever he was near—his very presence set her body humming. But the circumstances...the circumstances couldn't be more wrong. Her people were under attack from soul-eating monsters, her father had been murdered before her eyes. This was no time to selfishly think of romance. Especially with a man who had essentially *helped* kill her father.

She shook her head. "I can't think about that right now. Not until the soul-eaters are destroyed."

"This is a wise approach," Sarnak said. "Now, sit down."

Rika dropped onto the ground across from him, spent. She pressed a hand against the throbbing wound in her side, as if she could quiet it with a touch. Her and Vikal...fated? *Mates?* Her blood thrummed through her, refusing to succumb to reason. *No time for romance,* she told herself more forcefully.

Sarnak interrupted her downward mental spiral. "This is the thing about fate. It is fated to be. That doesn't mean it *will* be. I say you are fated to be our queen, but it will not be so if you walk from this cave and surrender yourself to a soul-eater."

"You're talking about free will."

"All have a say in their fate. Even the gods. To be Vikal's mate, or not, this will be your choice."

"That's good, I guess," she managed. Not that she had any idea what choice she wanted when it came to Vikal.

"Now, we return to the task at hand. You have learned, now you must awaken. To awaken is to become the goddess our people need." Or *my people* need, Rika thought stubbornly.

"So how do we… awaken me?"

"Meditation."

"Ugh." Rika grimaced. Her mother had gotten into meditation a few years back and had tried to make the whole family do it. Her father had lasted the longest, but even he couldn't stand it after a few weeks. As for Rika, her mind would never stop spinning.

"This is not the meditation where you sit and breathe and try not to think about thinking. This is different." Sarnak set aside the book, motioning for Rika to sit cross-legged across from him. It was nearly impossible in her tightly-wrapped skirt, but she did her best. He raised his hand and the orb lowered until it was floating between them. The surface dimmed, turning from bright white light to a dusky, swirling fog. Rika leaned in, fascinated by the patterns that played across the shining surface. "It's beautiful," she said. "The orb is your totem?"

"Look into the orb," Sarnak instructed with a sharp nod. "Slow your breathing. Relax your body. The orb will carry you where you need to go."

"Where is that?" Rika asked, trying to follow his instructions.

"Into the cycles. Your past."

"I have no idea what that means."

"You go to meet your past self."

Rika looked up in surprise.

He hissed, pointing. "Eyes on the orb."

Rika glowered but did as he instructed, letting out a deep breath. The silence of the cavern was broken only by the hushed sounds of her breath.

"Now. Imagine yourself inside the orb. Its swirling mist surrounds you. You are at peace within it. It begins to open. To disperse. A path is revealed. This is a familiar path."

Rika followed Sarnak's instructions one by one, walking in her mind's eye from a foggy darkness into a lush jungle like she and Vikal had first traveled through. It was a strange feeling. She knew she was imagining this all, yet things were appearing that she hadn't thought of. She pushed through the leafy fronds of forest until she emerged in some sort of garden. An explosion of plants and flowers surrounded a glassy pool. All around her, flowers bloomed and fountains tinkled with rivulets of water. The sky was dark, but for the brilliant stars and a bold, waxing moon.

"Hello?" she called. "Anyone here?" She spun around, looking for signs of life. It was peaceful in this garden, warm and soft. The edges of the world around her seemed to blur, turning the spilling jasmine and hibiscus into watercolor paintings. The stars above were impossibly big—bright enough to cast the garden in enchanted twilight, low enough to pluck like ripe fruit.

A lilting female voice sounded behind her. Rika spun to face her. "What an unusual iteration," the woman said. She was tall and willowy, wearing luxurious fabrics in the Nuan style—rich colors of gold and magenta. An elaborate headdress of gold crowned her brow and gold bangles adorned her wrists. Thick, dark lashes framed large eyes with strange irises that shimmered silver in the starlight. Rika blinked. Perhaps it was a trick of the light.

"Who are you?" Rika asked, trying unsuccessfully to smooth the tangles in her hair.

"I'm you. Your most recent past self. My name is Liliam."

As Rika stepped closer to the woman, a strange distortion occurred. Behind Liliam, she could see...a trail was the only way to describe it—a line of different women stretching out through the garden as far as her eye could see. Rika shook her head, overcome by the vision.

"If you stay directly in front of me, the image will be less overwhelming," Liliam said, repositioning her body so she and Rika stood face to face. The line of what Rika could only assume were her other past selves disappeared behind Liliam's form. Past selves. Did she really believe this strange vision? It was madness.

"Thank you," Rika managed.

"You are different than us," Liliam said. "Why?"

"I was born elsewhere. In another land." She couldn't stop staring at the woman. She had a grace and a regality about her that were impossible to imitate. *This is what a queen should be. A goddess.* Rika pressed her lips together to hide the gap between her teeth.

"Yet you have found your way to Nua. To the god of endings."

"Yeah. It's been a weird week. Nua is under attack. As is my land."

"Nua is your land," Liliam said. "You are tied to it. To all of us that came before you."

Rika pursed her lips. It didn't matter what this woman thought. She just needed to figure out how to use her powers and get back to her body.

"I see you doubt," the woman said. "But you speak our language. The stars that watch over Nua sing in your blood, as they did in mine."

"I can't speak..." Rika trailed off, realizing she *was* speaking in Nuan. She swallowed the lump in her throat. "Can you help me with our powers? I wasn't raised in Nua, so I don't understand them. I don't have our totem, either, though I hope to get it."

"It is not a thing to rush, this discovery of yourself. The constellations are our allies; they are not to be controlled or dictated to."

"Okay, that's good to know. The thing is, we're in a bit of a time crunch. In a few weeks, all of Nua will be taken over by evil soul-sucking monsters. And my land...where I was born, it will be taken over as well. It's important that you show me now."

Liliam's lovely face paled. "Very well. But you must listen very carefully to the things I say and meditate on each one until you come to understand them in your heart."

Yeah, yeah, Rika thought. "I promise," she said instead, in as solemn a tone as she could muster.

"Let us sit," Liliam said, moving to a stone bench next to the reflective pool. Rika squeezed her eyes closed as the line of past selves became visible once again, setting her equilibrium off-kilter. She hurried to sit beside the woman and realized that she was wearing her clothes from home. Leggings and a long, silver tunic wrapped with a white obi. A pang of homesickness overtook her as she smoothed her hands down the silk of her tunic. She may be speaking Nuan, but Kitina was her home.

"You understand how the gods and goddesses arise from the creator spirits that separated the parts of our world?"

Rika nodded. She thought she did.

"The endless sky is different because although it is a part of Nua's creation, it is also a doorway, if you will, a path that leads to other creations. We are the guardian of this path. By dividing Nua from the rest of the universe, the creator spirits had to create separateness. But there is still connection. The endless sky is that connection. Do you understand?"

"I think so," Rika said, not sure she really did. Other creations? Like Kitina?

"There is power in the stars beyond our world, but the farther you are from Nua, the more you will need your totem to access it."

"How do I access it?" Rika asked. "When I've used my power before, it was so unpredictable."

"You likely didn't know how to summon it correctly. Imagine you are tied to a star by a leash. It is tied to you. We call it tethering. It pulls you, but you can also pull it. All that is required to do this is knowing and will." Liliam lifted one of her hands and pointed at a star. It pulsed and surged, and when she swooped her hand back towards her, the light came too, skimming across the surface of the pool to rest above her hand. Rika squinted, shielding her eyes against the glare. Liliam flicked her hand again and the star shot back towards its source, quivering as it settled back into the obsidian sky.

"So…will…and knowing? What do you mean by knowing?"

"Know which star you are calling on and it will come to you. Different stars have different powers…intuition, love, battle. Different personalities. The character of the power you draw will be ever-so-slightly altered depending on what star you summon. Learn the identities and traits of the stars. Come to know them and they will come to know you. In time they will become like old friends."

Rika nodded, though she wouldn't have anywhere close to time enough for that. She'd have to settle for obedient acquaintances. "What about the constellations? I summoned a constellation once."

"The constellations have even more unique personalities. They have minds of their own, though their thoughts are simple." Liliam reached up again, focusing on a cluster of stars hanging over the horizon. The stars shimmered and shuddered, and when she pulled, they swooped towards the ground in the form of a massive eagle—a patch of night made manifest. Rika ducked as it flew over their heads, soaring up into the sky and turning for another pass. Liliam directed it back where it came from and it returned to its place in the heavens, filling the darkness so quickly that Rika could hardly believe she hadn't imagined it. "That was amazing!" she said, thinking of little Cygna, the night sparrow. Did she have the power to bring such huge constellations to life?

"It is really quite simple. They are our allies, each of them tethered to you. They will want to protect Nua. To obey you."

"How do you know which ones are constellations? Which can come to life? There are so many stars…"

Liliam frowned. "Your sight is blocked if you cannot see their life-forces—the ties that bind them to you." Liliam took Rika's hands in her own, her skin as soft as butter. The woman leaned forward and kissed Rika—first on each eyelid and then in the center of her forehead. It was a strange feeling, kissing yourself. "All our wisdom and skill is within you. You need only look within yourself and allow your mind to reveal it to you."

Easy for you to say, Rika thought. But when she opened her eyes, the world was transformed.

The stars shone with gossamer threads, hundreds upon thousands of lines of spiderweb silk running…to her. The constellations shone brighter, threaded together in images of leaping koi, prancing rams, and fierce dragons. Rika squeezed her eyes closed, overwhelmed by the connectedness of it all.

"Now you see," Liliam said. "We need only to ask and they will obey."

Rika opened her eyes and saw that she was threaded to Liliam as well—to all the women behind her. Generations of goddesses bathed in starlight.

"It's incredible. Now how do I turn it off?" She laughed weakly. Any movement shifted the shining threads, setting off her equilibrium. She thought she might throw up.

"You see this with your third eye." Liliam tapped the center of her forehead. "It sees what is there but not there. You may open and close it at will, though it takes practice. With your focus and intention placed upon it, ask it to close."

It all sounded very questionable to Rika, but she did as instructed. When she peeked through one eyelid, the world had returned to normal. She sighed in relief. "Thank you."

Rika felt a tug at her consciousness. She peered over her shoulder but found nothing there.

"The god of endings seeks your return," Liliam said, standing.

"I'm grateful for what you've taught me," Rika said. "I'll try to honor you all. To make you proud."

"Protect our people. That is enough."

Rika nodded, swallowing her guilt at deceiving the other woman. Herself. Well, she supposed she could help the Nuans while she was here. So long as it didn't interfere with getting back to Kitina.

CHAPTER 20

After her lesson with Sarnak, Rika tried to get some rest. Though the weariness of her body pulled her down like a stone, her mind was a whirlwind, her emotions like shooting stars. Around and around her thoughts went, wild spirals of sorrow to despair to hope and wonder. This place. The throb of her wound. The soul-eater destruction. Gods and totems and past selves and Vikal. The surprising burst of his laugh. His thumb on her cheek tethering her to this world as her lifeblood slipped away. The malevolent green of his eyes as he grabbed her ankle and dragged her back into the center of the tent, tossing her into the remains of her father's ashes. Her mother. Yoshai. What horrors were they facing? There had to be somehow she could know, that she could see. Liliam had said the stars were like doorways. Roads. Maybe she could find a window into her own world. But, a small voice demanded, what would she do if she saw the worst? Would she abandon Nua, now that she knew her history, had seen the threads tying her to this world? She traced the outline of her third eye tattoo, feeling its angles and curves. She wished she had a mirror to truly scrutinize it. She wanted to see herself—this Nuan version. She wasn't sure whether it fit, or if she still felt like a hopeless imposter.

She turned these things over in her mind for hours, wearing them down like a river wears a pebble until her very essence was borne away in a current of her own worries. Knees hugged into her chest, she peered into the darkness with unblinking eyes, longing for unconsciousness to take her. Would she never sleep again?

(⁺

Someone cleared their throat by her door, and Rika sat up quickly. "Yes?" she called, pressing a hand to her throbbing side.

Vikal stepped inside the entrance, his hands tucked in his pockets, a lock of hair falling over his forehead. "The people have planned a feast to honor our return. Would you like to come?"

"A feast?" Rika asked, wrinkling her brow. She wanted to itch at her third eye—when she moved it felt like she had something stuck between her eyebrows. "I thought there wasn't much food left."

"'Feast' is a generous term. But the hunters were able to kill a few deer, and they are roasting them. The people need something to lift their spirits. Especially the warriors that will come with us."

"The attack is planned?" Rika pushed to her feet, straightening her skirt.

"It is," Vikal said. Rika followed Vikal into the dark passageway towards the giant cavern—the Gathering Hall, Vikal had called it. "Nuanita castle is built on the sea. There are tunnels beneath that flood with the tides. They were designed as escape routes, but with Ajij's help, we'll be able to get inside. We make our way up floor by floor, killing any soul-eaters or thralls as we go. Stop at the treasury and pick up your totem and kill the rest of the soul-eaters we can find."

"What about the queen? You said killing her would destroy the rest."

"I believe she has traveled to your land. Kitina. She goes where there is the most...action."

"You mean the most to eat?" Rika asked, her words bitter.

Vikal looked apologetically at her. "The sooner we free Nua, the sooner we can return to Kitina. There will be soul-eater vessels with astrolabes in the harbor at Surasaya, behind the castle."

"Good," Rika said.

"It sounds nice on your tongue, you know," he said. He walked with his hands clasped behind his back, his head ducked to keep from brushing the tunnel ceiling.

"What?" Rika asked, feeling her cheeks heat at his mention of her tongue. He hadn't meant anything by it, surely.

"Our language. You speak it like a native. Not even Bahti will be able to find fault with your pronunciation."

Rika let out a half-laugh. "I didn't even realize we were speaking it. I guess my time with my past self opened up more than my third eye."

"I am sure it was strange. I remember my first time meeting my past self, and I had a lot more years of training to prepare for it."

"It was. Seeing all those versions of myself...even with what I've done...killing the soul-eaters...summoning Cygna...part of me hadn't believed it."

"What was she like?" Vikal asked. "Your immediate past self?"

"Patient. Savvy." *Unfairly beautiful,* Rika thought.

"I did not like him." Vikal said. "My past self. He behaved like a pompous ass."

"Sounds like the coconut didn't fall far from the tree," Rika joked.

He looked at her in surprise, and then smiled. "I am a work in progress," he said.

"How long does it take to get used to looking at the world through your third eye?" she asked. "It made me feel like I was going to keel over."

"That is normal," he said. "When I first opened mine, I got lost in the jungle. Lost! I was the god of the damn place, and it kept leading me away, these threads showing me things I had never seen before—plants, grottos, hidden places. My parents found me a day later in a little nest the jungle had made for me. I think the scolding was half for me, and half for the plants."

"I can't imagine you as a kid," Rika admitted.

"You think I just sprang from the womb, fully formed?"

"You know what I mean. You're so...serious."

"I did not used to be. As a child, I was quite the prankster. I would grow plant limbs to trip people right and left. My mother was ready to abandon me to the mountain when Sarnak came to begin my training."

"What happened?" she asked.

He grew quiet, his green eyes far away. "Something about your world being invaded, and your"—he paused—"loved ones dying...It sucks the joy from a person."

Rika understood. After seeing her father turned to ash...she would never be the same. There would always be a veil of shadow over her world. "Do you think you can ever get back there? To who you were?"

"I will never be that carefree person," Vikal said, looking at her. "But once the leeches are all dead...I would like to find some peace within myself. If there is any left to find."

"I'd like that too," she said, her words wistful. "Just don't ever trip me," she added. "I hate pranks."

"You had a little brother," Vikal said. "That makes sense."

"Koji was the worst!" Rika said. "Is the worst," she corrected herself, trailing off.

"We will go back before it is too late," Vikal said, sensing what she was thinking. "I promise."

Even though she knew it was a promise he couldn't make, she clung to it, wrapping her worry and her doubt in it like a warm cloak.

They reached the end of the tunnel, where it opened into the soaring Gathering Hall. Fires danced below where they stood, casting flickering shadows on the glistening walls. A heavenly scent of roasting meat and spices perfumed the air, making her mouth water. The sound of a single wooden flute cut through the buzz of chattering voices, the melody cheerful despite its loneliness.

Tamar bounded up to them, a tornado of enthusiasm. She grabbed Vikal's hand, bouncing on her feet. "The deer is almost done cooking!"

"It smells delicious," Rika said.

Tamar's eyes grew as round as the full moon. "You can understand me?"

Rika pointed to her forehead. "I'm a real Nuan now."

"How did you learn it so fast?"

"I knew all along. I only needed to remember."

"Are you going to dance with Vikal?" Tamar asked as she led them towards the end of the hall where the rest of the gods stood talking.

Rika and Vikal exchanged an embarrassed glance. "I didn't know Vikal danced," she said, raising an eyebrow at him.

"Oh, yes," said Tamar. "After we eat! You should dance with him."

"I don't know how to do any of the Nuan dances."

"Maybe you can remember. Like you did with our language."

"Tamar, let Rika be," Vikal said with a smile as they reached the other gods.

"Here comes the imposter," Bahti said to Kemala, taking a swig from a cup that had been fashioned out of a coconut. Ajij stood with them as well, in addition to two well-muscled men who looked like soldiers.

"I go by Rika, actually," Rika said coolly, nodding her head to the others. "Kemala. Ajij."

Bahti spluttered in his cup at her words, and Rika only just managed to keep her satisfied smile in check.

"I see your time with Sarnak has been fruitful," Kemala said with a ghost of a smile. "You are looking more Nuan by the hour."

Bahti turned on his heel and stormed across the cavern, joining another group of men chatting by a brazier.

"Do not mind him," Ajij said. "I for one am glad to see your third eye is working. The sooner you kill the leeches on the island, the sooner we can get out of this gods-forsaken cave."

"You don't like it here?" Rika asked.

"Do you?" Ajij asked. "Cut off from the sky, the stars, the mountain pressing down upon you? Bahti may feel as comfortable as a worn pair of sandals here, but I have been too far from the sea for too long."

Rika nodded. It did feel oppressive to be underground, as if her soul was anxious within her—anxious to be freed from this cave, to return to Kitina. "Vikal said there's a plan." Rika said.

Vikal appeared beside her. "We will discuss it at length tomorrow. Tonight, we celebrate. The food is ready. We should begin the feast." Vikal placed his hand on the small of her back, leading her towards the edge of the cavern. Her skin pebbled at his touch, and she felt a surge of disappointment when he broke contact.

"Gather 'round," Vikal shouted as they came to a stop next to a table ladened with food. His voice boomed through the cavern, and the people turned as one, the din falling silent. The other gods and goddesses fell into a line next to them, facing the crowd. Rika had never seen all the inhabitants together at once—it had to be a thousand people, maybe more. "This cycle has been difficult," Vikal said, his voice grave. "We have lost many loved ones. We will not forget them. But neither will we linger in the past. The future is filled with hope. The goddess of bright light has returned to us!" Vikal hoisted a fist in the air and the crowd roared. Rika balled her skirt in her hands, stilling her urge to step back. To run. "She came from a foreign world, to help us take our home back from the leeches. She freed me from their compulsion. She can kill them. I have seen it with my own three eyes. With the gods reunited, we will be victorious!" The crowd roared again, accompanied by clapping and whistling and stomping of feet.

Sarnak leaned over, his wizened face jovial. "No pressure, right?" he whispered. Rika gave a weak smile.

"We do not have much, but it will be enough. Tonight, we eat, and celebrate, and remember what we fight for. We remember joy, and love, and freedom. We have each of these things so long as we have each other. The leeches cannot take them from us!"

The crowd roared even louder this time. Vikal waved, soaking in their applause. It seemed that despite his fears, the Nuan people still had faith in Vikal as their king.

When the noise of the crowd finally died away, Vikal turned and ushered her toward the table of food. Rika hesitated, looking back at the mass of thin, hungry faces. There was no way this food could feed all these people. "I'm not hungry," Rika said, though her stomach ached within her.

"We eat first," Vikal said. "It is symbolic. They will not eat unless we do."

Rika sighed and helped herself to a spoonful of tana root, a plop of mashed orange that she knew would sustain her, though not be remotely satisfying. "Will this do?"

Vikal nodded. By the meager portion he put onto his own plate, she thought he understood.

Against the cavern wall was a low shelf of stone that had been covered with a green cloth. Rika sat down between Vikal and Sarnak—on display. It felt strange, sitting above the people who now lined up to place a few morsels on their plates. Rika's discomfort increased when a woman came forward, and with a reverent bow, offered her a single gold bangle. Not wanting to be rude, Rika took the bracelet from her, admiring it in the light. But when she looked up to return it, the woman was already gone.

Rika peered into the crowd. "Where'd she go? I can't keep this."

"It is traditional," Vikal said. "To make offerings to the gods and goddesses. Small tokens."

"Is that what those things are in the hallway outside my door?" Rika asked.

Vikal nodded. "People started leaving them as soon as word spread that you had arrived."

"But they have so little," Rika protested. "I don't want anything from them."

"They will be insulted if you refuse," Vikal warned. "And take it as a sign of your disfavor."

And so as the night wore on, more individuals approached Rika, handing her small tokens—a frangipani flower, a stick of incense, a strip of golden fabric, a piece of fruit. With each offering, Rika felt her heart open more and more to the Nuans, cherishing a spirit that could be so generous in the face of so little. She knew what it meant for these people to surrender some small piece of the outside world—how hard it must be to come by a flower or a piece of fruit after a month inside these caves. By the time the flutist began a new melody, and a space was cleared for dancers, tears trickled down Rika's face. Vikal said nothing but took her hand in his own, hidden behind the fabric of her skirt. She knew she should retrieve her hand from his, but she needed the comfort desperately, so she sat still as stone, soaking in the warmth that flowed between them.

The dancing began with a group of women who took to the floor, their feet bare against the rock. They began an intricate dance, weaving in and out of each other, moving towards the gods and away from them like waves. "It is the ashiak," Vikal said. "A dance to welcome the gods. And goddesses."

As the melody drifted away, the women floated off the stage. Cayono stomped into the center of the space to cheers and whoops. The flutist picked up another tune, this time faster and more serious. Cayono began to move and stomp and twist, his movements captivating. "He is depicting a warrior preparing for battle." As soon as Vikal explained, the movements of the dance sprang into context. Cayono moved effortlessly, seemingly weightless for a man so large. *Emi and Nanase would have been impressed.*

Cayono finished his dance to cheers and applause, and a new individual took the stage. The dancer wore a crude mask of black cloth tied into a semblance of shaggy hair. "Normally, when these dances are done, we have elaborate masks and costumes to depict the characters. They had to make do with what they had, obviously."

"What is this dance about?" Rika asked.

"The gods' defeat of great evil," he said.

"So just another day on Nua?" Rika joked.

"Exactly."

Rika watched as several dancers began to perform an elaborate fighting dance, sparring across the stage, several in black supporting the masked dancer, others in shades of faded green, red, blue, and white. When a woman in white battled one of the dancers in black, Vikal leaned over. "That is you. In the white. The goddess of bright light."

Rika turned in surprise and found her breath stolen as she realized how near his face was to hers. Her awareness narrowed to a pinpoint as the music fell away, the movement of the dancers dropped from sight. There was only Vikal. Caramel skin, dark stubble, three eyes as green as lily pads. He was looking at her with an intensity that radiated off him in waves.

A cheer went up from the crowd and his gaze was gone, ripped from hers, leaving a lingering absence. Rika let out a breath, looking back at the center of the cave. The dance floor was empty, and the people were cheering, hollering, yelling for the king. And for her. She looked around in confusion, utterly lost.

Sarnak rescued her. "They want you two to dance."

"I don't know how to do these dances," she said. The last thing she wanted was to stumble over her feet in front of all of Nua.

Sarnak tapped his third eye, and Tamar's suggestion sprang to mind. Maybe she just needed to remember.

Vikal turned to Rika with an apologetic look on his face. "Are you up for it?" He held out a hand.

"If you let me make a fool of myself, I will kill you," she said, putting her hand in his. The crowd went wild with cheering and clapping. Rika stood and saw Tamar with a group of girls dancing and jumping in delight. She couldn't help smiling.

She took a deep breath and willed her third eye to open. Thankfully, it complied, but the surge of light and sensations made her stumble.

Vikal was there at her side, his arm under her elbow. "Are you all right?"

She nodded, looking at him. In her new vision, she saw the threads of silver power tethered from her, running up through the cavern and past her sight, presumably to the stars far above. But when she looked at Vikal, all she could see was radiance, a green aura of fertile soil and broad leaves and all that was right with the Earth. He was exquisite to behold—like this, she could see his immortal nature. But that wasn't all. Between them stretched a thousand, a million tiny threads and fibers, weaving and twining and wrapping them together, pulling them towards each other. A hundred lives and pasts and loves, memories and sorrows. They were impossibly intertwined, so closely tied that there was no logic to separating. To being apart. They were supposed to be together. Fated.

CHAPTER 21

When Rika's third eye opened, it took Vikal's breath away. It was as luminous and shining as a diamond, as if a star itself shone from between her brows. Her breath caught as she looked around the cavern, looked between them. Vikal left his own closed. It was too painful to see the threads that stretched between them, that tethered them in a thousand minuscule ways. Past, present, future. He wasn't ready to face that destiny.

He gently pulled her into his arms as the flutist trilled the first notes of their ritual dance. Rika's body stiffened as his hand found her waist. "Do you remember the steps?" he asked.

She shook her head. "Go easy on me."

"They will come to you," he said, beginning to move across the rough cavern surface that had become a dance floor. Everything else had. Rika had taken to her heritage with effortless speed, as if it had been hovering just below the surface, waiting only for the doors to her soul's memory to be thrown open wide. Now the light was streaming through—celestial divinity made manifest in this tiny form. Even he had doubted when she had first freed him, that this girl from a foreign land could be their goddess. It had seemed a cruel joke. Now, seeing her in Nuan dress, with her third eye glowing and his language rolling off her tongue like honey…he was ashamed to have ever doubted her.

Rika stumbled through the steps, her cheeks flushed in a way that looked so lovely on her, though he suspected it was embarrassment. He spun her, pulling her hands and arms through and over his in the intricate dance, spinning and ducking and twisting. She laughed as they passed back to back, relaxing into the movements. When she met him in the next step, an instant before he was there, he knew she had remembered, that her soul had revealed to her another piece of their heritage.

"Ready to go faster?" he asked, and the grin split her face ear to ear. He whistled at the flutist and made a little motion for him to speed up the tempo. And then they were flying, in and out and twisting and turning, hands and bodies meeting and parting. Their people clapped and whistled and stomped their feet to the music, and when the music finally stopped, Rika was flush against him, a sheen of sweat on her face, her ebony hair wild. Their lips hovered inches apart, and she let out a breathless laugh. He stepped back, his body too painfully aware of how right it felt to have the length of her pressed against him, his lips wanting too much to connect to hers. He bowed to her, and she nodded back, her smile tight.

They returned to the dais and sank into their seats on the ground, leaving Bahti and Kemala to take the floor, to dance the dance that represented their union and powers. Bahti glowered at Vikal as he turned to take his wife's hand, shooting him a look of such ferocity that Vikal felt the heat from where he sat. Vikal stifled a sigh. There would be hell to pay from his friend later. He glanced at Rika. Her face was stony. She hadn't missed the exchange between the two men. She missed little.

She turned to him. "Why does Bahti hate me so much?"

"He does not hate you," Vikal said.

She snorted. "You couldn't convince a two-year old with that lie. The man has never done anything but glower at me. He'd strangle me in my sleep if he could."

"He is the god of the deep mountain. He has a fiery disposition." Vikal stalled. He should tell her about Sarya. He needed to. But how to explain that his heart belonged to another... yet he wasn't sure he wanted it to anymore. And that fact alone made him feel guiltier than he knew how to handle. He owed it to Rika to work through his own feelings before he burdened her with them.

"He doesn't look that way at anyone else. What aren't you telling me?

I'll find out from Sarnak," she threatened.

Sarnak coughed into his cup. "Leave me out of this."

Vikal ran his hand through his hair. "I will explain everything. But not tonight. After we defeat the leeches, we can talk about it for days. Just know that it is not really about you."

Rika's lips thinned to a line. She turned to Sarnak, who was looking at Vikal like he was trying to communicate something only through his furry eyebrows. As soon as Sarnak saw Rika's gaze on him, he feigned innocence, taking another drink from his coconut.

She turned back to Vikal, who also had schooled his features into a neutral expression. Rika hissed in frustration. "Fine. After we defeat the leeches."

Vikal suppressed a sigh of relief. He *would* tell Rika when the time was right.

They watched Kemala and Bahti finish their dance, an energetic number filled with leaps and stomps and lifts. It was mesmerizing to watch Bahti's raw strength and Kemala's grace. Kemala was just as skilled with a sword in her hand, Vikal thought gratefully. They would need those skills before the end. He looked around at the smiles on the faces of his people, the temporary reprieve from hunger and dirt and dark. He would bring them out of this mountain if it was the last thing he did. Back into the green spaces, to the turquoise of the sea. He glanced at Rika, whose third eye had closed. With Rika, they could do it.

Bahti and Kemala's dance ended in an elaborate pose where Bahti held Kemala high above his head. They smiled and waved as the crowd cheered and whistled their applause, but Bahti didn't return to his seat, instead disappearing through the throng of people.

"Excuse me," Vikal said to Rika, and he jumped off the platform to follow.

Vikal jogged through the Gathering Hall, catching a glimpse of Bahti's white shirt and red sash. "Bahti," he called. His friend disappeared into the tunnel, and Vikal picked up his pace to catch him. He grabbed Bahti's arm and spun him around.

"What?" Bahti's red eyes flared in the darkness of the tunnel.

"Enough," Vikal said. "I need you to try with Rika. She is one of us."

"She is not one of us!" He exploded, stepping towards Vikal. "She will never be one of us."

"Are you blind? Can you not see her third eye? Can you not see the threads of starlight connecting her?"

"I do not care if she has a third head. She was not born here. She does not know us, she does not know our people. She does not care for them as we do."

"She is learning. She is trying. It was not her fault where she was born this incarnation. Without her, we are doomed. Or did you forget? We are completely defenseless against the leeches."

"We will find a way." Bahti crossed his huge arms over his chest, looking away.

"There is no way. Not without Rika. We tried, remember? We were arrogant and foolish and Sarya died for it."

"Now you see fit to bring up my sister? When it suits you? When you can use her to make your point? Funny, you have been walking around here pretending like she never existed. I thought you had forgotten."

Vikal shoved Bahti, his anger flaring. "I think of Sarya every day. Every hour. I see her when I turn my head. When I close my eyes. How dare you?"

"It does not seem like it when you walk about with your new girlfriend, batting your eyes at each other and dancing the Prashia!"

"It is not like that, Bahti," Vikal said, though the voice in the back of his head flared to life. *Lies,* it said. Vikal shoved it down. "We need Rika. To save Nua. I would do anything to secure her aid."

"So you swoon at the new girl while pretending Sarya does not exist. In one move, you betray two women. Very kingly," Bahti said mockingly. "Does Rika even know that you have a wife?"

A gasp sounded in the tunnel behind him. Vikal whirled to meet the sound and caught a flash of white disappearing around the corner.

"Damn it, Bahti, now you have done it!" He barreled down the tunnel after Rika.

☾

Rika's breath stuck in her throat—she couldn't get it free. She felt like she was drowning, air coming in quick gasps.

"Rika, wait," Vikal cried, grabbing her arm and spinning her around against the tunnel wall. She could hardly process the rough treatment. Their words kept ringing in her mind. *"I would do anything to secure her aid." "Does Rika even know you have a wife?"*

"You're...married?" she finally managed, shoving Vikal away from her, needing space between them. "Married?"

His face was twisted in pain. "Rika, I am so sorry. I should have told you. I was married. She...She died. She is dead," he amended, closing his eyes.

Rika took a shuddering breath, pressing her hand against her chest to still her heart. "Dead."

"The leeches killed her. When they first came. Like...Like your father." He slumped against the wall opposite her, closing his eyes. "She was so damn naive. She embraced the thing. Hugged it! In welcome. And it sucked her into ash."

Rika's thoughts were returning to semi-coherence. Okay, he wasn't married. That was good. He wasn't a lying scoundrel. Only a liar. *"It's not like that, Bahti. I would do anything to secure her aid."* Including make a foolish girl think he was in love with her, that he was destined to be with her, just so he could use her. Even though her third eye was closed, she finally saw Vikal clearly. He was a sad, lonely king still in love with his dead wife. Desperate to save his people. Even at the expense of her heart. Strangely enough, Bahti had been trying to protect her!

"I am sorry I did not speak of her. I should have. I did not know how, or when, or what was the right time."

Rika shook her head, feeling the stone walls creep up around her heart. Her voice was flat when she replied. "You didn't owe me an explanation. There's nothing between us."

"Rika..." he said, pushing off the wall, approaching her. She held up her hands to him, and he stilled. She could hardly be angry at him. If their positions were reversed, she would have done the same thing to secure his aid. She really only had herself to blame for being naive enough to walk into his trap. "We need each other. That's how it started, and that's how it will end. You need me to free Nua from the leeches, and I need you to take me back to Kitina so I can protect my people."

"That might be what this started as—" Vikal began, but she cut him off with a shake of her head.

"It's all it is. All I want it to be. I need to get back to my people."

"These are your people," Vikal said softly.

She shook her head again. "No. They are yours to care for. I will do my part and go. Now excuse me." She turned and hurried down the corridor, slowing her feet, clenching her fists against the tears that wanted to flow. She walked back into the cavern full of revelers and music and dancing, keeping her head down. The scene that had been exciting and joyous only moments ago had turned alien. A desperate homesickness washed over her. She wanted Yoshai and burners and seishen and all the people who made sense to her. How had she thought for one minute that she belonged here? That these could be her people? That Vikal cared for her, or she cared for him?

Then she was through the Gathering Hall and in the tunnel headed towards her cave. The tears broke through her makeshift dam, and she began to run, her sandals slapping on the hard ground. She wanted to see the stars, breathe the fresh air. Instead all she felt was this mountain pushing down, down upon her. Crushing her beneath its weight.

INTERLUDE

The soul-eaters kept coming. Day and night, hour by hour, their assault on Yoshai's walls was relentless. The pattern and intensity of their assaults was becoming predictable. Blast the gates and foundations of the wall with sickly green magic. When Yoshai's forces responded with fireballs shot from the back of koumori and lightning drawn from the sky, the soul-eaters would withdraw, leaving the smoking corpses of their soldiers. Their slaves. Who seemed endless in number. The soul-eaters would attack at another location along the wall, and when Kai would divert her forces to deal with that attack, another unit would attack again at the original spot. Or elsewhere. She didn't have enough soldiers and burners to defend the entire stretch of Yoshai's walls around the clock, whereas the soul-eaters seemed to have no end to their resources or numbers. Kai couldn't help but feel that her city was being slowly eaten alive by locusts—a slow, painful death of a thousand, million bites.

Kai stood with General Daarco on the balcony of a temple that had been requisitioned as the headquarters of the war effort. She let the telescope drop, handing it without a word to Daarco. He let out a hiss of breath as he surveyed the scene beyond the walls.

"We were wondering what they're building. Now we know."

"Siege towers," Kai said. "It's hard to imagine they traveled all this way just to destroy. But the proof is before us."

"We could send another emissary…" Daarco trailed off.

Kai shook her head. "I will not doom any more men to their deaths. These creatures have been clear in their intentions." Despite Koji's insistence that she not send anyone to treat with the soul-eaters, Kai had needed to try one last attempt at diplomacy. She couldn't help but hope that her son had been wrong, that he had misunderstood what he had seen. Her emissary had never returned. It was as clear an answer as she would get.

"Send a squadron of burners to torch the siege towers. Incapacitating those towers is our top priority."

"Consider it done," he said. "I hope it's enough."

"It has to be," Kai said. "If not…we need to consider evacuation."

"I think that's premature. There's nothing to stop the soul-eaters from pursuing any refugees from the city and overtaking them on the roads."

"Better a fighting death than being penned up like cattle for slaughter," Kai said. "If we aren't able to destroy the siege engines, we'll have to fall back to the inner city. Only a third of the population of Yoshai can fit within those walls. I can't just leave the rest. I'd rather evacuate them. Let people make their own choices. We'll try to cover their retreat as long as we can."

"With what burners? They've all been run ragged. The koumori are sluggish from exhaustion."

"All we can do is what we can do," she snapped. "It will have to be enough."

"I can fight," a new voice said, and Kai turned to see her son summiting the ladder up to the balcony. "Me and my classmates." He was wearing the golden armor of the sunburner regiment, gray smudges under his eyes bearing testament to his lack of sleep. But still he stood tall, his shoulders squared. Had he grown in the last few days? In that armor, he looked so much like his father.

Kai rubbed her face wearily, as if she could wipe away the heavy sorrow that fogged her mind and clouded her thoughts.

"I won't put you at risk," Kai said. "You or your classmates. You're children."

"I'm not a child," Koji countered. "If I'm old enough to watch my father die, I'm old enough to kill the bastards who did it."

"We need you where you are. Running messages. Letting the people see you and Enzo. It raises morale."

"Anyone can run messages. You need burners. General, tell her," Koji pleaded with Daarco. "You need us."

Kai looked at Daarco, whose face was written with apology. "They're a dozen burners who can fly and fight. They've been training for years for this. They're raw, but they're fresh."

Kai narrowed her eyes. Traitor. Part of her knew he was right, that they needed every hand, that her sentimentality couldn't get in the way. But she couldn't risk her son. Wouldn't. Her heart twisted at the thought so hard that it took her breath. He was all she had left. "My decision is final. Koji is the heir to the throne. We need him safe."

"Heir to the throne? What about Rika? Have you forgotten your daughter so quickly?" Koji said, his voice strangled.

Kai's hand flashed out like lightning, striking Koji across the face. The sound of her slap resounded in the silence as Koji looked at her, his hand to his cheek, his eyes wide with betrayal.

"I will never give up on your sister," Kai whispered, horrified at herself. She was not a woman who struck her children. But she wasn't a queen who failed her people, either, and what hope could she truly give her city? She could feel herself coming unmoored. Without Hiro to ground her, without her daughter's rapt gaze on the heavens...she did not recognize this world she was living in.

"Koji," she said, reaching out a hand.

"With your permission, my queen," he said formally, tears rimming his eyes, her handprint bright across his cheek, "I'll take my leave."

She gave a sharp nod, and he backed down the ladder quickly.

"I've seen enough for today," Kai said. "You have your orders, General."

"Yes, Your Majesty," Daarco said softly. Whatever he wanted to say, he swallowed it, and she was grateful.

She descended the ladder next, coming into the wood-paneled library of the temple. Three people filled the room, startling her as she found her feet. "Colum?" she asked. "I thought you left after the festival."

Colum shook his head. "We saw an armada of black ships and turned around in a jiffy. Didn't Koji tell you we were here?"

Kai shook her head. "He was...distracted."

Colum huffed. "Youth. We came across something on the road I thought you'd want to see."

She found herself glad to see the old adventurer. She could use a little of his unfailing optimism right about now. She was less grateful to see the woman with him. "Mesilla." Kai nodded to the moonburner, whose silver hair was pulled back in a simple plait. The woman nodded back warily. There was much history between her and this moonburner—who had once been called Geisa. The past two decades may have changed the woman, but Kai would never truly trust her.

Daarco clearly had the same thought as he dropped from the ladder and blanched at the sight of their new visitors.

"What have you brought me?" Kai asked, looking at the third figure in the room. A person. A person whose hands and feet were tightly tied, whose head was covered with a burlap rice sack.

Colum stepped to the prisoner and pulled his hood off with a flourish. "We found a scout."

Kai's eyes narrowed as she took in the man dressed in all black. One of the soul-eater's soldiers. His hair was jet-black, his skin tanned—a darker complexion than most inhabitants of Kitina. He wasn't unattractive, though his features were foreign. But his eyes. His eyes glowed that evil green. The color of the soul-eater's magic.

"I don't know how these soldiers follow those monsters." Daarco spit on the wooden planks of the floor at the man's feet. "What could possibly be in it for them?" There had been a time when Daarco's anger and menace had frightened Kai, but now she was glad to have it on her side.

"Life," Kai said softly. "It's easy to justify atrocities when the alternative is death. Where did you find this one?"

"Like I said, he appeared to be scouting. Ever since we captured him, he's been raving about how they're going to kill us, destroy us, eat our bones, etc."

"That's hardly worth dragging him all this way," Kai said.

"He raves and yells," Geisa said. *No—Mesilla,* Kai corrected herself. "Until he doesn't. And then it's as if there's something else inside him. We think the creatures speak through him. That one or more of the things can see through him."

The thought chilled her. That dark magic could be looking through this man's eyes right now, watching her. She straightened, setting her jaw. "I am Queen Kailani Shigetsu of the consolidated lands of Kita-Miina. Who am I speaking to?"

The man blinked at her, his eyes burning like green coals. "Twenty-six," the man hissed.

Kai looked at the others. A number? "You have unlawfully invaded my country. Killed my husband, the king. But despite these offenses, I can be persuaded to see reason. Can there be a peace between us?"

The man laughed a hissing, hacking laugh that stood the hairs on the back of Kai's neck on end. "No peace."

Kai pursed her lips. "Surely, there is something you want. Something we can give you in exchange for you leaving this place."

"Your lives," he said. "Your land. Your souls."

"Those items are non-negotiable." She wasn't going to waste her time with this man. Kai motioned to Colum. "Will you make sure he is delivered to the dungeon? I want to see what else we can learn from him. Perhaps we can find out how he is under the creature's power. Find out a way to free him."

The man chuckled, and again, the sound didn't fit the vessel. "Your husband had a warrior's soul. It fought until the end. It was delicious," the man said. "Your daughter, on the other hand, yielded to us like a willing whore."

In a blink of an eye, Kai had pulled Daarco's sword from its scabbard and sliced the man's head off. The others stood with wide, shocked eyes as Kai's breast heaved and crimson blood dripped from the sword's point onto the ground. She handed the sword back to Daarco, who took it mutely.

Kai brushed her hair back from her face. "Colum, I've changed my mind. Please see that this man's head is displayed on a pike above the Sea Gate and his body is disposed of."

"Aye, Queenie," Colum managed.

And with a calmness she did not feel, Kai walked from the room, down the stairs, and out into the open air.

CHAPTER 22

V ikal hovered in the dark outside Rika's room, too cowardly to enter. He had followed her through the crowds of the Gathering Hall and the empty hallways, yet now that he was here, he didn't know what to say. Were there words of comfort he could offer her—should he even try? Rika had made it clear where her heart was—with her home and people in Kitina. It made sense. It was logical. So why did part of him feel an aching disappointment? He leaned against the cold stone wall, letting his head fall back. Gods above. He had wanted her to fall in love with Nua. With their people. And…with him. His decision not to tell her about Sarya had been entirely selfish. He had told himself that he'd spared her the pain of his confusion, but part of him had known that mentioning Sarya might make Rika pull back. And he hadn't wanted that.

A swirl of white materialized in his vision before swooping away down the hallway. He squeezed his eyes closed, rubbing them with the heels of his hands as if he could scrub away the image. Whatever strangeness he was seeing…it couldn't truly be Sarya. Could it? But it felt like her. There were even moments he swore he could smell her jasmine scent perfuming the musty stillness of Goa Awan. He looked down at the offerings lining the hallway outside Rika's door and bent to pick up a single jasmine bloom, wilted and dry. Perhaps this was what he'd smelled.

A light came into view at the end of the hallway, and Vikal unglued himself from where he stood. It wasn't the wisp of white this time.

"There are things to discuss," Sarnak said, unblinking in the glow of his floating totem. The light shadowed the craggy lines in Sarnak's face, lending him a ghostly look. So many ghosts in this place. Vikal nodded and fell in behind him, recognizing a Sarnak summons. It wasn't the type of thing you turned down.

A pang of loss vibrated through Vikal as he watched Sarnak's orb bob in the air. He shoved his hands in his pockets, keeping them from fluttering uselessly for a smooth wood staff that wasn't there. That would never be there again. When he and Rika had fled the soul-eater camp, there had been no way to get it back and escape alive. He should know; he had considered and discarded about every plan he could conceive of. In the end, Rika was more precious. But it didn't stop him from missing it, from feeling naked without it. It was one of the great relics of his ancestors, and he had lost it. Just another in his long line of failures.

They rounded the door into Sarnak's chamber and the old man gestured at a little chair. Vikal eyed it warily, but sat, the chair groaning under his weight. Sarnak himself perched on the bed, his crossed legs disappearing under his orange robe. Somehow, despite everything that had passed in the last few weeks, Sarnak still wore his mischievous smile.

"There were days I was not sure I would see you again," Sarnak said. "You walk an interesting path this cycle."

"Interesting?" Vikal said. For some reason, Sarnak's unflappability needled at him. "I wouldn't call it interesting. Nua is as good as destroyed. My wife is dead. I was enslaved to the worst kind of monster, forced to watch as my hands killed my own kinsmen. I wouldn't call it interesting."

"It's certainly not uninteresting," Sarnak retorted.

"What do you want, Sarnak?" Vikal asked wearily.

Sarnak didn't respond but simply sat, looking at him.

With a grunt, Vikal stood and paced across the chamber. "I don't have the patience for your enigmatic lessons right now. Speak your piece, or I'm leaving." He couldn't be here, pinned under the weight of Sarnak's ink-black stare. Looking deep into his soul, to the things Vikal couldn't face himself.

"Do you remember when you used to spar with Goji?"

Vikal slowed, looking back warily. The god wanted to talk about Vikal's childhood? "Of course," he said gruffly. "What about it?"

"The man was a seasoned soldier, one of the best on Nua. Even the king before you couldn't beat him. You were a thirteen-year-old boy. But every time you lost, you sulked like a little girl who'd had her doll taken away."

Vikal grimaced. "I did not like losing. I still do not."

"This much is clear. You are too hard on yourself. You always were. You expect perfection, and such a thing does not exist. Not for a king. Or even a god."

"This is not a sparring match! This is Nua's future. Sarya's life. The souls of our people…the threads of the jungle…" He trailed off as a lump grew in his throat. "Because I was not strong or smart enough, I failed them."

"The people do not seem to think you failed them. They want you as their king. No one even suggested voting you out while you were gone."

"They should have! I abandoned them. Fought for the enemy. Look what has become of us!" He motioned to the dark space around them.

"They believe in you. Even when you do not believe in yourself. The island is with you still. I felt its rejoicing when you landed on our shores once again. It led you and the goddess of bright light to this place, back to your people. Nua needs you."

Vikal pressed his fists to his forehead, trying to calm himself. "The forest," he said. "They burned so much. Poisoned the lakes…Nua will never be the same."

"Nua is stronger than you know. It will rebound. And now the words you will not voice, though they are defeating in their silence. Sarya. You must forgive yourself for Sarya."

Vikal fell back into the chair with a heavy heart. Sarnak's words were meant to comfort, but they only brought new feelings of wretchedness. Even if he somehow forgave himself for his prideful hand in Sarya's death, could he forgive himself for what came after? He loved Sarya with all of his heart. So why was he lingering in the hallway outside Rika's room? Why had the look of betrayal in her eyes twisted his heart?

"I did not deserve her love," Vikal finally said, running his fingers through his hair, cradling his head in his hands. "She has only been gone a matter of weeks and I am having…thoughts."

"About the lovely young goddess you rescued from a foreign land?

Yes, I can see how that would encourage…thoughts."

He couldn't meet Sarnak's eye. "Sarya deserved better than me." *Rika deserves better.*

"She says she chose you anyway, you sand-headed water buffalo."

Vikal's head whipped up. "What did you say?" His heart skipped a beat within his chest. Those words…they were Sarya's. It was the name she called him whenever he was being bull-headed. Well…she had said it a lot.

"She said she should be drinking tea with her ancestors, but you keep her tethered to you as tightly as a babe on his mother's apron-strings."

Vikal couldn't comprehend what Sarnak was saying. "Sarya. Is here? She's speaking to you?" The whips of white he had been seeing…so subtle he was sure he'd been going mad. Could they truly be Sarya?

Sarnak sighed and stood. "The god of endings sees souls into the next cycle. Helps them move on. But in some cases, they are not the one who needs help. It is those still living who refuse to let them go."

Vikal found himself on his feet, looking around the cavern, lit only by Sarnak's glowing orb. A breeze tousled his hair, bearing the scent of jasmine and coconut. They were inside. There should be no breeze here. He froze, feeling unmoored. "Sarya?"

"I will leave you two alone," Sarnak said, reaching up and spinning his totem with a single finger. "If I cannot get you to see sense, perhaps she can."

The light of the orb cast wobbly shadows on the walls. Sarnak disappeared into the hallway, but Vikal knew…he wasn't alone. The hairs on his arms stood on end. "Sarya?" His voice was small.

As the orb spun, it began to knit together an image in the air, as if a spell was being cast, added to by each revolution of the sphere. Sarya began to take form. Her delicate brow, cascading black hair, soulful brown eyes. She wore the same dress she had the day she'd died, magenta silk trimmed with golden thread, a fold of fabric falling gracefully over one shoulder. A sob escaped his throat and he ran to her—only to find his arms embracing nothingness.

"You can't hug me, you…"

"Sand-headed water buffalo," he said with her, tears beginning to fall. "I know. Because you are not real."

"Of course I am real. I am just lacking a body at the current moment."

"How is this possible?" Vikal asked. "Your soul…it was consumed. I was certain it would be the end for you. Your last cycle."

"Even the soul-eaters do not have the power to rip a soul from the cycle of rebirth forever. I was a captive, much as you were, within the soul-eater's essence. When the goddess of bright light destroyed the soul-eater, I was released."

Vikal's elation dimmed at Sarya's mention of Rika. Had she been alongside this whole time…watching? Shame burned his cheeks. He had dishonored her by how quickly he had grown to respect Rika. Grown…close to her.

Sarya clucked her tongue. "I am not hovering over your shoulder every moment, Vikal. We always knew this was a possibility. When we chose each other, we knew there was a risk. That a goddess of bright light would be born. That the fates would take you down another path."

"I choose my own fate," Vikal said. "And I chose you. I still choose you."

"You have always been honorable to a fault, Vikal. That is one of the things I love about you," Sarya said, raising a translucent hand as if she could reach out and grab his nose. He let out a choked laugh. It was such a Sarya gesture. Whenever he was being too serious, caught up in the stress of his duties, she would reach out and grab his nose. It had never ceased to bring a smile to his face. It seemed it worked even after death.

"Better," she said. "It pains me to see you so full of despair and mourning."

"It pains *you?*" he said. "What of my pain? How am I supposed to get through this life without you? I cannot do this alone."

"You are not alone," she said. "You have someone new to stand by you. It brings me great comfort to know that you are loved, that you will love again."

"Never," he said, though the hated part of himself whispered that was a lie. "I will never love anyone but you."

"Is there no end to your stubbornness, water buffalo?" Sarya said. "It always was your destiny—to love the goddess of bright light. To have had the time I had with you was a great gift, and one I will cherish into the next life. But you were only ever mine for a time."

"That's not true. I am forever yours. And you are forever mine."

She looked at him with kindness in her brown eyes. "A heart is capable of loving more than one person. Do not limit yours. Let it grow to make room for what is new."

"I would never betray you like that," Vikal said, desperate to believe his own words.

"It is why I asked Sarnak to speak to you. It is not a betrayal when one cycle is done to move to the next. It does not diminish what has come before. The cycle of our love is complete. It is time for me to move on, to be reborn into my next adventure. But I cannot do so unless you release me. Unless you move on as well."

"What do you ask of me?"

"To let me go. To be happy for all the rest of your days."

Her words cut him to the quick. "I...cannot. I do not know how."

"Then we will both be nothing more than ghosts." With those words, she stamped her foot and vanished.

"Wait!" he cried. "I am sorry! I will do whatever you want. Just come back. Stay with me."

But she didn't return, didn't rematerialize. The light of Sarnak's orb cast lonely patterns on the wall as it continued to spin in a lazy circle.

Vikal sank onto the floor, feelings of wretchedness overtaking him. Bahti was right. Somehow, despite his best of intentions, he had betrayed two women.

CHAPTER 23

R ika's tears had started falling before she reached her room. She hated those tears, cursed them. Her father deserved tears. Her mother and brother and the brave defenders of Yoshai who were probably under attack right now deserved tears. Vikal did not deserve her tears. These people—this land—didn't deserve her tears. They didn't care about her. They cared about what she could do. What power she had been born into. They cared about some ancient goddess who was wearing her skin. The goddess was just as bad as the leeches. Stealing her life for her own purpose.

Rika pulled her father's sword out from under the little cot that she called her bed, curling around the cold metal like a lover. She traced the etching on the scabbard, the leather of the grip, the ruby of the pommel. Her father had held this sword, had walked through life with it on his hip. It had rested by his side when he'd met Rika's mother. When he'd fought to overthrow the mad moonburner Queen Airi. It had sliced through tengu, saving their lands from destruction. It had sparred and parried, been sharpened and oiled. It had rested at his bedside when he'd gone to sleep each night. Rika let out an incredulous laugh through the darkness of her tears. She was jealous of a sword. She set it back down on the ground with a sigh.

She lay on the hard bed in misery, trying not to think about Vikal. As much as she had tried to focus on learning how to use her power and getting home, something had crept in—something more. In those moments when Vikal's stoic mask fell, she saw glimpses of who he had been before the soul-eaters had taken him, and it was someone she wanted to know. Wanted to be near. And that fire had flamed brighter for thinking he might feel the same. But now, she saw the truth. Everything had been carefully calculated to win her aid, to convince a lost girl that a god like Vikal could fall for her. She felt like a fool. He was in love with another woman. And she could hardly blame him. She was his wife! Rika squeezed her eyes shut. "Stupid, stupid, stupid."

At least she hadn't thrown herself at him. A sliver of kindness crept into her angry thoughts. She hadn't told him how she felt, or tried to kiss him, or flirted shamelessly with him. She knew, inside, what she had been feeling, but *he* didn't. She could pretend that nothing had passed between them, that it was nothing but a business arrangement that had brought her here. Free his people, then free hers. It was this thought that finally settled her mind enough to sleep. She would complete her side of the bargain. Then get the hell out of Nua and never look back.

When Tamar came to fetch her in the morning, Rika dragged herself from bed. Exhaustion pulled at her, and the claustrophobia of being away from the sky and movements of the sun and moon was beginning to drive her mad. She wanted to open her third eye, to summon a star to blow the walls off Goa Awan and expose it to the open air. But she was too cautious to even try her powers, keenly aware of what had happened when she had summoned Cygna. As much as she longed to practice with her powers, she couldn't risk exposing the last remaining Nuans by summoning a shooting star like a bullseye, could she? Though she had gained insight and control from Liliam…it still seemed an unnecessary risk.

"How long have you been in this cave, Tamar?" Rika asked.

Tamar considered, scrunching up her face as she skipped in front of Rika. "One passing of the moon?"

"A month?" Rika blanched. "That's a long time."

"I am very sick of tana root," Tamar said.

"I don't blame you." Rika chuckled. She couldn't help it, being around the girl lifted her spirits. How could she be so delightful when her father was such a brute? "What are you looking forward to eating the most when you get out of here?"

"Laklaks!" Tamar's eyes rolled back in her head as she pantomimed the ecstasy of eating whatever it was.

"That sounds like a duck call," Rika said.

"They are these little green cakes." Tamar sighed. "My auntie makes the best. They are so good right out of the fire. You can try them after we defeat the leeches!"

"I'd like that," Rika said, shoving down her guilt. Tamar was a sweet kid, but she couldn't stay here just to keep from hurting the girl's feelings.

"What do you want to eat when we defeat the leeches?"

Rika's heartstrings twanged. "In my homeland, there are these little round pastries called honey cakes. They are gooey and flaky—you can't eat one without getting it all over yourself. I'd like one of those."

"That sounds good! I'll have one of those too."

Rika smoothed the hair on Tamar's head. "It's a date."

Tamar stilled and she looked up to see Bahti standing at the door of the cave, his red eyes glowing reproachfully. His arms were crossed, and in one massive fist, he held a gleaming hammer the size of Rika's head. His totem. "Tamar, what did I tell you?"

"Yes, Father," Tamar whined, looking sidelong at Rika. "Bye!" Then the girl scampered down the tunnel, quick as a shadow.

Rika squared her shoulders, facing off against the big man. She refused to be intimidated. She was here to help him. "Bahti." She nodded at him and shouldered by him into the meeting room.

The other gods and goddesses were already waiting, together with Cayono, who polished the short knife that he kept in his belt. "Good morning," she said coolly before going to stand beside Sarnak at the far end of the table from Vikal. She needed as much distance between them as possible.

Vikal looked at her intently for a moment, as if trying to communicate something with his eyes. She turned to Sarnak. "How did you sleep?"

"Huh?" Sarnak said, raising a bushy eyebrow. "Would have slept better with some wine. Time to get out of this cave."

Vikal cleared his throat. "Sarnak and Rika met with Rika's past selves yesterday, and as we can all see, her third eye is open. She is ready to enlist the aid of the stars in defeating the leeches. Right, Rika?"

"Correct." She nodded curtly.

"The plan is simple," Vikal said. "We sneak into the palace by way of the hidden stairs. Ajij will control the tides to get us in. We locate Rika's totem, staying out of sight for as long as we can. Each of the soul-eaters are connected to the queen, and each of the human thralls are connected to the leech that turned them. Therefore, once we encounter anyone, they will know we are there."

"I can keep the humans out of our way," Kemala said. "But I will not be able to help with the leeches."

Vikal continued. "Once we retrieve Rika's totem, we will help her eradicate the soul-eaters from the island. Hopefully they will come to us—drawn by our attack."

"Can starlight over there handle this?" Bahti asked.

"My name is Rika," she snapped. "And in case you forgot, I'm the only one who can save your sorry asses. And if you want me to keep helping you, you could treat me with a little bit of respect. Just one grain of rice's worth." She held her fingers together.

"That is a scary little bark, but if we are betting everything on your newfound power, we need to know you are ready. I would not send a newborn foal into battle as a war-horse, and I cannot help but think this is what we are doing."

Kemala recovered first, laying a hand on Bahti's shoulder. "Rika does not have to prove herself. If Vikal and Sarnak vouch for her, that is enough."

"He's right," Rika said. Kemala turned in surprise. As much as it bothered her to have Bahti question her control in front of everyone, she needed to know too. It was one thing to use her powers in the dark spaces of her mind, under the watchful eye of her past self. It was another to do so in the heat of the moment, with the glowing eyes of the soul-eaters bearing down upon her. She needed to know she was up to the task. Rika opened her third eye, steeling herself against the nauseating wave of threads and connections that bloomed into view. Each of the gods were surrounded with them—tethering them to each other, to things invisible beyond the walls of the cave. Kemala's dark threads were intricately tied to each of them, and as Rika examined the shimmering ebony thread that tied the goddess into her, she got the feeling that Kemala could see her, really see her. She flicked her attention beyond Kemala, following a familiar silver filament. She traced along it, letting her consciousness flow through the bedrock of the mountain into the clear night sky above. *Cygna,* she thought, tugging gently on the thread. *I need you.*

The tether connecting her to Cygna vibrated, trilling like a bell as the stars shuddered in the sky, beginning to fall towards her. She willed Cygna to travel through the opening far above Sarnak's chamber, through the strange concoction of tunnels that filtered the light deep below. Cygna's speed astounded her.

When Rika opened her eyes, silver light was already blooming in the hallway, speeding towards them. And then Cygna was in the cave with them, soaring above their heads in a sweeping arc, coming to rest on the table between them. A grin stretched across her face. It had worked much better than last time, when she had accidentally destroyed their boat and dumped them into the ocean. When she saw Vikal's matching grin, her smile faltered. She looked away.

"This is Cygna, the night sparrow," Rika said, and with a flurry of his wings, Cygna alit and landed on her shoulder, illuminating the side of her face in silver light. "It's a constellation."

"What is it going to do, fan the soul-eaters to death? Peck them?" Bahti set his giant hammer on the table with a heavy thunk.

"It's more powerful than it looks," Vikal said. "That little thing blew our ship into slivers."

"Pardon me for not destroying the whole cave and announcing our presence to the leeches," Rika said.

"It is remarkable," Cayono said, his face childlike with awe. He held a hand out and the little constellation flitted over to him, landing on his outstretched index finger. He laughed in disbelief. "What wondrous magic!"

Rika's fondness for Cayono increased dramatically.

"This...constellation..." Ajij said. "It can kill a soul-eater?"

"I believe so," Rika said. "When I killed the other ones, I used the light of individual stars. But the constellations should be even more powerful. Concentrated." She looked to Sarnak, who nodded.

"This is my theory..." Sarnak said. "The leeches are from the stars. Travelers on the star-paths that connect our world to others. The power and might of the forces of this world cannot touch them because they are different in nature. But Rika's power draws on the power of other worlds—stars—planets. She is a traveler on the star-paths too, though it was her spirit that took the journey, not this current incarnation. Because their power is drawn from the same source, she can defeat them."

Sarnak's explanation rang true in her heart. Liliam had spoken of the star-paths, had explained that the heavens formed a doorway, a connection to another world. Could they connect to Kitina? Take her home?

"I believe Rika has sufficiently proven herself," Vikal said, looking pointedly at Bahti.

Bahti grunted, which seemed to be as much of an agreement as they would get.

Rika released Cygna's thread, gently ushering the little creature back towards the stars. *I'll be seeing you soon,* she thought.

Vikal continued. "We'll take a small party. Cayono has six other warriors who will come with us. One will stay with each of us. We need to travel quickly and quietly to make it through the jungle undetected. I think this is the best way."

"So there will be thirteen. An unlucky number," Ajij said.

"This is untrue. There will be twelve," Sarnak said. "I am not to come."

"What?" Vikal said. "What do you mean?"

"Someone needs to stay to guard the Nuans. If all of you brave foolish gods get yourself killed, the people will fall into chaos. They need a leader. This is my task."

Vikal's cheeks reddened. *Hadn't thought of that, had you?* Rika thought with satisfaction. Not perfect after all.

"Very well," Vikal nodded. "We leave at dusk."

CHAPTER 24

K emala paused before Rika as the gods filed out of the meeting room. "There is something I would like to show you, if you have time." Kemala up close was even more frightening than Bahti, her eyes like pools of liquid black, her beauty almost stifling to behold.

Rika managed a nod.

"Follow me."

Rika trailed Kemala through the tunnels back into the Gathering Hall. The jubilee of yesterday's feast and merriment had dimmed—hungry, gaunt expressions followed the two goddess's passage through the low light of the cavern.

Kemala led Rika into a tunnel tucked against the far wall—no more than a sliver of an opening between a cluster of glistening stalagmites. She wanted to ask where they were going, but her nervousness in Kemala's presence stilled her tongue. What did the goddess want with her?

The tunnel ran downhill, twisting and turning until Rika was hopelessly lost. A sheen of sweat beaded on Rika's brow. It was getting warm. Hot even. The smell of sulphur tickled her nose. The tunnel took a final turn and opened into a long, low-slung cavern arching gracefully over a steaming pool. "A hot spring?" Rika asked in surprise. "Why did you want to show me this?"

Kemala was already unwrapping the black sash around her waist. "It is a Nuan tradition to consecrate ourselves before battle with a ritual bath. And it affords us a good opportunity to talk. For me to know your heart, and you to know mine."

Know her heart? Kemala had hardly glanced her way since Rika had woken up from her injuries, and now the woman wanted to talk? Rika bit her lip. She was nervous to be alone with this strange goddess, but the water looked inviting, and she did feel disgusting from living in a cave and sleeping on a hard bit of ground. Kemala was completely naked now, but for her jewel-encrusted necklace, her caramel body lithe and muscular as she slipped through the steam into the water. Kemala seemed to sense her hesitation, though if she sensed its cause, she tactfully ignored it. "These are healing waters. They will speed your recovery as well."

Rika let out a little sigh and began to unwrap her sash. She stepped into the water and yelped, jumping back. "It's scalding!" She eyed Kemala with amazement. The woman was now covered up to her chin, her dark hair floating on the surface.

"You adjust."

Slowly, Rika inched into the water, taking her final step with a little gasp. It felt divine; the coiling warmth was almost enough to banish the insistent pangs of hunger. Rika untangled her hair from its knot and sighed. "Who else knows about this place?"

"A few of the women. They found it when exploring and told Bahti, as he is the god of the mountain. They have stayed away, believing it is his holy place."

Rika couldn't disguise a twist of her mouth. She had half a mind to get out right now, rather than float in Bahti's holy place.

Kemala laughed, a throaty sound that echoed through the cavern. "He deserves that. He has been unkind to you since your arrival."

"That's putting it mildly."

"I wanted, in part, to clear the air between us. To explain. Sarnak has told you of my gifts, yes?"

"He said you were the goddess of dark spaces. Human emotion."

"Indeed. I can sense human emotion, and I can also manipulate them. These are not gifts I use lightly," Kemala said quickly when she saw the look of disbelief on Rika's face. "But the disharmony between you and my husband is strong. It is my duty to soothe what I can."

"It's not my fault," Rika said. "He seems to object to the fact that I exist. I can't help that."

"Bahti still grieves over the death of his sister, Sarya."

"Vikal's wife."

"Yes. They were twins. The night of their birth there was a star-fall unlike any the island had ever seen. There were those who said it heralded the arrival of two gods."

"Sarya was a goddess, too?" Rika wrinkled her brow in confusion. The water was cutting through the aches in her muscles, leaving her almost drunk with relaxation.

"No. But they thought she was. Wanted her to be. They thought she was the goddess of bright light. And when Vikal and Sarya began to fall in love, it seemed confirmation of this fact."

"Because the god of green things and the goddess of bright light—"

"Are destined for each other. According to the cosmic order, anyway. But Sarya's powers never manifested. When it became clear that she was not divine, Bahti cautioned Vikal not to marry her, as he thought it could endanger her. Put her at odds with the fates."

"What do you mean?"

"If Vikal was fated for another, and Sarya was married to Vikal, then the universe would find a way to...eliminate her."

Rika blanched. Did they really think that was how their world worked? "That's awful. But Sarnak said...he said you could choose..." Rika trailed off. He had told her that she could choose. Was that not the case? Was there some cosmic power out there that would force her to be with Vikal, even though he loved another?

"I agree with Sarnak. Bahti has always been the most traditional among us. And the most pessimistic," she added. "The man has many good qualities, but this tendency I have struggled to counteract."

Rika didn't think she had seen many of these supposed good qualities but kept the thought to herself. "So...when Sarya died and then I appeared, Bahti saw this as confirmation of his worst fears?"

"Essentially. In his heart, he does not blame you. He blames himself and he blames Vikal. It was they who allowed this to happen."

Rika considered this. "Vikal...does he blame himself?"

"Vikal blames himself for the ills of the world. Including things he had no hand in, like the arrival of the soul-eaters. But yes, he sees Sarya's death as his fault."

"He still loves her," Rika said.

Kemala nodded.

Though Rika had known the answer, it still stung to hear the confirmation. And that made her angrier than ever. She didn't want to be with a man who didn't want her. She didn't want to be anyone's second choice. She knew these things, yet there was still a part of her that was drawn to him. Cords of silver thread tethering them together. Their past. But *not* their future. It couldn't be. She would be in control of her own life, not some etheric power. "Would you and Bahti have chosen each other if it wasn't your destiny?" Rika knew it was a personal question, but Kemala was her only resource on this subject. Well, and Sarnak, who was infuriatingly opaque.

"Perhaps it made us consider each other when we might have passed each other by. But it did not dictate our choice or make us fall in love."

"I'll be honest—you seem nothing alike."

Kemala smiled. "We are nothing alike, which is what makes us such great complements. He is the fire, and I am the cool breeze. A person wants both, needs both. Tamar is the perfect illustration of the balance of our opposite natures."

"She is very special," Rika agreed. "But I don't like the idea that something as important as whom I'm meant to be with is dictated for me. "

"I found it to be a relief in the end. Confirmation that what I desired on the inside was in fact what was best for me."

"I guess you lucked out. Your destined mate wasn't in love with another woman."

"It is not so simple. Vikal is waging a great war within himself. I wish I could help him, but only he can decide what path his heart shall tread."

Rika wrinkled her forehead. "What is he deciding between?"

"Sarya's ghost. And you."

Her? Vikal had feelings for her? Rika met Kemala's inscrutable gaze, trying to tamp down excitement that leaped within her. *No, no, no,* she told herself. "I thought you said you didn't read people's emotions without their permission."

"It doesn't take a goddess of human emotion to see that he has feelings for you. And you for him. Even if you would prefer to deny them."

Rika lifted her hand from the water, watching the droplets plunk onto the surface. Kemala knew Vikal better than she did. Could she be speaking the truth? And if it was true, what did that mean for Rika? Did she want to be with Vikal if he wanted to be with her? True, he had fought with her and saved her from the soul-eaters not once, but twice. He had softened her with unexpected humor. He seemed an honorable ruler who had the unfailing devotion of his people, and he treated her with respect—like an equal. Then there was the fact that her body came alive at his simplest touch, that when she closed her eyes in the dark she saw the green of his eyes and the ripples of his muscular form and smelled the verdant scent of him. But…there were haunted memories that transformed him into the thrall—the man in black leather who had stabbed a moonburner through the heart. There was her father. And Yoshai. "I can't think about Vikal right now," Rika finally managed when she had thoroughly tied herself in knots. "Not until we defeat the soul-eaters. And my people are free."

"It is natural to compartmentalize in times of strife. It is not an unwise approach. But it will not serve you forever. He will need to decide. As will you."

It was easy for Kemala to say. She wasn't torn between two worlds. Two destinies.

"Follow your truth, Rika. Everything you need is within you, if you only have the courage to look within."

"When I look within…it's a mess," Rika finally admitted, her emotions breaking over her like a tide.

"That is what it is to be human," Kemala said with a smile, softening the severity of her beauty. Perhaps Kemala wasn't as scary as Rika had thought.

"I thought we were gods?" Rika asked. "Doesn't that make things any easier?"

"Unfortunately, no. It only means you have a hundred lifetimes of baggage to work through."

Rika let out a hollow laugh.

"But," Kemala said, her dark eyes glittering, "it also means you have a divine family to help you through it."

Rika was as loose and relaxed as a willow tree when she bid Kemala goodbye at the junction of the Gathering Hall and the tunnel to her room. The goddess's unexpected kindness had given her much to think on. Perhaps suppressing her feelings weren't the best way to handle them. She collapsed onto her bed as she reached her cave, flipping off her sandals. Her body was bone-tired, but her mind still raced. It had been good having someone to talk to. She hadn't realized how much she had missed that over the last few days. Kemala's comment swam to the surface of her mind. "Everything you need is within you." Well, not everything. Though she sometimes felt she had several personalities, she couldn't talk to herself. A thought flashed through her mind, and she sat up, the wound at her side throbbing slightly. She pressed a hand to it. It was healing remarkably well, considering how close she had come to death.

Rika willed open her third eye and took in the luminescence of tiny filaments connected to her. It was like every cell of her being was connected to a star. Was Liliam right? Could she ever truly know them all? For now, she put that thought aside. There was only one she wanted to get to know. Cygna.

She called to the night sparrow, recognizing the thread the color of smoky quartz that tethered them together. She willed it to come to her as silent and stealthy as a shadow. As the seconds ticked by, Rika began to wonder if she had done something wrong. But then, as she went to tug on his thread again, it soared into the room, alighting on the end of the bed. Its brilliance was muted and dark and dimmed even further as it folded its wings. It almost looked like a regular sparrow, but for the shimmering sparkles about it.

"Hello, Cygna."

"Mistress." It flourished its wings in a little bow. Rika couldn't help but smile. It was no seishen, but it was her own personal bit of magic.

"Cygna, what do you know of the other constellations?"

"Much. We have been brethren for eons."

"Perfect," Rika said, lying down on the hard bed. "I want to know everything."

CHAPTER 25

Finally, they were leaving. The tunnel out of the caverns was long and winding. But with every step—every breath, the weight of the mountain lifted from Rika's shoulders. When she felt the first tickle of fresh air against her face, she could have wept for joy. Soon she would be free to gaze upon the sky, to behold her newfound celestial allies. Cygna had spoken to her long into the night, telling her of the constellations guarding Nua's night sky. The little night sparrow rode on Rika's shoulder, its muted shimmer matching the strange new light in Rika's irises. It didn't seem inclined to leave her to return to the sky. And she was just fine with that. It was a strange comfort—its soft feathers nestling against her neck. At her hip hung her father's sword, heavy and solid. Another comfort.

The currents of fresh air joined with a wet mist that stuck to Rika's face and neck. "What is that?" she asked.

"The entrance is hidden behind a waterfall," Cayono explained, his bulk hunched over in the tunnel. "You were delirious when we brought you in. I'm not surprised you don't remember."

Soon, she was making her way down a precarious, slippery path that was hardly deserving of the name. It was little more than a few abutments of rock sticking out of the mountainside to the left of the torrent of the waterfall.

Vikal navigated the path in front of her, offering his hand to help her across a particularly wide step. She took it begrudgingly, stepping across to find herself pressed next to him on the ledge. His features looked achingly beautiful silhouetted in the moonlight. His warmth and eucalyptus scent washed over her, quieting the voice in her mind that said she should pull her hand away, tear her eyes from his.

"Anytime," Ajij said from behind them. She looked over her shoulder with a start. The muscular man was clinging to the side of the mountain like a goat, his toes balanced on a thin ledge of stone.

"Sorry," Vikal said, and Rika slipped past him, letting Vikal help Ajij across. Her skin felt flushed even against the humid night air, and when Kemala looked at her with a knowing gaze, she blushed fiercely.

They picked their way down to the forest floor, where the flow from the waterfall turned the ash of the forest into slick mud. In the distance, the lush green jungle silhouetted the sky, and the clicking of bats and the cries of birds filled the air. Before them, in the direction of their destination, lay only the destruction of ruined trees and underbrush.

Rika's breath caught as she opened her third eye and finally beheld the full wonder of what she was connected to. A million points of light tied to her with silver tethers. Constellations sat heavy in the sky, almost moving, writhing, waiting for her to wake them and bring them to life. "Look at them all, Cygna," she breathed.

Next to her Bahti's threads shone red, Ajij's blue, and Kemala's black, tying her to the individuals in their party. Vikal's green threads strung towards the jungle in the distance, but many more were broken, severed and trailing, bearing witness to the part of the island that had been lost.

Rika slammed her vision shut as sorrow overcame her, rushing like a wave. "The forest," she gasped, looking at him. "Does it hurt?"

"Yes. And no," he said, his gaze set on the devastation before them. "It is a phantom pain. I feel what has been lost, though I know it is no longer there."

"It can grow back, right?"

"Yes. But I fear it will never be the same." Vikal hurried down the hillside, and she understood that this was as much as he could say. Could admit to himself.

She fell into line behind Ajij—Cayono and the human soldiers bringing up the rear. Her thoughts turned to Yoshai, to Kitina. Were the fields of blue grass burned, people driven from their homes? Had the walls fallen, the people sucked into ash or enslaved, destined to kill their families while their trapped minds screamed at them to stop? Out here in the open, she almost imagined she could reach far enough to see, to pull at threads that led all the way to Kitina. But when she tried, she felt herself stretched too thin, too far from herself. Who knew how far the soul-eater's astrolabe had brought them when delivering them to Nua. "I wish I could see," she whispered to herself. "If I could just ask the black tortoise that guards the north star…or the clever fox. He must see it all. I wish I knew what was going on,"

"I know the clever fox," Cygna chirped at her side. "It considers itself a trickster. Even if it sees, it might not speak the truth."

Rika's heart leaped. "You know the clever fox? The constellation. You know where to find it?"

"It lives far along the star-paths. A long flight from here. But the goddess of bright light and I have been on many journeys, some to the end of the cosmos."

Rika let out a delighted laugh. Vikal turned back to look at her with a questioning eye, but she ignored him. Was it truly that simple? Had the solution been sitting on her shoulder all this time? "Cygna, can you visit the fox? And the land it watches over? The soul-eaters are attacking my home. It's a city called Yoshai. Can you travel there and find out what's happening?"

"Certainly. If this is what you wish."

Rika seized Cygna from her shoulder and kissed its feathered head. "It is what I wish more than anything. Fly as swift as an eagle. My mother is the queen. Queen Kailani. Find out if…she still lives. If she still fights. And bring news back to me as fast as you can."

Cygna shook itself, its feathers fluffing up until she held a fat little puff-ball in her hands. "This sparrow is swifter than the eagle. But yes. I will go." And it took to the air, its shimmering light disappearing into the night sky, one more pinprick of light against the black, bearing her hopes with it.

They walked for hours under the light of the full moon, navigating their way down towards the sea. They eventually found their way onto a road, which made the travel significantly easier. It had the unwelcome side effect of taking them past abandoned homes, burnt-out shells that had once been thatched roofs, empty woven cages that had once held chickens. They passed a fire-ravaged temple—its once-proud three tiers leaning precariously, a breath away from collapse.

"Meru Karkita," Ajij said, pausing to stare, glassy-eyed at what was left of the building. "This was once our most glorious temple."

Little piles of ash littered the courtyard in front of the temple, scraps of clothing intermixed with the gray powder. Rika looked away, her stomach churning, the memory of gray cracks running through her father's skin filling her mind.

"We saved as many as we could."

"Why do they take some...?" Rika asked.

"And eat the others? We can only speculate. Those they think will be useful to the war effort, fighters or those with special knowledge...they keep. The rest..." Ajij trailed off.

Gods. What monsters.

"Will we stop soon?" Rika asked, hastily changing the subject. Her feet ached from walking in flat sandals and she felt weak from hunger.

"An hour or so. We will camp by the beach, lay low and try to avoid the attention of the leeches."

Rika nodded, rallying her strength. Every step brought her one step closer to Kitina.

☽

Rika woke to a flutter of soft feathers against her cheek. They had made camp by the beach about midnight, and Rika had dropped gratefully into a heavy slumber. She squinted, shielding her eyes from the brightness that hopped before her on the ground. "Cygna?"

"I did as you asked. I found the clever fox."

Cygna's words banished all traces of sleep. Rika shot up, pushing strands of hair from her face. "Tell me."

"It showed me this Yoshai you spoke of. The soul-eaters lay siege to the city. They surround it like flies on a carcass. Much of the city is overrun."

Rika's hand flew to her mouth. It was no less than she had expected, but still, to hear how bad things were... "What of my family? Queen Kailani?"

"I could not tell one person from another. But there is a walled structure that has not been taken."

"The palace?"

"Perhaps. There are many soul-eaters and thralls surrounding it. It is vulnerable."

Rika could see it in her mind's eye—the sandstone walls of the palace swarming with black-clad thralls with the glowing green eyes of the soul-eaters. If her mother were still alive, she must be despairing. And what of the people in the rest of the city? Rika shut her eyes, willing the images to leave her. They were too horrible to contemplate. "What of the constellations? The fox? The black tortoise? Can they not help?"

"The stars do not concern themselves with the rise and fall of men. Unless they have a goddess to demand it of them."

A goddess. Her. She needed to be in Yoshai, not here. She didn't know how to command constellations a world away. It already might be too late. She couldn't wait any longer. Rika looked around, resolve growing in her. The sounds of measured breathing and soft snores marked the rest of the party, who were stretched out on the ground, arms thrown over eyes to shield them against the morning light. Vikal and Bahti sat by a fire, talking in low tones, spinning some sort of small creature on a spit.

She stood and made her way over to the fire and settled into a cross-legged position. She wanted to shout at them, to flail her arms about the plight of Kitina, but she tried to remain calm.

"Couldn't sleep?" Vikal asked.

"I asked Cygna to travel to Kitina to see what has become of my family. Our city."

"It can do that?" Vikal interrupted.

"It can. And it did. The soul-eaters have breached the walls of Yoshai. The remaining survivors are barricaded inside the palace. My family's probably in there. They can't hold on much longer."

Vikal paled, his thick eyebrows furrowing. Bahti avoided her gaze, writing words she didn't recognize in the soft sand with a stick.

"I am very sorry to hear that," Vikal said.

Rika bit her lip, trying to quell her panic. "I need to leave now. We need to find a ship with an astrolabe. They can't hold on much longer! What if the soul-eaters break through? I'll get there too late."

"You swore you would help us," Bahti growled, looking up. His red eyes glowed bright as the fire.

"That was before I knew helping you would result in the deaths of everyone I know!"

Vikal held up his hands to calm her, shooting a look at Bahti. "We do not know that. And you cannot return without your totem. You forget, I have been to your land, and I was near powerless without my staff. Your Nuan powers will not be strong enough to make a difference without your totem."

"Then let's go. Now. I can't wait any longer."

"We are not going to go off half-cocked just because your mother is in trouble," Bahti said, and Rika lunged at him, fingers curling into claws. She was done. Done with his abuse, done with playing the meek girl.

Vikal caught her around the waist, heaving her back towards his side of the fire.

"Scary," Bahti said, and Rika lunged again, trying to slip through Vikal's grip.

"Bahti, enough," Vikal snapped. "Imagine how you would feel if Kemala and Tamar were about to be killed by those things. Have a little empathy. And Rika, calm down. We have a better chance at slipping in under cover of darkness. You know we are not powerful enough to go up against the leeches and their guards man to man. We need the element of surprise. It will not help your family if you get yourself killed."

"Argh," she cried, collapsing back onto the ground. "Let me go," she said, and Vikal released her, holding his hands up as if she had burned him.

"Fine," she said. "But the second I get my totem and end the soul-eaters here, we're gone. Promise?"

"I promise," Vikal said. "Now, I need you two to make peace. We are going into battle together; I need you on the same side."

"I've never been the problem." Rika crossed her arms. "I didn't ask for this, you know."

"Hush." Kemala appeared, hands in the air.

Vikal stood, suddenly alert. "What are you looking for?"

"Two of Cayono's soldiers are missing," Kemala said. "They were here when I went to sleep, but now they are gone."

"Have they gone to scout? Forage?" Vikal asked.

Cayono joined them around the fire, shaking his head. "I gave orders for nobody to venture off alone."

"Kemala, see if you can find them."

Kemala stilled, peering into the skeletal graveyard of trees. Was it Rika's imagination, or was that a branch snapping? She narrowed her eyes, trying to see through the mass of blackened limbs.

"Someone is coming," Vikal whispered.

Kemala hissed. "Thralls in the woods. Everyone to me. I will try to confuse them."

In an instant, the party gathered around Kemala. Cayono's men had scrambled to their feet at Cayono's urgent call and now stood looking into the forest through sleep-bleary eyes. A line of ten black-clad men emerged from the edge of the trees. From behind them, like a creature from a nightmare, stepped a soul-eater.

Rika's lip curled at the sight of the black chitinous armor and deep shadowy pit where the creature's face should have been. She hadn't seen a soul-eater since the ill-fated battle her first day on Nua. The sight of it set her blood singing with thoughts of vengeance. Finally. No more waiting. She could do something.

The line of soldiers faltered, seeming to balk at coming any closer. Perhaps Kemala was filling their mind with horrors that even the bravest man dare not face. The soul-eater hissed in its low tones, screeching at them, no doubt to move forward. Vikal winced, seeming to steel himself against the sound. He slowly unsheathed his two swords, tightening his grip around their hilts.

"Anytime, bright light," Bahti grunted, his hammer at the ready above his shoulder.

Rika opened her third eye. The threads were harder to see during the daytime, the rays of the sun turning them translucent. But she could feel them and their sure strength, and she tugged at one now, inviting the star to join her, to lend her its light.

It came to her, barreling towards them like a comet. Rika lifted her hand, trying to direct its path, steady it, guide it towards its target. The leech didn't see what was coming until it was too late. The pearlescent starlight barreled into its chest, tossing it off its feet like a leaf in the wind. The light burrowed into the creature's chest through the seams of its armors, sending it into convulsions. Its screams of agony were mirrored by the soldiers, who grasped their heads and fell to their knees, crying out against the pain of the cleansing magic.

Finish it! Rika thought with a bloodthirsty impulse, and the light flashed, breaking the soul-eater into a hundred pieces. Rika held up her hand to the glare. In the after-glow of the explosion, she saw that three of the soldiers' eyes still grew green. "Those three! Subdue them!"

The men turned and ran into the forest, compelled by some master other than the soul-eater she had just killed. Cayono and the human soldiers dashed after them, returning quickly with the howling men—still thrashing in the power of the leeches' thrall. Rika strode forward, power of the star filling her with its nearness.

The group stood, chests heaving at their near-miss. Rika turned to the others and saw Bahti, red threads streaming from him into the Earth, looking at her with a newfound respect in his two open eyes. "These ones must have been turned by another leech," Bahti growled.

"What do we do with them?" Ajij asked. "Tie them up?"

As Rika looked at the men struggling against their captors, her third eye revealed something she hadn't noticed before. A tether running from these men into the depth of the woods—faint, but very real. She stepped forward, examining it. It glowed the evil green of the soul-eaters' power, throbbing and vibrating with unnatural movement.

Kemala stepped up beside her. "You see the thread of their compulsion, tying them to their masters," she said. "I have tried but have never been able to affect it."

"Do you think…maybe I could do something? It could backfire, though," Rika said.

"Try it," Bahti said. "They are dead to us anyway as they are."

Rika looked to Vikal with a questioning gaze, unsure if he would be so cavalier about the men's lives. He gave a resigned nod.

She called to the star that had attacked the soul-eater, for it still hovered, waiting for instructions. She gestured at it with her fingers, willing the star to slice through the connection, severing it as it had destroyed the soul-eater. And it did. The man convulsed before her, but then fell still, the green light slowly draining from his eyes. "*Dewa*," he sobbed when the fog of compulsion had fully burned away. "Thank you."

Rika quickly willed the star to sever the other two men's' tethers. When it was done she thanked it for its assistance and released it back into the sky. When she closed her third eye, the world was quiet and still. Almost disappointingly normal.

INTERLUDE

"How long can the gates to the inner city hold?" Kai asked, squinting at the task at hand.

"Maybe twenty-four hours," Emi said quietly, though her tone said otherwise.

"Hand me those scissors?" Kai asked, pulling the needle through the man's flesh, the last in a series of neat stitches. Quitsu sat at her side, his black nose twitching.

Emi complied, and Kai tied off her thread, unrolling a patch of gauze to cover the wound. She tried to ignore the cries and groans of those in the hospital ward still waiting for care. So many. Too many. The room was bursting at the seams, the bedsides of patients crowded with family members. Normally, she'd shoo them away, but they had nowhere to go. The inner city was overwhelmed with the citizens they'd managed to evacuate from the lower city before the walls had fallen. So many, but still not enough. So many left behind. Twenty-four hours. Twenty-four hours until all these people were sucked dry by the soul-eaters.

Emi watched silently while Kai finished dressing the man's wound. Kai stood and stretched, her knees popping. She nodded to Emi and they walked silently through the throngs of people to the washbasin, where Kai rinsed the blood from her hands.

"There has to be a way to get these people out of here," Kai said, her voice low.

"They're surrounding the inner city. The time for evacuation has passed."

Kai hissed, wiping her hair from her eyes with her forearm. "You've sent burners to the seishen elder to ask for any aid it can give us? To the gods?"

"Yes. I already told you. They left yesterday."

"Of course." Kai closed her eyes for a moment. "I forgot."

"Kai, you need to rest. You're no good to us if you collapse of exhaustion."

"Thank you," Quitsu said. "I've been trying to tell her for days. You know when *I'm* feeling tired, things have gone far enough."

Kai looked at Quitsu crossly. He did look ragged, his silver fur gray and dull. "I have a few more injured to see," she said. "Then I'll rest for a few hours. I promise."

Emi crossed her arms, arching an eyebrow. "I've heard that before."

Kai huffed. "That was before they blasted through the sea gate, and hundreds were crushed in the panic. I can't very well tell my city I'm headed to bed when they're dying around me."

"No one doubts your dedication. But the people need to see you strong. Sure. If we're going to hold these walls, we need every man and woman filled to the brim with bravery and patriotism."

Exhaustion surged through Kai, and she put a hand on the wall to steady herself. "Hold these walls for what?" she whispered to Emi. The words that had been dancing in the back of her mind, refusing to be banished. Words that she hardly would allow herself to think.

"Reinforcements. If the seishen elder, or the gods can send someone to help…"

"You and I both know there will be no reinforcements. Even if they send aid, how could it be enough? I look over these walls and I see an endless sea of black. They just keep coming. Even the light of the lunar and solar crowns wasn't enough to kill *one* of them." Kai pushed from her mind that foolhardy experiment. They had hoped that the light from a moon and sunburner together would be enough to kill one of the creatures. Instead it had killed one of Daarco's best burners. The creatures' armor seemed impenetrable, even to the most powerful burning.

Emi took Kai's hand in hers and gripped it. "The prophecy said that Rika's powers would fight the great shadow. Even if it seems impossible, we have to have hope."

"I'm losing hope," Kai said, tears glistening in her eyes. She was so tired. How many days had it been since she had slept? Four? Five? How many days had this siege been continuing? It seemed like it was all she had ever known.

"There's always hope," Emi said fiercely.

"Maybe if Hiro were still here...and Rika..." Gods, she missed her husband. If he were here, he would have taken some of this burden. She didn't realize how heavy it felt until she bore it alone. And Rika...she couldn't process that her daughter was gone. She couldn't face it. Wouldn't face it. It didn't feel real.

"Hiro wasn't what made you strong, or brave. Hiro didn't make you foolhardy enough to take on the queen of a nation when you were eighteen, untrained, and powerless."

Kai let out a little laugh at that.

Quitsu piped in. "She's right. Hiro didn't banish the tengu from our world when they threatened to rip it apart."

"I had the Creator's help with that," Kai said.

"But the Creator knew only you were worthy to wield his power," Emi said. "I miss Hiro too. But you have always been enough. Just you. We need you to be enough now."

Kai nodded, though she knew it was a lie. How could she be in this world when her husband and daughter were gone? All these people depending on her...

"For Koji," Quitsu said, knowing in that seishen way what her heart needed. "We hold the walls for your son."

Emi nodded. "And my daughter."

A surge of weary determination swept through Kai, and she nodded. "We hold the walls. And pray for a miracle."

"And if the time comes," Emi said. "We'll go out fighting. Together."

Kai pulled her friend into a tight embrace. "Together."

CHAPTER 26

E nergy thrummed in Rika's veins. She was done waiting, done convalescing, done worrying about her and Vikal and her feelings. She wanted to fight, to storm the castle, to end these creatures, and then ride home on a star to save her people. She briefly imagined her mother's face as she blasted the soul-eaters from the walls of Yoshai—love, awe, relief. She had disappointed her family—herself—for so long. It was time to change that. "Vikal, I know you wanted to rely on the element of surprise. But our position's been compromised. We should attack now."

Vikal frowned, rubbing the dark stubble covering his jaw. "The leeches are a hive. Information travels between soul-eaters, and between those they hold in their thrall. They know we are here. They know we are coming."

"It is unfortunate," Kemala said, "but we must retake Nuanita. We have little choice."

"I do not like it," Vikal said, shaking his head.

"What is to like?" Ajij asked. "Our world has been invaded by hostile soul-eating monsters. But we finally have a chance to hit back. We should attack."

Vikal held up his hands, as if he needed quiet to think. "I know, I know. Something just…seems off. Did they just happen upon us?"

"They must have found our soldiers, who led them back to us. The island is crawling with leeches. There's no time to wait, *bak*," Bahti said.

Vikal closed his eyes, as if working on a complex problem.

Ajij tried again. "They know we are coming, but they do not know how. The tunnels to Nuanita are secret. I am the only one who can access them. We will be under their noses before they know what hit them."

Cayono chimed in. "We could send some men to advance towards the palace walls, to distract them, draw their attention while the rest are sneaking in the tunnels."

Bahti nodded. "That sounds like fun. I will go with Cayono."

Vikal shook his head. "It is a good idea, but I will not send you in undefended. Bahti, you are powerful, but Rika is our only true weapon against them. If you walked up to the front gate, you would be eaten or compelled in seconds."

Rika looked at the sky, her power thrumming. She had an idea. Perhaps a crazy idea, but she needed to bear it out. To see how deep her powers lay. "What if… What if they weren't undefended?" she asked.

They looked at her quizzically.

"Just…let me try something." Rika opened her third eye, eager to feel the power fill her again, to see the threads tying her to the heavens. She squinted into the blue, following the silver filaments past the daylight to the stars beyond. The twinkling lights spread across the cosmos, but some clustered, bonded together in a form that Rika could just make out. The constellations. Like Cygna. If she could send Cygna all the way to Yoshai, perhaps she could instruct a few constellations to attack the front gate while they snuck in through the tunnels. She called to a constellation in the form of a roaring lion, its forepaw raised to strike. Then a strange water buffalo with fierce twinkling horns and a hump on its neck. Their threads in her hand, she willed these great beasts to come to her aid, to take form and descend to Earth.

Rika shivered with excitement as she felt the answering vibration through the tethers. They were coming.

The constellations landed with a shuddering crash upon the seashore, talons and sharp hooves tumbling sparkling furrows. They were fierce, wild and untamed, utterly unlike Cygna. They towered above her—as tall as two men. Powerful muscles rippled under coats that shimmered like diamonds in the sunlight, and when the lion roared, Rika could swear she saw the darkness of a black hole within its maw. Doubt flickered through Rika, but she cast it down, stepping up to the constellations with far more confidence than she felt. With her third eye open, the shimmering threads ran from her hand to the constellations' hearts. Liliam's voice flickered through her memory. All she needed was within her. They were hers. She was theirs. She needed only the boldness to claim them.

"My allies. My friends." She addressed each one with a deferential bow of her head. "Travel with these men." She pointed to Bahti and Cayono. "Protect them. Destroy any who try to harm them."

The lion let out a great roar that reminded her painfully of Ryu. The buffalo tossed its horns, snorting and pawing the ground. They would comply. They had no other choice. No—that wasn't true. They wished to obey her. Because she had their respect. She needed to be careful to earn it. To keep it.

She turned to Bahti. "Treat them with respect. And they will clear your path."

Bahti nodded, backing away slightly. Awe softened his hard features. "I will do as you say, goddess. Do not let them eat me."

"Better be nice," Rika said with a wicked grin.

Cayono and Bahti took half the men, whose ranks had swelled with the thralls Rika had freed from the soul-eater's compulsion. Vikal, Rika, Ajij, and Kemala took the others, picking a path down to the beach and along the surf.

"How are we so sure that the soul-eaters haven't discovered these paths?" Rika asked Kemala in a low voice.

"Because they do not have Ajij," Kemala replied.

"I don't understand." Rika said, unable to disguise the hint of annoyance in her voice.

Ajij, who was leading the group, stopped at the sea's edge. Nuanita castle stood in the distance, its golden roofs glinting in the sunlight. It was like a palace from a dream, perched on dark rock above an aquamarine sea. Its pale walls, bleached by the light of the tropical sun, rose in four graceful tiers of balconies and wide verandas. "This is as far as we should go on the beach. We are close."

Rika pressed her lips together in confusion. On the beach? What did he mean? Where was this godsforsaken tunnel?

Ajij raised his hands and his fingers undulated in an intricate motion. He was moving the tethers of the sea. Masterfully—pulling together many moving parts in a complex pattern. The waves began to shudder, white foam tumbling as the surf swept apart. At their passage, they left a sandy path leading into the ocean, water hovering on either side as if held back by invisible walls.

Kemala grinned at Rika. "The leeches do not know about the tunnel because it is normally underwater."

"Stay close," Ajij said. No one required additional encouragement. The group huddled around the god of the deep sea. The waters closed behind them as they began to move forward. Their little circle of wet sand grew darker as the walls around them grew higher. An enormous shape flickered in the water to Rika's left, her steps slowing as she searched for it, trying to catch sight of it in the gloom. Was it a fish? A shark?

Vikal's hand closed around hers and she looked up, surprised, to see that the group was now a few steps ahead of them. "Incredible, is it not?" he said. "Easy to get distracted."

She merely nodded, her body flushing hot and prickling cold, the heat of his hand contrasting the misty coolness around them. "Have you done this before?"

"We would sneak out of the castle to come to the beach some nights," Vikal said. "Ajij stepped on a sea urchin once and almost killed us both. He was so surprised, he let the walls go and it all came crashing down on us."

Rika's eyes widened in disbelief as she looked up to the spot of blue in the distance above them. If the weight of this water fell upon them, they'd be crushed.

"We were not so deep as we are now," Vikal admitted. He was still holding her hand. He hadn't let go, and she didn't want him to. She wanted...she banished the thoughts. What did it matter what she wanted? All that mattered was what was before her. Get her totem, kill the leeches, find an astrolabe, and get back to Kitina before her family was sucked dry.

A set of cracked stone pillars covered with rosy coral appeared like a specter before them out of the ombré water. "We are close," Vikal said. "The pillars, then the upside-down man, then we are at the doorway."

"The upside-down man?" Rika asked. But she saw what he meant as they passed the pillars. A giant stone head appeared before them—its hair buried in the sand. It looked like it had toppled off a statute many eons ago.

"We were not very creative at naming when we were young."

"Some things don't change," Rika muttered, and Vikal flashed a grin. That grin. Gods. It lit up his whole face. This must have been the Vikal that Sarya had known. Bright and joyful and alive. Sneaking out of a palace to play with his friends. How much of that person was left after the leeches had had their way with Vikal?

Rika's foot bumped against a step, and Vikal steadied her. A slimy stone staircase ascended before them, its edges rough with barnacles and coral. As they walked up the stairs, the waters receded until they found themselves in a sort of cavern with an elaborate doorway carved into the far wall.

Vikal helped Rika up onto the ledge that bordered the cave, and once the remaining soldiers stepped onto the ledge, Ajij let the waters fall, closing his third eye. The ocean was no more than a gentle pool lapping at their feet.

"Amazing," Rika breathed. "You'd never know it's here."

"When the tide is low, you can see some of the steps. But no one but Ajij can get in and out." Kemala said.

Vikal released Rika's hand and she tried not to mourn its absence. "We are two floors under the main level. The floor above us holds the treasury, which should have Rika's totem. Be careful. Silent. We could encounter anything out there."

Kemala took the lead, followed by Rika and Vikal. If they ran into any unsuspecting soldiers, Kemala would confuse their emotions and fill them with fear long enough for the group to slip by. Rika freeing them was a last resort. Vikal had explained that the leeches might know when they lost control of a thrall and would be alerted to their presence.

They encountered no one as they ascended to the next floor of the Nuan royal castle—Nuanita. Here, Rika caught her first glimpses of the life that Vikal used to live—bright woven mats dampened their footsteps while elaborate carved mirrors reflected their silent progress. She caught a glimpse of herself and started. Between the Nuan clothing, the gaunt planes of her hungry cheeks, the tattoo crowning her forehead, and the glittering silver of her irises, she hardly recognized herself. She looked fierce. Nuan. Not like a burner of Kitina. Not like herself at all. She wasn't sure how it made her feel. She glanced at Vikal, but his face was set in stone, intent upon their mission. He must have his own ghosts to face, coming back here.

Kemala took a right turn and slowed as they reached a set of double doors with handles of brass carved like a sinuous dragon. "Do you think it has stayed locked?" Kemala asked in hushed tones.

"Only one way to find out," Vikal replied, brushing past Rika to push open one of the doors. It swung open on silent hinges. The room inside was dark. Vikal stood aside and motioned for the group to slip inside, out of the exposed hallway. Rika was the last one through, followed by Vikal, who latched the door behind them, plunging the room into darkness.

"Vikal," Kemala whispered. "We are not alone."

One by one, pairs of glowing green eyes winked open in the darkness. Four, five, ten, a dozen. Rika's breath hitched in her throat. The soul-eaters were waiting for them.

CHAPTER 27

What happened next was a blur of frantic screams and shadowed movements. Rika snapped her third eye open, threads filling her sight like glowing strings in the darkness. She pulled starlight towards her desperately, acting purely on instinct. Someone barreled into her from the side, knocking her to the ground. She hit the stones hard, her elbow exploding with pain that blurred her vision. She groaned, calling on more stars, who finally arrived, exploding through the ceiling above, showering them with debris. The celestial light illuminated a scene of chaos. There were three soul-eaters crowded into the treasury, their shell-like helmets almost grazing the ceiling. One had Kemala by the throat, while Vikal and Ajij did their best against the other. The third— the third was a few feet away, its malevolent gaze locked on her.

Acting on pure instinct, she scrambled to her feet and leaped onto the creature's back, hooking her arms around its armored shoulders. It shied back in surprise, whirling, but she hung on, refusing to relinquish her grip. Bile rose in her throat as the creature's sulfur smell enveloped her. Reaching out desperately with one hand, she grasped a tether connected to one of the waiting stars, yanking it towards her, willing it to burrow into the leech's face.

When the star hit, the monster let out a keening wail that raked across Rika's eardrums. She dropped to the ground, her ankle twisting painfully under her. She grunted in frustration, scrambling to her feet. No graceful warrior here. Ignoring the dying screams of the soul-eater, she turned her attention to the creature that had Kemala, willing a tethered star to blast into the cracks in its armor.

"Rika!" Vikal screamed. She whirled and dropped to the ground—a thrall's blade slicing through the air above her. *Thank you, Emi, for your endless drills,* she thought gratefully as she directed a star to savagely sever the green tether pulsing from the man to the final soul-eater. Ajij was pummeling the final leech with powerful blows from his trident, but they were clanging uselessly off the creature's armor, serving only to keep it distracted. Rika willed the stars she had summoned to join together into one massive, pulsing ball of purifying fire. "Ajij, duck!" she cried before releasing the light at the leech like a rock from a slingshot.

The soul-eater saw her attack coming. It dodged to the side—impossibly fast. The blow struck it in the shoulder, glancing off, without the force she was hoping for. But still the starlight obeyed her intentions, clinging to the monster, worming into its armor like a deadly plague. It was enough. The last soul-eater fell to the ground, thrashing and screaming until it cracked apart, the light in its green eyes dying.

Rika brushed her hair out of her face and released all but one of the stars with a fervent *thank you.* The light zipped back through the gaping hole in the ceiling of the treasury while she pulled the light from the final star to float on her palm, fashioning it into a little ball like the moon orbs back at the citadel in Kyuden.

"I think she is getting the hang of this goddess thing," Kemala remarked, a hand on her hip, the other rubbing the red patch on her throat. It appeared her totem had saved her windpipe from being crushed, its glittering form hard as armor.

The freed soldiers were shaking their heads and groaning, coming to. Rika surveyed the damage. They had lost three of their own men and had killed two of the compelled soldiers. It could have been much worse. *It wasn't enough,* Rika thought as the heat of battle cooled. She couldn't fight the soul-eaters one by one. There were too many of them. She needed to summon the constellations—it needed to be as natural as breathing.

Vikal watched her, seeming to understand her thoughts. "You did well. We will find your totem, and you will be able to fight the whole hive in your sleep."

"What are we waiting for?" she asked.

"Everyone, look for a peculiar weapon. It has curved blades on each side of its handle," Vikal said.

"Here's the lasso of the goddess of open air," Kemala called, already deep into the shelves of sparkling treasure. "I think I found it!" She emerged from between two tall shelves, holding a weapon on her outstretched palms. It matched the drawing in Sarnak's book perfectly. The weapon's handle was wrapped with creamy white leather, and from each end came a curving blade, about half the length of a regular sword. The keen blades curved away from each other, lending the weapon an undulating look, like a wave on the sea.

"It's beautiful," Rika breathed, though she had no idea how to wield such a weapon.

"According to the legends, when you throw it, it will come back to you," Vikal explained.

"Come back to me and stick me straight between the eyes?" Rika asked doubtfully.

"I doubt it is designed to do that," Ajij said. "Take it!"

With a deep breath, Rika reached out and took the weapon from Kemala. The moment her fingers touched the leather of the handle, her third eye blew open. She reeled, her hand over her forehead, grasping the weapon in the other. The threads of the stars and constellations glowed brilliantly, nearly blinding her sight. And there were more—thousands waiting for her to summon. It was the most beautiful and most terrifying sight she had ever seen. She had believed in her power—believed she could summon stars and constellations—but a small part of her had still doubted she could ever be a true goddess. Had still felt human. Weak. Like someone had made the wrong choice, and she would be found out. But with this weapon in her hand, she could travel the worlds. She felt invincible.

The others were grinning at her. "A heady feeling, is it not?" Ajij asked.

Rika nodded. "It's extraordinary!"

"I miss my totem," Vikal said wistfully.

"We will get it back from these leeches," Kemala said.

"Try it out," Ajij said eagerly.

"Okay. Back up. I don't want to kill anyone by accident." Everyone backed against the sides of the treasury, leaving Rika free in the middle.

A powerful connection pulsed between her and the totem, down her arm and into the weapon. She thought that if she threw it, she could likely use this tether to tug it back.

"Here goes nothing," she said, and she tossed the blade in a spinning arc at a suit of armor at the far end of the room. It flew across the room and stuck, quivering, in the breastplate. Kemala clapped politely and a few of the men whistled their approval. Now came the hard part. Rika tugged on the tether and the weapon flew back towards her, its point outstretched towards her heart. Every fiber in her being told her to dive out of the way, but she held her ground, her hand out with far more steadiness she felt. At the last moment, the blade rotated vertically and the handle landed in her outstretched hand, tight as a glove.

Rika let out a laugh of disbelief, turning to Vikal. He was wearing his smile—the broad one she so rarely saw. Pride. With this power, she had a chance of saving Yoshai.

"Can we finally kick some soul-eater ass?" Ajij asked. The comment was met by nods and grunts of determination. He turned to lead the way out the door, but Kemala doubled over, her head in her hands. "Bahti," she groaned.

"What is wrong?" Vikal was at her side in a flash, helping to hold her up.

She straightened slowly, wincing. "He tried to send me a message. He is not known for his subtlety."

"What was the message?"

"They are under attack."

Vikal led the way through the halls of the castle, pausing to look around corners to be sure they weren't walking into an ambush. The castle seemed deserted. They entered the main courtyard through a side door, keeping to the shadows under the wraparound balcony. Green vines trailed down from above, lending further cover. The gates were open, and the sound of fighting resounded from outside the castle walls.

"How many?" Vikal asked.

"Twenty men. I cannot sense the leeches, so I am not sure."

"It doesn't matter." Rika hissed. "Let's go. I'll kill them all."

"Easy," Vikal said, laying a hand on her shoulder. "I know the totem makes you feel invincible, but you are not. No need to rush into a trap."

"They could be dying!"

"I will investigate. Everyone stay here until I signal." Vikal trotted along the stones of the outer courtyard as he began to make his way through the gate underneath the massive walls of the castle, disappearing from sight.

Rika huffed, narrowing her eyes at his retreating form.

"He is not wrong," Kemala said. "No need to take unnecessary risks."

"I don't see saving your husband as an unnecessary risk."

"Worried about Bahti now?" Kemala arched an eyebrow. "He is tougher than he looks. But I am worried about Cayono and the others. At least they are alive. For now."

Vikal reappeared around the corner and held up six fingers. He motioned them to follow. Rika's blood sang with anticipation. Urgency called her forward. She needed to finish these leeches so she could go home. Her mother's face flashed before her eyes. Were they holding on, or was it too much?

Their group surged across the courtyard, their sandaled feet sending up silent swirls of dust. As she moved, the battle came into view. Six soul-eaters and their thralls, crowding around Bahti and Cayono and the other men. The two constellations were the only thing keeping the men at bay. The soul-eaters were keeping their distance—away from the threat posed by the starlight. Well, it was time to end that.

Rika opened her third eye, readier this time for the overwhelming sensations that poured into her sight. She summoned six stars—strong, powerful light forces that now hurdled towards the Earth. One to destroy each soul-eater. They crashed to the ground in an explosion that blinded her with its terrible power. The men and gods threw their hands up, shielding their eyes.

In the fading after-glow of the starlight, the scene became clear. All six soul-eaters were dead—no more than smoking piles of armor littering the ground. Rika stumbled on her feet as she released the star-threads, releasing her celestial allies back into the sky. A wave of vertigo swept over her.

"You're bleeding." Vikal appeared at her side, his hand hovering by her face.

She touched her upper lip and her finger came away red with blood. "It's nothing," she said, wiping it on her sleeve.

"That was a lot of power to use at one time. You have to be careful not to overdo it."

"I'm fine," Rika snapped. She had just saved their sorry asses. She wasn't in the mood for a lecture. "Shouldn't we go kill the rest so I can get home?"

Vikal turned back to the castle gate, which yawned above them. "Yes. But where are the other soul-eaters? The castle should be swarming with them. Why does it feel...?"

"Deserted?" Ajij said. "You are right. What are they up to?"

"Kemala," Vikal said. "Can you sense where the soul-eater's forces are marshaled? I do not want to walk into a trap."

"I do not sense other humans close by," she said. "Give me a moment." She closed her eyes and opened her third eye. It glowed as black as obsidian, glittering brighter than the gems at her throat.

Rika examined her totem as they waited. The delicate stitching on the leather handle, the sheen of the blades, quicksilver and deadly. It felt right in her hand. With this, she had a fighting chance against the leeches. Even if using her power made her bleed. She shoved the worry away. She would drain every ounce of life from herself if it meant defending Yoshai and defeating the leeches once and for all. Her soul itched within her, desperate to fly, to go, to live her purpose. To save her people. It was what the prophecy had said.

Kemala let out a hissing breath. "I found them."

"Where are they?" Vikal asked. "Have they laid an ambush?"

She shook her head, her arching brows knotted together in horror. "They took advantage of our absence. I do not know how they knew, but... there is no mistaking it."

Bahti put his arm around Kemala, steadying her. "What are you saying, my love?"

Her voice shook. "They have found Goa Awan. They are going to kill everyone."

CHAPTER 28

Shock hung silent and heavy in the humid air. "How did they find it?" Bahti whispered.

Ajij shook his head. "We always knew that it would only take one enthralled Nuan to give the secret away, whether they wanted to or not."

"They must have decided to move after they found our camp this morning," Vikal said. "They enthralled two soldiers who were with us. Gods!" He spun away from them, muscles tensing, hands balled into fists. "Idiot! I should have realized the moment it happened!"

"It does not matter. We have to go, now," Bahti said. "What are we standing around waiting for? We have to stop them."

"We might already be too late," Kemala said, her hands tightening on Bahti's arm. "Tamar…"

"We have to try," Vikal said, turning back. "We go now—we travel as swiftly as we can. Bahti, can you collapse the tunnels, keep them from getting in?"

He nodded. "Consider it done. But I cannot bring down too much rock, or it could jeopardize the whole cavern system. At best, it will buy them an hour or two."

"It will have to be enough. Let us move."

Rika's feet seemed glued to where she stood. Goa Awan…all those people. Tamar, Sarnak, everyone who had laid a flower or bracelet at her feet, who had feasted on tana root with joy and thanksgiving, like it was a roast pheasant glazed with the richest sauce. She cared for them, worried for them…but there was another people who needed her more. Her own. She could delay no longer.

"I'm not going," Rika said quietly.

Every face turned to her, expressions of surprise and betrayal chipping away at her resolve.

"What?" Vikal asked, stalking back towards her like a predator.

"Cygna…my people had just hours before the leeches broke through the palace walls. If I go back to help in the caverns…I'll be too late."

"These are your people," Bahti said.

"Oh, now I'm one of you?" Rika shot back. "When it serves you?"

Vikal held up his hands in a placating gesture. "If you do not come, we will not be able to defeat them. Everyone on this island will die."

"If I don't go, thousands of my people will die. I was their princess first. My mother is there. My brother. You promised me, Vikal. You promised me you would get me home."

"You promised you would help us defeat the leeches here. That job is not done."

Tears pricked at Rika's eyes. "Can't you see what an impossible position you put me in? Either way, thousands will die. I care about the Nuans; of course I do. But I can't abandon my people. Would you do that for me?"

A storm of emotion crossed Vikal's face. He didn't answer.

"I didn't think so," she said. He had his duties, and she had hers. Whatever the fates had planned in other lifetimes, this god of green things and goddess of bright light weren't destined for each other. There was too much distance between them.

"This is insanity!" Bahti said. "Every minute we wait is another minute the leeches are tunneling through the rocks I just dropped. Take her with us." He stepped towards her and Rika pulled her totem from her belt, facing him down. "I'd like to see you try."

"Bahti," Vikal said with exasperation. "You are not helping. Rika, please. Do not abandon Nua. We need you."

"So does Kitina! I can't save both."

"What if you could?" Ajij asked, stroking his beard. "You were able to send constellations with Bahti and Cayono, though you were not with them. Lend them, if you will."

"So?" Rika said.

"Now that you have your totem which links you to Nua, do you think you could lend them over longer distances?"

"Send constellations with you...while I'm in Kitina?" she asked. "I don't know. It's a long way." *And I need all the firepower I can get to defeat the horde at my mother's door,* she thought. But as she took in their pleading, desperate faces, she knew she would not be able to refuse Ajij's suggestion.

She sighed. "I'll try. How many do you need?"

"All of them," Bahti said.

Rika rolled her eyes. "I don't think me killing myself by overusing my power will serve anyone. How many leeches are there?"

"I believe two dozen were left on the island to manage things here. The queen has moved most of her forces to your world," Cayono said.

"So if I leave a half a dozen constellations? We already killed nine here today," Rika said, her mind reeling at the thought.

"Can you summon that many? You will be significantly weakened for defense of Yoshai," Vikal said.

"If you all end the fight here before I have to face the leeches in Kitina, it should be fine. My power will be freed up to summon more constellations."

"And if we do not finish it in time?" Vikal asked, concern written on his face.

"Just—finish it. Now. You promised to show me how to use the astrolabe. Let's go."

"You are not coming with us?" Bahti asked Vikal accusingly.

"Let me see Rika off. I will catch up." A silent exchange passed between the two gods—clenched jaws and flashing eyes and balled fists. "I promised," Vikal said softly.

It seemed to be enough. Bahti looked away first, with a sharp nod of his head.

With one hand on her totem, Rika began to summon constellations. The lion and the water buffalo stood silently watching, and she looked for the fiercest among the stars to join them—the eagle, the scorpion, the tiger, and the centaur with its bow and arrows. As she pulled their silver tethers, the inhabitants of the sky met her call, glowing hooves and paws and talons crashing into the soft earth. Wings stretched, roars bellowed. When her celestial army had been summoned, even her feet threatened to shy away, intimidated by the huge glowing beasts that towered over the other gods and men, ready to rend black armor and unnatural flesh. But she held her ground, hoping that they understood, that they would obey. "You are under Kemala's command. Your task is to destroy the soul-eaters on this island and to save the people of Nua. When this task is complete, with my thanks, you may return to the sky." They acknowledged with roars and cries and hisses.

Kemala nodded at Rika, and in a rush, the woman ran to her, pulling her into an embrace. "Thank you," Kemala whispered.

"Go save Tamar." Rika gave Kemala a little shove. "Go."

The others looked at her with thanks and waves before turning, disappearing into the skeleton forest. Ajij was last, giving her a little salute with his trident. "You are worthy of the mantle, goddess of bright light." And then he was gone.

"Let's go," Rika said, movement hiding the lump in her throat, the tears in her eyes.

She followed Vikal through the empty castle. The carved walls and twisting staircases felt familiar somehow. Ajij, Kemala, Sarnak, even infuriating Bahti, their souls felt familiar as well, though she had known them for only days. And Vikal. As much as she wanted to feel nothing more than cold indifference—believe that their relationship was a mutually-beneficial business arrangement—her treacherous heart kept telling her otherwise. It didn't matter, she told herself. Even if she felt one way, there could be no future for them. They were from different worlds, loyal to different lands. And Vikal was married to a ghost.

The doors of the castle opened onto a majestic stone patio leading down to the sea. A half-dozen black ships bobbed beyond the surf, their charcoal hulls staining the crystal waters of the idyllic turquoise bay.

"Come on." Vikal jogged down onto the soft white sand, shoving a rowboat towards the sea. She took the other side and together they pushed the little boat into the surf before hopping in. Vikal took the oars and with powerful strokes rowed them towards the nearest of the soul-eater vessels.

"How do you feel?" he asked. "Stretched thin?"

She nodded. It was an apt description. The power she was using to maintain the constellations here on Nua pulled at her, stretching her back towards the island. It was as if part of her soul was fighting her, wanting to be there—fighting beside them. How bad would she feel once she traveled thousands of miles from Nua? A world away? Would her power be ripped from her like a babe from the womb? She ran her fingers along the stitching on the handle of her blade. *Please be enough to tether me here,* she prayed.

"Do you think you will be able to hold the constellations when you get to Kitina? To have anything left to fight with?"

Why did he have to ask these questions? The questions that burned in her own mind. What if the only thing she accomplished with this foolish division of her powers was to doom both lands to destruction? By not choosing, would she fail them both? "I'll have to," was all she finally managed to say.

The rowboat bumped against the hull of one of the ships. Rika grabbed the ladder. She climbed up over the rail, followed closely by Vikal. He tied the rowboat to the rail and took the cover off the astrolabe. It looked the same as the others, glowing sickly green. "It draws its power from the leeches," he said. His handsome face twisted with regret.

"Okay." She shrugged, unsure of his meaning. Until it hit her. "If you kill the leeches here on Nua—these will be useless. You couldn't get to Kitina, even if you wanted to." *And if I succeed in killing the leeches in Kitina...I will never be able to return to Nua,* she realized. This was the end. Her and Vikal's end.

He nodded. "I promised to go back and help you defeat them. To free your land. I have to break that promise."

Rika pursed her lips. So she was truly on her own. She didn't know why she had thought that Vikal would come to save her once he defeated the leeches that threatened Goa Awan. But part of her had. Part of her had hoped. That she wouldn't have to do this alone. She forced a smile. "I suppose I broke my promise too. I said I would help you rid your land of the leeches before going home. But I couldn't do that."

"You are doing that," he said softly, turning the dials of the astrolabe in some unknowable pattern, tuning it back to her home.

As he finished, he met her gaze—unspoken words charging the air between them. She was sick of words unspoken. "Do you wish she had been goddess of bright light?" Her. Sarya. His wife. The memory that seemed to hover over him, clouding the destiny that they might have shared.

He shook his head. "It was always supposed to be you."

She nodded. *Say something,* she thought, wanting to shout it at him. *Say something,* she shouted at herself. *Say something, do something, don't let the last time you ever see each other be an awkward goodbye.* She opened her mouth, unsure what would come out, but he beat her to it.

"Good luck, Princess Rika. Goddess of bright light. I am honored to have known you, and to have called you friend." He bowed low before her, his dark hair shining in the sun.

She nodded, swallowing her disappointment. So that's how it would be. She cleared her throat. "Thank you for all you did for me. For my people."

"Likewise. You will free Kitina from the soul-eaters. I know it."

"I better get to it then," she said. "You too. You don't want Bahti to take all the good action."

He grinned that brilliant smile, and this time it pierced her heart through as surely as an arrow. It was gone just as quickly as it appeared. "You can manage the sails?" he asked.

"Yes." Her voice was thicker than she wanted it to be.

"The astrolabe will transport you when you get far enough away from shore," he said, turning. He walked to the rail where the rowboat was tied, his steps jerky. He looked back at her, and the whole world seemed to pause for a moment. Would he say something? A true goodbye? But no. The world sped up again as he threw his leg over the rail and began descending the ladder.

She watched him go, longer than she should have. She watched him settling onto the little bench, taking the oars in sure hands. She watched him row back towards the castle with steady strokes. She couldn't tear her eyes away from his, for it seemed that he watched her too. Like they couldn't give up the last image of each other, the last moment, the last glimpse.

When the bow of his rowboat hit the shore, she tore herself from the rail and launched into action, letting the routines of readying the ship crowd out the emotions, the thoughts that screamed at her. Untie the sails, instead of thinking of that bow. A bow? What in the gods' name was that? Pull up the anchor—rather than dwelling on how she should have kissed him. Should have said something. Should have done something, anything other than stand like a limp fish waving goodbye.

Hoist the sails, tie off the lines, take the wheel, these things grounded her, focused her. Nua, Vikal, her destiny as goddess of bright light, all of it. It was a dream. A strange interlude to her life. Kitina, Yoshai, her mother, her brother. This was real life. Her reality. It was time she wake up.

"Hold on, Mother," she said, wiping the tears from her face, tightening the main sail. "I'm coming."

INTERLUDE

It was less of an evacuation and more of a feeding frenzy. Screams from below punctuated the air, ringing in Kai's ears. She dropped the telescope with a hiss, smashing the castle wall with her fist in frustration.

"The dragons are helping," Nanase said, her voice tired and flat. "At least more will get away. We should be grateful to Tsuki and Taiyo for sending them."

"They are helping like a bucket of water helps a forest fire," Kai said. Koji stood next to her, swaying with exhaustion in his armor, soot and dried sweat crusted on his face. She had finally relented and allowed Koji and his classmates to join the fight. Their koumori squadron had helped hold the walls of the inner city as long as they could, to allow as many people as would fit to flee into the relative safety of the palace. The only evacuation happening now had been taken over by a dozen serpentine dragons sent by the god and goddess of their world. Deities that were pacifists, not fighters. Where was a god of war when you needed one? Half of the dragons were shuttling people out of the palace a few at a time, depositing them with the rest of the fleeing citizens to the north.

The others were razing her city, destroying as many of the enemy's forces as they could find, blocking streets and burning bridges. Dragon fire was as useless against the soul-eaters as burning, but the dragons *could* incinerate the soul-eaters' followers, their shadow army of black-clad soldiers. That was something. Though it wasn't enough. Soul-eaters strode ahead unimpeded, following the fleeing citizens to the north. Even the people who were getting out couldn't escape forever. They would be picked off one by one until every inhabitant of this land was dead. And she, their queen, would cower in her palace until death came through the gates for her.

Kai turned and strode to the other side of the courtyard, training her telescope on the creatures that worked to break down the palace gates. "You're sure that's the one who killed your father?" Kai asked Koji, who had followed in her wake like a shadow.

"I'm sure," he said. "Three fingers. I recognize that staff, too. He's the one, all right. And traitorous Master Tato is at his side. "

Kai wanted to rain fire and brimstone down upon these ungodly creatures. She wanted divine justice. She wanted to slice off their heads and watch them roll down the steps of the palace. Anger burned within her as hot as a furnace, but she was impotent to release it. There was nothing they could do against these creatures. It would burn her up inside.

"Remind me again why we can't make a last charge? At least go out like warriors instead of rats cowering in the dark?" Kai asked Nanase.

"It's too soon," Nanase said.

"We've tried everything," Kai said. "No word from the seishen elder. I don't think I'll be getting back the power of the creator anytime soon, even if it were enough. I've even thought about summoning the tengu into this world to fight the soul-eaters for us, but Geisa says they're just as likely to turn against us as fight for us. More so."

"We certainly don't need another set of superhuman evil demons to fight. We've got our hands full with these ones," Quitsu remarked from his perch on the castle wall.

"We still have Rika," Koji said quietly, his jaw set, his eyes trained on the horizon.

Kai's heart twisted. She reached out and stroked Koji's golden hair, the back of his neck. "I miss her too," she whispered. "But she's not coming back."

"We don't know that. We don't know what happened to her."

"The creatures said they killed her."

"They're liars," Koji said. "I know she's not dead."

Kai sighed, swallowing the question she wanted to ask. If she isn't dead, where is she? Why hasn't she come? "I want to believe it too, but it's wishful thinking. A ruler has to face facts, not make decisions based on prophecies and prayers. We rally the troops for a final push. I want to distract the soul-eaters and take out as many of their followers as we can before we go. Give the remaining people in the palace the best chance of escaping."

"Mother, no!" Koji shouted, his voice cracking. "Don't give up."

Quitsu stood as well. "Listen to your son. You're not thinking clearly."

"All I've been doing for the past week is thinking, thinking. At some point, it's time for fighting. I've made my decision. It's not up for debate."

"Your Majesty..." Nanase began, but Kai cut her off, her voice softening. "Not you too, Nanase."

Nanase inclined her head, resigned. "It will be done. We will show them a last charge worthy of the burners."

"That's the spirit." Kai stroked the jade pommel of the dagger at her side. Her fingers itched to drive it into flesh. This anger...it was stronger than she had ever felt. Burning, burning.

Koji turned on his heel and stomped towards the stairs. Not that there was much room downstairs. The palace was packed with refugees, soldiers and burners. But he paused before descending the stairs, looking into the mute sky. "Is that a shooting star?" He pointed to the south, towards a shimmering streak moving through the hazy smoke.

"During the day?" Nanase asked.

Kai watched it, her heart leaping into her throat. It was close. Too close. A surge of knowing flooded her—a mother's intuition. She grabbed Nanase's arm to steady herself, her gaze locked on the object. It was drawing nearer. "It's not a shooting star. It's my daughter."

"What?" Nanase looked at Kai with concern, and Koji returned to her side. "What do you mean?"

"Wait," Kai breathed. The streaming star surged closer until it wasn't moving across the sky but down, barreling towards Yoshai, towards the Earth, towards *them*. It hit the roof of the palace with an explosion of light. Kai and the others shielded their eyes, blinking into the blinding whiteness to make out what had fallen.

"Rika?" Kai cried, running towards it, throwing caution to the wind. Her arms longed to embrace her daughter, her baby; her breath was ragged in her throat. The light dimmed, dying to only the brightness and size of a moon orb. Swooping above the stones of the courtyard was a tiny, perfect sparrow. Instead of feathers and flesh it was made of pure spirit and celestial power. "Are you the queen of Kitina?" it asked, its voice tiny but strong.

"Me," Kai said eagerly. "I'm the queen. Are you from Rika?"

"Rika lives," it said, and Koji whooped beside her. "She is returning. She says to hold on. She is coming as soon as she can."

Returning? From where? Kai thought. The creature began to rise back towards the sky. "Wait!" Kai cried. "Where is she? When is she coming?"

"As soon as she can," the sparrow repeated, and then it took to the air, soaring back towards the southern horizon.

Kai's heart sang within her as she watched the creature depart, the burning anger quenched by the surge of another emotion. Hope.

"A little light on the details," Nanase remarked. "How long will we have to hold?"

"As long as it takes," Kai said, wrapping her arm around Koji. "As long as it takes."

BOOK THREE

CHAPTER 29

Though Rika expected the shift this time, it still surprised her. The astrolabe flared to life, its unnatural green glow launching the little ship through space or time or…she didn't know how it worked. All she knew was that when the spinning and lurching stopped, she vomited onto the deck before collapsing onto the wooden boards. She was lightheaded from eating so little over the past days, and her head pounded from the journey. And then there was the deep abiding sense of thinness, like she would look behind her and find herself stretching all the way back to Nua. It was hard to breathe. She placed a firm hand on her chest, as if she could hold her spirit inside with her palm, press back together the pieces of her heart that had shattered upon the sight of Vikal's boat hitting the shore. He had left her. Yes, she had left him too…but a foolish, desperate part of her had hoped. That he would come with her. That she wouldn't have to do this all by herself. She spit again on the deck, a cough and a sob mingling with the taste of her bile. How could she defeat the soul-eaters like this? She felt as if she had been turned inside out.

She slowly lowered herself back to the wood of the deck, rolling onto her back. The cloudless afternoon sky was hazy—a sickly gray color that spoke of ashes and fear. Kitina's sky. Her sky. The urge to wallow in self-pity flickered and went. They were counting on her. And every moment could be the difference between saving them and being too late.

She pushed herself to her feet and took in her surroundings. Her little ship had deposited her amongst the soul-eater's fleet, nestled her against the edge of the silent armada. Smoke drifted across the shoreline, adding to the pallor of the sky. Rika narrowed her eyes. It was time these leeches paid for what they had done.

Rika undid the rowboat and made her way through the fleet towards the shore. In places, the boats were so tightly packed that she could hardly navigate between them. It felt claustrophobic with their tall black sides stretching up above her, her oars bumping wood on wood. Though she had seen it before, the size of the fleet astounded her once again. How many men had these ships carried? How many soul-eaters? How did her mother and the burners stand any chance of holding them off, let alone defeating them? How did she?

The rowboat reached the shore and Rika hopped out into the surf. She left it behind. Rika hiked up the slippery dunes of the beach and crested them into the sparse grass. The sight stopped her in her tracks. As far as the eye could see, the grass was destroyed. Burned in places, trampled in others by the boots of thousands of thousands. It was a day's ride from here to Yoshai, and once she got there, Rika had absolutely no idea what to do. The city would be surrounded by soul-eaters and their soldiers. Was she going to work her way through from the back, killing as she went? Here she was to save her people, and she had no plan, let alone a horse. Some prophesied savior she was. Rika sighed, rubbing her temples in a fruitless attempt to rid herself of the pounding. Well, there was only one thing to do: Start walking.

In the distance, if she squinted, Rika could see the palace at Yoshai, high on the hill above the city. She had always loved the view from the very top courtyard, the broad expanse sweeping across the green valley to the sea. She couldn't help but imagine what that view looked like now, with swarms of soul-eaters and their soldiers covering the land and polluting the city. Was she already too late? Was her mother dead? If so, what would she do? There were a few burners in Kyuden and Kistana, the capitals of the former countries of Kita and Miina before they had been joined in unity by her parents. Perhaps she could rally those burners...save some.

She looked back at the sea, darkened by boats. There were so many soul-eaters. There was no way she could fight them all individually. She needed to kill their queen, hope that when the queen fell, the numbered soul-eaters and their thralls would fall also. But where was she? Finding her would be like a needle in a haystack. Neither Vikal or Cayono had learned much of use during their time as thralls. They knew only of her rise to power, of the reverence with which the other soul-eaters spoke of her. Thinking of Vikal sent a waterfall of emotions through her, surging and bubbling. What was happening in Nua? Were they facing the soul-eaters? Would the constellations be enough? As thin and weak as she felt now, she knew that leaving the constellations with them had been the right thing to do. Perhaps Nua wasn't her home, but it had embraced her. She couldn't leave them to die undefended. And Vikal...whom she would never see again. Vikal who was deep enough to drown in, bright enough to burn. Her destiny. And she had sailed away. Chosen a different path. "For you, Kitina," she said softly. "You are my destiny."

The sun was setting behind her, staining the hazy sky the color of blood. She stopped for a moment to look, catching her breath and uselessly adjusting the straps of her sandals that were rubbing her raw. She turned back towards Yoshai, panic rising in her. She wasn't going to make it. By the time it took her to walk to Yoshai, let alone get through the hordes, her mother and brother would probably be dead. But what could she do?

She took the blade out of her belt, her totem, and hefted it in her hand. Turn it into a koumori and fly? She growled in frustration, marching forward again, her totem in her hand. She had to be the worst goddess of bright light ever. Bedraggled, dirty, weak with hunger, blisters on her feet, no transportation, and no plan. "Your savior has arrived!" she said mockingly to no one. She felt nothing like the queen in Sarnak's book, fierce and terrifying—three eyes burning with starlight, hair flowing in the wind, borne by a star, totem in her upraised hand.

Wait. Borne by a star...an idea surged within her, so all-consuming that she tripped over a rock, nearly tumbling to the ground. She cursed and stopped.

"Cygna!" she called, opening her third eye. She hadn't seen him since she had sent him warn her mother. To tell her she was coming. But she thought of the sentiment that had been shared by Liliam, Sarnak, Cygna, Kemala. Though the words had been different, she thought she was beginning to understand. All she needed was within her. The threads here were fainter than the powerful set of strings in Nua, but she could still see them clearly. Where was the sparrow's thread? There! The familiar tether vibrated, stretching low in the sky. She gave it a tug while examining the other personalities in Kitina's night sky. The blue dragon of the east, the great tortoise, the southern phoenix, the white tiger of the north. These constellations were powerful protectors of their land— told in the stories to watch over the four corners of the world. They would be her first summoning. Next would be the clever fox with his bushy tail. Because she had always wanted to meet it.

The erratic vibration of Cygna's thread brought her focus back. She closed her third eye, and a bolt of white light came into view. It was Cygna. She sighed in relief, happy to see a familiar face, even if it was a tiny bird.

"Did you find her? My mother? Does she live?"

"She lives."

Relief surged through Rika in a powerful tide. "How are they doing?"

"Badly," Cygna said. "The soul-eater army is pushing through the palace gates."

Rika's spirits plummeted. "I won't get there in time. Not like this. Cygna, the goddesses before me, did they ride constellations?"

"Yes. They can be made corporeal. It takes much concentration, but can be done."

"Let's do it," Rika said. "I need a ride. Something with wings."

Cygna hopped on her shoulder, fluttering its wings. "Your past selves have ridden me. It can be so again."

Rika let out a startled laugh before clapping her hand over her mouth. Cygna was cocking its little head to the side in an expression that could only be annoyance.

"But...you're so small," said Rika. "No offense."

"Size is relative. In the sky, my wings stretch across cities."

"So get bigger. Please." Rika motioned uselessly with her hands.

"The goddess of bright light controls this change."

"Me? How the heck am I supposed to do that?"

"All you need—"

"Is within me," Rika finished, rolling her eyes. "Okay. Give me a minute. Maybe...stand back. In case this works." It had to work. Rika closed her eyes, acting purely on instinct. *Spirits of the former goddesses of bright light,* she prayed, feeling silly. *I know my soul remembers, though my mind does not. Help me to remember how to make Cygna grow large and strong so we can soar together.*

Then she waited, listening, wondering what she was supposed to feel or hear. Three words floated to the surface of her mind, so soft she wasn't sure she didn't imagine them. *Knowledge and will.* They were the words Liliam had spoken to her when she'd been teaching her how to summon the stars. But she didn't have the knowledge, that was the problem!

But even as she protested, a little voice inside her trilled. She didn't have to know how to do it; she had to know the stars. The constellations. And she did. She knew Cygna—she had for generations. The night sparrow was loyal and stealthy and brave and patient. Together, they had swirled through stars, soared through galaxies, along star-paths to distant worlds, including this one. Rika gasped. She remembered. Remembered her spirit traveling with Cygna along the paths to this world. To deposit itself into a tiny growing babe inside Queen Kailani Shigetsu. She had come here for a reason. For a purpose.

Though she was stunned by the revelation and wanted nothing more than to contemplate it and all it meant, time was running out. Rika opened her three eyes and with practiced hands began tugging at Cygna's threads, lengthening and firming the constellation's essence. When she was done, Cygna stood as large as a house, its wings stretching and shadowing the ground. It was magnificent—a glittering mass of stars and blackness, as if a piece of the night sky itself stood before her. A grin split across Rika's face.

She clambered up Cygna's wing, grasping its silken feathers, wincing when she slipped and pulled a bit too hard. It felt real beneath her, but the glow emanating from the sparrow made it impossible to forget that she was not walking upon just any wing.

"To the palace," Rika said, settling into a little valley atop Cygna's neck. She buried her hands in its feathers, silently apologizing. If this was anything like riding a koumori, she would wish she had a saddle. Better hold on tight.

"It will be done," Cygna said, and it launched into the air. Even with her tight grip, Rika was nearly unseated by the power of Cygna's wingbeats as they rose through the air. As they reached altitude, she let out an incredulous laugh. Well, this would make more of an impression than walking in on blistered feet.

They swooped towards the palace, and Rika's hair streamed behind her, the wind pulling tears from the corners of her eyes.

It only took a few moments to close the distance to Yoshai. The scene below her wiped the grin off her face. Hordes of black-clad soldiers moved throughout the city like a plague. The soul-eater forces were concentrated around the palace, completely surrounding it on all sides. At the gate was a mass of men with a battering ram, crashing against the wooden gate with fearsome blows. As she soared overhead, thousands of green eyes looked up to follow her progress—soul-eaters and thralls alike.

Rika couldn't help it. She opened her third eye and pulled at a thread of a star, sending it down towards the men and soul-eaters attacking the gate. It hit with a satisfying explosion of light, tendrils of starlight searching, penetrating the soul-eaters, burrowing into their armor. Rika's head swam from the effort, and she held tight to Cygna's feathers as her world spun around her. Or was it just Cygna banking towards the courtyard at the very top of the palace?

The night sparrow landed in the courtyard with a thunderous crash, sending moonburners and sunburners scrambling. It let its wing down and Rika launched herself from her perch, half-tumbling, half-running down its side. She didn't care about appearances. She was home. "Mom!" she screamed, scanning the faces. "Koji?"

The blue uniforms parted as someone pushed their way forward through the crowd. "Rika?" It was her mother. Her silver hair was wild, her uniform dirty and torn. But she was alive. Real and solid and *alive*.

Rika ran for her, and they crashed together in an embrace as forceful as Cygna's landing.

"My daughter," Kai said, her thin body wracking with sobs. "You're finally home."

CHAPTER 30

Vikal tore through the trees, pumping his arms and legs as fast as they could carry him. Blackened limbs blurred by, bleeding into strange specters silently observing his passage. His thoughts were before him— on Goa Awan. Had the others reached the caverns? Had the soul-eaters? Were they too late? His heart, though…his heart was behind him. Sailing on a ship plunging through a hole in space. He should have kissed Rika. He had longed to…lingered far too long while he'd debated and doubted…and then it had been too late. It would only have made things worse. They were never going to see each other again. Either they would defeat the soul-eaters, and he would never be able to journey to Kitina, or he would die here, defending his land. So what good would a kiss have done? He groaned. He still should have kissed her.

Vikal's steps slowed as he began to lope up the mountain, his sandals straining against the soft earth. From the corner of his eye, he swore he caught a glimpse of Sarya floating beside him, a silver wraith against the green of the jungle. Once she had been a comfort, a constant reminder of how real their life, their love, had been. Now, part of him wished her gone, and that part was growing. It shamed him—the guilt festered in his gut. What kind of man loved two women? He had promised he would love Sarya forever, forsaking all others. But he had been so quickly undone by the bright-eyed, fiery foreigner who had saved him from compulsion—who had looked upon the face of the horrors he had perpetrated without flinching. Who now sailed across the sea alone to defeat an army. What tremendous courage. Rika was a remarkable goddess. A remarkable woman. She deserved better than his ruined heart.

A root tripped him, and he pitched forward onto his hands and knees. The forest had always worked with him before, not rejected him. "What do you want from me?" He hissed at it, scrambling to his feet and resuming his climb. "I'm here to save your people. I can't save Rika's too." The jungle seemed to thicken around him, and he screamed with frustration, snapping his third eye open and using the threads of power to force the forest to make him a path. "I know she's your goddess too," he said, panting, the words scraping his throat. "And I'm worried about her as well. But it has to be this way. She's on her own. She chose that." *No*, his inner voice seemed to say. *You chose that for her. You promised you would help her and you abandoned her.*

The waterfall came into view and Vikal redoubled his efforts, ignoring his ragged breath. There were no soul-eaters or thralls in sight, but the shuddering threads of the jungle revealed that they had passed this way. They must already be inside. What was going on? Were they already pulling Nuans into their sick embrace, turning them to ash?

Vikal clambered up the slick hillside parallel the waterfall, his muscles quivering and spent from the climb. His foot slipped, leaving him hanging in space, his feet kicking, his fingers straining against the wet rock. A vine took pity on him and snaked beneath him, hardening into a foothold. "Thanks," he panted, climbing the rest of the way up and hauling himself over the ledge. He flashed back to the memory of clamoring up this face while watching an unconscious Rika strapped to Cayono's back. He'd had the strength of ten men when it had come to saving her.

Vikal slipped behind the rushing waterfall into the dark of the tunnels. He moved through them by feel, his heart hammering in his throat. Where were the others?

The tunnel began to brighten before him with the light of a hundred stars. He must have been close. He heard Bahti's voice booming from the cavern beyond. What was going on? Why were they talking, not fighting? He lowered his head and sprinted to the end of the tunnel into the illuminated light of the huge cavern. What he saw…was nothing like he'd expected.

A tall soul-eater stood in the middle of the Gathering Hall, surrounded by thralls and soul-eaters. Vikal quickly counted ten of the leeches. Less than they had feared. Still far too many. But it wasn't that fact that stunned him. Or even the fact that the creature held Sarnak by the throat, the god's toes barely brushing the ground. It was that everyone was gone. Where were all the Nuans? Where were his people? Had they already been killed? Devoured?

Bahti apparently had the same question. "Where is my daughter?" he cried, pointing his hammer at the soul-eater like a promise.

Vikal slipped behind Kemala, pulling his swords from their sheaths in a whisper of steel. "Where are they? Are they alive?"

"I don't know," she said. "They've…vanished. But this place doesn't have the residue of fear or death that I would expect if we had arrived…too late."

"They're safe," Sarnak groaned. "But you better get to killing these things." With ferocious strength, the soul-eater tossed the old man across the cavern. Sarnak tumbled to a stop against the far wall, his disheveled robes a riot of orange. As he hit the wall, the cavern flickered somehow, as if reality itself had tripped and stumbled. Suddenly, the cavern was full to the brim with Nuans, wide-eyed with fear, hands clutched together in prayer.

Kemala gasped, her hands flying to her mouth. "Tamar!"

Bahti roared, running for his daughter. And then they were gone. Tamar was gone.

"Sarnak…" Vikal said to himself, realization dawning on him. The god's power controlled the cycles—did that include the cycles of time? Somehow, he had shifted their people…out of time. Out of this ending. He didn't understand it, but his eyes didn't lie. He focused on the god, who was still clutching his head, lying prone on the cavern floor. The soul-eater who had been holding him locked its evil gaze on Vikal, and then swiveled slowly to look at Sarnak.

"No!" Vikal screamed, launching forward to do something—anything—to stop the soul-eater from reaching Sarnak. The distance was too far—the creature moved with impossible speed. Vikal had hardly made it two steps when the creature lifted Sarnak's body and tossed him across the cavern with a sickening crunch.

Instantly, the cave shifted, the fabric of reality snapping back into place. Once again the Gathering Hall was full to the brim with Nuans. Vikal bowled into a group of women, knocking them onto the floor, tangling in their skirts. "Attack them!" Vikal said, scrambling to his knees and pointing at the stunned soul-eaters. It was the only time he had seen the creatures surprised.

Kemala took up his cry. "Constellations! In the name of your goddess, attack!"

The constellations surged to life, swooping and pouncing at the nearest soul-eaters. The Nuans screamed and ducked, scattering every which way.

Vikal plunged towards the nearest thrall, knowing the humans were the only ones he could fight. The other gods were fighting some of the soldiers, even some of the Nuan men were joining ranks. The constellations attacked the soul-eaters, pouncing upon them with glowing rage, snarling teeth and raking claws. The centaur's arrows were vicious—in short order the constellation had peppered a soul-eater with shafts, its arrows piercing the soul-eater's armor like knives through warm butter.

The soul-eater who had attacked Sarnak was clearly the leader of this unit. It moved with lightning speed, tossing people before it like leaves in the wind, seizing others and making them thralls, desperately trying to turn the tide in its own favor. It was ruthlessly efficient and thus far, none of the constellations had been able to touch it. The scorpion lashed out at it with fearsome claws and tail, but the soul-eater rolled and ducked, wrecking more havoc in its wake. Vikal headed towards it, wading through the fray. Until he froze, realizing who stood next in its line of sight. Tamar.

The frightened girl had lost her caretaker and was standing amongst the chaos and screams, her tear-streaked eyes wide with fear.

"Tamar!" Vikal screamed, launching into a run. "Come here!"

She turned to him, recognition written in relief on her face. She didn't see the soul-eater coming for her. But it saw her. And it saw Vikal.

She was too far. The soul-eater was going to get to her first—crush her small body with one of its armored fists. "Rika, help me," he breathed, saying a prayer to the goddess of bright light.

It was as if she heard him. An arrow of starlight streaked from across the cavern and thunked—quivering—into the soul-eater's body. It was enough to slow its progress and Vikal altered his path, barreling into the leech with all the force he could muster. Pain exploded through his shoulder as he hit the creature, bearing it to the ground. He reared back and punched it right in the face, feeling that there was flesh in the dark recesses of the helmet. He punched it again and again, pouring his anger and rage into his attack. The month of being under its mind control. The destruction of his island. Sarya's death. Displacement of his people. Bringing Rika into his life and then ripping her away again. These creatures were pure destruction. Evil and chaos and cruelty. He longed to smother it with his bare hands—to feel its life slipping away, as these things had taken his.

"I think you got it," Bahti said from behind him. Vikal looked around. The bodies of the other soul-eaters were strewn about the cavern. Dead. The men who had been enthralled were beginning to wake from the nightmare, shaking their heads and looking around with clear eyes for the first time.

Vikal slumped back on his heels, his breath hissing through his teeth. His fist was bloody, the clean red of his own blood mixed with sickly green of the leech's.

"Vikal," Cayono called from across the Gathering Hall. "Sarnak's in bad shape."

Vikal hauled himself to his feet, hurrying to where Cayono knelt over the crumpled body of his friend and mentor. Flecks of blood speckled Sarnak's lips, and when Vikal delicately probed at the back of Sarnak's head, his fingers came away wet. He exchanged a look with Cayono. Sarnak's injuries were grave.

The god's eyes fluttered opened to reveal pools of black. "Are they dead?" he asked, his words thick and slurred.

"We got them. Thanks to you. You saved our people."

"'Course I did," he said. "This was fated to be."

"Of course." Vikal smiled at Sarnak's conceit despite himself. "Now hold on. We will get you help."

"Nothing for it," Sarnak said. "I see my ending bright and clear."

"No, Sarnak." He didn't think he could bear to lose another friend. "This is all my fault. I should have known that the soul-eaters had something up their sleeves. I should have protected Goa Awan. Protected you."

"My totem," was all Sarnak said, reaching out his hand towards the orb, which had rolled a few feet away. Cayono fetched it and placed it in Sarnak's hands. "She was..." He coughed again, a wet hacking sound. "Right. You are a rice-headed water buffalo." Sarnak spun the orb, and with a sluggish orbit, it began to glow, throwing light into the cavern. Rotation by rotation, another figure came into view, in a magenta skirt and sash.

"Sarya? Bahti cried, running to her but pulling up short, holding his hands up to her incorporeal face.

"If I had known how you two would martyr yourselves, I would never have agreed to die," Sarya said, clucking her tongue, hands on her hips.

"Agreed..." Vikal trailed off. "What do you mean?"

"Sarnak and I agreed it would be best not to tell you, as you would just as soon kill him for it. But now that he is dying anyway, it is time you knew the truth."

"What truth?" Bahti's voice was hesitant.

"Sarnak told me what was going to happen the day the soul-eaters landed on our shore. I knew I went to meet my executioner."

Vikal looked from Sarya's ghostly face to Sarnak's bloodied one, confusion coursing through him. "Then why? Why did you go?"

"Just like the day of absolute silence. The island needed a sacrifice."

"That is a children's story! A fable!"

"But are not all fables based in a grain of truth? If I had not been killed, they would have taken you. And if they had taken you, you would never have become a thrall. You would never have journeyed to another land and brought back the one person who could save us."

"There had to be another way!" Bahti said. Kemala had come to stand beside him, her fingers lacing through his.

"The god of endings sees all possibilities. There was no other way. So I took this burden gladly, knowing it would save my love, my family, my niece, my people."

Vikal's thoughts stuttered and stopped, unable to comprehend what Sarya said. She had stepped forward to embrace that soul-eater, knowing what it would cost her. Knowing what it would do. He hadn't thought it possible, but this only made him respect Sarya more.

"So will you please stop blaming yourselves? Throwing away your lives with guilt and sorrow. I chose this. Me. So you could live. So live!" She fluttered her hands like a mother ushering her children out to play.

Sarnak's floating orb fell from where it floated with a resounding thunk, making Vikal jump. He fell to his knees at Sarnak's side, but Cayono shook his head. The god was gone. Vikal looked up to see Sarya slowly disappearing. But at her side, hand in hand, was Sarnak. The god gave him a little salute before they both vanished into the dark.

CHAPTER 31

Rika didn't want to let go. It only took the first breath of her mother's orange blossom scent for the dams to burst—for the careful walls and makeshift barriers she had built around her feelings to evaporate completely. She was a girl again in her mother's arms, scared and sorry and missing her father down to her bones. "I'm sorry I couldn't save Father," she sobbed into her mother's silver hair. "If I had known how to use my powers..."

"Hush," Kai murmured, stroking her back. "Not you too. It wasn't your fault, it wasn't Koji's fault. It is not a child's job to protect their parents. It's our job to protect you."

Rika sniffed, pulling back from her mother.

Kai traced her face, running a thumb over the third eye tattoo on her smooth forehead. "But you are not a child anymore. You have grown into a woman, and I can see you have a story to tell."

"I'm sorry I was gone so long. I couldn't come back sooner."

"No apologies. You're here now." Kai pulled her into a hug again, rocking her back and forth.

"Rika?" an excited voice called. Surprisingly deep. She pulled back from her mother and saw Koji standing in a red leather uniform, dirt and blood smeared on his face. Apparently, she wasn't the only one who had grown up. "Koji!" she said, and they ran towards each other, pausing awkwardly just before embracing. It had been years since they had been close enough to hug.

"I'm glad you're back," he said, rubbing the back of his head. She laughed and pulled him in, crushing him in her embrace. "I can't believe Mother let you put that armor on!" she said, her voice muffled in his shoulder.

He laughed. "It took some convincing." He looked her over. "Where in Taiyo's name have you been? What are these ridiculous clothes? And what is that, some dirt on your forehead?" He wet his thumb and went to wipe at her third eye tattoo, a grin on his face.

"Don't even think about it," she said, opening her third eye and giving him a fierce glare.

"Woah!" he said, stumbling back. "Mom, look at this!"

"Remarkable," Kai said, peering into Rika's face. "What does it do?"

Rika opened her mouth to explain, but someone cleared their throat across the courtyard. It was Emi. "I hate to interrupt the family reunion, but we're getting our asses handed to us down there. Rika, does that big bird of yours do anything besides sit there blinding all of us?"

Rika pursed her lips to keep from grinning, her heart singing with gladness to be back amongst her family. "I missed you, Emi."

"I missed you too, panda. Now can you hop to on the prophecy and start ridding Yoshai of these monsters?"

"Leeches," Rika said, striding back towards Cygna. "We call them 'leeches.'"

"We?" She heard Kai say as Rika scrambled her way up Cygna's wing to her seat behind its neck.

"Where do you need the most help?" Rika called to Emi.

"The palace gates are about to fall. If that happens, we're all doomed," Emi replied.

Rika nodded. Cygna launched into the air. It did one pass above the lower courtyard, where a new group of three leeches and their thralls had resumed the attack on the thick wooden doors. A cloud of dark-clad thralls lined up behind them, waiting to push through once the doors were breached. *Not going to happen*, Rika thought.

"If we swoop by," Rika shouted to Cygna, "can you grab one of the leeches with your feet?"

Cygna complied, beginning to come around. "I guess that's a *yes*,"

Rika said, tightening her grip on the bird's feathers, flattening herself to its back. She opened her third eye again, and the threads and filaments of Kitina jumped into view. It felt so good to be home. The stars here shone brightly beyond the blue sky, eager to lend aid to defend this land. She located the threads of two particularly bright stars and pulled them, summoning them to her aid, directing them to the two other leeches that hammered at the door. The action sent a pounding through her head—lights bloomed in her vision, and a wave of nausea swept through her. She tightened her grip in Cygna's feathers until her fingers creaked with effort, clinging to consciousness even as she clung to her mount.

They struck as one. Cygna swooped, burying its talons into the most exposed of the three leeches. The silver light of Rika's stars slammed into the other two, tossing their heavy armored forms into their men in a wave of tumbling destruction. The light burrowed its way into the creatures' armor, filling it with purifying fire that burned out the monsters inside. Cygna flapped its immense wings, making their way back to the upper courtyard, where her family watched with awe. It tossed the soul-eater it had retrieved with its talons down onto the stones before settling onto the edge of the wall once more.

Rika swung a leg over and stumbled down Cygna's wing—her feet heavy, her steps ungainly.

"That was awesome!" Koji whooped and hollered, jumping up and down.

"You're hurt," Kai reached out a hand as Rika passed by her, her eyes fixed on the soul-eater Cygna had dropped in the courtyard. Green blood was oozing from puncture wounds in its armor, but it was still alive. Still dangerous. Rika wiped the blood from beneath her nose and pulled her blade from her belt. Having her totem in her hand sent a surge of strength through her, steadying her steps.

She came to stand over the creature, to look in its green eyes. She could see through her third eye the sickly threads that tied this creature to so many soldiers, that held the poor men in its thrall. But there were other threads too—threads that tied this creature to the heavens, to the stars. At one time perhaps, this had been a celestial being. Before it had been perverted. Warped into this thing of evil and destruction.

"Where is your queen?" Rika asked. Her voice was clear and strong. She was grateful for this.

"Why would I tell you?" the creature rasped, a wet cough following its words. It was dying.

"Because if you do, I won't feed you to my constellation," she retorted.

"I care little about my life. I am part of the whole. I live only to serve my queen."

Rika grimaced. How did one torture an impossibly scary evil being for information?

But then a thought occurred to her like an arrow of light. She could see the threads connecting the thralls to the soul-eaters. Could she see what connected the soul-eaters to their queen? She peered at the soul-eater. Dozens of threads splayed from it in all directions like a spiderweb. But one…she squinted, examining it. One was different. Darker, thicker, pulsing with an unnatural heartbeat. She stepped back and let her gaze travel along it, let her spirit be born along the tether as it stretched across Yoshai's walls, south towards Antila, and towards the sea. To where it ended. In a floating galleon ten times the size of the other vessels. The queen's ship. Rika snapped her attention back into her body and turned to the soul-eater with a grin. "Thank you for the information." Another idea came upon her, and she took the soul-eater's thread in her hand. If she could sever the thralls from their masters, could she sever this one from its queen?

The creature lunged at her, its movements faster than the eye could see. But Rika's third eye was open, and her totem was in her hand. Almost like it had a mind of its own, her arm was up before the soul-eater reached her with outstretched talons, and so the only contact made was the soft exposure of its face connecting with her blade. She cringed at the squelching sound as her arm reverberated with the force of the creature's attack. It spasmed and shook, and Rika pulled out her blade, her blood singing with adrenaline. The creature fell to the stones and vanished in a surge of white light, leaving only empty armor.

Rika blew out a deep breath and wiped her blade on her sash before turning back to those who stood behind her. She supposed she would need to find out on another subject.

Kai had her hands to her mouth, eyes wide, while Koji had his sword half out of its scabbard. Emi just stood with her arms crossed, a look of—*was that pride?*—in her dark eyes.

"What?" Rika asked.

The soul-eaters and their army pulled back from the palace gates after the destruction of the three soul-eaters left many of their thralls milling about in confusion, freed of their compulsion. Though Rika longed to let the men through the gates, to shelter them from being retaken as thralls, the palace was already full to bursting. It was too dangerous to open the doors.

They had moved to her mother's council room and were sitting around the long table. General Daarco had joined them, giving Rika a bone-crushing hug. "Oma will be thrilled you're back," he said. "She's been beside herself." Colum was the last to arrive, his curly salt-and-pepper hair wild. "I can't wait to trade adventure stories." He winked at her before taking a chair. He seemed as unflappable as ever.

The chair to her mother's right sat empty, the memory of Hiro nearly as palpable as his presence. She couldn't stop looking at it. Being here, being back—memories swam to the surface unbidden—his big, booming laugh, sitting on his lap listening to a story by the fire, riding Ryu like a horse when she couldn't have been more than four. Her parents' ever-present love—the stolen kisses before official functions, nights retiring early, Hiro's arms wrapped around Kai, his chin resting on her head. Rika met her mother's eyes and there was such deep sorrow there that tears sprang forth unbidden.

Kai reached out her hand, and Rika took it. "He's waiting for me in the spirit world," Kai whispered "Someday we'll all see him again."

Rika could only nod, words failing her. Someday.

"Rika," Emi said, drawing them back to the moment. "We couldn't be happier to have you back. Even Koji's happy to see you, and that's saying something." Rika chuckled and wiped her nose. "We want to sit by the fire and drink sake and hear all about where you've been and who's your bird friend and how you've grown a new eye. But we've got an annihilation to avert."

"What have you learned about them? These—leeches?" Daarco asked. "Emi said they have a queen. Can she be bargained with? Kidnapped and ransomed?"

"Killed," Rika said. "If we kill her, this is all over."

"How do you know?"

"Vikal…a friend. He had been under their compulsion but was freed when I killed the soul-eater who had turned him. He learned things while he was a thrall. The thralls send information back to their masters, but some comes the other way, too. They're a hive structure. Like honeybees."

"I'd prefer to face a hundred hives of those over these leeches," Koji muttered.

"They have a queen that controls the soul-eaters. The soul-eaters in turn control the thralls. If the queen is killed…"

"Then all the soul-eaters die too?" Kai asked.

"I think so. Hopefully. Best case scenario, they all die. If not, at least, they will be disoriented—without orders. We'd have a much easier time of picking them off one by one."

"Do we know anything about this queen?" Daarco asked. "What kind of guard she's under? What abilities she might have? Are you sure you can defeat her?"

"No," Rika admitted. "I know only what my friend told me. And he didn't know much."

"It seems risky. Now that we have a way to kill them, why don't we go out there and kill them the old-fashioned way? Rika, summon more of those lightning bolts and a few more birds and it'll be over in no time."

Rika hesitated.

"That would likely kill Rika," Kai said quietly. "Wouldn't it? Your powers…they drain you."

Rika sighed. "They're connected to another land. Nua. It's where I've been. They're fighting the soul-eaters there too, and I left constellations there for that fight. I'm far from the source of my power and my strength is already divided. There are hundreds of leeches out there. I couldn't kill them all."

"So we kill the queen," Koji said. "What are we waiting for?"

"We wait for a plan, my son," Kai said wryly. "Do you have one?"

"No." He crossed his arms.

"I have one," Rika said. "And it just might be crazy enough to work."

CHAPTER 32

Vikal sat on the floor, numb with shock. It was done. Nua was free. But at what cost? He would never see Sarya again. Or Sarnak. He had lost so much. And Rika…she wasn't even his to lose. Yet somehow he had lost her anyway.

Kemala came to kneel beside him, her voice velvet. "Are you all right?"

"She says to live. How do I live without her?"

"You know how."

Vikal averted his eyes from Kemala's penetrating gaze. She knew his secret, he was sure. The truth he tried so hard to hide from even himself. "Is it possible for a man to love two women?" he whispered.

"All things are possible when it comes to the human heart."

"Does it not betray her memory?"

"She did not seem to think so."

"Daddy," Tamar said. She was tucked against Bahti's leg, hugging it fiercely. "It's moving." She pointed to the soul-eater Vikal had pummeled. One set of its black claws was curling ever-so-slightly. It wasn't dead.

Vikal was on his feet in a flash, his swords in his hands.

"Let one of the constellations finish it off," Bahti said.

Kemala motioned to the eagle constellation, who perched on a nearby stalagmite, its bright eyes gleaming in the dark. The creature swooped down, landing on the soul-eater's chest. The brilliant bird was as large as the black-clad monster.

"Wait!" Vikal cried, sheathing his swords. The eagle cocked its head at him in confusion.

"Have you lost it, *bak?*" Ajij asked.

"If we keep one alive, the astrolabes will still work. In the boats." He had been moving through these past days like a ghost. But no more. Despite what he had done, what he had seen, he *was* still alive. He still had a future. It was time to act like it.

"Keep one alive?" Bahti asked. "You crazy? Kill it!"

"You want to go help Rika," Kemala said, exchanging a look with Bahti.

"She left," Bahti protested, his tone petulant.

"She lent us her strength to free this land, even though it jeopardized her ability to help her own people."

"Rika deserves our aid. But can we leave our people so soon?" Kemala asked gently. "What if other soul-eaters lurk on the island? We should be sure before we leave them unprotected."

"If we do not help her defeat the soul-eaters there, what is to prevent them from coming back here? The queen knows what we have done," Vikal said. "And we would not have Rika to help us then. We would be helpless."

"I am in," Ajij said. "She is one of us. We help our own. Leave one constellation here to protect the island. Take the others and the soul-eater with you. Help her. Kill the queen. Make sure these creatures never set foot on Nuan soil again."

Tamar turned her face to Bahti, wiping her tears with the back of her fist. Her voice was small but strong. "If Rika needs help, you should go."

Bahti stroked her hair and pulled her into a hug. "I could not refuse my girl anything. We go."

The centaur had pummeled the soul-eater a few times with a hoof to the helmet to ensure the monster was truly unconscious. They had wrapped it in cloth, and now Bahti dragged the leech behind them, complaining the entire way.

Vikal turned, looking over his shoulder, asking for the third time. "Do you want help?"

Bahti dropped the end of the fabric, his barrel chest heaving. "No." He turned and gave the bundle a vicious kick. "That is for Sarnak, you disgusting leech!" He kicked again, his sandaled foot clanging against creature's armor.

"I doubt it feels that through its armor," Vikal said, doubling back and picking up one corner of the fabric.

"Still makes me feel better."

Kemala shook her head and turned, continuing to trudge down the hill. No doubt she was used to her husband's antics.

"And what is that smell?" Bahti asked. "Ugh. Sulfur."

"Imagine being trapped on a boat with them. Sleeping near them. Killing for them."

Bahti's face grew grim. "I forget that however much we have been through on Nua, you went through more. You have lost more."

Vikal had never thought he would feel a pain as deep as losing Sarya. But now, in doing his best to avoid such pain again, he might lose Rika, too. He couldn't think of that right now. "We have all lost much."

"Sarnak will want a shrine built in his honor," Bahti said.

"A shrine? A temple!" Vikal said. "A palace!" He quieted. "In truth, he deserves all that and more. He was like a father to all of us. As angry as I am at him about Sarya, I cannot believe he is gone."

"He will be back," Ajij said from a few steps behind them. "I feel it. We will see him again soon. He will put on quite a show when he is reincarnated."

"Biggest star-fall in fifty years," Bahti agreed.

"Not the biggest," Vikal said, remembering his childlike wonder as stars fell like confetti across the heavens, heralding the birth of the goddess of bright light.

"Do you believe what Sarya said?" Bahti asked. "That she knew? Before the end."

"Oh, yes," Vikal said. "She was brave and stubborn enough to try to take on the world herself. I believe her."

"I have been blaming you, *bak*," Bahti said. "It was not fair of me."

"I blamed myself too. I still do."

"Even the god of green things cannot control all the world," Bahti said.

"So I have learned."

Silence stretched between them, marked by only the swishing of their steps.

"You truly care for her," Bahti finally said. Bahti didn't say Rika's name, but Vikal knew whom he spoke of.

"I will always love Sarya," Vikal said quickly. "But...yes. I care for Rika. More than I thought I was capable of."

"I suppose..." Bahti's voice was gruff. "I have not been entirely fair to that girl. She did leave behind the constellations that saved us. That saved Tamar."

"True," Vikal said, a small part of him enjoying Bahti's discomfort. Was his friend actually going to apologize?

"What I am saying is...if you want to love her...then I guess I am all right with that."

"That was downright civilized," Kemala chimed in without turning around.

Vikal nodded. "That means a lot, *bak*."

"Right!" Bahti said, his face flushed. "We go get your girl! Well, assuming she feels the same about you. She does feel the same?"

Vikal looked at the ground, avoiding Bahti's piercing red gaze. He had asked himself the same thing many times. There had been moments where something had passed between them. Something deeper. Something more. But he had abandoned her. Left her to return home on her own, broken his promise. Could she forgive him? Would she want anything to do with him? A broken man from another world... "I do not know," he finally admitted.

"She does, you foolish man," Kemala said, again not turning. Her black hair swished behind her as she walked. "And it should not take the goddess of dark spaces to see it. You are fated. And the fates are not about to let you two screw things up."

Bahti raised his eyebrows at Vikal, who flushed with hope. "Do not mess with the fates," Bahti said.

"No." A smile broke across Vikal's face. "I would not dare."

The soul-eaters' ships sat quietly, spots of shadow in the crystal-clear water of the bay. They made quick work of dropping the unconscious soul-eater into a rowboat and making their way out to the nearest vessel anchored in shallow water. Vikal's heart thudded in his chest, remembering making the same voyage with Rika just hours ago. Had she made it? Was she safe? Locked in the battle of her life against hundreds of soul-eaters? Would he arrive too late…only to find her gone?

"She is strong," Kemala said, placing her hand over his where he was drumming his fingers on his knee. "And smart. She will survive."

He nodded. She would survive. He would accept no other outcome.

They had banished all the constellations but two, an eagle, who soared before them to the ship, and the scorpion, who guarded the caves. The others had disappeared back into the sky, their energies released to return to where they had come from, borne on threads invisible to all but the gods.

Upon arriving at the ship, they rigged a rope to haul the dead weight of the soul-eater from the rowboat onto the deck. It was too heavy for one or two men to lift—the creature was huge, and its armor weighed a ton. But with Bahti straining against the rope, and Ajij and Vikal steadying it, they got it on board, dropping it into the deck with a crash. The centaur's blows had left it out cold, but Vikal still eyed the cloth-wrapped bundle with unease. Being near the creatures made his skin crawl. The leeches weren't natural.

Ajij set to work readying the ship to sail while Bahti and Vikal pulled up the anchor. Kemala pulled the cover off the astrolabe, examining its gears and points. Part of Vikal couldn't believe he was leaving Nua again so soon, heading back to the foreign world he had been forced to travel to before against his will. But this time it would be his own choice.

Vikal and Bahti had just tucked the anchor into its compartment below deck when a strange keening noise sounded behind them. Vikal turned in time to see the soul-eater rearing to life, bursting through the cloth they had wrapped it in. With tremendous speed, it darted towards the astrolabe, tossing Kemala across the deck with a powerful backhand.

"No!" Vikal cried. The soul-eater turned its green eyes to him, seeming to understand his concern, his fear. He could have sworn it smiled at him, though it was impossible to truly see into the dark recesses of its helmet. The creature plunged its armored claws into the delicate mechanisms of the astrolabe and crushed the device beyond recognition before turning and advancing on the gods.

"Kill it!" Bahti cried to the eagle, who perched atop the mast, its claws buried in one of the stays.

"Wait!" Vikal screamed at the eagle, but it was too late. The bird of prey heard its order and dove, its claws burying into the exposed face of the soul-eater. The eagle launched into the air, its wingbeats blinding flashes of light. It wrenched the soul-eater apart with razor-sharp talons, pulling the creature's head clean off its body with a pop.

Vikal fell to his knees as the soul-eater's head dropped from the eagle's claws into the water with a splash. So quickly. His last chance had slipped through his grasp so quickly.

The eagle screeched, stretching its wings, spiraling back up towards the heavens. Its work here was done. The soul-eaters were dead.

"It needed to die," Bahti said as Vikal let out an incredulous laugh. The lights on the other vessels had gone dark. The last soul-eater in this area had died, and the energy to fuel the astrolabes had died with it. Now, the ships sat as floating hulks, dead pieces of metal and wood.

He staggered to his feet, his focus narrowing on Ajij. "You," he said.

Ajij jumped at the intensity of Vikal's comment. "What? I did nothing."

"No. You can help. You are the god of deep places. God of the sea. Get this sea to carry this boat to Kitina. As fast as you can. It is not too late to help Rika."

"Vikal." The regret in Ajij's voice needled at him. "Even with fair winds and tides and the help of the sea, I do not think…I do not think Kitina is on our world. Only someone who can navigate the stars can get there."

"No!" Vikal punched his fist into the railing, the wood splintering under the force of his blow. "There must be a way."

"Vikal." Kemala's gentle words scalded him. "It was a good plan. But there is no other way to get there in time. The boats have gone dark. It is over."

Vikal turned his back on her, on all of them, looking into the darkening sky. Somewhere, Rika was out there. Fighting. Dying. Alone. And it was his fault. Without meaning to, his third eye opened, and he saw the threads of Nua, of this world, stretching from him back to the plants and green things of the island. But threads stretched before him too, faint and thin. The tether of his totem, which had been a part of him and this island for so many years, now lost to him, clutched in some soul-eater's hand. Lost to his progeny. The gods that would come after him would be weakened, always missing a part of themselves because of his failure today. And then there were the shining threads stretching from his heart leading into the distance. So strong and unyielding, he almost felt like he could pull himself upon them. Rika. His connection to her. They had never shone so clear before, with his eyes fixed on Sarya. But here they were. Proof of their connection—their destiny.

He took the strongest tether gently in his hand, wishing with every part of him that he could jerk it towards himself and bring Rika flying. Or that she would do the opposite. But instead he ran his thumb along its fine filament, pouring every bit of sorrow and regret and emotion into it. "I will not be able to come. I cannot keep my promise. I hope you defeat them and have a long, happy life. I am sorry."

Somewhere in the distance, the thread trilled back at him. Rika heard and understood. It should have soothed his unhappy heart to know that she was still fighting, still alive. But it only made it ache more. To know she was out there. Only an impossible world away.

CHAPTER 33

"We disguise ourselves," Rika explained. "Dress ourselves in their uniforms, sail one of their ships to the main galleon, where the queen must be waiting. Once we get as close as we can, I unleash the constellations on her. Kill her, the rest of them die, the thralls are freed. Done."

"Is it as easy as that?" Emi asked, her words dripping with sarcasm. "Why didn't we think of it?"

"What makes you think they'll let us anywhere near them? The thralls never go anywhere without a soul-eater commander. Plus, our eyes don't glow green. We'd be found out before we got close," Daarco pointed out.

Green-glowing eyes, Rika thought. She did know someone like that, though his eyes glowed with the lemon green of palm fronds and banana leaves, not the evil of these diseased soul-eaters. But Vikal wasn't here. "They won't see us until we get to the main vessel. Then, we only need a few moments to get onboard." Rika jumped from her chair as a flash of inspiration hit her. "Run upstairs and grab the helmet of the soul-eater, will you?" she said to the nearest soldier, who disappeared from his post at the door to follow her command.

"What are you up to?" Koji asked.

The soldier returned, his chest heaving, the huge helmet in his hands.

Rika took it from him, its weight almost too much for her. She hefted it aloft. "We find the largest soldier you have. He will be our soul-eater."

Koji shuddered. "You couldn't get me to put that thing's armor on for all the gold in Yoshai."

"You're far too scrawny anyway," Rika shot back, dropping the helmet onto the table, where it sat between them, radiating menace.

As she went to sit down, a wave of energy passed over her. She stumbled, steadying herself on her mother's chair.

"Are you all right?" Kai asked.

Rika nodded, sitting slowly. "Some of my energy has returned. The constellations I left behind have been released to the heavens. Most of them anyway." There were two threads that still drew energy from her. What did it mean that Vikal had sent most of the constellations back into the heavens but had kept only two? Had they defeated most of the soul-eaters, but not all? Were they on the hunt? She desperately wanted to know what was going on in Nua. Were they safe? Had they freed the island? But in the end, it didn't matter. They were there, and she was here. She needed to focus on saving her own people.

"What do you all think about the plan?" Rika asked.

Daarco shook his head. "It's madness."

"So naturally," Emi chimed in, "we love it."

"It is a bold plan," Kai said. "I approve of it. Even with your power and constellations to assist us, there are too many soul-eaters to defeat one by one. None of us would be left in the end."

"Great!" Rika clapped her hands. "Let's go."

"Aren't we forgetting something?" Koji asked. "Like, how are we going to get from here to a ship that's over a league away when we're surrounded by soul-eaters?"

"We'll take Cygna," Rika said. "It can carry more than just me."

"Fly your glowy star-bird to a ship that then approaches the galleon? I think even they might figure that out."

Rika frowned.

"Koji is right. The constellation is too conspicuous. We have three koumori and one golden eagle here in the palace that haven't been killed or fled. We will take them."

"Only four can go?" The number seemed so small. Four against the queen. Four against the destruction of their world.

"I'll wear the armor," Daarco said. "The eagle should carry me."

"I'm going," Koji said. "I want to stick this queen right through her eyes."

"Koji," Kai said carefully. Rika knew that tone, and Koji apparently did too, because he crossed his arms and stuck out his chin even before she continued. "You must stay here. If Rika and I fall…we cannot risk the entire line of succession. You will be in command of our remaining forces here."

"You're coming with us?" Rika asked. She knew her mother had been a great moonburner in her youth, but her father had done most of the adventuring for as long as Rika remembered while her mother handled the affairs of state.

"Oh, yes." Kai's hazel eyes flashed dangerously. "These leeches killed my husband. I have a score to settle."

Rika and Koji exchanged a wide-eyed look. This was a side of their mother they hadn't seen before. But it couldn't be more welcome.

They worked through the rest of the details of the plan—securing thrall uniforms, optimal timing, sharing the plan with the leaders who were staying behind to defend the palace. Emi was going to take the third koumori. When they finally finished the discussions and trailed out of the room to make their arrangements, a powerful message washed over Rika. She stumbled against the sandstone wall, leaning into it for support. It overwhelmed her—a flood of emotions so vivid that they competed with her own. Regret. Sadness and words left unsaid. Love. Pure, sweet love, an intoxicating elixir that took her breath and brought tears to her eyes.

"Are you all right, my daughter?" Kai asked, laying a hand upon Rika's shoulder.

Rika shook her head to clear the surge of feelings. "Yes. No. I thought…I thought we might have reinforcements. It was a long shot; I don't know why I even let any part of me hope. But it looks like he…like they won't be coming."

"I'm sorry," Kai said simply, and in those words, Rika knew her mother understood. That Rika had lost something…the chance at something. Someone.

"I miss Father," Rika whispered. "I still can't believe he's gone."

"He's not gone," Kai said. "He's puttering around the spirit world, second-guessing our battle strategy, annoying Ryu with his pacing. He's waiting for us. Cheering for us."

A little laugh bubbled up as Rika pictured the exact mannerisms her mother described. "We can do this, right? This plan can work?"

Kai smoothed Rika's hair back behind her ear. "It can work. We've been in dire straits before. We managed to find our way out then. We'll do it again."

"To think of all the nights I spent wishing that prophecy would come true. That I would just get my powers."

"Power isn't all it's cracked up to be," Kai said. "It usually comes with heavy responsibility."

"I should have listened to you."

"If you had listened to me, we might all be dead right now."

"Instead of all being dead in a day or two?"

"That's the spirit!" Kai said, wrapping an arm around Rika's shoulders. "Now come, panda. It's time to don our black."

When Rika returned to the courtyard atop the palace, Cygna was gone. She frowned, spinning in a circle. She hadn't released him. Where had he gone? She could feel his thread far to the south, moving swiftly. Why had he left? She should return his power to the stars, to free her energy to summon other constellations. She opened her third eye to do so—

"Rika." She turned to find Koji standing behind her. He had washed the blood and dirt from his face. His beard seemed to be coming in fuller. How was it possible for him to look so much older in just a few days? Though she supposed she had changed as well.

"Do you think you could spare a constellation to guard the palace here? In case the soul-eaters try to make another push?"

"Of course, Ko," she said. "I was planning on it. Any requests? I was thinking I could summon the great tortoise…"

Koji rolled his eyes. "The tortoise! What's it going to do, sit on them? Summon me something dangerous. Like the blue dragon."

"Consider it done," Rika said with a grin before it faltered. "It suits you, you know. The crown. King."

"I'm holding it temporarily until you return," Koji said.

A cloud passed across Rika's face. "I don't know. The queen is required by law to be a moonburner. I'm not one." And a part of her realized that she didn't feel entirely tied to Kitina anymore. This was her home, yes, but part of her heart was tugging her to the south. To the lush forests of Nua, with its pink sand and aquamarine waters. She banished the thought. She couldn't return there. Not if they killed the queen. But she didn't know where that left her, here in Kitina.

"Nonsense," Koji said. "Laws can be changed. No one will dispute that you have the power to rule, or that you deserve it. Especially after you save the country."

"After *we* save the country," Rika corrected.

Koji nodded before hesitating, examining the stitching of his armor. "I'm sorry I left you," he finally said, the words tumbling out in a rush. "I never should have left you. I thought you had died as well as Father, and it was all my fault."

"We can't both be to blame for Father's death, can we?" Rika said. "I'm starting to realize. It's the soul-eaters who are to blame. It's them we have to make pay." She unbuckled her father's sword, which had hung heavily around her waist for so long. She traced her fingers down the engraved length of the scabbard before offering it to Koji. "He would want you to have it. It's a sunburner weapon."

"I couldn't!" Koji said, though the longing on his face was as clear as day. He had played with that sword every chance he'd gotten as a boy, despite their father doing everything in his power to keep it from his son.

"I want you to have it. And though there's nothing to forgive, I want you to know I forgive you."

Koji took the sword silently, and then sprang at Rika with an embrace of surprising ferocity.

She softened, patting his back. "I love you, brother."

"I love you too, sister. Now go end this."

Koji's words echoed in Rika's mind as Yoshai's defenders climbed into the night sky, borne aloft by silent wings. Daarco looked demon-like in the soul-eater armor, though his constant complaining about the smell took away some of the drama. They selected a ship near the back of the anchored armada, directing their koumori to land gracefully on the deck. With whispered footsteps, they swept through the vessel, finding it empty. They hoisted the sails, heading towards the queen.

The queen's vessel was larger than anything Rika had ever seen. The side of the galleon, armored in dark metal, rose above them, seeming to drown out the sky. No words passed between them as they tied off to the stern of the vessel, where angled stairs stretched up above them.

Daarco went first, his spine as straight as an arrow, the dark armor glittering in the moonlight. The two extra arms hung limply at his side. They had stuffed them with cloth and hay, but they wouldn't pass even a glancing scrutiny from a real soul-eater. Rika came next, Kai after and Emi bringing up the rear, half-marching, half-climbing up the steep metal staircase. Rika kept one hand on the rail and the other on her totem, worrying the stitching of its leather handle with her fingertips. One blow. One blow to the queen was all it would take. All she needed to do was get close enough.

The summit of the stairs was a few steps above them, and with her heart hammering in her throat, Rika crested the stairway, making her way onto the black deck of the galleon. Daarco stumbled to a stop before her, and she narrowly avoided crashing into the back of him. "What is it?" she hissed, but then she saw what had halted him. Saw what he had seen.

"Gods almighty," Kai whispered.

Emi offered a muffled curse.

They stood on a balcony at the stern of the ship, high above the long, broad deck. Below them, standing in neat squares, were a thousand dark bodies, a thousand pairs of glowing green eyes—their malevolence directed at the four interlopers.

Across the deck was a raised dais, topped by an elaborate black throne. On the throne, flanked by two soul-eaters, was a creature as strange as any Rika had ever seen. Six arms, four green glowing eyes, and a gaping maw that leaked green light. Larger than any of the other soul-eaters. Larger by far. "Welcome, starburner." The queen's rasping voice carried across the silent distance. "Welcome to your end."

CHAPTER 34

"I think we were expected," Daarco muttered.

"No shit," Emi retorted. "My love," she amended.

"Keep to the plan," Kai said, drawing her sword. "Rika? A little backup?"

The thralls nearest them marched up the stairs towards their platform, urged on by their masters. Daarco took a swing at the first two men, knocking them backwards into the crowd of their brethren.

Star-threads sprang into sharp relief as Rika opened her third eye. The constellations called to her, aching to lend their aid to the fight. She summoned the fiercest among them—the great bear, the fiery phoenix, the wasp, the clever fox. One by one they took form, answering her call and sliding down from their heavenly homes to land on the deck before them with concussive force that rocked even the huge ship. The thralls shied back at the sight of the massive glowing creatures but were spurred forward by their masters.

Rika drew her blade from her black sash. "Each of us sticks with a constellation. We kill the thralls; the constellations take care of the soul-eaters. Rendezvous at the queen," Rika said.

The others nodded. Rika took aim and hurdled her blade with all her strength directly across the deck at the queen's bulbous eyes. The blade winked in the moonlight, spinning directly towards its target…only to be deflected at the last moment by a wooden staff. Rika grunted and pulled the thread of the blade back to her. Worth a try. The blade sang as it spun back at her; she caught it in the air next to her head. Her gaze was fixed ahead at the soul-eater that had blocked her strike. The soul-eater holding a wooden staff carved with the leaves and palms of Nua. The soul-eater with three fingers.

"That's the one that killed Father," Rika said, her voice stiff. "With the staff."

It was all Kai needed. She sprang into the crowd of men, her sword clearing a path, fire jetting from her outstretched free hand. Moonburning may not be able to kill the soul-eaters, but it could certainly damage their minions. "Mother!" Rika called, exasperated. "Stay with her," she directed the phoenix, and the constellation launched into the air, soaring after her mother.

"She can't have all the fun," Emi said. With a whoop, she tore down the stairs after her, the great celestial bear in tow.

Daarco was busy removing pieces of the heavy armor, throwing them down at the men who made their way towards them. "What's our move, princess?"

"Kill some leeches," Rika said, wrapping the threads of the wasp around her fingers. She spun them out like throwing a spiderweb, and the constellation darted towards the queen in answer, stinger at the ready. The queen moved in a blur of black and green, narrowly avoiding the wasp's glittering barbed stinger.

"She's not just an ugly face," Daarco said.

"No." Rika frowned, searching frantically for the queen. There! Escorted by three leeches, including the three-fingered one. A handful of thralls hurried behind them, including one with golden hair. Anger flared in Rika. Master Tato. The traitorous librarian. She yanked a handful of threads, pulling starlight down in a fiery rain upon the retreating soul-eaters, taking special care to send one towards Tato. The world spun as the starlight flashed and shimmered.

"Are you all right?" Daarco put a steadying hand under her arm. "It won't do us any good if you burn yourself out."

"I'm not a burner," Rika panted.

"Doesn't mean you can't burn yourself out," Daarco commented. "Look out!" He bore her to the ground just in time to miss a quivering spear that impaled itself in the boards behind her.

Rika looked up in shock and saw one of the queen's guard making his way towards her. And the three-fingered soul-eater. The shooting star had killed the third, but other soul-eaters had filled in around the queen, protecting her. Daarco snarled and leaped at the nearest one, who raised its armored arm to meet his powerful sword strike in a shower of sparks. "Help him." Rika motioned to the giant fox, who sprang at the soul-eater who was wrapping one of its fists around Daarco's throat.

The three-fingered soul-eater took an impossible leap from the deck of the ship and with a thunderous crash, landed before her, Vikal's staff in hand. Rika reached and yanked desperately at the threads of the wasp, all the while throwing her blade at its face with all the force she could muster.

The soul-eater deflected her throw with the staff—metal ricocheting off wood—and her totem tumbled into the crowd of thralls below. Rika pulled its thread while dodging a lunge from the soul-eater. "That doesn't belong to you," she panted, coming into a crouch. The wasp was closing in...

"Its owner was unworthy," the soul-eater said before ducking to the side at the last moment. The wasp overshot, missing him completely before spinning, buzzing in anger. "None of you are worthy. Of this world. Of living."

"Funny," Rika said, summoning the wasp again, gauging her attack. "I was thinking the same thing about you." The wasp attacked the soul-eater again, and this time the leech wasn't so fast. The constellation locked on to the creature's torso, stinging him in quick succession. Rika darted into the creature's reach and stabbed her totem through the neck joint in the creature's armor. The soul-eater bellowed with pain, and with a blow of its iron gauntlet, tossed her into the air like a piece of chaff.

Pain exploded behind Rika's eyes as she crashed to the deck in a tangle of limbs, tumbling to a stop. Her totem skidded over the rail, falling to the deck below. Her vision blurred as she tried to push herself to hands and knees—reeling from the strain and the trauma. She squinted and saw that the three-fingered soul-eater was grappling with the wasp constellation. It had the star in its four-handed grip—it was pulling, pulling, pulling, and with a sound like splintering armor, the wasp's segmented body cracked. The constellation keened in anger and pain, scrambling away from the soul-eater, flopping onto the deck. The soul-eater had *wounded* a constellation. Rika hadn't known that was possible.

"Rika!" Emi's scream from the lower deck pulled her attention, and she saw that Kai and Emi were surrounded by half a dozen soul-eaters, black talons grasping, ready to suck their souls' essence until they were no more.

In a panic, Rika yanked at threads of starlight, sending them to her mother and Emi's aid like a deadly meteor show. The handful was too many, and while the devastating light rained down upon the soul-eaters, burning them through and causing others to scatter in fear, the power it required left her panting and weak. Pain snaked through her head and behind her eyes, and the threads blurred and swam. "Daarco!" she called, but she didn't know where he was—couldn't tell where her constellations were. She cried for them, but all around her the fighting was thick. The constellations and burners fought for their lives.

Black-booted feet swam into her vision, the wooden end of a staff thunking ominously on the deck. She had been an overeager fool running into this mess, thinking she could take on a thousand soul-eaters and thralls with only the heavens for backup.

The soul-eater knelt down and buried its fingers in her shirt, lifting her onto her feet, pressing her against the rail. The smell of sulfur overwhelmed her, and she spit the bile building in her mouth into the soul-eater's face. It laughed. Laughed!

"I thought perhaps I had found a foe worthy of me. Of my queen. But I see now that you are deficient. Like all the rest. How disappointing."

Rika's third-eye vision flickered in and out, but she jerked at a nearby thread, summoning it to come to her. It whistled down towards the soul-eater, who dodged at the last moment. Rika used that distraction to pull her legs up and shove off the soul-eater's armored chest with her feet, wrenching herself free of its grip. She scrambled across the deck towards the staircase at the far side of the balcony, her legs rebelling, her head swimming. Daarco and the fox constellation were on the lower deck, locked in brutal combat with a swarm of black. Rika was halfway down the stairs when another figure appeared at the bottom, blocking her exit. The queen.

Rika's mouth went dry and she backtracked up the stairs—the queen matching her steps with alien grace. The creature was huge, even more monstrous up close. She wore no helmet to shadow her gruesome face; instead, her four green eyes burned above a maw filled with black teeth and flanked by two clicking mandibles. Long hair like black, slick ropes hung down her back. *If this is what passes for beautiful in soul-eater territory,* Rika thought, *they have very different tastes indeed.*

She found herself back on the upper balcony, the queen towering before her, the three-fingered soul-eater behind. This was her moment. Her chance to kill them both. To end this war, to save her people. And she was empty. Weak as a mewling lamb. She jerked on the thread of her totem and it spun up from below into her hand. That effort alone was enough to nearly undo her—it took all her effort to stay on her feet. Her vision flickered. She needed time to regain her strength.

"Where do you come from?" Rika asked boldly, trying to stall. Her third eye was staying open, and she eyed a thread, a large and powerful star, fierce and unyielding.

"We come from the stars. Just as you do," the queen hissed. "But we have been at this a thousand thousand years."

"So have I," Rika said, and with a twitch of her fingers, she summoned the star, willed it to send its fiery radiance into the soul-eater queen, to devour and consume her. The light streaked down above, strong and sure... And the queen sidestepped. One instant, the queen stood before Rika, the next, she was beside her, watching the light explode onto the deck in a maelstrom of sparks.

Pain exploded across Rika's back as the three-fingered soul-eater struck her with Vikal's totem. She sprawled forward onto the planks, hitting hard, her totem sliding across the deck. She tasted blood. The soul-eater's booted foot connected with her ribs, sending a wave of agony through her torso. Through the railing, Rika could make out blurry forms of the constellations, snarling and clawing. There was no one to come to her aid. Emi and Daarco and her mother were fighting for their own lives, the constellations the only thing holding back the tide of thralls and soul-eaters. But if she died, the constellations would vanish. She needed them. She desperately grasped at the thread of the fox constellation, pulling it towards her. It slipped from her fingers as if she grasped at air. She wasn't strong enough—couldn't see it clearly.

The soul-eater queen knelt over her, filling Rika's vision with green-eyed horror. "Your soul is a delicacy I won't soon forget," the queen rasped, her mandibles quivering, opening.

"Never," Rika said, raising her hand to rake the queen's eyes with her fingernails. She didn't know what else to do.

The queen shied back, avoiding Rika's labored effort. "So

determined," the queen said before pinning Rika 's shoulders to the deck, puncturing skin with her talons. A scream ripped from Rika's throat, summoned by the pain, by the fear and hopelessness and sorrow. The scraping sound of the queen's laughter filled Rika's world as the nightmare curled over her like a lover, beginning to drink.

CHAPTER 35

I t had been the strangest ride of Vikal's life. Sandwiched between Ajij and Kemala, his eyes squeezed closed as they slipped through time and space. Somehow, Rika had known, and she had sent Cygna to them— the tiny sparrow now a massive creature with wings as broad as a temple roof. Cygna had climbed and climbed, past the point where the sky met the velvet stars, flying onto ethereal paths of light and energy that no human had tread before. Vikal felt Rika's energy all around him, pure and clean and powerful. In this place of beauty, of light, Cygna cut through the universe, bearing them towards its mistress.

Vikal had expected the situation in Kitina to be dire, but when they descended down out of the heavens, his stomach dropped at the sight.

"That's a lot of leeches," Bahti said, his teeth clenched against the cold and the height.

A fight to the death played out across the yawning deck of a massive black galleon. The leeches appeared to be winning.

"Where's Rika?" Vikal shouted, clutching Cygna's feathers as the bird banked, soaring lower.

"God and goddess," Kemala breathed. "At the stern. Vikal…"

His eyes desperately searched for where Kemala indicated, and when they locked on to Rika's form, sanity left him. "Cygna, kill that leech!" he bellowed, and the night sparrow narrowed its wings, pulling into a dive. The sweet essence of Rika's soul was vaporizing above her body, being sucked out by a horrific soul-eater. Were they too late?

"Hold on!" Vikal bellowed.

Cygna hit the feasting soul-eater and ripped it off Rika, grasping it with its talons. Or so Vikal imagined because when he looked back as Cygna flapped its immense wings, the leech was gone. Another leech stood over Rika's body now, watching them with baleful eyes. It held a staff in its hand. His totem.

"Set us down!" Vikal cried. "By Rika!"

The great bird wheeled about, coming to a screeching stop on the upper deck of the ship, the power of its wings driving the soul-eater back. Vikal and the others leaped off the creature's back, sandals hitting the deck. The strange soul-eater who had been feasting on Rika was writhing underneath the bird's huge talons, pierced through.

"You have what is mine!" Vikal shouted at the soul-eater, who turned to face him. He wasn't sure he only meant his totem. He wanted to run to Rika, to cradle her face in his arms, but he was intent upon the soul-eater. He had learned the hard way not to turn his back on these creatures.

"Our little thrall, back so soon? I am not surprised that you could not live without us. Free will is not for the weak."

Vikal spit on the deck, unsheathing his swords. "I would rather die than be under your control again."

"We can arrange that." The soul-eater was upon Vikal in an instant, yielding his own staff like a weapon against him. Vikal ducked out of the way, ready for the leech's blows, having seen them time and again as he had stood mutely by these creatures' sides.

Kemala knelt over Rika's prone form, and from the corner of his eye, Vikal saw Rika move. She was alive. "Help the others," Kemala called.

Ajij and Bahti plunged into the battle below, forces of nature turned against the tide of thralls and leeches that were threatening to overwhelm the little knot of desperately fighting burners and constellations.

And then all his focus was pulled back to the task at hand, dodging and ducking, striking blows that glanced off the soul-eater uselessly. He needed the power of starlight to kill this creature. "Cygna!" he called, risking a glance over his shoulder. Horror welled within him. The huge, distorted soul-eater grappled with the constellation, raking Cygna with her armored claws, clambering over it with insect-like grace. Cygna thrashed and clacked its beak, trying to throw her off. Could a constellation be killed?

"Magnificent, isn't she?" the soul-eater said. "A queen to be worshipped. Worthy of our devotion."

"She has you in her thrall, just like I was in yours." Vikal grunted, leaping over a swing of his staff. Gods, he wanted that staff back. "You are a slave, just as I was."

The soul-eater bellowed, and this time, when it swung at him, Vikal dropped one of his swords and caught his totem, his arm flexing and straining to wrench it from the monster. Power flooded through him, filling him with knowledge of the threads of the green things of this world. He laughed with relief at the surge, redoubling his efforts to wrench his staff from the leech.

Cygna let out a scream of pain behind him, drawing Vikal's attention for an instant. It was enough. The soul-eater punched him in the face with its other arm, its armored gauntlet connecting with a sickening crunch. Vikal crumpled to the ground, stars exploding in his vision.

The soul-eater hovered above him, the black eternity within its helmet mocking him with rasping laughter. "To come all this way only to die at my hand. The gods of your world surely are the sorriest lot I have ever encountered."

Anger burned in Vikal, swimming through the pain. He tried to rise, but his body rebelled, still in shock from the power and pain of the blow. The soul-eater drew his sword, its attention locked on Vikal. So intent that it didn't see. It didn't see Rika coming onto unsteady feet, her face ghostly pale and grim as the grave. Rika pulling the thread of her totem, summoning it to her hand. And pulling the thread of a star, infusing it into the blade so it glowed with white-hot starlight.

As the soul-eater moved to make its killing blow, it hesitated, seeming to recognize the incongruity of Vikal's teeth bared in a smile of triumph. But it was too late. Rika plunged her blade up under the leech's helmet, into its spine and brainstem, if the soul-eaters in fact had such things. Starlight snaked into the recess of its helmet, cracking and expanding until the soul-eater exploded, the weight of its armor crashing at Rika's feet. "It forgot about the goddesses," Rika said, her breast heaving, her eyes glowing and wild.

Vikal laughed incredulously and heaved himself to his feet. He crashed into Rika, pulling her up into his arms, not able to stand another second of separateness. When his lips met hers, she tasted of blood and stardust and the rightness of coming home. The pain and adrenaline coursing through his veins vanished as she wrapped her arms around his neck, crushing her lips to his, she as desperate as he to make up for the foolishness of their parting. Why had he ever left her?

She pulled away with a gasp, doubling over in pain. "Cygna!" she said. "The queen!" The constellation and the queen of the soul-eaters were locked in deathly combat, and it seemed killing blows had been given on both sides. Sickly-green blood leaked from the queen as she snarled and leaped at the bird again with slashing claws; Cygna ducking and slashing with its talons. Starlight leaked from one ravaged eye, and its movements were labored.

The others were running up the stairs now—two silver-haired women and a man with golden hair followed the other gods. "Together," Rika said. "She's too fast for me to get her alone. Hold her, and I'll strike."

"With pleasure," Bahti said, aiming a jet of fire at the soul-eater, sending her tumbling off the back of the constellation. They quickly moved around the queen, flanking her, surrounding her in a circle. Fire from Bahti and water from Ajij and lightning from the two silver-haired women pulverized the queen, pinning her to the deck even as she struggled to rise and flee. The bear and fox constellations flanked the queen, threatening her with gnashing teeth and rending claws. Rika moved in, her totem flashing, her three eyes glowing bright as stars. Vikal's breath caught as Rika raised her blade for the killing blow, feeling as if all the world and past and future hung in the balance of this blow.

Rika struck true. Her blade dropped, burying itself to the hilt in the soul-eater queen's face. A shower of light exploded from the contact, searing his vision. When he blinked away the brightness, relief flooded him. The queen's armor had fallen to the deck, empty and limp. Rika fell to her knees, leaning her forehead onto the deck. When she finally straightened, two crystal tears trickled down her cheeks. "Is it done?"

Vikal turned and looked over the deck, praying that their theory had been correct—that without the queen, the soul-eaters would fall. All across the deck, the black-armored creatures were spasming and screeching, dropping to the deck, rolling into the fetal position. It seemed that they had no minds of their own without the instructions of their queen. It would be a simple matter of putting them down. "Almost," he said, unable to believe it himself. The black-uniformed thralls milled about, rubbing their foreheads and looking about with confusion at their former captors, who now lay prone beside them.

"Come on, fox," Bahti said to the constellation that stood next to them, its bushy tail twitching.

"I will assist," Daarco said, motioning to the other constellation with a jerk of his chin. "Let's finish these creatures so they'll never hurt anyone again."

Vikal turned back to Rika, weary to his bones. He didn't need to watch the extermination of these creatures. He'd had enough killing for a lifetime. He crouched down beside her. "Can you stand?" he asked.

She shook her head, stumbling back onto her rear, leaning against the rail of the upper deck. "I think I'll sit here for a moment," she said, tilting her head back and closing her eyes. Vikal sat beside her, stretching out his legs, taking her cold hand in his. She squeezed.

The two silver-haired women sat down on either side of them, leaning back against the rail with a groan, laying down their weapons.

The woman next to him had smooth skin and freckles across her nose, but her hazel eyes were deep and knowing. She wore her exhaustion like a fine cloak, regal even smeared with blood and covered with a sheen of sweat and dirt.

"You must be Rika's mother," he said. "Nice to meet you."

"You must be the one she was waiting for," she replied.

His cheeks heated and he looked down at Rika, barely conscious, her head leaning against his shoulder. "I should have been here sooner."

"You made it. That's all that matters. I'm Queen Kailani Shigetsu. But you can call me 'Kai.'"

"Vikal," he replied.

"And I'm Emi," the other woman interjected, her scarred face shining in the moonlight. "If you hurt her, I'll be the one who comes for you."

Vikal's eyes widened. Perhaps she was joking? But the woman had a certain ferocity that made him not want to cross her. "I do not intend to hurt her," he said. "Not again, anyway."

Emi nodded. "As long as we understand each other, we'll get along just fine."

Vikal looked down at Rika, her eyes still closed. A ghost of a smile danced on her lips. Yes, they'd all get along just fine.

CHAPTER 36

Rika's ride back to Yoshai passed in flickers and glimpses. It was all she could do to cling to consciousness, to keep feeding her energy to the constellations that were finishing off the remaining soul-eaters. The one steadiness was Vikal's presence next to her—carrying her down the stairs into the rowboat, lifting her into his arms as they stepped back onto the sand of Kitina. Vikal gently brushing her hair off her forehead, running his thumb along her temple. Finally, she heard the words her soul had been longing for, praying for. "It's done," he said. "Rest now." And she did.

Rika awoke in her bed in Yoshai, sunlight streaming through a crack in the dark curtains. The down of her bed felt luxurious and heavenly beneath her aching body. Everything about her room looked the same. The gauzy canopy over the bed, the lacquered wardrobe covered with soaring cranes, her bookshelves piled with astrology notebooks and journals. It was as if the past weeks had been a dream. Strange and horrible at times, powerful and heady at others. She squinted in the darkness, and her gaze fell on a figure sleeping next to her. Her heart stuttered. Vikal. Sitting in her armchair, dragged over from the fireplace to her bedside. He snored gently, his head tipped against the brocade wingback of the chair. No, it wasn't a dream. Rika's hand strayed to her forehead, where she ran her fingertips across the marking of her tattoo.

Vikal looked so peaceful; she didn't want to disturb him. But her stomach growled and her bladder urged her to emerge from the warm cocoon of her bed, so she threw back the covers and tiptoed to the bathroom to relieve herself. When she returned, wrapping herself in a colorful silken robe, Vikal was just beginning to stir.

She sat on the bed facing him, watching the dark of his lashes flutter against his cheeks as he groaned. He was as exquisite as a statue, too handsome to be fair. Her lips tingled at the memory of their kiss, of the heat and salt of his mouth pressed against hers, his hands firm on her back. Had it been a moment of madness birthed by the heat of battle? Was their connection some imagined thing manufactured by danger and adrenaline and mortality? True, they were soulmates according to legend, but was that real? Was it what her heart felt?

Vikal opened his eyes, the lemongrass green of his irises meeting hers. A jolt of heat burned through her—awareness and anticipation. He smiled sleepily at her, and all reason fled. All she wanted was to see that sleepy smile every morning for the rest of her life. There was no denying what her heart felt.

"You're finally awake," he said. "How do you feel?"

"Good," she said. "Refreshed. Starving, though."

He chuckled, stretching his arms out, arching his back. "I'm not surprised. You slept for the better part of two days."

"Two days!" Rika squeaked, shooting to her feet. "Where's my mother? What's going on? Are any of the leeches still fighting? Is Cygna okay?" The last she had seen of the night sparrow, it had been grievously wounded in its battle with the queen.

"Relax," he said. "We did it. The last leeches are dead. Cygna survived and has returned to the stars to mend. The thralls are all free. A little confused about where in creation they are, as most of them are Nuan. But your mother and her council have been distributing food and arranging temporary housing. She is a very efficient monarch. A little scary how good she is at handling everything, actually. I could learn a thing or two."

Rika sank back onto the bed in relief. "Yes, my mother always made being queen look easy. As a kid, I was certain I'd never measure up."

"That is not the case anymore. You should hear her go on and on about how proud of you she is. It is almost like you saved your entire nation singlehandedly.""

Rika blushed. "Not exactly singlehandedly."

"Perhaps not, but do not discount your contribution. You are a more magnificent goddess of bright light then I could have ever imagined."

Rika's blush deepened. "Thank you for coming, Vikal. All of you. If you hadn't..."

"I should have come from the beginning. I promised."

"I released you from that promise. I understood why you stayed. You needed to protect your people. Were you able to defeat the soul-eaters? Did everyone...make it?"

He shook his head. "Everyone but one. Sarnak. He used his powers to hold the cavern and all our people out of time until we could arrive. They killed him for it."

Rika closed her eyes. Sarnak. Another man who had felt like a father to her, albeit briefly, dead. He had been an infuriating, but wonderful, teacher for their short time together. "I'll miss him," she finally said. "But it sounds like his sacrifice saved many."

"It did. And in Nua, we do not mourn the passage of a god. Not really. We celebrate their life and what they accomplished in this incarnation. He will be back."

Rika smiled wryly. "Can you imagine Sarnak's grumpy face on some tiny baby body? His poor parents."

Vikal laughed. "I hope I am alive to see it."

"Me too," she said, but the words stalled in her mouth. She pursed her lips. She wasn't Nuan, even if she was their goddess.

Vikal stood and in one swift step came to sit on the bed by her side. When he intertwined his fingers through hers, her body came alive with awareness of his presence. "Rika," he said. His voice was tentative, unsure.

She wanted to encourage him. "Yes?" she asked.

"It will be time for the gods to leave soon, to return to our people. And before I do, there is something I must say. I do not have much to offer a woman. A half-burnt island across a universe of stars. A scattered people, shell-shocked by war and death. A heart so deeply scarred that I thought...I thought it would never be whole again. Memories that I do not want to forget, but that I am ready to set aside. So they no longer own me. These things are a meager offering for a goddess blessed by the heavens themselves…" He trailed off, raising his gaze to hers. Her breath was tight in her throat, but she didn't respond, letting the silence stretch between them. She needed to hear. Needed to hear how he felt. That *he* chose *her.* That he wasn't just a god giving himself over to the whims of fate.

He continued. "What I can offer, however, is my love. Because you have brought to life a part of me that I thought was long dead and buried. What I thought was only darkness is light once again. I love you, Rika. I've loved you from the moment you, a tiny scrap of a woman, looked a soul-eater in the face without a trace of fear in your eyes and destroyed him with purifying fire. I did not see it for what it was until I almost lost you, and you hovered near death in the caverns. And even then, I was too afraid to feel it, to let it be true, until you were gone, sailing away and I realized I could never deny what is between us. It is as deep a part of me as my arm or my totem or my magic. I love you, Rika, and I hope beyond hope that despite all my foolish missteps, that you might love me too." The words had tumbled out, faster and faster, until they were all spent. Finally, Vikal looked up, gauging her reaction. "You are crying," he said, raising his hand to wipe away one a tear.

She nodded. "I love you too," she whispered. "Sure took you long enough."

A wide grin split Vikal's face, and he took her other hand in his. "You do? Truly?"

"Truly." And then she kissed him.

After an instant of surprise, Vikal wrapped his arms around her, pulling her flush against him. Her heart sang with the rightness of it, the taste of him, the heady elixir of passion and possibility. His tongue expertly parted her lips and his hands tightened as they ran up her back to tangle in her hair.

She lost all her moorings, her thoughts swept away in the delicious tide that was Vikal. All she wanted was him, more and more until she knew every part of him, every bright space and dark place alike.

She melted into him, hooking a knee up to push him back onto the bed, but her momentum was cut off by a knock on the door.

Vikal broke off their kiss with a gasp. "Should we get that?"

Rika pouted. "They can come back later."

Another knock. She sighed and broke off the embrace, wiping the corner of her lips, which were pleasantly buzzing from Vikal's ministrations.

"Come in!" she called, straightening her robe.

"It's so dark in here," Koji said, striding into the room. "What were you two doing?" He crossed the room and threw the curtains open.

Rika squinted, raising a hand to block out the sudden influx of light. "Sleeping?" she retorted, her heart hammering in her chest.

"Whatever you call it." Koji smirked. "I'm glad you're awake. Saves me the trouble of shaking you back to life. Mother wanted me to tell you that you have two hours until Father's wake. She wanted you to have enough time to get ready before sundown."

"Wake?" Rika's soaring heart thudded back down to earth.

"We were so busy defending against the soul-eaters that we haven't had a chance to honor him. Tonight is the full moon; Mother thought it would be best."

Rika nodded. "I'm glad I'll be able to be here."

"Me too," Koji said. "It wouldn't have been right without you." Koji stood awkwardly for a moment before turning to leave.

"Thanks, Ko," Rika said softly.

He nodded, closing the door behind him.

Vikal stood, taking a step back. "I will let you get ready. Perhaps we can talk after this wake?"

"You're not coming?" Rika asked, grabbing his hand, trying to keep the disappointment from her voice.

"I did not know your father. Except…" He trailed off. Oh, yes, she remembered. When he helped the soul-eaters kill him. "I want to be respectful," he finished.

Rika thought for a moment. She wanted Vikal at her side, but she wasn't sure how her mother would feel. "Perhaps it's best if you don't attend. I'll find you after."

He nodded, standing. "I understand. I should check on Kemala and the others anyway."

Rika walked him to the door, not wanting him to go. It was a silly sentiment, she told herself. They would only be apart a few hours.

Vikal hesitated. "I will see you soon, *dewa*," he said before leaning in quickly and kissing her on the forehead. He disappeared out the door.

She leaned her head against the door jamb for long after he was gone, her skin tingling from the touch of his lips. *Dewa*. For the first time since this mad adventure had begun, she liked the sound of that.

CHAPTER 37

Hiro's wake was held in the great temple in Yoshai. After Vikal had left, Rika bathed, braided her hair, and scarfed down a quick meal the servants had brought her. She moved through the motions like a ghost, her mind firmly fixed upon its dilemma. Could she really leave Kitina forever? Give up being queen—the role she had studied and prepared for her entire life? What would her mother say? Would it break her heart to have her daughter leave so soon after losing her husband? Would she think it was a foolish gamble, to leave for a man Rika hardly knew?

Rika opened her wardrobe and selected a white dress embroidered in gold. As she pulled it on, she pushed thoughts of Vikal aside. It wouldn't do for her to be distracted, not tonight. The memory of her father deserved her undivided attention.

Rika had always thought the temple was one of the grandest spaces in the city, but tonight, it blazed even brighter with light from thousands of candles. Its soaring ceiling, inlaid with gold and silver celestial scenes, glimmered above their heads. Those scenes were familiar to Rika now, those constellations beginning to feel like friends. They didn't just watch over the people of Kitina from a dispassionate distance. They had saved them. Fought for them. Fought for her. She couldn't wait to get to know them in the calm of peace. Their personalities, their quirks. She could sense that each was unique. But if she left, would she ever have that chance?

Rika walked up the polished aisle between the rows of guests. The temple was packed to bursting with people—everyone had streamed back into the city when they'd heard of the defeat of the soul-eater queen and her hordes. Sunburners in full red and gold armor, silver-haired moonburners, nobles in glorious colors. Tears pricked at Rika's eyes. This was her father's legacy. The love and devotion of everyone he'd met.

She settled into a seat in the front row between Koji and Nanase, who gave her a tight hug. "Good work, Rika. I knew you had it in you." As she settled back, Koji took her hand in his and squeezed. She looked at him in surprise, and he offered a smile. It seemed that the soul-eaters had changed him, too.

Rika's mother ascended onto the dais between larger-than-life statutes of the gods Tsuki and Taiyo. She wore a white gown with billowing sleeves, her waist wrapped in a white obi. The lunar crown was woven into her silver hair. She held up her hands to quiet the crowd.

"We're here to honor the life and death of my husband and your king. I like to think that Hiro died like he lived—without regrets. He died with honor. Fighting to protect us, his people. To give us the chance to barricade our gates against the storm that was to come. He died to give his children a chance to escape from that same fate and return to us with the key to defeating the greatest foe we have ever encountered. He would ask us not to mourn him. But to celebrate the exceptional life he lived."

One by one, people came forward to tell a story or a tale of Hiro, how he had lived. So many Rika had never heard; she had never known that her father had made those impressions. When it was her turn, she couldn't find the words, so she asked those attending to follow her outside into the warm spring night. When everyone had gathered, she cleared her throat. "I don't have the right words to tell you what my father meant to me. He was always there for me. Even when I thought I knew better or pushed him away, he would be there to pick me up when I fell, or to kiss the pain or sorrow away. That's who he was. A protector, a guardian, a friend—and the best dad. I don't feel like he's gone. He will always be there, watching over me. Watching over all of us. His family, the people of Yoshai and Kitina, the burners whom he loved. I can think of no better way to honor my father than to give him a place in the heavens, so he will truly, always be with us."

Rika had been planning it out in the hours before the wake, unsure if she could even do what she was about to attempt, if the stars would cooperate. But she had reached out and stroked the threads and found willing stars, those who were eager to be part of something more—something bigger. So she opened her third eye, and reached for the heavens, gathering stars to her, pulling them across the sky into a patch of inky blackness that would be the constellation's new home. She formed the stars into an image of an armored man with a sword, a lion at his side. When it was done, and her father's likeness winked at her from the sky, she turned and walked back to her mother's side.

Tears were flowing freely down Kai's face. "Thank you."

Rika stood with her mother and brother and thanked their guests as they left, receiving hugs and handshakes and kisses and murmured condolences until her feet throbbed. When they were finally alone, Kai wrapped her arms around her children and pulled them close. Rika laid her head on her mother's shoulder, her heart aching at her father's absence. It wasn't fair. He should be here with them. "I miss him too, dear ones," Kai said. "But he'll never be gone. Not really."

Finally, as the rays of dawn were lightening the horizon, Koji claimed he was tired, heading back to his rooms. Kai's seishen, Quitsu, jumped into Rika's arms, and she clutched him to her chest, taking in the offered comfort and warmth.

"I'm starving," Kai said. "Come with me to the kitchen to sneak something delicious?"

Rika set Quitsu down. "I don't think the queen can sneak anything. It all belongs to you."

"Sometimes it's more fun to sneak," Kai said, and Rika shook her head with a little laugh.

"Sure."

The kitchens were nestled into the palace walls, their hearths forever chugging out fragrant smoke. Kai and Rika managed to find and commandeer a batch of steaming soup buns that had just come out of the pot. The cook handed them two bowls and waved them out of her kitchen with a good-natured flick of her apron.

"I've had some interesting conversations with your fellow, Vikal,"

Kai said as they made their way out into a quiet courtyard to sit.

Rika's breath caught as she sat down on a wooden bench carved like two facing dragons. "Oh?" she said, trying to feign disinterest.

"He seems like a good man," Kai said. "He's been through much. They all have."

Rika took a bite and hissed, letting the bun drop back into the bowl. "Hot," she said, fanning her mouth. "He *is* a good man. He saved my life."

"And you saved his. Or so he told me many times."

"I guess we both saved each other."

"That's the best way. That's how me and your father..." Kai trailed off for a moment. "That's how we started. We spared each other's lives. Have I told you the story of how we met?"

Only about a hundred times. But Rika wanted to hear it again. "Tell me," she said.

"I was just leaving Kita to make my way to the citadel in Kyuden for the first time. I had been sentenced to death and had barely made it out of the desert alive. I wouldn't have, if it weren't for Quitsu." Kai scratched her seishen's head. "Daarco knocked me off my koumori. I almost fell to my death. I was almost dying a lot back then."

"Clearly," Rika commented, grinning. "So Father comes out of the darkness..."

"Right," Kai said. "Daarco has a knife to my throat— he's ready to kill me for my silver hair, but your father commands him to halt. There was something about him—in that moment, I knew he was something special. That there was a connection between us." Kai shivered.

"You knew you were supposed to be together," Rika said, thinking of Vikal, of the likelihood that he would be there in that tent the night her father had died, of all the thousands of thralls in the soul-eaters' clutches. That she would have killed the soul-eater that had had control of him...that he would have helped her escape. What were the odds?

"I was never one to believe in fate," Kai continued. "But sometimes it's hard to argue with. I have no doubt your father and I were meant to be together. As infuriating as that man was sometimes."

Rika smiled. "I always loved that story."

"I sense that you and Vikal are making such a story yourselves. He told me he loves you, and that he wants you to return to Nua with him.

He was very candid with me."

Rika's eyes widened and she fought to keep her heart grounded. "He said that?"

"It surprises you?"

"No. Sort of. Not the sentiment, but that he was so upfront with you. We haven't had much time to talk."

"Do you love him?" Kai asked, innocently popping a steaming bun into her mouth.

"Yes," Rika said, closing her eyes for a moment as the image of his face swam up before her. "I tried not to. We were fighting the soul-eaters, Father had just died, I was in a foreign place trying to figure out how the heck I had grown a third eye." She laughed ruefully. "But somewhere in all of that, in trying to deny it…I fell for him."

"I thought so," Kai said. "This is something to celebrate! Why do you look so forlorn about it?"

"I was worried you'd be…disappointed in me," Rika admitted, shoving a bun in her mouth so she didn't have to say any more.

"Disappointed? That my darling daughter has found a unique and capable man to love, who loves her back? What kind of mother would I be?"

"You and Father have been preparing me from birth to be queen of Kitina. I can't just abandon it for love. Can I?" She looked up with hope.

"Your grandmother gave up her country for love, and though she had many joys in her life, I know that was a piece of sorrow she carried with her all her life. For me, I'm not sure what I would have chosen. Your father was smart enough to never make me choose. We were lucky. For you, though…you have always been different, my daughter. With your head in the stars, you weren't bright sun like your father or cool moon like me. Perhaps your path was always to lead elsewhere. Perhaps when we were teaching you to be queen, we just didn't have the imagination to see what country you would rule."

"Do you think that's true? That Nua is my destiny? That those are my people?"

"Only you can know that, deep in your heart. But Vikal told me something of the cycles of Nua, and your divine destiny as goddess of bright light. As much as I selfishly want you here with me, I must be honest. It seems to be the role you were born for."

"But what about Kitina?" Rika said. "I couldn't leave you and Koji and Emi and Nanase… Everyone I've ever known is here! And Koji would be king?"

"Yes, Tsuki help Kitina with your brother at the helm," Kai joked, then turned serious. "We raised him too, you know. You may think of him only as your annoying little brother, but he will make a good king. I see much of Hiro in him."

Rika's mind raced as she took in what her mother was saying. She was saying…to go. To go to Nua. To be goddess and queen and…more. Tears sprang to life, threatening to spill down her cheeks. "Will you be…all right?"

"Me?" Kai said, setting her bowl down on the ground. She cupped Rika's face in her hands, gazing at her with hazel eyes. "I am stronger than you think. I refuse to let you abandon this new adventure because you are worried about your dear old mother. This is your destiny, Rika. I feel it."

Rika nodded as the tears came in earnest. "I feel it too. But I'm going to miss you so much. Everyone. Everything here. How can I say goodbye?"

"It won't be goodbye. That massive star-bird thing brought your boyfriend and those other gods—it can bring you back to visit. Or bring me over to Nua! Vikal makes it sound like a very nice place to vacation."

She laughed. "It will be once the forest grows back."

"Just you wait and see, you'll never be rid of me. Especially if you have grandchildren." Kai's eyes lit up, and she rubbed her hands together. "Oh yes, once the babies come, you'll be wishing you had more than a galaxy between us!"

Rika rolled her eyes and pulled her mother into her arms, squeezing her tightly. "I'm holding you to that."

"Vikal!" Rika ran down the hallway of the guest wing, lit by the light of the rising sun. Which room was he in? "Vikal!"

A door opened behind her and she whirled, skidding to a stop. "Vikal?"

It was Bahti, rubbing his eyes, a scowl on his face. "What time is it, crazy goddess?"

"Time for me to find Vikal!" Rika said, grinning like a madwoman. "Which room is he in?"

The door across the hall opened, and Vikal stepped out. "Is everything all right?"

Rika's whole body thrummed at the sight of him, shirtless, his dark hair tousled. "Nothing's wrong," she said, coming to stand before him. "I talked to my mother about everything. I've decided. I'm going to Nua!"

Vikal's face lit up. "You're coming to Nua?"

"That's what she said," Bahti said grumpily.

Rika nodded her head. "I'm going to Nua. I'm going with you."

Vikal swept her up in his arms and with a laugh of disbelief, spun her around and around. She buried her face in his shoulder and grinned until her cheeks hurt. When he finally set her feet on the ground, his lips met hers, his arms pulled her to him—his embrace saying more than his words ever could.

"Ugh, young love," Bahti said. "There will be so much kissing."

"Shut up," Kemala said softly, and then Rika stopped listening. Kissing Vikal was like floating, a weightlessness she had never experienced. Together, they would fly.

EPILOGUE

With the destruction of the soul-eater queen, the astrolabes had gone dark, now just complex decorations adorning the ships. Thousands of Nuans had been brought to Kitina by the soul-eaters, and they needed a way home. Kai had extended an offer of land or work to any who wished to stay and make a new start in Kitina, and an adventurous few took her up on the offer. But for the majority, they had family and a home they longed to return to. Cygna, the one constellation who could make the journey, would have a busy few months, shepherding them across the star-paths a few at a time. Kitina would generously keep them fed and clothed until they all made their way home.

It took a few days for Vikal to see his people settled and prepared for the wait. Rika knew that her goodbye would come sooner than ever, so she relished her last few days in Kitina, riding beside Koji and Enzo, snuggling with Quitsu, laughing with Oma, sparring with Nanase with her new totem in the evenings. And then she would slip away from her friends and family263

into Vikal's arms, lingering tension and worry and doubt unwinding beneath his soft kisses.

"Someday soon, when we're not surrounded by a thousand people, I'm going to show you how much I really love you," Vikal murmured into the curve of her neck, sending a shiver down her spine.

"I look forward to that day," Rika replied, leaning into the hard planes of his chest. And while she spoke the truth, part of her savored this moment too. She was done wishing for life to be different, longing for the future or some grand adventure. She was content to take each day as it was, savoring the pleasures and frustrations it offered in turn. Because that, she was beginning to realize, was what life was all about.

The morning they were to leave dawned sooner than Rika had been ready for. For now, it was just Rika, Vikal, and the other gods who would ride home on Cygna.

They were to take off from the palace's upper courtyard. Rika stood at the wall, looking down at the shimmering stretch of sea where the lifeless soul-eater vessels bobbed.

Kai and Quitsu approached, and Kai wrapped her arm around Rika's waist. "Whenever I look at the stars I'll think of you. I'll know you're just across the way. You do the same, yes?"

Rika nodded.

"Just what I need," Koji said, coming to stand on the other side with Enzo. "My sister watching me all the time. Creepy!"

"Don't get into any trouble, and you won't need to worry about it." Rika reached her other arm around Koji's waist and pulled him close, despite the groan that escaped his lips. "When did you get so tall?" she asked, looking up at him.

"I ask myself the same thing daily," Kai muttered.

Koji just smiled. "Maybe I'll come visit you someday, sis."

"I'd like that. Lots of pretty girls in Nua."

"Why didn't you say so? I'll come *now*. Any room left on that giant bird?"

Vikal came to stand beside Kai, keeping a respectful distance. "The people of Kitina are always welcome in Nua. Our shores are always open to you."

Rika beamed at him, and then laughed as Kai snaked her other arm around Vikal's waist and pulled him into the embrace.

"I already told Rika that I'm visiting. Especially once there are grandbabies."

"Mother." Rika groaned, mortified.

Vikal just laughed, a throaty chuckle. "Let's take it one day at a time,

Your Majesty. Today, we go home."

Rika met Vikal's eyes over her mother's silver head and excitement trilled in her. Was it possible to have two homes? Yes, she thought it was. Part of her heart and soul would always belong to Kitina. But Nua called to her too, a siren song welcoming her return.

Today, together, they were going home.

THE END

FROM THE AUTHOR

Thank you so much for taking the time to read *Starburner*, the final book in the *Moonburner Cycle*! I hope you've enjoyed reading about Rika and Vikal's adventures as much as I've enjoyed writing them!

Reader reviews are incredibly important to indie authors like me, and so it would mean the world to me if you took a few minutes to leave an honest review wherever you buy books online. It doesn't have to be much; a few words can make the difference in helping a future reader give the book a chance.

If you're interested in receiving updates, giveaways, and advanced copies of upcoming books, sign up for my mailing list at www.claireluana.com and receive a free gift!

Have you read Burning Fate, the prequel to the Moonburner Cycle? Grab your copy now!!

ABOUT THE AUTHOR

Claire Luana grew up reading everything she could get her hands on and writing every chance she could. Eventually, adulthood won out, and she turned her writing talents to more scholarly pursuits, going to work as a commercial litigation attorney. While continuing to practice law, Claire decided to return to her roots and try her hand once again at creative writing. She has written and published the Moonburner Cycle and is currently finishing a new trilogy about magical food, the Confectioner Chronicles. She lives in Seattle, Washington with her husband and two dogs. In her (little) remaining spare time, she loves to hike, travel, binge-watch CW shows, and of course, fall into a good book.

Connect with Claire Luana online at:

Website & Blog:
www.claireluana.com

Facebook:
www.facebook.com/claireluana

Twitter:
www.twitter.com/clairedeluana

Goodreads:
www.goodreads.com/author/show/15207082.Claire_Luana

Instagram:
www.instagram.com/claireluana

Amazon:
www.amazon.com/Claire-Luana/e/B01F28F3W4